Loving Rose

STEPHANIE LAURENS

Loving Rose

THE REDEMPTION OF MALCOLM SINCLAIR

AVON

An Imprint of HarperCollinsPublishers

The name Stephanie Laurens is a registered trademark of Savdek Management Proprietary Ltd.

AVON BOOKS
An Imprint of HarperCollins*Publishers*
195 Broadway
New York, New York 10007

Copyright © 2014 by Savdek Management Proprietary Ltd.
ISBN 978-1-62953-091-8

Loving Rose

The Honorable Barnaby Adair's Previous Investigations

Cornwall, June 1831
Assisting Gerard Debbington, brother of
Patience Cynster, brother-in-law of Vane Cynster
and Miss Jacqueline Tregonning
In: The Truth About Love

Newmarket, August 1831
Assisting Dillon Caxton, cousin of Felicity Cynster,
brother-in-law of Demon Cynster,
and Lady Priscilla Dalloway
In: What Price Love?

Somerset, February 1833
Assisting Lord Charles Morwellan, Earl of Meredith,
brother of Alathea Cynster, brother-in-law of
Gabriel Cynster, and Miss Sarah Conningham
In: The Taste of Innocence

London, November 1835
Assisting Miss Penelope Ashford, sister of Luc,
Viscount Calverton, sister-in-law of Amelia Cynster
In: Where the Heart Leads

London, October 1837
Assisting Heathcote Montague, Cynster man-of-business,
and Miss Violet Matcham, companion to
Lady Agatha Halstead
In: The Masterful Mr. Montague

1833
The shores of Bridgewater Bay, Somerset

Pain.

Excruciating, relentless, it razed his senses and shredded his mind with fire-tipped claws.

Agony seared, brilliantly bright, successive lightning bolts devastating and eradicating all ability to think, to know—even to remember.

Death.

He'd chosen it, accepted it—welcomed it.

This was his necessary suffering, his torment along the road to hell.

It was nothing more than he deserved.

He couldn't move, could no longer tell if his body was even there, if he still inhabited it.

His mind lost its final tenuous tether and fell away, conscious thought a ribbon drifting out of his reach.

Gradually, battered by the onslaught of unrelenting pain, his senses, too, started to fail. To stutter. Then . . .

Oblivion lay ahead, a void of nothingness toward which he sank.

Beyond would lie the flames of hell, of eternal damnation.

He waited.

"**B**rother Roland—look!"

Stifling a sigh, Roland, Infirmarer of the priory of Lilstock, straightened from the tangle of seaweed he'd been picking over. As usual in this season, he'd brought the youngest novices to help him harvest the medicinal bounty the sea provided. It was a weekly chore and he was glad of their help, even though he sometimes wondered if the benefit was worth the cost; the youngest novices were so very easily distracted.

Expecting to have to deal with a wandering sheep, or perhaps to identify some unusual bird, Roland raised his head and looked down the beach.

Only to see the entire bevy of novices eagerly scrambling down the dunes, their focus a tangle of wet rags bundled every which way and cast up, flotsam on the rough sand.

Roland focused on the rags; he'd been at the priory, above the bay on the southern shore of the Bristol Channel, for the last decade—he recognized the tangled bundle for what it was. "Wait!"

His bellowed command brought every boy up short. None had got within twenty yards of the body. All turned puzzled faces his way.

Roland ignored them. Robes flapping, he strode swiftly down the dune on which he'd been working; for their still-innocent sakes, better he view the body first. The Lord alone knew what state it would be in.

The Channel was one of the busiest shipping lanes in the world. Captains needed to bury their dead before putting into Bristol, and sometimes storms prevented them from doing so on the open sea. So said captains performed last rites once they were in the calmer waters of the Channel. But the Channel, although deep, was a maze of strong, swiftly running currents. Bodies regularly fetched up along the southern shores.

Quite aside from their faith's command to see all such bodies treated with due respect, there was also the danger of disease to be assessed.

And, needless to say, legitimate burial wasn't the only reason bodies washed ashore.

Tramping over the sand, the grains shifting beneath his booted feet, Roland studied the rumpled heap of wet material—dark suiting with a glimmer of dirty ivory—and wondered if this body belonged in the latter category.

By the time he crouched beside the body, he was certain that was, indeed, the case. For a start, the man—for it was a man—was almost certainly English. Fair hair, now lank and sodden, but nevertheless well-cut, clung to a broad forehead and cheeks that, originally, had held the sharp angles and clean planes that were hallmarks of the aristocracy.

This man had been well-born. But now . . .

Experienced eyes scanning the ungodly tangle of long, once elegant limbs, tracing the unnatural angles and impossible contortions of bones forced into positions they simply could not—should not—ever be in, Roland felt something in him seize—with pity, with horror, with outright shock.

What manner of rack had this man been placed upon?

The man had fetched up on his stomach, his head turned toward the sea, his shoulders askew, his spine twisted, arms and legs hanging like limp twigs. Roland looked down on the man's face, on the side he could see, once handsome but now battered, the skin pallid, holding the leaden tinge of death.

This man had been broken, hideously and utterly, before death had claimed him.

Roland made the sign of the cross, instinctively murmuring a prayer for the man's soul. He started to turn to give orders to the novices—a sibilant *shush* from the sea made him pause.

A wave rolled in, higher than the most recent; the tide had turned and was coming in.

The wave reached the man, washing up around his body, lapping at his sodden clothes. The water came high enough to briefly cover the man's chafed and parted lips and his nose.

Roland had seen no reason to try and prevent that.

Then he saw the thin stream of bubbles escape from the man's mouth.

"Good God!" Roland shot to his feet. His heart was pounding.

But he was the Infirmarer.

The sea receded. Roland swung to the novices, now gathered in a curious group fifteen paces away. "You— Godfrey." Roland pointed to the leanest and fittest of the bunch. "Run back to the priory and fetch the stretcher. Ned and Will—you go, too, and bring back my medical bag, and the bag of splints and bandages. Go. Now—and *run!*"

He didn't need to make any further exhortation; the three boys shot off like hares, racing and leaping up over the dunes, making for the path to the priory on the headland. Turning back to the unknown man, Roland wondered if he was doing the right thing—if there truly was any point, any hope. If what was to come would ever be worth the price . . . yet he was God's man; he had no choice. He had to try.

That he had no guarantee that the man would live was beside the point. Also irrelevant was that, if he lived, the man would likely not thank him for rescuing him into a life of unending pain and misery.

The man had literally been cast up at Roland's feet, a wreck, but yet alive. This wasn't a matter for Roland to judge or question. He was the Infirmarer, and he knew his duty.

To him fell the task of saving this life.

Mind reengaging with that task, Roland swiftly assessed, then blew out a breath. For the novices' benefit, he said, "I don't want to risk shifting him until we've done all we can to stabilize his limbs." That was what the splints and bandages were for; thinking of how many splints he had in his bag, and how to use them, he ordered, "Ben and Cam—do you have your knives with you?"

Both boys nodded.

"Good." Roland pointed down the beach. "There's a stream that runs into the sea along there. Follow it back a little way and you'll come to some reed beds. Cut as many reeds as you can carry and bring them here as soon as you can."

"Yes, Brother Roland," the pair chorused, then turned and jogged off.

"Brian and Kenneth—collect all our baskets and stack them by the path to the priory. We can pick them up later, on our way back. Then return here."

"Aye, Brother Roland."

Roland turned to the six boys left. "We can't move him yet, but we need to keep the water from him as best we can. So we need to build a wall of sand to keep the tide back until the others return with the supplies and I can bind him. So . . ."

All he had to do was point to where; the novices were still young enough to enjoy building walls in the sand.

He'd thought he would have passed through the inferno's portal by now, but no. The pain went on.

Stoically, locked deep within a mind he was somewhat amazed still existed, he endured.

He waited. Still. For death to claim him.

While the agony rolled on.

Still, he remained. Fleetingly conscious now and then. Distantly aware.

Although of what, he had no idea.

Gradually, he realized he was still within the mortal world. That his physical body still existed, albeit as nothing more than a dull ache. That his mind, trapped within a head he couldn't really feel, still functioned.

He lived. Still.

Why, he couldn't fathom.

The pain had receded, not disappearing so much as becoming an integral part of his being.

An integral part of the new him.

If this existence—this non-death—continued, at some point he would have to open his eyes and find out what had happened, but, like the rest of his body, his lids did not seem to actually be there, not physical entities he could command.

So he waited.

To see what came next.

At last, he was able to raise his lids. Only a sliver, and the light was blinding, so he instantly lowered them.

But someone was there—someone he now realized had often been there, someone he'd sensed even through the haze of pain—and that someone had seen.

Cool water touched his parched lips. He parted them, and the trickle of water down his throat—the sensation of it—was unimaginably intense, his senses, so long dormant, unused, abruptly flaring to life.

"Can you hear me?"

So his ears still functioned, too. The voice was deep, a man's, resonant, the tone calming, caring. A flicker of his lashes was all he could manage in response.

"Your name. If you remember it, if you can manage to speak it, that's all I would ask of you."

His name . . . they would need one to put on his gravestone, of course. But the man he'd been was now dead, even to him; not even in death did he wish to lie beneath that man's name.

More water was offered and he took it, grateful enough as he accepted that he should answer—that he should give the caring man a name.

His mind roamed, sorting through his memories; gradually, his past took more definite shape. Recollections solidified, what that now-dead man had done, what had happened—and all that had happened even earlier in his life . . .

There *was* another name—an alter ego he'd created long ago and had used on and off until the end. He'd killed off the man he'd been, but that other . . . he'd forgotten about him.

As he was dying—and given the weight of his sins, he

expected no other outcome—perhaps this was Fate's way of giving him the opportunity to tie up even that loose end?

He did like neat plans.

"Thomas." His voice was raspy, harsher than he recalled, dulcet tones ruined by his ordeal. Breathing deeply enough to speak took conscious effort and multiplied the ever-present pain by several orders of magnitude, yet as he sensed the caring man lean closer, he forced himself to lick his cracked lips and say more clearly, "Thomas Glendower."

Pain lanced through his side; darkness swept across his consciousness and he let himself flow with the tide.

"Will he live?" Prior Geoffrey, white-haired and ageing, rested a hand on Roland's shoulder.

In the tiny end cell of the infirmary, seated on a stool by the narrow cot on which the man they'd rescued from the shore had lain for the past weeks, Roland looked up and answered truthfully, "I can't say, but as he's lived this long, through all of this"—Roland gestured to the countless splints and braces, the outward signs of the long list of procedures he'd had to employ to patch the man up and put right what he could—"and he hasn't faded yet, I have to assume he will recover, at least as far as that's possible."

His gaze on the man's damaged face, Roland paused, then drew breath and put into words the issue his conscience had been wrestling with ever since he'd found the man on the shore. "I still don't know if we've done the right thing—if saving him was the right thing to do."

Prior Geoffrey didn't immediately answer, but then his long fingers gently gripped Roland's shoulder. "Ours not to know the workings of the Almighty, my son. If Thomas Glendower lives, you, at least, can be assured that you will have performed exactly as you should have."

Roland hoped so. Inclining his head in acceptance, he said no more.

Thomas sat on the bench in the medicinal garden of Lilstock Priory, the stone wall of the infirmary warm at his back, and stared unseeing at the profusion of plants filling the neatly laid-out beds.

He could feel the sunshine on his face, could sense the light waft of the summer breeze. Could smell the rich aroma of freshly tilled loam and the tang of fruit ripening in the nearby orchard.

He could hear the soft thuds and grunts as two monks worked further down the garden, could hear the birds chirping and twittering in the trees. Even though one eyelid now drooped, and the orbit of that eye would never be perfect again, he had regained normal vision in both eyes; he could follow the swooping flight of swallows across the blue expanse of the sky.

He wasn't sure if that—the return of his senses and his faculties—would ultimately prove a blessing or a curse.

Months had passed since the man he'd been had died.

Yet he was still alive, and that he didn't understand.

He'd been beyond ready to go, to leave this world for all time. To spare the rest of the world his continued presence.

But that, apparently, was not to be.

According to Brother Roland, the Infirmarer, the man who had cared for him, who had saved him and had prevented the him he now was from dying, he was improving and would improve further with time.

He was convalescing, as yet unable to move without assistance, but otherwise able.

Able, at last, to think.

He still suffered constant pain, but although he could feel

it, he no longer heeded it; pain had become such an unre-
lentingly insistent companion that he took it for granted and
it no longer distracted him, no longer interfered with his
ability to function.

He heard footsteps on the gravel, and from their steady
pace he knew who was approaching before Roland appeared beneath the archway from the priory courtyard.

Roland glanced around, spotted Thomas, and walked
across to the bench.

Thomas managed a crooked smile and waited as, returning the welcome with a nod, Roland gathered his robes and
sat alongside him.

For several minutes, they looked out over the garden, silently savoring the tranquility of the scene, then Roland
asked, simply, bluntly, as was his way, "So who is Thomas
Glendower?"

Thomas felt his lips curve. He'd been expecting the question, had known it would come soon enough.

And because he liked Roland, he was prepared to answer.

Roland was a type of man Thomas recognized, a man
who almost certainly shared a similar background to himself but who had taken a very different path. There was
much in Roland that Thomas understood and, with his new
understanding born of death, could now appreciate and ad-
mire.

Without shifting his gaze from the greenery and the bobbing flower heads, Thomas said, "I was born into the minor
aristocracy, but my parents died in an accident when I was
six. I had no close relatives, so was passed into the care of a
guardian, one of my father's friends who held a lofty position socially and politically, but who, by no stretch of the
imagination, could have been termed a good man. Under

his tutelage, I evolved in ways that, perhaps, had he been otherwise, I would not have, but as he took his own life at the time I reached my majority, how I lived the rest of my previous life lies entirely on my own head."

He paused, reflecting, then continued, his damaged voice still guttural, but clear, "I was warned, at that time, to mind my ways, warned that I needed to exercise caution, but, as young men are wont to do, I thought I knew best and set out to explore all life had to offer me. In material terms, I prospered, yet by choice I remained largely alone, for I did not feel any need for personal connection. That, more than anything else, was my downfall. Because I didn't think of others, I caused others—many others—pain. More, I brought desolation, and even death. I caused others to die. And for that . . . I died."

Roland remained silent for some time, then asked, "You killed people?"

"Yes."

"By your own hand?"

It was tempting to lie, but he owed Roland the truth. "No. I never killed anyone directly, but I did cause them to be killed."

Brow furrowed, Roland cast him a sidelong glance. "You ordered others to kill them?"

It would, Thomas reflected, have been easier to lie. Resting the back of his head against the wall, he said, "No, but the orders I gave caused them to be killed." Having gone that far and sensing Roland's utter confusion, he felt compelled to explain, "It wasn't straightforward. I wanted something—several somethings over the years—and so I ordered others to arrange it, to get those things for me. I never knew about the deaths until the end, but had I thought things through . . . but I didn't, you see? I never thought about others at all—that was my failing. I operated as if my actions had no impact on anyone else, but I was entirely wrong, and they did. And when I eventually realized that, I put a stop to it."

Another pause ensued while Roland digested that. Then he said, "Thomas Glendower isn't the name you were born with, is it?"

Thomas nodded. "But the name I was born with died with the man I was—I killed him not only physically but in every other way as well. I made sure reparation was paid on every level." He paused, inwardly acknowledging how right that decision still felt, then went on, "The man I was is dead, and no good—indeed, much harm to others—would come from resurrecting him. And I'm prepared to swear to that on the priory's Bible."

Roland humphed.

Thomas simply waited, with a patience the last months had taught him, to learn what his fate would be now that he'd admitted to the crimes of his past.

Eventually, his gaze, like Thomas's, on the garden, Roland shifted, leaning his forearms on his thighs and clasping his hands between his knees. "There were times, especially during the first days you were here, when I didn't expect you to live. I had to break bones and wrench tendons to reset your joints—I had to dose you against infection, I had to sedate you against the pain. I had to straighten your spine and hope I didn't kill you in the process. You were unconscious throughout—I couldn't tell if you wished to live or die. So I held aloof. I didn't pray for your death, yet neither did I pray for you to live."

Hands gripping tightly, Roland continued, "Prior Geoffrey had a different view. He saw your survival as likely, even assured, because, in his eyes, the fact that you had been delivered into my hands, especially in the state you were in, was a sign of divine intervention."

Thomas blinked. "That can't be right."

Roland snorted. "After what you've just told me, I can see why you might think so, but . . . I've known Geoffrey for years. He was my mentor when I was a novice. He is unbelievably shrewd and farsighted, especially when it comes to his fellow men and their foibles." Roland paused, then said, "I'm coming around to his way of thinking."

"What?" Startled, Thomas let his cynicism show. "That because of my attempt to pay for my sins, the Good Lord has forgiven me?"

Roland chuckled, dryly, wryly. Turning his head, he met Thomas's gaze. "No, not that. Geoffrey believes you've been spared for a reason. For a purpose. He believes Our Lord has some task in mind for you—something only you can do, and you've been spared so that you can do it."

Thomas saw the solidifying certainty in Roland's eyes.

As if to confirm Thomas's insight, Roland nodded. "And after what you've just told me, I'm even more inclined to agree with Geoffrey. No matter what you might think, Our Lord is not finished with you."

Thomas didn't know what to make of that. He was tempted to point out that he wasn't religious, that he wasn't even certain he believed in any deity. In Fate, perhaps, but in God? He couldn't claim any conviction.

But sitting in the sunshine, meeting Roland's level gaze . . . he had to think to do it, but he slightly raised one shoulder—the less damaged one—and said, "Well, no doubt we'll see."

Months passed before Thomas, propped up on crutches, could manage well enough to reach the priory library.

There he discovered, as he'd hoped, the news sheets from London, delivered every afternoon, although for whose benefit he could not say; no one else in the house seemed interested enough to read them.

Another month saw him petitioning Prior Geoffrey to be allowed to repay the priory by assisting with their investments. Geoffrey, every bit as shrewd as Roland had painted him, agreed, and for the first time in a very long time, Thomas started to feel as if he was living, rather than simply existing.

As he'd told Geoffrey, if he'd been spared for some reason, then presumably that reason would make itself known in good time. Until then, in keeping with the ethos of the house, he should make himself useful. And the only skill he had lay in making money—in taking money and making it into more.

Other than requesting a vow that any action Thomas took would be entirely legal and aboveboard, Geoffrey had been agreeable, not to say enthusiastic, and had personally shown Thomas the priory's records and ledgers.

Several months later, the priory's investments were steadily improving.

Seated at his now habitual place at the end of a table in one corner of the library where winter light spilled through the diamond panes in the leaded windows, Thomas was working through the details of a proposition the priory's investment agent—immensely invigorated now that someone was actually encouraging him—had submitted, when Roland entered the library and saw him.

A benevolent smile on his face, Roland walked over, pulled out the chair alongside Thomas, and sat.

Thomas merely arched a brow in greeting, but otherwise kept working through his figures until he reached the end.

Then he looked up and met Roland's steady gray gaze. As usual, the big, broad-shouldered man—as tall as Thomas, but heavier, stocky and strong, and where Thomas was fair and brown-y blond, Roland was fair and dark; Thomas felt certain Roland had French blood somewhere in his recent ancestry—had settled with his forearms on the table, his big, well-shaped hands clasped before him. Leaning back in his chair, Thomas arched a brow, this time in open question.

Smile deepening a fraction, Roland said, "When I asked for your name, you were in extremis, barely conscious and nearly out of your mind with pain, yet you answered. Until you told me otherwise, I believed that Thomas Glendower was your name. You've been answering without hesitation to that name for months. So . . ." Roland's gray gaze studied Thomas's hazel eyes. "Am I right in assuming that Thomas Glendower actually exists?"

Thomas nodded. "He does. He is"—he gestured, something he could at last freely do, and with reasonable grace— "an alter ego of mine, one I set up before I attained my majority, but which I had rarely used, at least not for the schemes that were my other self's undoing." He paused, considering, then said, "If I'm to live in the world long enough to fulfill whatever purpose Fate or the Deity wants me to achieve, then I need an identity, and Thomas is . . . not perfect, not completely free of sin, but he is resurrectable, useable for this purpose at least."

Roland nodded. "You mentioned that you, at least as you were, had a tendency not to think of others—to be less than aware of the impact of your actions on others." Fixing his gaze on Thomas's eyes, Roland said, "So I feel I should ask—does Thomas have any dependents? Anyone for whom his—your—disappearance, and prolonged absence, will cause difficulties?"

Thomas blinked; slowly, he sat straighter. "Not immediate difficulties—not even after this amount of time. But eventually . . . yes."

"Indeed," Roland said. "So consider this a jog to your elbow. Although you might choose to remain in seclusion here, pending enlightenment as to your purpose, you can write now"—with his head, he indicated the pen Thomas had set down—"and you should reestablish contact with those dependents, to reassure them and keep your affairs in order."

Thomas thought that through, then met Roland's eyes. "Thank you."

Roland's ready smile appeared, then he pushed back from the table. "I'll leave you to it. Any letter you want sent, simply leave it on the salver on the table outside Geoffrey's study."

Thomas nodded.

As Roland walked off, Thomas debated, then reached for a fresh sheet of paper.

Half an hour later, leaning heavily on his crutches, Thomas struggled into the hallway outside the prior's study. Pausing by the table set against the wall, chest heaving, he drew in a deeper breath and dropped the two missives he'd clutched in one hand onto the waiting salver. Both letters bore London addresses; the first was to Drayton, Thomas Glendower's business agent, and the second was for Marwell, Thomas's solicitor.

Balancing on the crutches, Thomas stared at the letters, lying on top of a small pile. They were his first foray back into the world outside the priory—a step the magnitude of which he felt certain Roland had appreciated.

But, indeed, it had had to be done; the letters had had to be written, the step taken.

Gripping his crutches, Thomas turned and clomped away.

The library became his workplace and the seasons rolled on. Winter passed, and spring arrived, along with the abbot of the abbey to which the priory was attached. Having seen the recent financial reports from Prior Geoffrey, the abbot wished to inquire whether Thomas might manage to perform a similar miracle with the abbey's fortunes.

Thomas was pleased to accept the challenge; managing more funds would keep him occupied, keep his mind engaged, and sharpen his faculties. It would also force him to deal with more people, and he was starting to realize that he needed steady practice in the art of, as Roland, with telling simplicity, put it, thinking of others.

For Thomas, that had never, and still did not, come naturally. He had to remind himself to do it, to think his actions and their ramifications through from the perspectives of others involved.

As he still had no clue as to the purpose for which he'd been spared, he accepted that, in order to remain even within the world enclosed by the priory walls, he needed to learn how to live with others without inadvertently causing harm through his habitual self-absorption.

The priory was Benedictine, and somewhat to his surprise he found himself falling into the pattern of monastic hours; there was comfort in the regimen. Roland remained his closest associate, although he also spent many hours with Geoffrey. Both men had minds that, if not the equal of his, were at least close enough to foster mutual appreciation.

Slowly, his body healed. His face would never be the same again, and he would carry his many scars for the rest of his life, but one by one the various braces and strappings Roland had devised to realign Thomas's bones and support his wrenched joints were permanently retired. Two years after Roland had found him washed up on the nearby shore, he could walk fully upright, with only a single cane for support.

Despite his ordeal, his health, previously unassailably rude, hadn't deserted him; as the months rolled on, he spent his afternoons away from the library, helping in the gardens, stables, and workshops, wherever an extra hand was needed. And his strength grew, and his abilities increased. The latter he viewed with a somewhat cynical pleasure; in his previous life, he had never had the chance to lay his hands on an adze, much less a mattock. As for his strength . . . if he had been spared in order to fulfill some function, perform some deed, then, he reasoned, he would need sufficient strength to accomplish it.

Three years after he'd arrived at the priory, Geoffrey died. Thomas was somewhat surprised to feel sorrow, grief, and regret at the old man's passing. Those weren't emotions he'd experienced before, not for an acquaintance; he took their existence as a sign that he was, indeed, learning the ways of connecting with others.

After Geoffrey was buried with all due ceremony, the remaining brothers met and elected the next prior. Thomas wasn't surprised that the brothers' unanimous choice was Roland.

"To you, Prior Roland." Leaning back in the armchair to one side of the hearth in the prior's study, Thomas raised his goblet to Roland, seated in the chair opposite, in which Geoffrey had used to sit.

Roland's lips twisted, half smile, half grimace. "I wish I could say I'm thrilled, but I would much rather Geoffrey was still here with us."

For once, Thomas could understand. He inclined his head. "Indeed."

For a moment, both were silent, then Roland raised his goblet. "To absent friends."

"To Geoffrey." Thomas drank, as did Roland.

Then Roland sat back and eyed Thomas. "And, in some ways, to you—it's you I, and my colleagues, have to thank for the priory being in such robust financial health that we will, it seems, never have to worry about our continued existence."

Thomas waved the thanks aside. "I was here, bored—and it was appropriate that I repay you and the house for this." Another wave indicated his healed body. "Incidentally, can I expect any further improvement, or is this as nimble as I'm going to get?"

Roland's lips quirked. "You will get stronger—I've seen that in you over the last months. But you'll find that your strength will be in different areas. For instance, your hands grip harder because they so often must support your weight, and your arms and shoulders will be stronger than they were, but your legs will always be weaker than before. As for nimbleness"—Roland's tone gentled—"you will always walk with a hitching limp . . . I couldn't fix that. And you will almost certainly always need a cane, but other than that, as you've already discovered, you can ride, and, in time, you'll be able to walk much further than you presently can."

His gaze on his weak left leg, Thomas nodded.

"But," Roland continued, his voice strengthening, "to return to the point I was intending to make before you so glibly deflected me."

Thomas smiled wryly.

Roland nodded. "Indeed. To return to that point, I have

clearly found my place, my path leading on into the future. Like Geoffrey, I will be prior here until I die. I actively sought that path—I worked and put myself into a position from where, if my colleagues so chose, I could become prior and attain my life's goal. As Geoffrey did before me. But what of you, Thomas? You've been biding time since I brought you here, but you are not the sort of man to live life by default. You're like Geoffrey, like me, in that regard. So what is your goal?"

Thomas sighed. Raising his head, he rested it against the well-padded leather. After a moment, he met Roland's gaze. "I expected to die. But I didn't. If I accept yours, Geoffrey's, and, indeed, this house's thesis, then I've been spared for some reason, presumably to fulfill some purpose—one I am uniquely qualified to carry out." He spread his hands. "So here I am, waiting for Fate, or God, or whatever force determines these things to find me and set their ordained task before me." He paused, then, knowing Roland was waiting for the rest, continued, "I intended, and still see my death—the true and final death of the man I was—as an inescapable payment for my sins, for the sins I committed as that man. In that context, that I've been spared to perform a task that only I can accomplish . . . fits, in a way." Thomas paused, then drained his goblet. Lowering it, he murmured, "I feel like I'm on a journey of penance—almost dying, yet not being allowed to get off so easily, my consequent convalescence, and, presumably, eventually, my task to complete. The way I now view it, only once that task is done will I be allowed to know peace, to finally finish paying my full penance for my past deeds."

Roland regarded him in silence. A minute ticked past, then Roland said, "I can see that you believe that, and I can mount no argument against your logic. Your view is much as mine would be were I in your place. However, to return to the aspect of your situation that remains to be addressed, you are well enough now to actively seek your path—the one along which your task to complete lies. Yet to my mind, you're still waiting—still passive, not actively seeking."

Thomas frowned. After several moments, he said, "I had thought—assumed—that Fate, or the Deity, would find me when they were ready . . . when they felt I was ready. I assumed that all I needed to do was wait here, and my task would find me."

Roland's lips twisted. "That might be so, but the priory is a highly circumscribed world. Your task may well lie beyond our walls, and you might not find it unless you actively seek it."

Thomas said nothing, simply stared, unseeing, at his feet.

Roland waited several minutes, then murmured, "Just open your mind to the question. Clarity will come to you in time."

That night, Thomas tossed and turned on his narrow cot in the last cell of the infirmary. Roland's words, their implication—that to complete his penance and find true peace he would need to leave the confines of the priory, and the safety its walls afforded, and seek his ordained task in the wider world—and the ramifications of that churned through his mind.

He knew he was the sort of character who liked to be in charge, and in control of his own destiny, most of all. And he was manipulative, more or less instinctively. Was staying here, supposedly waiting, simply another way of him trying to exert some control?

Trying to force Fate, or God, to play by his rules?

One thing he knew beyond question, beyond doubt—he hated stepping into unknown situations. He always had.

And he still had no clue, no inkling at all, of what his ordained task might be.

To accept the risk and simply set out, and trust that his task would find him, that by seeking, he would find it . . .

Having faith in anything but himself had never come easily.

"It's time I left the priory." Using his cane for support, Thomas let himself down into the armchair beside the hearth in Roland's study.

Sinking into the armchair opposite, Roland studied him, then nodded. "You've achieved all that you set out to achieve here."

Rather grimly, Thomas nodded back. "I made a pact with myself—if, by the time I amassed sufficient funds for the priory and the abbey to undertake the building works you and the abbot have set your hearts upon, my fated task had yet to find me, then I would accept that verdict and go forth and actively search for it. As of this morning, that time is upon me—as I'm aware you've always thought, my task is clearly not fated to find me within these walls."

Head tipping, Roland searched Thomas's face. "I've never understood your reluctance to go back into the world. It's not as if it and its ways are unknown to you."

"No. And to be perfectly candid, I'm not sure I understand my . . . antipathy toward it, either." Thomas paused, then continued, self-deprecation clear in his tone, "I can only surmise that some deep-seated self-preservatory instinct would prefer I remain in relative comfort here, rather than expose myself to the vagaries of life in a world where many have every reason to loathe, if not hang, me."

Roland's gaze remained steady; Thomas could feel its weight—a weight that had grown over the last two years as Roland had matured into his priorship.

"There's one thing," Roland eventually said, "that you often seem to forget."

When Roland didn't immediately continue, Thomas met his gaze and arched his brows inquiringly.

"You are not the man that the world knew. Trust me, your death, as you call it, and your years here have ineradicably changed you."

Thomas inclined his head. "Perhaps so, and perhaps that, in part, is what's behind my reluctance to leave, to chance my hand in the wider world."

Roland blinked. "I don't follow."

"Put simply, I don't know who Thomas Glendower now is, and I don't know how he'll fare outside these walls."

Roland's lips curved in wry understanding. "That's the challenge, isn't it?"

Thomas arched his brows. "A part of it, I suppose. But I think you and I can be reasonably certain that amassing the fortitude to quit this place will be merely a prelude to my fated task." A moment passed, then, more pensively, he concluded, "But to address that task, it's now abundantly clear that I need to go forth and seek it, or, more likely, to allow it to find me."

Chapter 1

March 1838
Lilstock Priory, Somerset

Thomas rode out through the gates with the sun glistening on the frosted grass and sparkling in the dewdrops decorating the still bare branches.

His horse was a pale gray he'd bought some months previously, when traveling with Roland on one of his visits to the abbey. Their route had taken them through Bridgewater, and he'd found the dappled gray there. The gelding was mature, strong, very much up to his weight, but also steady, a necessity given Thomas's physical limitations; he could no longer be certain of applying sufficient force with his knees to manage the horse in stressful situations.

Silver—the novices had named him—was beyond getting stressed. If he didn't like something, he simply stopped, which, in the circumstances, was entirely acceptable to Thomas, who harbored no wish whatever to be thrown.

His bones already had enough fractures for five lifetimes.

As Thomas rode down the road toward Bridgewater, he instinctively assessed his aches and pains. He would always have them, but, in general, they had sunk to a level he could ignore. That, or his senses had grown dulled, his nerves inured to the constant abrading.

He'd ridden daily over the last month in preparation for this journey, building up his strength and reassuring himself that he could, indeed, ride for the four or five days required to reach his destination.

The first crest in the road drew near, and a sense of leaving something precious behind tugged. Insistently.

Drawing rein on the rise, he wheeled Silver and looked back.

The priory sat, gray stone walls sunk into the green of the headland grasses, with the blue sky and the pewter of the Channel beyond. He looked, and remembered all the hours he'd spent, with Roland, with Geoffrey, with all the other monks who had accepted him without question or judgment.

They, more than he, had given him this chance—to go forth and complete his penance, and so find ultimate peace.

Courtesy of Drayton, he had money in his pocket, and in his saddlebags he had everything he would need to reach his chosen abode and settle in.

He was finally doing it, taking the first step along the road to find his fate.

In effect, surrendering himself to Fate, freely giving himself up to whatever lay in wait.

Thomas stared at the walls of the priory for a moment more, then, turning Silver, he rode on.

His way lay via Taunton, a place of memories, and of people who might, despite the disfigurement of his injuries, recognize him; he rode straight through and on, spending the night at the small village of Waterloo Cross before rising with the sun and continuing west.

Late in the afternoon on the fourth day after he'd ridden out from the priory, he arrived at Breage Manor. He'd ridden through Helston and out along the road to Penzance, then had turned south along the lane that led toward the cliffs. The entrance to the drive was unremarkable; a simple gravel avenue, it wended between stunted trees, then across a short stretch of rising open ground to end before the front door.

He'd bought the property years ago, entirely on a whim. It had appealed to him, and for once in his life he'd given into impulse and purchased it—a simple, but sound, gentleman's residence in the depths of Cornwall. In all his forty-two years, it was the only house he'd personally owned, the only place he could imagine calling home.

A solid but unimaginative rectangular block constructed of local bricks in muted shades of red, ochre, and yellow, the house consisted of two stories plus dormers beneath a lead roof. The windows of the main rooms looked south, over the cliffs, to the sea.

As he walked Silver up the drive, Thomas scanned the house and found it the same as his memories had painted it. He hadn't been back in years—many more than the five years he'd spent in the priory. The Gattings, the couple he'd installed as caretaker and housekeeper, had clearly continued to look after the house as if it were their own. The glass in the windows gleamed, the front steps were swept, and even from a distance the brass knocker gleamed.

Thomas halted Silver at the point where the track to the

stable met the drive, but then, in deference to the old couple who he hadn't informed of his impending arrival, he urged Silver nearer to the front steps and dismounted. Despite the damage to the left side of his face and his other injuries, the Gattings would recognize him, but he didn't need to shock them by walking unheralded through the back door.

Or clomping, as the case would be.

Retrieving his cane from the saddle holder that the stable master at the priory had fashioned for it, then releasing Silver's reins, Thomas watched as the big gray ambled a few steps off the drive and bent his head to crop the rough grass. Satisfied the horse wouldn't stray much further, Thomas headed for the front door.

Gaining the small front porch, he was aware of tiredness dragging at his limbs—hardly surprising, given the distance he'd ridden, combined with the additional physical effort of having to cope with his injuries. But he was finally there—the only place he considered home—and now he could rest, at least until Fate found him.

The bell chain hung beside the door; grasping it, he tugged.

Deep in the house, he heard the bell jangling. Straightening, stiffening his spine, adjusting his grip on the silver handle of his cane, he prepared to meet Gatting again.

Footsteps approached the door, swift and light. Before he had time to do more than register the oddity, the door opened.

A woman stood in the doorway; she regarded him steadily. "Yes? Can I help you?"

He'd never seen her before. Thomas blinked, then frowned. "Who are you?" *Who the devil are you* were the words that had leapt to his tongue, but his years in the priory had taught him to watch his words.

Her chin lifted a notch. She was tallish for a woman, only half a head shorter than he, and she definitely wasn't young enough—or demure enough—to be any sort of maid. "I rather think that's my question."

"Actually, no—it's mine. I'm Thomas Glendower, and I own this house."

She blinked at him. Her gaze didn't waver, but her grip on the edge of the door tightened. After several seconds of utter silence, she cleared her throat, then said, "As I'm afraid I don't know you, I will need to see some proof of your identity before I allow you into the house."

He hadn't stopped frowning. He tried to look past her, into the shadows of the front hall. "Where are the Gattings? The couple I left here as caretakers?"

"They retired—two years ago now. I'd been assisting them for two years before that, so I took over when they left." Suspicion—which, he realized, had been there from the outset—deepened in her eyes. "If you really were Mr. Glendower, you would know that. It was all arranged properly with . . . your agent in London—he would have informed you of the change."

She'd been smart enough not to give him the name. As she started to edge the door shut, he replied, with more than a touch of acerbity, "If you mean Drayton, he would not have thought the change of sufficient importance to bother me with." With a brief wave, he indicated his damaged self. "For the last five years, I've been otherwise occupied."

At least that served to stop her from shutting the door in his face. Instead, she studied him, a frown blooming in her eyes; her lips—quite nice lips, as it happened—slowly firmed into a thin line. "I'm afraid, sir, that, regardless, I will need some proof of your identity before I can allow you into this house."

Try to see things from the other person's point of view. He was still having a hard enough time doing that with men; she was a woman—he wasn't going to succeed. Thomas stared at her—and she stared back. She wasn't going to budge. So . . . he set his mind to the task, and it solved it easily enough. "Do you dust in the library?"

She blinked. "Yes."

"The desk in there—it sits before a window that faces the side garden."

"It does, but anyone could have looked in and seen that."

"True, but if you dust the desk, you will know that the center drawer is locked." He held up a hand to stop her from telling him that that was often the case with such desks. "If you go to the desk and put your back to that drawer, then look to your right, you will see a set of bookshelves, and on the shelf at"—he ran his gaze measuringly over her— "about your chin height, on the nearer corner you will see a carriage clock. In the front face of the base of that clock is a small rectangular panel. Press on it lightly and it will spring open. Inside the hidden space, you will find the key to the center drawer of the desk. Open the drawer, and you will see a black-leather-covered notebook. Inside, on the first leaf, you will find my name, along with the date—1816. On the following pages are figures that represent the monthly ore tonnages cleared from the two local mining leases I then owned." He paused, then cocked a brow at her. "Will that satisfy you as identification?"

Lips tight, she held his gaze steadily, then, with commendable calm, replied, "If you will wait here, I'll put your identification to the test."

With that, she shut the door.

Thomas sighed, then he heard a bolt slide home and felt affronted.

What did she think? That he might force his way in?

As if to confirm his incapacity, his left leg started to ache; he needed to get his weight off it for at least a few minutes or the ache would convert to a throb. Going back down the three shallow steps, he let himself down to sit on the porch, then stretched his legs out and leaned his cane against his left knee.

He hadn't even learned her name, yet he still felt insulted that she might imagine he was any threat to her. How could she think so? He couldn't even chase her. Even if he tried, all she would have to do would be to toss something in his path and he would trip and fall on his face.

Some people found disfigurement hard to look upon, but although she'd seen his scars, she'd hardly seemed to notice—she certainly hadn't allowed him any leeway because of his injuries. And, in truth, he didn't look that bad. The left side of his face had been battered, leaving his eyelid drooping, his cheekbone slightly depressed, and a bad scar across his jaw on that side, but the right side of his face had survived with only a few minor scars; that was why he'd been so sure the Gattings would know him on sight.

The rest of his body was a similar patchwork of badly scarred areas and those relatively unscathed, but all that was concealed by his clothes. His hands had survived well enough, at least after Roland had finished with them, to pass in all normal circumstances. The only obvious outward signs of his injuries were his left leg, stiff from the hip down, and the cane he needed to ensure he kept his balance.

He was trying to see himself through her eyes, and, admittedly, he was still capable sexually, but, really, how could she possibly see him as a threat?

He'd reached that point in his fruitless cogitations when

he realized he was the object of someone's gaze. Glancing to the right, he saw two children—a boy of about ten and a girl several years younger—staring at him from around the corner of the house.

As they didn't duck back when he saw them, he deduced that they had a right to be there . . . and that they might well be the reason for his new housekeeper's caution.

The little girl continued to unabashedly study him, but the boy's gaze shifted to Silver.

Even from this distance and angle, Thomas saw the longing in the boy's face. "You can pat him if you like. He's oldish and used to people. He won't bite or fuss."

The boy looked at Thomas; his eyes, his whole face, lit with pleasure. "Thank you." He stepped out from the house and walked calmly toward Silver, who saw him, but, as Thomas had predicted, the horse made no fuss and allowed the boy to stroke his long neck, which the lad did with all due reverence.

Thomas watched the pair, for, of course, the girl trailed after her brother; from their features, Thomas was fairly certain they were siblings, and related to his new housekeeper. He'd also noticed the clarity of the boy's diction, and realized that it, too, matched that of the woman who had opened the door. Whoever they were, wherever they had come from, it wasn't from around here.

"Nor," Thomas murmured, "from any simple cottage."

There could, of course, be many reasons for that. The role of housekeeper to a gentleman of Mr. Thomas Glendower's standing would be an acceptable post for a lady from a gentry family fallen on hard times.

Hearing footsteps approaching on the other side of the door, rather more slowly this time, Thomas picked up his cane and levered himself back onto his feet. He turned to the door as the woman opened it. She held his black note-book in her hand, opened to the front page.

Rose looked out at the man who had told her what date she would find in the black-leather-covered notebook in her absent employer's locked desk drawer—a drawer she knew had not been opened during all the years she'd been in the house. Hiding her inward sigh, she shut the book and used it to wave him in as she pulled the door wide. "Welcome home, Mr. Glendower."

His lips twitched, but he merely inclined his head and didn't openly gloat. "Perhaps we can commence anew, Mrs. . . . ?"

Her hand falling, Rose lifted her chin. "Sheridan. Mrs. Sheridan. I'm a widow." Looking out to where Homer and Pippin were petting Glendower's horse, she added, "My children and I joined the Gattings here four years ago. I was looking for work, and the Gattings had grown old and needed help."

"Indeed. Having added up the years, I now realize that was likely to have occurred. I haven't visited here for quite some time."

So why had he had to return now? But Rose knew there was no point railing at Fate; there was nothing for it but to allow him in, to allow him to reclaim his property—it was his, after all. She no longer had any doubt of that; quite aside from the date in the book, she would never have found the hidden compartment in the clock if he hadn't told her of it. She'd handled the clock often enough while dusting and had never had any inkling that it contained a concealed compartment. And the clock had been there for at least the last four years, so how could he have known? No, he was Thomas Glendower, just as he claimed, and she couldn't keep him out of his own house. And the situation might have been much worse.

Stepping back, she held the door open and waited while, leaning heavily on his cane, he negotiated the final step into the house. "Homer—my son—will bring up your bags and stable your horse."

"Thank you." Head rising, he halted before her.

She looked into eyes that were a mixture of browns and greens—and a frisson of awareness slithered down her spine. Her lungs tightened in reaction. Why, she wasn't sure. Regardless, she felt perfectly certain that behind those eyes dwelled a mind that was incisive, observant, and acutely intelligent.

Not a helpful fact, yet she sensed no threat emanating from him, not on any level. She'd grown accustomed to trusting her instincts about men, had learned that those instincts were rarely wrong. And said instincts were informing her that the advent of her until-now-absent employer wasn't the disaster she had at first thought.

Despite the damage done to his face, he appeared personable enough—indeed, the undamaged side of his face was almost angelic in its purity of features. And regardless of his injuries, and the fact he was clearly restricted in his movements, his strength was still palpable; he might be a damaged archangel, but he still had power.

Mentally castigating herself for such fanciful analogies, she released the door, letting it swing half shut. "If you'll give me a few minutes, sir, I'll make up your room. And I expect you'd like some warm water to wash away the dust."

Thomas inclined his head. Stepping further inside as the door swung behind him, he reached for the black notebook she still held. His fingers brushed hers, and she caught her breath and rapidly released the book.

So . . . the attraction he'd sensed moments earlier had been real, and not just on his part?

He felt faintly shocked. He hadn't expected . . . straightening, he raised his head, drew in a deeper breath—and detected the fragile, elusive scent of roses.

The effect that had on him—instantaneous and intense—was even more shocking.

Abruptly clamping a lid on all such reactions—he couldn't afford to frighten her; he needed her to keep house for him, not flee into the night—he tucked the notebook into his coat pocket and quietly said, "I'll be in the library."

One glance at the stairs had been enough to convince him that he wouldn't be able to manage them until he'd rested for a while.

"Indeed, sir." His new housekeeper shut the door and in brisk, no-nonsense fashion informed him, "Dinner will be ready at six o'clock. As I didn't know you would be here—"

"That's quite all right, Mrs. Sheridan." He started limping toward the library. "I've been living with monks for the last five years. I'm sure your cooking will be more than up to the mark."

He didn't look, but he was prepared to swear she narrowed her eyes on his back. Ignoring that, and the niggling lure of the mystery she and her children posed, he opened the library door and went in—to reclaim the space, and then wait for Fate to find him.

Washed and dressed in fresh clothes, Thomas made his way down the stairs to the drawing room, reaching it with five minutes to spare. He amused himself by examining the room; he hadn't used it often in the past, but as far as his recollections went, nothing had changed.

The door opened and Mrs. Sheridan stood revealed in the doorway. "If you'll come through to the dining room, sir, dinner is waiting."

He nodded. Leaning heavily on his cane—managing the

stairs had proved a challenge, one he was determined to conquer—he crossed to the door and, with a wave, gestured for her to precede him. He followed her across the hall. The lamp there and those in the dining room cast a steady, even light, illuminating his mysterious housekeeper and allowing him to see her more clearly than he previously had; as he limped to the head of the table and sat, from beneath his lashes he watched her go to the sideboard on which serving platters were arrayed. Her gown was of some dark brown material, of decent quality but severely, indeed, repressively, cut, with a high collar and long, tight sleeves. Her hair, thick, lustrous locks of rich walnut brown, was restrained in a knot at her nape.

She picked up a soup tureen and turned, and he fixed his gaze on his plate. He already knew her eyes were a soft mid-brown, fringed by lush lashes and well-set beneath dark, finely arched brows. Her complexion was fair, cream with a tinge of rose in her cheeks; her features were delicate, her face heart-shaped with a gently rounded chin.

He'd already noted her straight, no-nonsense nose and her full lips of pale rose, but as she leaned across to offer him the tureen, he saw that, as before, those lips were compressed into a tense line.

The sight . . . displeased him, which, on one level, he found curious. He rarely cared about how others were feeling, at least not spontaneously.

"Thank you." Availing himself of the ladle, he served himself.

As he picked up his soup spoon, Mrs. Sheridan ferried the tureen back to the sideboard, then turned and, clasping her hands before her, took up station at the end of the sideboard, ready to serve him the subsequent courses.

He took a mouthful of the soup while debating how best

to say what he wished to convey. In the end, he said, "This soup is delicious. My compliments to the cook."

"Thank you."

"If I might make a suggestion, there's no reason for you to wait on me, Mrs. Sheridan. If you place all those platters on the table where I can reach them, you might then go and take your meal with your children." Sidelong, he cast her an inquiring glance. "I presume the pair are dining in the kitchen as we speak?"

From the look on her face, he knew he'd guessed aright. Six o'clock was standard dinnertime in the country, especially in gentry houses. And he was fairly certain both she and her children were gentry-born.

She hesitated, and for a moment he wondered if what he'd suggested might in some way be construed as an insult, but then he realized she was wrestling, in two minds.

Inwardly smiling, he said, "I really don't mind." *And I find having a lady standing while I'm seated off-putting.* He swallowed the words before they escaped, but . . . that was, he realized, how he felt, and wasn't that revealing? His facility for gauging people, especially their social standing, had always been acute; it might be a trifle rusty from disuse, but it was clearly still functioning.

"If you truly don't mind, sir . . . ?"

"I wouldn't have suggested it if I did."

"Very well." Turning, she picked up two of the covered platters and carried them to the table. Two more trips back and forth and he had everything he needed, including condiments, within easy reach.

Still, she hovered, as if unsure if he truly was capable of serving himself.

Fleetingly irritated—he might be a partial cripple, but he

wasn't incapacitated—he dismissed her with a wave. "Thank you, Mrs. Sheridan. That will be all."

She stiffened at his tone. She started to turn away, then remembered and paused to bob a curtsy. Then she left.

Leaving him to slowly finish his soup, his mind already toying with various scenarios that might explain who she was and why she was there—pretending to be a house-keeper in an isolated country house.

He'd finished the soup and had moved on to a second course of lamb collops before the relative silence impinged. Once it had, with every passing minute he grew more rest-less, less settled, less content. He wasn't alone in the house, but only by straining his ears could he detect any sound from the kitchen—a clink, a muted sentence. Regardless, his awareness shifted and fixed on it, on there . . . it took him a few minutes to identify his problem, to understand what was wrong.

The solution was obvious, yet he hesitated—he knew how the man he once had been would have behaved, but he was no longer that man, and, apparently, the man he now was had different needs.

Surrendering to the insistent impulse—and, after all, it wasn't the Gattings, who would have been more shocked—he quickly gathered his plate and all else he deemed necessary for the rest of his meal, piled everything on the big tray Mrs. Sheridan had left on the sideboard, then, hefting the tray in one hand—something he'd learned to do at the priory—and gripping his cane in the other, he headed for the kitchen.

They heard him coming, of course.

He pushed past the green baize door at the rear of the front hall, then went along the short corridor to the kitchen. When he appeared in the archway giving onto the good-sized room, he saw the table sited squarely in its center; all three occupants seated at the board, knives and forks in their hands, had turned surprised and, at least on the children's part, frankly curious faces his way.

Seated at the far end of the table, Mrs. Sheridan set down her cutlery and pushed back her chair, preparing to rise.

"No." He answered the question in her face as he limped out of the shadows into the lamplight. "There's nothing whatever amiss with the food." Halting at the nearer end of the table, he lowered the tray to the scrubbed surface. "The truth is that, through the last five years of convalescing in a monastery, I've grown accustomed to taking my meals in the refectory, surrounded by lots of monks." Raising his gaze, he met Mrs. Sheridan's eyes. "I've just discovered that I find eating alone somewhat unsettling, and I wondered if you would object to me joining you here and taking my meals in your company."

That was the truth, just not the whole truth; he was also insatiably curious about the small family he'd discovered living under his roof.

Sinking back onto her chair, Rose stared at him and swiftly weighed her options. His request was outlandish, entirely outside the norm, yet he owned the house, so how could she deny him? She needed this place, this position—the safety of this house—for herself and even more for the children; she wouldn't risk that over such a minor matter. Moreover, he had explained his need for company, and that she fully understood. How many years had it been since she had conversed with another adult? Yes, she understood that craving for company, yet . . . she glanced at the children.

They had lived there for four years, and their story was established and sound. Homer, three years older than six-year-old Pippin, understood enough to be careful, and Pippin simply didn't remember enough to pose any real risk of exposure.

She looked up at Glendower, fleetingly studied him anew, confirming the presence that, despite his infirmities, still shone clearly. Still had an impact. She consulted her instincts, yet, as before, they remained undisturbed; no matter the circumstances, she sensed no threat from him. She nodded. "If you wish it, then, indeed, you are welcome to join us." She glanced at Homer. "Homer—please fetch the other chair for Mr. Glendower."

An eager smile lighting his face, Homer leapt up and brought the fourth chair from its place by the wall.

Glendower took it from him with a smile and a nod of thanks, set the chair, and sat, facing her down the short length of the table. He glanced at Homer. "Homer, is it?"

"Yes, Mr. Glendower," Homer brightly replied. "That's me."

"As we're to share a table, Homer, you may call me Thomas." Glendower's gaze passed on to Pippin, who had been equally eagerly, but rather more shyly, regarding him. Glendower smiled, an easy expression that despite the damage to one side of his face remained unimpaired in its charm. "And you are?"

Rose waited to see if Pippin would deem Glendower worthy of her words.

After eyeing him for several seconds, during which Glendower simply waited, unperturbed by her scrutiny, Pippin made her decision and beamed and piped, "I'm Pippin—like the apples."

Glendower's smile deepened. Gravely, he inclined his head. "I'm delighted to make your acquaintance, Pippin. And please, call me Thomas."

"I will," Pippin assured him.

Glendower's gaze moved on to Rose; before it reached her, she made a show of studying what he had brought in on his tray. "Do you have everything you need there?" Raising her gaze, she met his hazel eyes.

His easy expression in place, Thomas held her gaze for a long moment, but she gave no sign of wavering. No first names between them, it seemed. Glancing down at the tray, he nodded. "Yes, I believe so." It wasn't in his best interests to annoy or irritate her. He started to lift the various platters and plates from the tray, setting his plate before him and spreading the platters along the table, clearly inviting Homer, Pippin, and the curiously haughty and reserved Mrs. Sheridan to partake of the dishes.

Everyone returned their attention to their plate.

Thomas waited. The little girl, Pippin—six or seven years old?—had the same color and fine texture of hair as her mother, and similar eyes, too. The girl's features were younger echoes; between the two females, the resemblance was strong. The boy had darker hair, more sable than walnut, and dark blue eyes, somewhat differently set in a broader face, but while his features in general were stronger, the resemblance to his mother was there.

Thomas had had very little to do with children, yet he did remember what being a boy was like. His money was on Homer, and the boy didn't disappoint.

"Did you really live in a monastery for five years?" Homer's big blue eyes overflowed with curiosity.

Mrs. Sheridan opened her mouth—no doubt to quell the imminent inquisition.

Thomas spoke before she could. "Yes. It was up by the Bristol Channel." He'd long ago learned that the best way to invite confidences from others was to offer information first.

"Was it old and ruined, and were there ghosts?" Pippin asked.

Thomas smiled encouragingly. "No—it was only built about thirty years ago. The monks came over from France during the . . ." *Terror.* " . . . upheavals there, about fifty years ago now."

Now the gate had been opened, both children came barreling through, posing question after question about life in the monastery; both possessed what Thomas considered healthy curiosities, and he was entirely willing to indulge them.

Still alert, still wary, Rose watched her employer charm the children, but there was nothing in his manner that struck her as worrisome; indeed, time and again, he stopped and thought before he answered. She'd already noticed that about him; his responses were, more often than not, considered.

As for the children, as he'd all but invited their questions, she was content to let them pose them—so she, too, could learn the answers.

She was as curious, if not more so, than they.

When she'd first opened the door to him, she'd instinctively catalogued his clothes, his hairstyle, his deportment, his manners, his diction, and all the rest—all the telltale signs of class—and had pegged him as upperrange gentry, perhaps with a knighthood or a baronetcy in the family. That also fitted what she'd gathered about Thomas Glendower. Now, however, as the conversation between him and the children continued, steady and unforced, and she had time to study the clothes he'd donned for the evening and his more polished appearance, had time to note his precise diction delivered in that faintly raspy voice, and the manners and assurance that seemed an intrinsic part of him, she had to wonder if his origins weren't a rung or two higher.

Somewhat to her surprise, the meal passed in unexpectedly and uniformly pleasant fashion.

And at the end of it, he set the seal on her approval by offering, and then insisting, albeit with consummate grace, on helping her and the children to clear the table, and to wash the dishes and put them away.

"It's only fair if I'm to share your meals." He made the comment to the children but then looked up, questioningly, at her.

When she didn't look convinced, he added, with a suggestion of a grin, as if he understood her position perfectly, "Put it down to my years in the priory—there, everyone helps with the chores."

With the children looking on, it was impossible to refuse him, so the four of them worked together to clear, clean, and tidy the kitchen.

When all was done, the children went up to their rooms to read. She fetched her sewing basket and set it down beside her chair. When she looked up, Glendower was watching her. In response to her questioning look, he inclined his head.

"I'll be in the library should you need me," he said.

She nodded, then asked, "Would you like me to bring you some tea?"

"Later." He glanced at the clock on the wall. "Perhaps sometime after nine?"

She nodded again. "I'll bring it in to you."

He turned away and, using his cane, gimped toward the archway, but then he paused and glanced back at her. "I daresay it will take a little time for me to adjust to life outside the priory. I would appreciate it if you could see your way to humoring my what might occasionally seem rather eccentric ways."

She met his gaze, held it, and equally directly replied, "As long as those ways hold no harm for the children or myself, I see no reason we won't be able to reach an accommodation."

His lips curved in that peculiarly engaging smile he had. Inclining his head, he turned and left her.

Unwillingly intrigued, Rose watched him go and wondered at the conundrum that was Mr. Thomas Glendower.

Thomas's first day at the manor had, in fact, proved more interesting than he'd expected.

Draining the cup of tea Mrs. Sheridan had duly delivered, along with two shortbread biscuits that had proved decidedly delicious, he swept his gaze once more over the shelves of the small library he'd so long ago assembled. It wasn't extensive, but all the works he regarded as critical were there.

Setting down the empty cup, he glanced out of the window, but it was full dark, with only a glimmer of moonlight; he couldn't make out much at all.

Grasping his cane, he levered himself up and headed for the door.

The stairs were a trial; he had to step up with his right foot, then pull his left up to the same step before repeating the process. Still, purely from having gone up and down earlier, the ordeal was easier, the effort less.

Reaching the head of the stairs, he paused to marshal his strength, then limped along the corridor to the door to his room. The largest bedroom in the house, it faced south. He'd left the window uncurtained. Closing the door, he didn't bother to light the lamp but walked through the shadows to stand before the window and look out at the view across the cliffs to the rippling darkness of the sea beyond.

Moonlight shafted from the heavens to his right, a silver beam lancing down to dance on the waves, leaving eerie phosphorescence gilding the crests. Clouds gathered in clusters, splotches against the black silk of the night sky, blocking the faint light of the stars.

Often along this stretch of coast, the view would be stormy, turbulent, the seas a churning mass of green-gray. But tonight, the wind was mild, the ocean calm. All was peaceful.

He looked, saw, and drank in that peace.

He'd bowed to Fate and had taken the next step, had come out into the world, and here he was.

What now? was the question in his mind. He was there, ready, waiting, and willing to do whatever Fate would decree as his final act of penance.

Yet beyond being there, out in the world, he wasn't sure what more he could do to actively seek his true path.

After five more minutes of staring at the view, during which nothing further occurred to him, he sighed and turned to the bed. He was safe enough there, and his unexpected housekeeper and her children—learning to live alongside them, learning to live in the world again—would be interest and challenge enough for the nonce.

And if he could do anything to help them, he would.

While he waited for Fate to summon him.

After doing her nightly round of the house, and noting with approval that her employer had taken himself upstairs, Rose climbed to the upper floor; hers and the children's rooms were nestled under the eaves.

Going first to Pippin's small room, then to Homer's, she

tucked them in firmly. Both were already asleep, their innocent faces beatific; she smiled down on them, then left them to their slumbers.

Earlier, when she'd come up to shoo them into their beds, both had still been chattering about Mr. Glendower—Thomas as he now was to them. She didn't think it wise to relinquish the formal mode of address herself, and he, sensibly, hadn't pressed. But with the children he'd already stepped far beyond the "distant employer" state; both had many eager and curious questions, none of which, she judged, were of the sort to cause him any difficulties, and she had to admit she was curious herself.

If someone had asked her to imagine what her absent employer would be like, she would never have dreamed of such a man—of such a very complex, rather fascinating man.

Oddly, despite being on obvious display, his infirmities had not, and did not, materially influence the way she or the children saw him—and that, she suspected, was because he, himself, did not see himself as damaged and unable, as somehow lesser because of his injuries. It was his self-confidence and assurance that others responded to; that had been demonstrated beyond doubt throughout the evening.

Still, as she slid beneath the covers and settled in her bed, she forced herself to take a mental step back and evaluate, coolly and logically, whether Thomas Glendower and his advent into their lives posed any threat to their concealment.

She'd already dismissed the possibility that he might be any threat to either her or the children personally; her instincts really were too well honed by now for her to doubt their verdict, and on the subject of Thomas Glendower, her instincts were entirely certain: He posed no direct threat to her or the children.

That aside . . . she weighed every likely possibility, thought through every scenario she could imagine, and ended concluding that, if anything, his presence at the manor, as the owner of the property, someone who, despite not having been there for years, was known by name and reputation, made their situation better, not worse.

He was, effectively, an extra shield, strengthening and making more impenetrable the façade she'd constructed to hide behind. Him being there, and by inference accepting her and the children for who they purported to be, made their disguise even less transparent.

She considered that conclusion for several minutes and finally accepted it as sound.

Satisfied, she turned on her side and snuggled down, pulling the covers over her shoulder.

Having Thomas Glendower return to live at the manor might be a very good thing, indeed.

And that was not at all how she would have expected to feel about having a largely unknown man sleeping under the same roof as her and the children.

Lips curving in a wry, faintly intrigued smile, Rose shut her eyes and let sleep take her.

The following morning, before Rose could set a tray for him, her employer arrived in the kitchen and took his seat at the end of the table.

"Good morning." He nodded to Homer and Pippin, both of whom grinned back, then he raised his gaze to Rose, where she stood rooted before the stove. "What's for breakfast?"

Rapidly consulting her memory, Rose realized he had, indeed, mentioned taking his meals—all meals—with them. She reached for the coffeepot. "Would you like coffee to start with?"

He nodded and she poured him a cup, then carried it to him.

He reached out and, with both hands, took it from her. His fingers brushed over hers and, once again, she felt a sensual shiver.

Which she ruthlessly quashed; developing any degree of

susceptibility to her employer was very definitely not part of her plans.

Without any sign of awareness of his impact, he buried his nose in the cup, and, relieved, she retreated to the stove. "Bacon and eggs in just a few minutes." She glanced over her shoulder at him. "Are scrambled eggs all right, or would you rather fried?"

"Scrambled will suit me very well." He looked at Homer and Pippin. "So what are you two doing today?"

They told him, filling his ears with all the little details of their days while she laid the bacon to drain, then tipped her prepared eggs into the skillet.

Three minutes later, she set a plate piled with a mound of fluffy golden eggs and trimmed with three slices of the local bacon before him.

"Oh, that does look good." Picking up his knife and fork, he addressed himself to the food.

Rose set Homer's and Pippin's smaller serves before them and they, too, fell silent.

Satisfied, she slipped into her chair and joined the gustatory indulgence. But she remained alert, feeling that this was all going too easily and expecting some catch, some less-than-helpful aspect to make itself known at any minute, yet none did.

And, she had to admit, having him take his meals with them would make catering for his presence significantly easier.

As if to demonstrate yet another advantage, on finishing his meal he pushed away his plate, reached for the coffeepot she'd set on the table, and poured himself a second cup, sipped, then his hazel gaze focused on her. "I have to ride into Breage, and then on to Helston this morning. Is there anything you'd like me to fetch—more eggs, butter, ham?"

She blinked. "I get groceries, eggs, and meat delivered every week—the last delivery was earlier this week—but . . ." She hadn't allowed for his arrival, and she'd just used up a good half of the eggs. "In the circumstances, perhaps I could give you a list, just to get us through until the next delivery comes. I can increase my orders then."

He held her gaze for a moment, long enough to have her thinking over her words and wondering what she'd said. But then he nodded and pushed away from the table. "By all means give me your list of immediate extras, but you can also give me a list of those merchants with whom you have standing orders. I'll call on them, look over the orders, and increase accordingly, then the deliveries from next week will be sufficient." He paused, his gaze growing momentarily distant, then he refocused on her face. "I believe my original arrangement was that all the merchants send their bills to Drayton. Is that system still in place?"

She nodded, casting about for some way of asking the question the discussion had raised.

As before, his lips quirked—and this time she knew it was in understanding; he had read her mind—and he said, "I don't know how long I'll be remaining here. It could be for weeks, or even months."

She blinked. "You have no definite plans?"

Still holding her gaze, he shook his head. "No." After a moment, he added, "You might say I'm awaiting a summons of sorts, but I can't say when it will arrive."

So he was there potentially indefinitely. She inclined her head, accepting, for what else could she do?

He got to his feet, smiled as he nodded to the children, then he glanced at her. "I'll be in the library for a few hours. I'll come and find you before I leave."

She nodded again and watched him pass under the archway into the corridor to the front of the house. He still limped, still used his cane, but, she noticed, he wasn't leaning as heavily on it as he had been the previous day.

While the children finished eating, then helped her clear and clean, she replayed her conversation with Glendower.

There was, she acknowledged, a chance that he would realize their truth, or at least see through some part of their disguise. He was certainly observant and, she judged, intelligent enough. Piercingly intelligent; she could see that in his eyes, and it was more than enough to make her wary.

She and the children could leave before he had a chance to learn too much, but, against that, she and the children were settled and comfortable there, and, despite all, her instincts continued to tell her that she had no reason to fear him—no reason to suppose that, even if he knew all, he would wish them any harm.

And he had voluntarily lived in a monastery for the last five years; presumably he had a healthy notion of right and wrong, of good and evil.

With the dishes dried and stored, she turned to the children and smiled at their bright faces. For them, still, each day was an adventure. "Come along, then." She reached out to stroke their shiny heads. "Let's get you started with your lessons."

Until she had some reason to decide otherwise, they would go on as they had been, but, regardless of her instincts, she would remain on guard.

Two hours later, armed with his requested lists, Thomas made his halting way to the stables. The neat brick structure at the end of the drive appeared in good order; he suspected that ensuring that order was one of Homer's chores.

Pulling open the wooden door, Thomas limped inside

and paused in the central aisle to take stock. His gray was placidly, but expectantly, eyeing him from the stall closest to the door. The next stall housed a smaller horse, little more than a pony, no doubt used for drawing the light trap that sat at the rear of the stable. The third stall was currently empty, its winter occupant no doubt the cow he'd seen cropping grass in the small field beyond the manor's back garden. The side of the stable opposite the stalls was piled high with bales of straw and hay, and several bags of grain.

Noting the tack area just inside the door, Thomas crossed to where his saddle sat atop a wooden horse. Collecting the saddle in one arm, he lifted bridle and reins from a peg, then went to saddle the gray.

He was just settling the saddle across the gray's broad back when a clatter of rushing footsteps approached, then Homer came racing through the door. He skidded to a halt facing Thomas and the gray.

The gray snorted. Thomas grinned.

Eyes wide, Homer blurted, "Ma sent me to help you." Straightening, he blinked. "But you've managed it all yourself."

"Indeed." Balancing against the horse's side, Thomas expertly cinched the girth. "As you can see, I'm perfectly capable of performing such tasks." He glanced at Homer; the boy appeared faintly crestfallen. "But please thank your mother for the kind thought, and thank you for rushing out here to help."

Homer brightened. "Oh, I was happy to." Approaching the gray's head, he patted the long nose. "It meant I could come outside for a spell."

Thomas inwardly frowned. Settling the reins, he asked, "How old are you?" He'd been careful not to ask too many questions, even the obvious ones, last night, not in front of the still suspicious and watchful Mrs. Sheridan.

"Nine," Homer readily volunteered. "Pippin's only six."

Thomas hesitated, then asked, "Why is it you're not attending school? If I remember correctly, there's a village school not far away, just this side of Breage."

Unperturbed, Homer nodded. "Ma schools us. She gets books when we go into Helston or Exeter." He shrugged. "It's been all right, I suppose, but . . ." He grimaced. "I'm sure I could learn more—things like geography, and more Latin, and history, too. Even arithmetic. I'm as good as Ma at that already. And I would love to learn astronomy— about the planets and the celestial bodies."

Watching the boy's face, absorbing the eagerness lighting his eyes and the fervor in his tone, Thomas noted that Homer saw no contradiction in being a housekeeper's son and having access to tutelage in such subjects. "Have you looked through the books in the library?" He tipped his head toward the house.

"No." Homer sighed. "Ma doesn't let us go in there."

Gathering the reins, Thomas led the gray out of the stables. Homer kept pace on the horse's other side. Halting the gray, Thomas held his cane out to Homer. "Hold this while I mount."

Homer took the cane and watched with transparent curiosity as, standing on Silver's off-side, Thomas angled his body so he could slip the toe of his right riding boot into the stirrup; Silver had been trained to allow him to mount on the off-side, a necessity given his injuries. Grasping the saddle, Thomas pulled himself up, swinging his stiff left leg over and sitting. The stirrup on the left hung lower than on the right, but unless one looked closely, Thomas appeared to ride as easily as any other man.

He reached for the cane. "Thank you." Slipping the cane into its holder, he glanced at Homer. "If you like, when I get back, I could select some interesting books for you to read."

"From your library?" When Thomas nodded, Homer beamed. "That would be *wonderful!*"

Thomas found himself grinning back. He could remember having just such a ravenous thirst for knowledge; in his case, he'd had it fulfilled, more or less as part of his birthright. In Homer's case, Thomas could assist in expanding the boy's knowledge. He was more than qualified to act as the boy's tutor. But he should, he suspected, talk that over with Mrs. Sheridan before he raised Homer's hopes.

Yet he'd already decided that while he was at the manor he should do what he could to help the Sheridans, and letting Homer read some books from the library was surely an unexceptionable way to do that.

The gray shifted, eager to be off. Thomas reined him in long enough to nod to Homer. "Done. I'll look out a selection of books when I get back."

Then he let the reins ease, and the gray surged. As Thomas steered the horse down the drive, he heard a whoop of boyish delight fading behind him.

The gray was ready for an outing and settled into a well-paced canter along the road to Breage. Although Helston was Thomas's goal, and he could have reached the town by a more direct route, he'd elected to ride through Breage—just to see.

As it transpired, the baker Mrs. Sheridan favored for her flour and similar supplies was located in the small village. Thomas called there and spent a few minutes improving his rusty charm while adjusting the standing order for the manor.

Leaving the shop, he paused in the street, looking up and

down at the few shops and single alehouse. The baker's wife who he'd spoken with had evinced nothing more than a natural curiosity over meeting a long-absent landowner, one who was scarred and walked with a pronounced limp. As far as Thomas could recall, he had never had any real truck with anyone in the village; there should be no one there who would remember him from before.

From 1816, when, as a much younger man, he'd been party to a scheme to frighten locals who had owned tin mining leases to sell them to him. He'd done nothing more than spread false rumors, and that had been the one and only less-than-honest business venture Thomas Glendower had participated in. All the rest had been done under his birth name, the one associated with his now-dead other self.

Satisfied that there was no potential problem—either for him or the Sheridans—lurking in Breage, Thomas mounted up and took the high road for Helston.

Four uneventful and relaxing miles later, Silver clattered across the bridge over the river Cober, and Thomas turned the horse up the steep rise of Coinagehall Street. The only place in Helston in which, in 1816, he'd spent any real time was the Blue Anchor, a tavern frequented by miners. Walking the gray past the thatched building, he continued up the rise and turned into the stable yard of the Angel Hotel, a more superior establishment high on the rise and much closer to his goal of the post office.

Leaving Silver in the care of the Angel's head ostler, Thomas crossed the road and continued to the post office. He posted letters to Drayton and Marwell in London, and also dispatched a missive to Roland. After a congenial chat with the clerk behind the counter, he went into the tobacconist's next door, where he arranged for copies of the principal London financial news sheets, as well as *The Times,* to be delivered every day as soon as they arrived from the capital. Given this was Cornwall, that meant he would receive the early morning edition in the late afternoon. The delay wasn't ideal, but it had been the same at the priory, and he'd learned to work with the limitation.

Over the last years, he'd refashioned Thomas Glendower's investments into the equivalent of a philanthropic master-fund; despite having set out to seek his fated task, his ultimate penance, he did not see that as an excuse to cease his necessary oversight of that fund. While he waited for Fate to find him, he still had work to do; he did not intend to wait idly.

Aside from all else, idleness in one such as he invariably led to trouble.

His mind never ceased thinking, weighing, speculating: What if he did this, or that? What would be the outcome? Where would lie the gain? And would it be as much as he predicted? It was a persistent activity he'd long ago learned to live with; indeed, for him, such constant mental activity was the norm.

And, as one farsighted old lady had warned him long ago, therein lay the danger. His mind was all too adept at forming schemes for financial gain but, sadly, without due consideration of the law, much less morality. If such schemes remained inside his head, no harm was caused, but, once formed, the temptation to let the schemes out into the world, to give them a chance to play out to see if they worked . . . that was the lure, the constant, insistent temptation he had learned through hard experience he had to hold against.

Keeping his mind busy with legitimate, even desirable, moneymaking ventures was, for him, more necessity than choice.

Halting on the narrow pavement outside the tobacconist's shop, copies of yesterday's news sheets tucked under his arm, Thomas pulled out his fob-watch. It was well after twelve o'clock. The impulse to ride straight back to the manor was surprisingly strong, but by the time he reached there, Mrs. Sheridan and the children would almost certainly have finished their luncheon, and his arrival, hungry and wanting to be fed, would put his housekeeper out.

Tucking his watch back in his waistcoat pocket, Thomas straightened, tightened his grip on his cane, and made his way across the street to the Angel Hotel, and its purportedly excellent dining room.

The following day, Rose was tidying the kitchen after they'd had their morning tea when, through the window over the sink, she saw Glendower walking around the outside of the house.

He wasn't simply strolling; he held a notebook in one hand and was halting every now and then, eyes narrowing, to study the house itself.

Curious, she watched him. After one such instance of close scrutiny, he pulled a pencil from the pocket of his jacket, raised the notebook, and scribbled something.

He was wearing breeches and riding boots, a plain linen shirt, a neat but simply knotted cravat, with a hacking jacket over all; she had assumed he'd intended to go riding again, but no. As she watched, the light breeze ruffled his hair; the bright gold strands amid the light brown were what had caught her eye and drawn her to the window.

Standing before the sink, cloth in hand, she vacillated. She wanted to know what he was doing, what he was planning; in her role as the children's protector, she needed to know of anything that might pose a potential threat, that might bring the risk of exposure into their orbit. Against that, she was honest enough to admit, at least to herself, that her curiosity about Glendower was equally fed by a more unsettling, even disturbing, impulse.

She'd never felt attracted to any gentleman before; mildly curious, perhaps, but not drawn like this.

Drawn to venture closer, to discover whether the sensual thrill she felt at his touch was still there.

She knew it was, would be; every time his fingers inadvertently brushed hers, she felt that addictive thrill to her marrow.

But she didn't know if he felt anything at all, and she couldn't fault his behavior, not in the slightest degree; he'd made no move that even by the wildest stretch of anyone's imagination could be construed as inappropriate, much less as any definite advance.

He'd given her no reason to believe he wanted her, desired her, that he was any threat to her at all.

Was it wrong of her to want to . . . test him?

Was it perverse of her to want to learn more of him, the man, and so risk all the benefits his presence had brought them? Not just to her, but to the children, too?

Last night, after dinner when the children had gone upstairs, he'd spoken to her about Homer and had offered to find suitable books from his library to help satisfy Homer's burgeoning need for knowledge—a need she, herself, could not sate. Glendower had cast the act as a very little thing, something he could easily and painlessly do, but it had already made a difference to Homer and, therefore, to her. The look on Homer's face when, after breakfast this morning, Glendower had taken him into the library, piled his arms with leather-bound tomes, then dispatched him to the dining room, there to sit and read at the big table Glendower no longer used, had been beyond revealing.

Homer had been in alt.

She had been beyond grateful, beyond relieved, but when she'd taken Glendower's morning tea tray to him in the library and had tried to offer her thanks, he'd dismissed his part as insignificant, nothing worthy of further consideration.

He'd made no attempt to capitalize on her gratitude, not in any way. . . .

Rose shifted to keep him in sight as he moved further along the back of the house. Again he stopped, stared, then made a note in his book. She frowned. "What the devil is he doing?"

Tossing the cloth on the bench, she smoothed her hands down her skirts, then passed her palms over her hair, confirming that her chignon was still neat. Then, grabbing her shawl from the back of her chair, she headed for the back door.

Sunshine greeted her as she emerged onto the step, but the light breeze was still cool. Spring was only gradually stealing in and hadn't yet properly arrived. Swinging her shawl about her shoulders, she stepped down to the narrow paved path that led to the stables, but she immediately left the path for the coarse grass and lengthened her stride in pursuit of her quarry, now nearing the far corner of the house.

He glanced at her as she neared, but then went back to writing his latest note.

Halting a few feet away, she faced the house and studied the façade, trying to see what had caught his attention.

As if reading her mind, he murmured, still scribbling,

"The guttering. It needs clearing. If you look closely, there's grass growing up there."

Raising a hand, she shaded her eyes, looked, and saw that he was right. She glanced at him. "Is that what you're listing?"

He nodded. Shutting the book, he looked at the house again. "All the little things that need doing."

Closing his hand about the silver head of the cane he'd left resting against his thigh, he continued his slow progress around the house, examining each window, each piece of spouting, and all else of a structural nature.

Rose trailed after him.

When he stopped to check the paint on a windowsill, she said, "There's a local handyman we—the Gattings and I—have used over the years. He's reasonable and reliable. If you wish, once you have your list, I could get him in."

To her surprise, Glendower shook his head. "No." Almost as an afterthought, he added, "I'll do the work myself."

Rose blinked. She thought of how high the guttering was, thought of how stiffly he moved . . . wondered why a gentleman might wish to do such work himself. . . .

He halted again, this time to assess the sturdiness of a piece of latticework anchored to the side of the house.

Rose halted a few feet away. Her gaze on his face, she bit her lip, wondering how to phrase the question that had leapt to her mind.

Stepping back from the lattice, balancing his cane against his leg, he drew out his notebook and pencil.

She watched him open the book and saw his lips curve, distinctly wryly. "No," he said, his gaze on the page and the words he was writing, "I have plenty of money." He paused, then, as if sensing that more explanation was required, added, "I need the exercise or my muscles will atrophy— grow weak again. I need to keep using them, in lots of different ways."

She was intrigued, yet . . . "There's exercise, and then there's hard work."

He chuckled and put away his notebook. "Indeed." He sounded genuinely amused, not offended in the least by what another employer might have viewed as a temerity.

Reassured, Rose continued to keep pace with him as he walked further, rounding the next corner to examine the front of the house. She waited, hoping . . .

Halting to squint up at the front façade, he said, "The monastery was a Benedictine house—it was the done thing for everyone, including any laity within the walls, to contribute to the house's maintenance and repair, each according to their talents." He glanced briefly at her, long enough for her to glimpse the self-deprecation in his eyes. "When I first arrived there, I had no useful talents, not in that sense. But there were many brothers who did, and they consented to teach me. Subsequently, I discovered that I had an unexpected aptitude for . . . I suppose one could say crafting and repairing things. Working with my hands to make physical things work."

They strolled on, and, after a moment, he continued, "I know it's not a customary occupation for a gentleman, but I derive great satisfaction from it—from putting things right and making them work."

Thomas heard the words, his first attempt at explaining to anyone his liking for such activities, and realized the connection, the essential similarity between his habitual occupation through the morning—investing and managing funds to create money to put things right—and what had come to be his preferred means of filling his afternoons.

Two sides of the same coin, one largely cerebral, the other solidly physical.

Halting ten yards away from the house, in line with the front door, he turned to consider his housekeeper. "So," he concluded, meeting her soft brown eyes, "I'll do the necessary repairs myself."

She held his gaze for a moment, then inclined her head. Halting, too, she glanced at the house. "Do you have any thoughts as to the order in which you'll tackle the tasks?"

He shifted to face the house; they were standing close, only a foot between them. "The repainting should wait until the weather improves, so at the moment that goes to the bottom of the list."

Busy studying the façade, she hadn't seen him move. As she, too, swung to squarely face the house, her shoulder brushed his.

Sparks flared. That's what it felt like. He could all but sense their mutual attraction crackling in the air.

His muscles, more susceptible than most men's through habitually being tensed, trembled. He gripped the head of his cane tightly, his knuckles paling as he fought the impulse to react, as he ruthlessly quashed the instinctive urge to pursue that attraction. To pursue her.

No good could come of that.

From the rigidity that had gripped her, from the fact that she'd stopped breathing, he knew she was engaged in a similar battle, that she, too, felt the power of that flaring connection.

Then, surreptitiously, she drew in a shallow, somewhat shaky breath, and shifted so that her shoulder no longer touched his. "Well, then." Her voice was slightly breathless; she raised her chin a notch higher and with greater determination stated, "I'll leave you to it."

Inclining her head, without meeting his eyes, she turned and walked slowly back around the house.

He watched her go and had to wonder if, despite both their best efforts, this was one battle that might prove a lost cause.

After several moments of thinking further along those lines, he returned his gaze to the house.

If she could deny what was growing between them, could continue to suppress her reaction to him, then, clearly, he could, and should, and would do the same.

At the end of the first week after the return of Mr. Thomas Glendower to Breage Manor, Rose slipped into her chair at the dinner table and listened to the conversation already raging between Glendower—Thomas, as both the children had taken to calling him—and Homer regarding the correct way to interpret someone's theory about the moon orbiting the earth.

Pippin was busy eating, but between mouthfuls she was also listening, although Rose would have wagered it was the animation displayed by both Homer and Thomas— Glendower—that was holding Pippin's interest.

Rose looked down at her soup plate, took her first mouthful, then looked again down the table.

There he sat, large as life—her employer, a male who, regardless of his injuries, his obvious infirmities, regardless of his disfiguring scars, still managed to seize and hold her attention and interest like some emotional lodestone—and yet she felt . . . settled. Calm, assured, even serene, her instincts convinced beyond question that the situation was . . . good.

His presence in their household felt . . . simply right.

He'd proved to be a creature of habit and had settled into

a daily routine. After breakfasting with them—and he'd
yet to be late down, and most often beat the children
downstairs—he would shut himself in his library and work
through the morning. She usually found him still there, analyzing figures and reading news sheets, when she took him
his morning tea. Eventually emerging, he'd taken in recent
days to spending half an hour or so with Homer in the dining room, from which both would appear when she rang the
bell for luncheon.

After helping her clear the table, he would go outside,
either to ride or to work on whichever of the small projects
about the house was next on his list. While such actions
demonstrated a certain arrogance in that he clearly did not
care what others thought of him, for her part she considered
his stance commendable, and one she supported without
reservation.

Homer had, of course, noticed; since Glendower's arrival, Homer had revised his view of doing chores, like
mucking out the stable, previously a matter of argument,
and apparently now deemed all such activities to be perfectly acceptable, acceptably manly, occupations.

Initially, Pippin, as was her wont, had simply listened
or, with her doll in her arms, had silently trailed after
Glendower to watch him work around the house. Rose had
expected him to ignore the little girl, not in any dismissive
way but simply because she was a girl, but no. Over the
last days, Pippin had come in full of tales of how Thomas
had let her hold his nails, or pass him his hammer, of how
she had helped him complete whatever task he'd been
working on.

Rose had to own to surprise on that score . . . and also at
the fact that, despite the attraction that, like lightning,
seemed to streak down her nerves whenever she and

Thomas passed close to each other—an affliction she was increasingly suspicious he had guessed she was prey to—he and she had continued to manage to deal with each other without incident of any sort. At least, no incident they couldn't both ignore, or, at the very least, pretend hadn't happened.

She wasn't entirely sure how she felt about that, but . . . all in all, after his first week with them, she was feeling unexpectedly content.

She could even admit that she was glad he had joined them.

At the other end of the table, Thomas, too, was content with his first week's achievements. His days were settling into a rhythm of financial work, intellectual instruction, and physical labor that suited him well. Coming to the manor, and remaining even after he'd discovered his unexpected new caretakers, had been the right thing to do. He could remain here in comfort and in peace while waiting for Fate to summon him to perform his final penance. If somewhat deeper in his blackened soul lay a certain impatience over his ultimate task, an impatience to learn of it, accomplish it, and find . . . whatever lay beyond, somewhat to his surprise, the gentle distractions of the moment, of the house, the children, and the alluring Mrs. Sheridan, appeared to have sufficient weight to drown it, to suppress it.

Here, now, he was conscious only of a day well spent and a soothing, soporific sense of calm.

Pippin skipped around the table removing the empty soup plates. Mrs. Sheridan handed out the dinner plates, then brought a large casserole to the table.

Resuming her seat, she gestured for him to serve himself; it was one of those instants when he wished he could argue but accepted that she would prefer he take the path of least resistance. His instincts insisted that she—a lady no matter her standing—should be served first, but . . . to keep her peace, he served himself, then passed the spoon to Homer.

The meat was delicious; he'd made sure to increase not just the amount delivered but also the quality of the cuts. Mrs. Sheridan had, of course, noticed, but she had made no comment, simply adjusting her dishes to suit the better ingredients.

As a pleasant silence, broken only by the chink of cutlery on china and a murmured request from Pippin for Homer to pass the bread basket, enfolded the table, Thomas flicked a glance up the board and met Mrs. Sheridan's fine brown eyes, which had already been on him.

Their gazes held for a second too long, a fraction of a heartbeat beyond the excusable, then they both looked down at their plates.

Thomas resisted the urge to shift in his chair; she would notice, and . . . no. That was the only thorn to the rose of his days there—the attraction that, unrelieved and unsated, was building, building. It was, he knew, the sort of attraction that would not readily subside, not while they remained under the same roof, in such close proximity.

However, thus far, they'd both succeeded in suppressing any outburst, in keeping a lid on the pot that was slowly, steadily, inevitably, coming to the boil.

His hope was that, before it did, Fate would send for him.

The thought focused him again on the other three occupants of the table. He glanced at Homer, then at Pippin. He would only be in their lives for a short time, theirs and their mother's, and although he'd weighed the matter at some length, with every passing day he felt increasingly certain that his decision to interact with them and give them whatever support, whatever help, he could over the time he was with them was the right path to take.

Teaching Homer, and Pippin, too, what he could, and meanwhile living as normally as he could—as he needed to live—while avoiding setting what was fermenting between him and their mother alight . . .

His plate empty, his stomach comfortably full, he leaned back in his chair and looked down the table. "A very nice dinner, Mrs. Sheridan. My compliments to the cook."

She laughed, a spontaneous sound of pleasure, and while he managed to maintain an expression of nonchalant ease, something in him stilled.

When, after sharing a smile with the children, she shifted her gaze to him, he inclined his head, forcing himself to let his lips curve in gentle acknowledgment, making sure his lids and lashes veiled the leaping hunger in his eyes.

Days passed, then weeks. A month after he arrived at the manor, Thomas sat in the library, his financial work for the day not yet commenced; his admiral's chair swiveled so his back was to his desk, to the letters and news sheets waiting piled upon it, he stared broodingly out of the window.

The impatience in his soul remained, yet, even now, he felt a measure of calm, the soothing influence of the simple pleasures he was exposed to every day. Each and every day that he spent at the manor, an accepted part of the small household.

He wasn't sure he was supposed to be enjoying himself quite so much. So . . . effortlessly.

The man he once had been would have listened to his welling impatience, would have surrendered to it and found some way to press ahead; the man he'd once been would have had no hesitation in going forth and forcing the world to his bidding—forcing even Fate to his self-determined timetable.

Yet the man he now was had learned something of humility, had accepted that he was not the person about whom his world revolved. His destiny would, without doubt, be low on Fate's—or God's—list of matters to be settled.

She—or he—would get to him in due course.

Patience. That, too, seemed to be a virtue he needed to acquire.

Perhaps that was the lesson of this time.

He weighed that conclusion; in some ways it was self-serving, yet he could see no viable argument against it. He had to wait for Fate's summons, and Breage Manor, he was increasingly certain, was the place in which he was supposed to bide his time. Patching up the manor so Mrs. Sheridan and her children would be safe and secure once he left. Teaching Homer, and broadening Pippin's horizons as well.

And continuing his work as Thomas Glendower.

Accepting that verdict, he pushed his chair around and refocused on the various documents piled in readiness. Picking up the letters, he sorted them, then drew out a ledger and plunged into the work. Into taking funds and legally expanding them, then using the proceeds to support those who couldn't support themselves, the weak, the helpless, those most in need.

In atonement for the sins of his previous life, he'd devoted himself to that task.

And entirely unexpectedly had found a measure of balance, and of succor, and of guilt-free peace.

The following day rolled on much as those preceding it. Thomas spent his morning in the library analyzing the financial information culled from the previous day's London news sheets and any communication from Drayton or any of his other sources, and reassessed and decided on any necessary adjustments to the numerous portfolios he managed, after which he wrote to Drayton with instructions to execute those decisions.

But the investment world generally moved slowly; most days he had no letters to write.

Today was one of those days. Satisfied with the current state of all his funds, he tidied his papers, then sat back in his admiral's chair. After a moment of staring blankly at his desk, he swiveled the chair and stared, equally unseeing, out of the window.

Freed from the rigors of analyzing investments, his mind, predictably, turned to the next most intriguing and most immediate puzzle—his housekeeper and her children.

Mrs. Sheridan was far removed from the average housekeeper of a country manor, or a stately home, or even a London mansion. There was steel within her, and a directness and quickness of mind that did not sit well within any construct of servitude.

Rose. Pippin had let fall that that was Mrs. Sheridan's name. Both children usually called her Ma, which in itself seemed odd; given their poorly concealed gentility, he would have expected Mama, but no. And the children themselves . . .

What was a small, gently bred family doing living in such a way? Why had Rose chosen this as their life, for plainly she was the driving force behind that decision?

Their determined isolation was another oddity; both children were of an age to attend school, and the local school wasn't far, yet neither went. More, neither consorted with any other children, and, tellingly, neither expected to.

Admittedly, Homer already required more wide-ranging teaching of a higher level, the sort normally supplied by either a good grammar school or a private tutor, but Pippin was young, and would, Thomas suspected, have been happy with the other girls at the local village school . . . except for her social standing, which was definitely not "village."

A bell jangled in the distance, drawing him from his reverie. It was Rose's—Mrs. Sheridan's—kitchen bell, summoning them to morning tea. If he didn't respond and appear in the kitchen, she would bring in a tray for him.

Swiveling the chair back around, he reached for his cane, stood, and headed for the door.

He reached the kitchen on Homer's heels; the lad had been in the dining room, which Thomas had suggested Homer use for all his studies.

Homer fell into his chair and, his expression closed and unaccustomedly moody, reached for a slice of bread and butter. Pippin was already in her chair, happily consuming a slice of bread liberally spread with raspberry jam.

Rose turned from the stove, the teapot in one hand and the milk jug in the other. Seeing Glendower, she acknowledged him with a nod. Setting the teapot and jug on the table, she reached for the cup and plate she'd left ready on a tray to carry into the library; these days she never knew whether he would join them for morning tea or not.

She set the plate and cup before him and poured his tea before filling her own cup and sitting in her chair.

Homer reached for the milk jug and filled his mug, then Pippin's.

Aware of his disaffected state, Rose asked, as he set the jug down, "Did you finish that arithmetic?"

Homer pulled a schoolboy face. "Yes. But arithmetic's so boring!"

Rose opened her mouth, but Thomas—Glendower—caught her eye, and she paused.

And listened as Glendower said, "In some respects, but arithmetic—all that boring stuff—is the foundation for everything I do as an investor."

Instantly, he had Homer's undivided attention.

"Without arithmetic," Glendower continued, "I couldn't make all the money I do. Any landowner, too, uses arithmetic every day—considering returns on his crops, yields over his acres, prices for his farms' produce. Without arithmetic, no level of commerce could function. No banks, no shops, no government. And without arithmetic, you can't build anything—no houses, railways, ships, not even roads—not proper ones." Trapping Homer's gaze, Glendower concluded, "If you expect to do anything meaningful with your life, you'll need to conquer arithmetic."

Rose could have kissed him. She looked at Homer—in time to see him pull another face.

"But I can already do additions and subtractions, and I know all my tables by heart." Homer looked beseechingly at Glendower. "There has to be more to it than that."

Glendower blinked, then he glanced up the table at Rose, then looked back at Homer. "There is. There's multiplication and division using much larger numbers than in your tables—that's what knowing your tables helps you to do. Tables come first, then those two—and then there's many levels of manipulating figures after that."

Rose felt her heart sink as both Homer and Glendower looked at her. She'd already reached the limit of her arithmetical education. She had hoped to be able to guide Homer at least for the next few years, but he'd already outstripped her abilities, at least in arithmetic. Under Glendower's acutely observant, not to say piercing, gaze, she felt like squirming, but instead she held his gaze and tried to think.

As if he'd seen enough and understanding had dawned, Glendower sat back in his chair. His gaze still on her face, he said, "As I believe I've mentioned, I'm waiting for a summons and intend to remain here until it arrives. However, even with my investments and the repairs to this house, that still leaves me with free time—as now." He glanced at Homer, who was hanging on his every word. "Perhaps, with your permission, Mrs. Sheridan, I could assist in furthering Homer's studies?"

Thomas remembered what it had felt like when he had reached the limits of his tutors' capacity to expand his horizons and engage his questing mind. How different would his life have been—how many people would still be alive— had there been someone to take an interest in him and steer him on at that point? Instead, he'd been left to find his own way forward, to forge his own path, and that had not, in the end, turned out well for either him or wider society.

Now here was Homer, in many ways similar to his long-ago self, reaching much the same point, but at an even earlier age, and Thomas had the time, and the abilities, to steer Homer on in the right fashion.

Thomas looked up the table at his housekeeper. His expression as open as he could make it, he arched a brow.

She didn't immediately accept the offer—one that would solve what he knew she already recognized as a problem. Instead, her eyes searched his, scrutinized his expression; he could almost hear the thoughts clashing in her mind.

She didn't want to be beholden to him. Against that, Homer and his well-being were paramount to her, something she would—and almost certainly had—made sacrifices for.

Thomas paused, then opened his hands, wrists still

resting on the table, palms out, to her. "No conditions." He glanced at Homer and added to deflect the boy's mind from those words, "And not just in arithmetic but in all the other disciplines, too, and you'll have to promise to work hard."

His eyes huge, his expression stating that he hardly dared hope, Homer nodded eagerly and, with Thomas, looked up the table at Rose.

She met Thomas's gaze, held it for an instant, then said, "If you're sure you can spare the time?"

Thomas smiled easily, confidently. "I am." He looked at Homer as the boy drained his mug of milk; he'd already eaten two slices of bread and jam. As Homer lowered his mug, Thomas asked, "Are you ready to face more arithmetic—this time rather more challenging?"

"Yes!" Homer beamed and pushed back his chair.

With a nod down the table, Thomas rose, too, and followed the irrepressibly excited boy back to the dining room.

There, he got Homer to show him the last exercises Rose had set—basic and boring, indeed—then he devised a series of steadily advancing exercises that would lead Homer step by step into more challenging levels of mathematical manipulation.

Leaving Homer working his way through the first of those, Thomas reviewed the other subjects he himself had been exposed to at Homer's age. Recalling a book that had stirred his interest in geography, he returned to the library, tracked down a copy tucked away on a bottom shelf, and, triumphant, took it with him back to the dining room.

Homer was still busy, and would be for the next hour or so.

Thomas set the book down on the table. When Homer looked up, Thomas nodded at the tome. "When I was about your age, I read that—it's an adventure story set in Africa.

You can take it up to your room or even outside—it's not so much a schoolbook as a book that makes you want to learn more."

Homer smiled and reached out to draw the book closer. He read the title, then glanced up at Thomas, head tilting. "Did you learn at home, like this, or did you go to school?"

"A bit of both. My parents died when I was six years old, and after that I lived with my guardian. I had tutors at your age, but, soon after, I was sent to Harrow, and, later, I went to Oxford."

Homer's eyes had grown round. "You were an orphan, too?"

Thomas inwardly frowned, then sought to explain, "I was an orphan, yes, because I lost *both* my parents—my mother died as well as my father. You, at least, still have your mother."

Homer stared at him for a moment, then blinked. Gaze distant, he nodded, then bent over his workbook. "Yes. At least I have Ro—Ma."

Thomas, still standing, saw Homer clamp his lips shut. A wise move.

Looking down on the boy's shiny head, Thomas replayed the exchange.

Children rarely made good liars.

The following afternoon, Thomas hefted an axe, swung it up to his shoulder, and set out for the orchard. Enclosed within drystone walls, the orchard lay to one side of the rear garden, opposite the stables.

He still carried his cane, but more out of habit than necessity; he barely used it as he crossed the rear lawn. As summer rolled inexorably nearer, the warmer weather dulled the ache in his bones and joints, and the variety of exercise he'd been consistently engaging in ever since returning to the manor had steadily strengthened muscle and sinew.

Passing through the gap in the stone wall, he paused to survey the orchard. All eight trees within it were old, but they had been well tended, and from the buds forming on neatly pruned branches, seven were still healthy and would be nicely productive later in the season. Thomas had a hazy memory that Gatting had prized these fruit trees, and Mrs. Sheridan looked to have kept up Gatting's work.

But the apple tree three trees along the row to the right was blighted.

Axe still on his shoulder, Thomas walked toward it, passing the two damson plum trees, and ignoring the cherry tree, two pear trees, and walnut tree in the other row.

During his years at the priory, he'd spent as much time as he could outdoors, and almost all of that had been in one or other of the house's gardens—the medicinal garden, the kitchen garden, or the orchard. He'd learned a lot in that time, including how to spot blight and what the most effective treatment was.

Halting before the apple tree, he surveyed it, noting the dark stain of blight steadily overtaking so many of the branches.

Inwardly sighing, Thomas let his cane fall to the grass and lifted the axe from his shoulder.

Limping forward, he ducked under one of the lower branches, to where he had a clear field to angle the axe into the trunk. Setting his feet, he raised the axe—

"No-oo!"

The sound had him lowering the axe and looking toward the house.

Pippin came flying down the garden, her braids and her

pinafore flapping behind her. "*No!* No, Thomas! You can't cut down my tree!"

Her wail was anguished. Setting the axe-head on the ground, Thomas straightened.

Pippin rushed into the orchard. Thomas glanced at the house and realized she must have seen him from the window of her bedroom.

She raced through the long grass to fetch up near his cane. Her gaze beseeching, her expression imploring, she fixed her big brown eyes on his face. "Please, Thomas, you can't cut it down—it's my *name* tree. It gave me my name."

Thomas inwardly blinked. After a moment, he said, "I thought your name was Philippa, or something like that."

Pippin shook her head emphatically. "No, but I like apples, so when I had to choose a name, I chose Pippin." She nodded at the tree. "So that's my tree."

"Ah." So what was her real name? And why had she had to choose another? Thomas stared at her for a moment more, then glanced at the tree. Obviously, the most effective treatment wouldn't be the best treatment in this case. He looked at Pippin. "It's sick, you know."

Her little face deathly sober, Pippin nodded. Drawing closer, she reached up to trace a diseased branch. "It's not healthy, is it?"

"No, it's not." Holding the axe head down, Thomas ducked back under the branch to join her. "And if we don't do something, it will keep sickening and eventually die— probably by the end of this year."

Pippin faced him, her soft brown eyes, so like Rose's, locking with his. "But we don't have to cut it down, do we? Isn't there something we can do to make it better?"

Thomas held her gaze, then heaved an inward sigh and turned back to the tree, re-surveying it and cataloguing how

far the blight had spread. There was, just possibly, an outside chance that judicious pruning might save the tree. Was
it better to try, and give Pippin possibly false hope, or
should he simply insist that the tree had to come down
now?

He glanced around at the other trees. "The other trees all
look healthy, so this is most likely an apple-tree-only
blight." Again, he studied the apple tree, very conscious of
Pippin's gaze locked on his face, of the hope shining in her
eyes, and the faith, too, that if there was a way of saving the
tree, he would find it for her.

"If," he said, glancing down at her, "we carefully cut off
all the dying branches, every bit that shows any sign of going bad at all, and then take all the pieces away and burn
them, then we might—and I can only say might—save your
tree."

She stared up at him, then reached out and grasped his
hand. Squeezed as she said, "So can we? Please?"

We. It occurred to him that she would get more out of any
rescue if she helped—and if the worst came to be, at least
she would feel she had done all she could. "All right."

She clapped her hands and squealed. Thankfully briefly.

Hiding a grin at her exuberance—and wondering how
long it would last in face of the chore awaiting them—he
gestured with his chin toward the stable. "Come along,
then. We'll put back the axe and get the shears and saw."

She skipped along beside him, and he couldn't help but
smile.

After returning the axe, he collected all the tools he
thought they might need, along with an old, paint-splattered
tarpaulin. Letting Pippin carry the lighter shears, he bundled everything else up in the tarpaulin and slung it over his
shoulder, and together they went back to the orchard.

Spreading the tarpaulin out on the far side of the apple tree, on the slight slope that ran down to the rear wall of the orchard, he lifted the two saws and the heavier shears from the canvas, laid them aside, closer to the tree, then, taking the lighter shears from Pippin, he said, "Now, this is how we're going to work."

He explained that he would cut the branches and hand them to her, and that it was her task to make sure that each and every little piece of branch taken from the tree ended on the tarpaulin. "It's very important that every piece of bad wood ends up on our pile, and not on the grass near the tree. Then, once we've cut off all the diseased bits, we'll pull the tarpaulin down to the far corner of the orchard, and we'll make a pile there and burn all the bad wood."

Pippin nodded. He raised the shears, but as he reached to take hold of the first branch, Pippin slipped closer to the trunk of the tree. Crouching beside it, she laid a palm against the smooth bark. "I promise we're going to do everything we can to make you better so you can grow healthy again, and bear nice apples for us to eat."

She patted the tree, then, rising, she came to stand beside Thomas. Looking up, she met his gaze and nodded. "We can start now."

Entirely sober, Thomas nodded back and cut the first branch.

They quickly fell into a rhythm and worked steadily around the tree, with each successive circuit cutting deeper and deeper into the branches. Thomas lost track of time, but, eventually, with the tree branches trimmed to less than half of what they had been, he could see no lingering traces of blight.

Straightening, he stepped back and looked again, just to be sure. Pippin came to stand beside him. "Can you spot any more blighted bits?" he asked. Her eyes, after all, would be much sharper than his.

To her credit, she didn't immediately answer but instead searched the tree carefully. But, at last, she sighed, satisfaction in the sound. "No. I think we've got it all."

Thomas nodded. "Right, then. On to our next task. We have to destroy all the diseased wood."

"Burn it!" Pippin sang.

Understanding from the delight in her face that she liked a bonfire as much as any other child, he grinned and bent to grasp the lower edge of the tarpaulin. "No," he said when Pippin came to help him. "You go to the opposite side and lift the edge. That way, when I pull it down the slope, none of the pile will fall back and off the tarpaulin."

"Oh." Her delight didn't dim. "Yes, I see."

Together they dragged the tarpaulin down to the far corner of the orchard, where there was plenty of clear space for a fire. Dropping the edge he'd dragged, Thomas circled around and joined Pippin, and together, with much laughter from her and silent grins from him, they raised the tarpaulin, tipping the wood off it as they dragged the material free.

Thomas glanced at the resulting rather haphazard pile. "Let's make it up into a proper bonfire, then we should go back and gather our tools, take them back to the stables, and then we can come back and set our bonfire alight."

"Yes!" Pippin danced and darted, picking up loose branches and setting them atop the pile.

Swiftly Thomas shifted some of the larger branches to give the pile a better structure, then he largely let Pippin dance and have fun.

Her gaiety was infectious.

When the bonfire was built, they did as he'd decreed and

took the tools back to the stable. Pausing only to collect some dry tinder from the wood box, they made their way back to the far corner of the orchard.

The weather had been clear for some time, and in most of the branches they'd cut, the sap had yet to properly rise. It wasn't hard to set fire to their pile.

As twigs caught and flames started to crackle and lick their way through the stacked wood, Thomas stood back and checked that Pippin was maintaining a safe distance from the conflagration, then settled to watch.

Bit by bit, the greedy flames spread, until at last the pile erupted with a muted roar.

Pippin had gradually moved back. As the fire settled to consume the apple tree's blighted branches, she drifted to stand by Thomas's side.

Without warning, she slipped a small hand into one of his.

He glanced down, even as his fingers instinctively tightened about hers. Not too tightly, just enough to hold her hand, to respond . . .

Pippin sighed and leaned against him, nestling her head against his side.

Something inside him stilled.

Such innocent, unconditional trust . . . it rocked him.

He drew in a shallow, not entirely steady breath and, raising his head, looked at the flames.

A minute later, he heard from behind them, "What are you burning?"

Glancing around, he saw his housekeeper—Pippin's mother. He glanced down at the little girl and was no longer so sure of their relationship.

Straightening, Pippin barely glanced back, but, instead, jigged at his side. "Thomas and me are burning up all the bad branches off my tree." Pippin pointed to the apple tree. "See? We had to cut and cut to get all the sick branches off, and now"—with a sweep of her little arm, she indicated the bonfire—"we're burning them all up so my tree can get well without catching the sickness again."

She glanced up at him, met his eyes, smiled brilliantly, then looked back at the fire.

Her mother came to stand alongside her; over Pippin's head, Mrs. Sheridan met his eyes.

She studied them, studied his face, then she inclined her head. Gratitude shone clearly in the soft brown of her eyes.

Eyes she shared with Pippin, but . . . he had to wonder.

Rose stood silently beside Pippin and watched as the pile of branches burned steadily down.

She felt touched, truly grateful that Thomas—Glendower—had been kind enough, had empathized enough with a little girl's wishes, her childish feelings, to change his tack. She'd seen him walk across the rear garden with his axe, but she had gone into the sitting room at the front of the house after that; she'd heard Pippin rush out but hadn't known she'd joined him.

Hadn't known that he'd intended to attack the ailing apple tree.

A light breeze sprang up, wafting the smoke their way. She wanted to thank him but couldn't think how.

He waved at the fire. "It's low enough to leave." Turning, he gestured toward the house. "We should go in." He met Rose's eyes. "It must be time for afternoon tea."

She smiled, then drew breath and nodded. "Yes, it is—and thank you, Thomas." Before he, or she, could dwell on her use of his name, she glanced down at Pippin and smiled. "There are fresh scones, clotted cream, and blackberry jam for tea. After all this work, you must both be hungry."

Pippin whooped. But instead of tearing off to the house as Rose had expected, Pippin darted up the slope, retrieved Thomas's cane from where it had lain in the grass, and danced it back to him. "Come on, Thomas." She waited until he accepted the cane, then she took his free hand. Her other hand grasping Rose's, she started towing them both up the slight slope. "Let's go and have our tea!"

Rose glanced at Thomas—her enigma of an employer— took in his profile as he smiled down at Pippin, and silently fell in with Pippin's plans.

Curtis, the highly respected owner of what was arguably London's most respected inquiry agency, rounded his desk. Pulling out the chair behind it, he glanced at his client, seated before the desk.

"Well?" Richard Percival demanded. "Your note said you have news."

Elegantly turned out, his aristocratic features arranged in a mask of polite boredom—one that was, just fractionally, cracking—his dark hair fashionably styled in a windblown tumble with one dark lock sweeping across his brow, at first glance Percival appeared the epitome of the tonnish rake most in society assumed him to be. Curtis, however, knew Percival for a man obsessed; Curtis knew for how many years and to what extent and expense Percival had gone to trace his missing relatives.

Curtis also knew why, and so wasn't surprised by the hunger—the hope—behind the man's crisp diction. "We believe they might have headed into Cornwall."

"Cornwall?" Percival narrowed his eyes. "Why the devil would she have taken them there?"

"She has no connection with the area? No distant relatives, no old nurse—that sort of thing?"

Richard Percival thought, then, slowly, shook his head. "I've never heard of any such personal link, and, frankly, would be surprised. She's Leicestershire born and bred."

Curtis paused, then offered, "Cornwall is, more or less, as far as one can go from Lincolnshire. In fleeing Seddington Grange . . . it's possible she just ran as far as she could, and then stopped."

Richard Percival grimaced. After a moment, he looked at Curtis. "You said you *believe* they might have gone to Cornwall—on what grounds, and are you sure?"

"A woman fitting her description, with two children, was seen in Exeter, but it was years ago, exactly how long ago we can't be sure. We're certain enough of the identification—the man I've got down there knows his business. But as to whether she and they are still down there . . ." Curtis shrugged. "With a trail this cold, it's impossible to say."

Frustration broke through Richard Percival's mask. "Damn it! There *must* be some way of pushing harder, more decisively."

Unmoved by the uncharacteristic outburst, Curtis paused, then, clasping his hands on his blotter, quietly asked, "Your instructions were—still are—that you want this kept quiet, with no dust raised whatsoever." Curtis met Richard Percival's dark blue eyes. "Has that changed?" He let a moment elapse before adding, "Because, yes, I can go much harder. I could raise a hue and cry, the next best thing to a manhunt, if that's what you want."

Richard Percival blew out a breath. "No. No." After a moment, he drew in a deep breath and said, "Whatever reason she had for taking them and fleeing that night . . . until I have them back and can learn what that reason was . . ." Eyes narrowing, he stared into space, then murmured, "If at all possible, I want this kept entirely confidential."

Curtis nodded. "In that case, I'll send more men down tomorrow. We'll need to move slowly and carefully, but our information is that they left Exeter and headed west. Into Cornwall."

Richard Percival sat silently for several seconds, then he rose and crisply nodded. "Send in your hounds—and keep me apprised of anything they find." Turning, he strode for the door.

Curtis watched him go. Even after the door had closed, Curtis continued to stare at the panels, then he sighed, shook his head, and got on with his work.

The days rolled on, and with no summons from Fate eventuating, Thomas found himself looking for things to do, for activities to occupy his body and mind.

Recalling the Gattings, who had watched over the house since he'd bought it early in 1816, and who had always made his infrequent stays there comfortable and serene—comforting in truth—he decided that he should call on them and thank them for their years of exemplary service.

The following morning, over the breakfast table, he asked Rose—he and she had, by degrees, slid onto a first-name basis—where the old couple lived.

"In Porthleven, in a little cottage in Shute Lane. That's just off the harbor, before you start up the hill to the east. Their cottage is Number four."

He nodded, envisioning the town as he'd last seen it; it wouldn't have changed. "I'm going to ride that way this morning once I check over the news sheets. I'd like to call and wish them well."

Rose's expression as she set down her teacup was approving. "I'm sure they would like to see you . . ." Her words trailed off, then she recovered and shrugged lightly. "To know you're alive, if nothing else."

She'd realized that the Gattings would remember him as he'd once been, not as he now was. He smiled with wry understanding. "Indeed."

Rose colored faintly and reached for the teapot. "It's not as if you're incapacitated. Whatever your accident was, you've survived and continue to live. Continue to make something of your life."

He studied her, trying to decide which part of her view of him most confounded him—her apparent blindness to the scars that disfigured the left side of his face, to his habitual gimping gait, or her confident assertion that he was actively living and forging a life, by implication a life worth living.

To his mind, he was in stasis, not living so much as existing, waiting to make his final payment in retribution for his past sins.

Which of them was correct—her or him?

Or could they both be right?

Shaking aside the distraction, he glanced to his left, at Homer's bright head, then looked at Rose and caught her eye. "I was wondering if I might take Homer for a ride, too. An excursion for the day." He'd noticed the boy was growing physically restless; a day of exercise would do him good.

Homer's head shot up, his expression beyond eager. He fixed his blue eyes on Rose. "Please. I'll do my chores, too—I won't forget."

Rose hesitated. She wasn't immune to the plea in Homer's eyes; she understood, indeed, shared his longing to venture beyond the confines of the manor. More, she accepted that boys of his age needed to be out and about more, but she couldn't risk being seen with him. The pair of them together would be much more identifiable than either of them individually. Yet, equally, she couldn't allow him to venture forth on his own. . . .

Shifting her gaze to Thomas, she nodded. "All right." Thomas would keep Homer safe; she knew that to her bones. Allowing Thomas to take Homer out for the day was the perfect solution to her problems on that front; aside from all else, if the pair were seen, given the way they interacted—Thomas with Homer, and Homer with Thomas—they would be assumed to be father and son.

Yet another distracting veil to add to hers and the children's safety.

Homer whooped.

Rose glanced at Pippin, now frowning slightly, her lower lip starting to protrude. Rose looked at Homer. "Consider being allowed to accompany Thomas as a reward for working so hard at your studies, and, after all, your birthday is coming up."

Homer simply grinned. Stuffing the last of his toast into his mouth, he raised his mug and drained it, then pushed back his chair. "I'll go and check the cow and the stables." He glanced at Thomas. "Will you be long?"

"Maybe an hour." Thomas looked at Rose. "We'll have lunch there, and be back for afternoon tea."

She nodded crisply. A glance at Pippin showed a much more amenable, accepting face; the mention of Homer's birthday had done the trick.

Homer dashed to the back door and went out.

Thomas pushed back his chair. Rose glanced at him and

realized he'd followed her gaze to Pippin. "Pippin," he said, "you were going to show me the dress you've made for your doll. If you like, you could show it to me now—I have a little time before we go."

Pippin's little face lit. Nodding, she gulped the last of her milk, then flung a smile at Rose and pushed back her chair. "I'll go and get Dolly—she's still asleep."

Thomas nodded solemnly. "I'll be in the library—come and show me there."

Pippin raced off, shoes clattering.

Down the length of the short table, Rose met Thomas's gaze. "That was . . . brave of you."

His lips quirked lightly. "I'm sure I'll survive."

Pushing up from the table, he started gathering plates.

She rose and did the same, taking the stack to the sink.

He followed with the rest.

They'd fallen into a small domestic ritual; she would wash the dishes and he would dry them and put them away.

She was very aware that neither of them had been born to such duties, yet they performed them now without complaint; their lives, the decisions they had made, had brought them to this.

She knew that was true for herself, and she intuitively knew it was true for him, too.

But that morning . . .

Standing before the sink, the plates she'd ferried from the table already in the bowl, she waited for him to set the stack he'd carried on the bench-top beside her.

He did and paused, looking down at her. His gaze was on the side of her face; she could feel it.

And awareness flared—the sensual yearning both of them were being so careful to hide, to suppress.

Regardless, its very existence made her feel alive.

Alive in a way she'd never felt before.

Even though nothing could ever come of it, it still stole her breath, still made her blood sing.

Raising her chin, she stared out at the rear garden, fighting the compulsion to shift her gaze to him, to his face, to his fascinating eyes. Eyes that seemed so clear, so open—unrestricted gateways to his soul.

Her lungs had grown tight, but she found breath enough to say, "I'll take care of all this today—you'd better get into the library, or Pippin will be disappointed."

He didn't immediately move. After a moment, he said, "I really don't know anything about dolls."

She smiled. "But you do know something of dresses." She cast him a very brief sidelong glance. "The trick is to pretend the doll is real, like a frozen lady, and comment accordingly."

"Ah." He nodded, then dipped his head. "In that case, I'd better go and do my duty."

He moved away, heading for the door.

Before he reached it, she swung around and said, "Thomas." When he paused and looked at her, she met his gaze directly. "Thank you. From both me and them." *But especially from me.*

His lips curved cynically. "No thanks required. I wouldn't have offered if I hadn't wanted to—if I didn't think I'd enjoy Homer's company as much as he'll enjoy the outing."

She'd noticed that was a habit of his, downplaying his acts of kindness. She arched an equally cynical brow back. "And Pippin?"

The curve of his lips deepened. As he turned away, he said, "That, I believe, you should view as an attempt to keep the peace."

She snorted, then, shaking her head at his ways, reached for the kettle.

Several hours later, Thomas guided Silver down the hill into Porthleven, Homer on the pony trotting alongside.

The ride from the manor along the cliffs had been uneventful. Silver had wanted to canter, but the pony's shorter legs wouldn't keep up; Thomas had had to rein the gray in, and Silver was now disgusted, trudging along in the equivalent of a horsey sulk.

But the steep descent into the tiny harbor village had them all looking about, even Silver.

The day had started fine, but light clouds had blown up, intermittently blocking the sun. Now that they were by the shore, the breeze had stiffened a touch but remained more flirtatious than forceful.

They had come into the village around the western headland; the harbor and village lay in the steep cleft between the twin headlands, where the land descended sharply to meet the waves of the Channel.

Whitewashed buildings lined the cobbled road that encircled the small harbor. A seawall extended from the western shore across the harbor mouth, protecting many small sailing and fishermen's boats bobbing at anchor behind it from the sometimes destructive swells of the Channel. From the eastern headland opposite, a breakwater curved out and across, creating a barrier to shield the entrance to the harbor itself, the gap between the end of the seawall and the quay lining the eastern shore.

The village had grown up around the stone quays bordering the three sides of the harbor, with most houses scattered up the long slope of the eastern headland.

Shute Lane was easy to find, on the eastern side just

above the harbor. Thomas and Homer drew rein outside Number 4, a tiny fisherman's cottage with bright spring flowers in a box along the front window.

Gatting answered Thomas's knock. Now old and wizened, and heavily dependent on the cane over which he hunched, Gatting covered his shock at Thomas's injuries, yet, regardless, it was plain that the old man was pleased to see him.

Thomas hadn't intended to go inside, to, as he'd thought of it, impose on the old couple's hospitality, but Gatting would have none of it, and when he called Mrs. Gatting to the door and she added her entreaties, Thomas realized he couldn't—shouldn't—refuse them.

Sometimes, the rights and wrongs of how he should behave still escaped him.

Indeed, it was Homer who largely led the way; noting how the Gattings responded to the boy, who they knew from their shared years at the manor, Thomas decided he should follow Homer's lead.

So he and Homer sat in the cramped little parlor and allowed the Gattings to serve them morning tea. Homer and Gatting chatted all the while, and in between, Gatting inquired after Thomas's plans for the manor. The arrival of Mrs. Gatting, still round and plump with a cherubic face, carrying a tray that included a plate piled with slices of pound cake, created a diversion that saved Thomas from having to invent too much.

Settling on the settle, Mrs. Gatting railed at the fate that had seen him so badly injured, but, as he was learning was common with ordinary people, she accepted that life went on and thereafter largely ignored his state, treating him as she always had, with a mixture of deference and suitably restrained mothering.

All in all, the visit passed smoothly, with considerably more warmth than Thomas had expected. When they parted from the Gattings at the front door, he pressed a folded bank draft into Gatting's hand. "A small token of my appreciation for all you did for the manor, and thus me, over the years."

The Gattings both beamed. "Thank you, sir," Gatting said.

"And the best of luck to you," Mrs. Gatting added.

With a salute to them both, Thomas turned and followed Homer to where they'd left their horses. Mounting up, he wheeled back toward the harbor; pretending not to have noticed the shock on the Gattings' faces as they realized just how much he'd given them—enough to see them through the rest of their days in comfort—he led the way back through the town.

As they walked the horses along the stone quay across the base of the harbor, Thomas glanced at Homer and saw the boy's wide eyes fixed on the many sailing boats bobbing at anchor in the roughly rectangular pool.

Homer didn't look his way even though Thomas waited; the boy was beyond absorbed. Facing forward, Thomas scanned the curve of the road rising along the western side of the harbor—their route home. Just past the point where the harbor wall jutted out from the western headland stood the whitewashed bulk of the Ship Inn.

Thomas flicked a glance at Homer, who was still fixated. "Let's leave the horses at the Ship Inn and go for a wander around the village before returning to the inn for lunch."

Homer happily nodded and nudged his pony to keep up as Thomas turned Silver up the street to the inn.

There wasn't all that much to see in the small village. Thomas stopped at the blacksmith's to pick up some nails, then, noticing a small milliner's shop, braced himself and entered. With Homer's help, he selected a pair of lace mittens for Rose and three lengths of bright ribbon for Pippin. Tucking the packages into his jacket pocket, he followed Homer back into the sunshine.

Although the boy was too well behaved to push his case, the way Homer's gaze drifted to the harbor, to the boats, told its own tale. Understanding the fascination, Thomas waved his cane down the lane that led back to the harbor. "Why don't we walk out to the eastern headland before heading back to the inn?"

Homer looked up at him and grinned. "Yes. Let's."

They set out at a steady pace. After riding even the few miles there, Thomas appreciated the chance to stretch his legs. Marching along paved streets was quite a different exercise from walking over the less even but softer terrain about the manor; his gait was different, with different muscles drawn into play.

As they reached the headland, the last of the clouds whisked away and the sun streamed down, warming and embracing. They paused to look across the harbor, scanning the panorama from the white walls and lead roofs of the village, over the green rise of the western headland, and beyond, to the wide sweep of the sky and the sea. Sunlight glinted off the waves; gulls swooped on the currents high above, their caws a counterpoint to the murmuring of the waves, to the constant, sibilant *shush* of the sea.

Thomas stood and looked, breathed in, and felt unaccustomed contentment slide through him. He glanced down at Homer—and discovered the boy, even now, focused on the boats in the harbor.

Such unrelenting obsession made Thomas smile.

"Come along." With his cane, he pointed back along the street. "Luncheon calls."

Homer readily fell in with his direction, although whether it was the mention of food or the fact that their way took them around the harbor—and the boats—again, Thomas couldn't say.

Half an hour later, they were settled at a table at one of the windows of the Ship Inn, from where the view was all of the harbor wall and the harbor itself—and those bobbing boats.

A large slice of succulent rabbit pie and a glass of lemonade successfully vied for Homer's attention for several minutes, but once he'd cleaned his plate, his gaze once more shifted, and halted on the boats.

Smiling, still engaged with his own helping of pie, Thomas asked, "Have you ever sailed? Or is your interest merely a fascination with the unknown?"

Homer barely glanced his way. "No." Gaze on the small flotilla anchored behind the seawall, he sighed; the sound held all the abject longing only a child could muster. "I've never been sailing, at least not that I can remember, but I would so love to."

Several moments passed, then Homer looked at Thomas. "Have you ever sailed? In a small boat, I mean."

Setting down his fork, Thomas nodded. "I used to sail before my accident."

Homer's eyes widened to saucers. "You can sail? You know how to?"

Amused, Thomas reached for his ale mug. "Yes. I learned long ago, but it's not something one forgets."

"Could you teach me?" Hands on the table, eyes fixed in eager hunger on Thomas's face, Homer pleaded, *"Please . . ."*

Thomas kept his expression neutral while he weighed the pros and cons of a situation he hadn't foreseen.

Homer's eagerness built. He glanced at the harbor. "There are boats one can hire—I've seen other people take them out. Just for a sail—for fun."

Thomas couldn't see any reason he shouldn't grant the request, and, indeed, he wouldn't mind taking one of the smaller boats out on the water himself; it had been too long since he'd felt the sea air on his face and experienced the exhilaration of running before the wind. Nevertheless, he tried to put himself in Rose's—or any similar guardian's— shoes, tried to see if there was any reason he shouldn't oblige, and could find none.

Homer's gaze turned beseeching. "And my birthday is coming up—this could be your present to me."

Thomas stifled a laugh; no moss grew on his charge. But it was true that, not having known about the approaching birthday, he didn't have any gift organized. "Very well."

Had he harbored any doubt as to how much Homer had yearned to sail, the look on the boy's face would have slain it. Transformed by delight, Homer breathed, "*Thank* you." He glanced fleetingly at the boats, then looked at Thomas. "Can we go now?"

Thomas laughed, and nodded; pushing back his chair, he rose.

After he'd paid their shot, they walked back into the village to the main quay. Five minutes' brisk discussion with one of the older men sitting mending nets along the quay's edge, and Thomas had hired a small boat with a single sail. The old sailor's son rowed a small skiff out to the boat, drew in its anchor, and towed the boat to the steps leading down from the western quay.

Despite his stiff leg, Thomas stepped down to the bob-

bing deck easily enough. Setting down his cane, he beckoned Homer to join him. The boy was over the side in a
flash.

The sailor's son hovered close by in his skiff, but as he
listened to Thomas instruct Homer in the basics of sailing a
small, single-sail vessel, the sailor's son's concern vanished. With a brisk salute to Thomas, he bent to his oars
and rowed back to the main quay.

"Right, then." Instructions completed, Thomas sat on the
bench seat. "We need to take her out under oars, at least as
far as the harbor mouth. Once we're on the sea proper, we
can ship the oars and hoist the sail, but first, we need to
navigate well enough to get the boat out of the harbor."
Thomas patted the space to his left. "I'll need to manage
both oars to some degree, but my left arm's weak, so if you
sit here, you can man the left oar while I guide us."

Homer eagerly sat and gripped the oar. Thomas showed
him how to place his hands for best effect, then, with the
other oar, pushed off from the harbor's side.

It took a little adjusting, but their coordination rapidly
improved, and five minutes later, they passed through the
harbor mouth and rounded the seawall—and met the first
true ocean swell.

"Oh!" Excitement lit Homer's eyes, his whole face.

"Now we ship the oars." Thomas quickly brought the
right oar aboard. Homer leapt to do the same with the other.

Shifting to sit on the rear bench, locking one hand on the
tiller, Thomas pointed to the mast. "That rope's the one to
pull—firmly, but steadily."

Homer obeyed and the sail slowly—steadily—rose.

"That's enough," Thomas called. "Now tie it off like I
showed you, then come and sit with me, and we'll see."

He'd set the sail to catch just the right amount of ride from the brisk sea breeze. The sail billowed, filled, and the boat started to move, cleanly, smoothly cutting through the waves, gradually building speed.

"Oh, yes." Homer's eyes shone.

Thomas grinned, entirely at one with the feeling.

It was a perfect—*perfect*—day for sailing, with just the right amount of breeze to send them skimming over a largely glassy sea. The waves had subsided, and the sun shone down as they skated along the inner reaches of Mount's Bay toward Trewavas Head.

They didn't need words to share their mutual delight; exchanged glances were enough. The expressions on Homer's face, the dawning wonder and joy, assured Thomas that he'd made the right decision—indeed, the boy's reactions were a shining reward.

Once the first wave of sensory delight faded, Thomas showed Homer how to make this adjustment and that, how to bring the boat around, then set her running free again. They tacked and sailed before the breeze for more than an hour, then Thomas brought the nose around and they headed back to the harbor.

By the time they'd returned the boat, collected their horses, and were once more riding the cliff road toward the manor, the afternoon was well advanced, but Thomas estimated that as long as they didn't dally, they wouldn't be late for afternoon tea.

Homer chattered nonstop for half the distance back but then fell silent. Glancing at his charge, Thomas was reassured by the absentminded joy still evident in the boy's face. Homer had gone from talking to daydreaming.

Lips curving, Thomas faced forward and rode steadily on.

They reached the manor kitchen just as Rose was setting the teapot on the table.

She looked up and smiled. "Excellent. I've baked scones"—she waved at the platter in the center of the table—"and they're so much better fresh from the oven."

Pippin was already at the table. She grinned at Thomas and Homer, then reached for a scone.

Rose had paused, her gaze passing assessingly over Thomas, then Homer, taking in their tousled, windblown hair and somewhat damp clothes. She met Homer's eyes. "Did you have a good time?"

She turned away to pick up her cup and saucer as Homer—eyes lighting in an almost dreamy fashion as he drew out his chair and sat—said, "It was wonderful! Thomas took me sailing and we had an absolutely *magnificent* time."

"*What*?" Rose whirled to face them.

Startled, Thomas watched as all color fled her cheeks.

The cup rattled on the saucer. In a daze, she steadied it and set it down. She stared in what seemed to be abject horror, first at Homer, then at Thomas, now seated in his chair at the end of the table.

"You took him out on a boat?" Her voice hoarse, Rose gripped the back of her chair. "A sailing boat?"

Thomas had no idea what was wrong. It took conscious effort to suppress the instinct to lie, but he'd learned that much, at least. "Yes." He paused, then went on, "It was a perfect day for sailing, the sea smooth and the wind not too strong, and Homer said he'd never been out, so—"

"*How could you*?" Rose swung her gaze to Homer. Her voice was choked; she was clearly distraught. "You know how I feel—and why."

Thomas looked at Homer.

Far from retreating, the boy met Rose's accusatory gaze with a steady, unrepentant stare. His lips compressed, but then he replied, "I needed to know if I would like it or not, and I do." He gave heavy emphasis to the last words, then reiterated, "I had a wonderful time."

Thomas heard that last as an invitation to Rose to understand how important that had been to Homer.

Instead, she sucked in a breath and let it out with "That's not the point!"

"Yes, it is." Homer wasn't going to back down. His lips, his whole face, tightened, then, his eyes locked with Rose's, his voice harder than Thomas had ever heard it, he said, "I won't die like they did, you know."

Silence. It spread through the kitchen and trapped them all. Thomas realized he'd stopped breathing. A quick glance at Pippin showed the girl with her head bowed; her fingers, previously crumbling a scone, had stilled. Frozen.

He glanced at Rose. She was staring at Homer as if he'd grown two heads.

Homer, for his part, stared, mulishly determined, back at her.

The entire kitchen seemed to quiver on a knife edge.

Thomas inwardly sighed. Leaning both forearms on the table, he looked from Homer to Rose and evenly asked, "Would someone please tell me what's going on?"

His voice reached Rose. She glanced at him and blinked, then she drew in a shallow breath and replied, "Homer's father and . . . a friend died in a yachting accident." Breathing in again, she straightened and returned her gaze to Homer. "That's why I'm so upset."

Thomas knew he'd heard some of the truth, but he didn't think she'd told him all. Be that as it may . . . "I'm a tolerably good sailor, quite experienced, and it was a remarkably calm day. Neither Homer nor I were in the slightest danger."

His attempt at soothing failed. Rose's eyes flashed as she turned on him and snapped, "And if you *had* got into danger out there on the open sea . . ." She flung a hand toward the ocean. "Are you so *very* sure you"—her gaze flicked to his crooked left shoulder and weakened left arm—"*could* have got both of you to safety?"

He was shocked to feel the jab strike home, but in the face of her clear—if unreasoning—distress, he held on to his temper and, rigidly keeping his voice to a calm and even tone, replied, "If I had, at any point and on any level, believed there could possibly be any danger to Homer that I could not have guarded adequately against, I would not have consented to take him out."

Before he could add what to him was the most pertinent point—that nothing untoward had threatened, much less happened—Homer pushed back his chair and stood.

The boy held Rose's gaze unflinchingly. "I know you fear me sailing, but it's something I needed to do—to at least try it and find out what it's like. Today was my chance, and I took it. I'm not going to say I'm sorry that I asked Thomas to take me out, because I'm not. But I am sorry that you're still so bothered by it, when all that happened was that we had a wonderful time."

Homer stepped back from the table and turned. His gaze carried an apology as it passed over Thomas's face, but then Homer walked to the door and left the kitchen.

Thomas raised his gaze to Rose's face, watched as, her expression blanking, she stared after Homer.

Her eyes swam with such a confusion of emotions that Thomas couldn't make them out.

A second passed, then he shifted his gaze to Pippin. A

second later, he reached for a scone. "What did you and Dolly get up to today?"

Pippin shot him a sidelong look, then she straightened in her chair, settled Dolly more firmly in her lap, and proceeded to tell him.

Leaving Rose to draw in a shuddering breath, then, slowly, sink into her chair.

A moment later, she lifted the teapot and poured herself a cup.

Thomas gave Homer a few hours, then went in search of him. He found the boy in one of his favorite places, sitting on the stile at the side of the orchard looking out over the fields to the sea. At least Thomas now understood Homer's fascination with the wide and distant view over the rippling waters of Mount's Bay.

Ducking beneath the branches just coming into leaf, Thomas made his way down to the stile. Reaching it, he didn't say anything; he simply leaned against the wall alongside and looked out at the view, too.

Eventually, as Thomas had known he would, Homer stirred. His knees drawn up, his arms wrapped tightly around them, he kept his gaze on the fields and said, "I had to find out, you see?"

He continued, explaining his actions, expounding his excuses.

Thomas listened without interruption, his own youthful self-justifications of various indiscretions echoing in his ears.

Eventually, Homer fell silent. Resting his chin on his arms, he waited for Thomas's response.

Thomas debated; dealing with children wasn't an activity in which he had any experience. In the end, he decided that all he could offer was what he saw as the truth. "Your desire to go sailing is valid, but the way you chose to go about getting what you wanted was where you went wrong."

After a moment, Homer turned his head and looked at him. Questioningly, faintly puzzled.

Without waiting for further invitation, Thomas elaborated, with the wry self-abnegation only one with the same failing could show. "Manipulating others to get what you want, capitalizing on their ignorance, even if what you cause them to do brings no harm to them or anyone else, is still wrong."

Homer's dark blue gaze grew distant as he digested that. Eventually, he sighed and, in a quiet voice, said, "I'm sorry for manipulating you."

Thomas could only marvel that he, himself, had never been brought to utter those words; the knowledge only made his appreciation of Homer's simple honesty all the greater. He nodded, but hesitated, thinking through his words before he said, "This time, I'll let the transgression pass, but in the future, never attempt to manipulate me, or Rose, or, truth to tell, if you're wise, anyone at all."

Homer was quick-witted enough to hear the personal resonance infusing Thomas's last words. He looked at him quizzically.

Thomas let his lips curve. He settled his forearms on the wall and, after a moment of gathering his thoughts, went on, "If you want something, it's perfectly acceptable, even laudable, to make it your goal. To doggedly pursue it, even in the face of all opposition—as long as you do that openly, without guile or deception. As long as you own to your aims. If you stick to that path, then when you get what you want, you won't be left feeling like a thief—feeling that while attaining your goal should have felt so wonderful, the victory is somehow tarnished, and your achievement is no longer an unalloyed joy."

Homer thought that through for several minutes, then his eyes widened fractionally and his lips formed a silent O.

Another minute passed, then he said, "So I can still press Ro—Ma to let me sail?"

Thomas grinned. Straightening, he reached out and further ruffled Homer's already untidy hair. "Yes—but if you're wise, you'll wait for a few months to roll by."

In the distance, they heard a bell ring—Rose's summons to the dinner table.

Thomas glanced at Homer. "Come on. We'd better wash and tidy ourselves. We need to be on our best behavior until R—your ma forgives us, which, all things being equal, she will soon enough."

With a swift, answering grin, Homer clambered back over the stile. Landing in the grass beside Thomas, the boy hesitated for a heartbeat—then he flung his arms around Thomas's waist and hugged him as hard as he could. "Thank you."

The words were muffled against Thomas's jacket, but he heard them. For a second, he didn't know what to do, then he surrendered to impulse and laid a hand on Homer's shoulder and gently gripped. Held on.

After a tense instant, Homer dragged in a breath and released him.

Thomas loosened his grip but left his arm lightly draped about the boy's narrow shoulders.

With Homer matching his free and easy paces to Thomas's hitching ones, together they made their way back to the house.

Thomas waited until the children were abed before going to face his other Waterloo.

He found Rose in the kitchen, seated in a chair in the inglenook, her head bent over one of Pippin's dresses as she repaired a tear.

He paused in the archway, but she didn't look up; the rhythm of her needle did not falter.

Lips thinning, one hand in his jacket pocket, his other gripping his cane, he limped across the room; halting before the sink, he looked out through the window above it at the darkened fields, at the glimmer of moonlight that lent an elusive silver edge to every leaf, every blade of grass.

He'd thought of what he wanted to say, but finding the words hadn't been easy. Saying them was even harder. Eventually, feeling her gaze touch the side of his face, he drew breath and began. "Like Homer, I find it difficult to apologize for doing something that I had no reason not to do. That said, I am sincerely sorry that by taking him sailing, I unwittingly caused you so much distress. That was never my intention—that possibility never even entered my head. I realize, now, that perhaps I should have been more . . . careful. That perhaps I should have specifically asked Homer whether taking him sailing would go against any prohibition you had in place, but . . ."

He paused, then forced himself to go on. "I'm not very good at dealing with other people. I don't—habitually don't—think of how my actions will affect others, how what I do might impact on them. I have to stop and make myself specifically think about that, each and every time. It's a flaw, and I know it, so I try to stop and think things through before I act. I did so over taking Homer sailing. However, I lacked the information that would have stopped me from doing so—I didn't know that you had forbidden it."

Again, he paused to think his words through, then went on, "All that said, I wanted to apologize for our contretemps today, and to assure you that, the next time a similar situation arises, I won't agree until I know that you approve of whatever Homer or Pippin want to do."

He didn't know why giving that assurance and being able to continue to interact with the children was so important to him; it simply was.

Keeping Rose herself in his orbit, reclaiming his position within her good graces, also featured as highly desirable, if not imperative.

He heard her sigh, then material rustled. An instant later, she appeared beside him.

Like him, she stood staring out at the night. "I accept your apology—and I must apologize, too." Fleetingly, her gaze touched the side of his face—the scarred left side; he felt her gaze linger for a second, then she drew breath, faced forward, and went on, "I should have known better than to imagine for even a second that you would go behind my back in arranging such an outing. You couldn't have known about my feelings over Homer going sailing—my expectations of you were illogical, and I'm sorry I ripped up at you." She paused, then, voice lowering, continued, "And I'm even sorrier for my quite unforgivable remarks regarding your ability to keep him safe. I've watched you work about the house for weeks, and the jibe was unjustified and uncalled for."

When she paused, Thomas wondered if he was supposed to excuse her that last, yet her apology had only stated the truth.

Before he could decide on a response, lifting her head, she continued, "Homer and Pippin, as I'm sure you've guessed, are very precious to me. I've devoted my life to caring for them, so . . . I tend to get overprotective. But I know I can trust you—that I can trust in you to protect them."

He nodded. "That you may do without reservation. I would never let anything happen to either one."

At his tone, some of her tension left her. The line of her shoulders and spine, until then rigidly straight, softened.

Thomas hesitated, then said, "So that we're both clear on what happened, and where matters now stand, when I spoke with Homer earlier out by the stile"—he felt sure she'd seen them there—"I explained that while his wish to sail was valid and it's ultimately going to be his life to live, manipulating others to achieve that desire was where he had gone wrong, and that in general trying to manipulate either me or you, or anyone, for that matter, wasn't a wise idea."

Rose turned to regard him; through the soft shadows thrown by the lamp burning on the kitchen table, she met his eyes, read the sincerity—the straightforward honesty—in his gaze. She replayed his words; slowly, she inclined her head. "While I can't agree about the sailing, I appreciate your argument." She held his gaze for an instant more, then said, "Thank you for speaking with him."

In this instance, she was perfectly aware that Homer would pay more attention to Thomas's words than her own.

She started to turn away, but he stopped her with a hand—a fleeting touch—on her arm.

"So"—his shadowed gaze trapped hers—"are we . . . once again in accord?"

They were close; she could feel the radiant warmth of his body, subtly comforting, sensually distracting. No matter his injuries, his presence remained; it burned like a flame, strong and contained, unmarred by the physical imperfections—no, in some strange way made more potent by them.

Realization swept her; the fact that despite his disfigurement, his infirmity, he still affected her as he did only underscored just how powerful the attraction was—that it could overcome such hurdles, that the lure of him could so effortlessly reach over the barriers and snare her so completely.

The insight only served to further heighten her awareness of it, of him.

And replace her previously ebbing tension with tension of a different sort.

Her breathing had grown shallow, but he was due an answer. She moistened her lips—saw his gaze drop to them—and abruptly nodded. "Yes." Inwardly cursing her breathlessness, hoping he hadn't detected it, she forced more air into her lungs and met his gaze again. "Yes, we're in accord, as we were before."

"Good." The single word sounded deeper, almost a rumbling caress.

She had no idea of his background, but instinct told her he was more than experienced enough to know how he affected her.

Every time before, he'd drawn back, but as they stood inches apart in the kitchen in the night, she was suddenly unsure what she wanted—whether she wanted him to draw back or, this time, to step forward.

Her fascination with him was bordering on the dangerous.

His gaze shifted, and again he paused—thinking, she now realized, as he'd said. That was what was behind those curious little hesitations of his.

Then he eased back a fraction, and something within her deflated. Subsided.

Expectation. Anticipation. Hope. All those things.

Shifting back, he reached into his pocket and drew out two small packets. "These are for you and Pippin." He held them out.

As she took them, she glanced at his face. "Why . . . ?"

He shrugged. "Homer and I were enjoying ourselves, but the two of you weren't there . . . it seemed only fair." Gripping his cane, he stepped back. "The pink one is for Pippin."

"Thank you." She looked up as he turned away. "I'll leave it by her plate at breakfast."

Without looking back, he inclined his head. "Thank you."

No, thank you. Fleeting exasperation rose; he never accepted thanks, not readily, even when they were due.

She was tracing the edge of the green packet that by default had to be hers when the tap of his cane ceased. She looked up and saw him hesitating in the archway giving onto the corridor.

As if sensing her attention, he angled his head and, without looking back, said, "There's a danger inherent in attempting to restrain, or even limit, a boy of Homer's type of mind." He paused, but this time only for a second, then went on, "At his age, I was much as he is, quick-witted, intelligent, always wanting to know. So trust me when I say that I know—none better—the pitfalls of being a boy with a highly intelligent and *questing* mind."

Rose blinked, waited, but he didn't say anything more. Gripping his cane, he continued into the corridor. The shadows enveloped him, and then he was gone, the dull thud of his cane faintly reassuring as he made his way into the front hall, and then, slowly, up the stairs.

For a long moment, Rose stood and listened, his gift in her hand, a frown slowly forming in her mind as she replayed his last words, and their tone.

Only when she heard his bedroom door shut, and she stirred and returned to her chair, did she realize that the frown in her mind was not for Homer, not for her, but for him.

everal days later, Thomas was standing at the edge of the front lawn, a sketch pad in one hand, his cane propped against one thigh as he drew a plan of the new garden beds he thought would improve the front of the house, when the rattle of wheels on the gravel of the drive reached him.

Raising his head, he looked down the drive, inwardly frowning as he realized it wasn't the usual day for deliveries, and, more, that the wheels didn't sound like those of the carter's lumbering dray.

Lowering the pad, Thomas reached for the head of his cane and shifted to face the drive.

A light trap came bowling out of the cover of the thick band of trees that screened the manor from the lane. Two men sat on the board; even before the driver had reined in the horse and brought the trap to a halt beside Thomas, Thomas had recognized what type of men they were.

Not only had he seen their sort before but he'd also employed such men before; he knew very well what they were good for.

"Morning, sir." The nearer man, the passenger, tipped his hat to Thomas. Both he and his companion were middle-aged, soberly dressed, the sort of men one might pass in the street in any town and not think twice about.

Not unless one looked into their eyes and noted the constant alertness, the surveillance that, being their stock-in-trade, quickly became an entrenched habit.

Thomas returned the man's polite nod but, as was the habit in any part of the West Country, simply waited to learn what the pair wanted; westcountrymen didn't waste their words.

Both men had been scanning the manor's façade. The passenger nodded toward it. "Are you the owner?"

Thomas waited until both men looked back at him. "And you are?"

His tone and his manner answered their question, and less-than-subtly reminded them that they weren't of his class and had no right to demand anything of him. Not even his name.

The men instantly retreated into deferential politeness. "Begging your pardon, sir," the driver said. "It's just that we're looking for some people and wondered if you or anyone here might know where they are."

As Thomas had suspected, they were inquiry agents, men hired by someone to find someone else who, for whatever reason, did not wish to be found. "I see," he said, moderating his tone. He arched his brows in mild interest. "And who are you searching for?"

"A young lady—well, she *was* youngish, but she'd be a bit more than that by now, and two children. A boy who's nine years old and a girl a bit younger." The driver had the sort of reassuring face that invited confidences. "They disappeared from Leicestershire four years ago, and it's thought they might have come down this way. Few years ago, at least, it'd be."

Thomas shifted his stance, deliberately giving the impression he'd relaxed—a wordless lie. "Why are you searching for them?" His tone indicated nothing more than idle curiosity.

The passenger answered. "Seems the boy's in line to inherit some estate, but it's likely he doesn't know it."

"We're trying to find them to give them the news," the driver added.

Thomas frowned as if searching his memory—as if he'd swallowed what was one of the oldest lures in an inquiry agent's arsenal. "A lady with two children in tow, all from Leicestershire . . ." After several long moments, he slowly shook his head and refocused on the men. "I can't say I know anyone who would fit that description."

The driver had been holding his horse on a taut rein. The horse shifted, sidled.

Thomas watched as the driver settled the horse. So the men hadn't come to the manor by accident—someone had mentioned his housekeeper and her children.

Horse under control, the driver cast him a sharp, distinctly more interrogatory glance, but his tone was still even, still politely deferential when he asked, "What about your housekeeper and her children? We heard they might be the ones we're after."

Thomas smiled and worked to make sure that the expression reached his eyes, that there was nothing visible to alert the men, well-trained observers though they were, that the gesture was anything other than entirely sincere. "Ah—I see the confusion. My housekeeper would be about the right age, and the children, too, but she's a widow, and also a native of these parts, as are the children. The family hails from around Penzance, and to my certain knowledge they've never been out of the county. Her husband was in the navy, and she was a connection of my previous caretakers, so took over when they retired."

The men hesitated; his certainty and confidence had shaken theirs.

After a moment, the passenger stirred. "We did hear as she was well spoken, your housekeeper—like a lady."

Thomas nodded a touch more curtly. "Indeed. She's gentry-born, but married beneath her. Consequently, now she's lost her husband, she clings to the outward trappings of her previous station, because, of course, that improves her chances of better employment—for instance, as my housekeeper."

He paused, wondering if he should offer to bring his housekeeper forth, but from a gentleman of his standing that would be one step too far in pushing his argument. Instead, gripping his cane with both hands, he straightened and said, "If there was any chance that she was the lady you seek, and her son the boy in line for an inheritance, I would summon them to meet you, but as I know they aren't—that their background is entirely different to that of those you seek—I see no reason to disturb them."

That, he felt, hit just the right note.

The men thought so, too; they all but visibly deflated.

Resigned, the passenger asked, "You can't think of anyone else 'round about who might fit our bill, sir?"

Again, Thomas pretended to think before shaking his head. "No." He paused, then said, "I presume someone's sent you to search for these people—are they, the people behind the search, sure the lady and the children are still in the area?"

Lifting the reins, the driver grimaced. "As I heard it, the gent himself didn't know much, but the agency tracked them down this way, and they haven't been seen anywhere else since, so . . ." He shrugged, then tipped his head politely to Thomas. "Thank you for your help, sir."

The passenger also bobbed his head.

Thomas stood and watched as they turned the trap and headed back down the drive.

He'd glimpsed Rose surreptitiously watching from the drawing room window, screened by the curtains. He didn't look her way.

After several moments of rapid thinking, he raised his sketch pad and returned to his previous occupation.

He couldn't tell whether the two agents had swallowed his lies whole; he thought they had, but he wasn't willing to take the risk—wasn't willing to risk Rose's, Homer's, and Pippin's safety—by doing anything that might alert the agents if they remained suspicious enough to halt the trap in the lane and slip back through the tangle of bushes and trees to see how he had reacted to their news.

No. He was far too old a hand at manipulation, at creating an illusion to make people believe what he wanted them to, to not play the role he'd scripted to its end.

He remained in the front garden for half an hour more, pretending to work on his plans.

And every minute his mind seethed with possible answers to the now-critical question of who his housekeeper and her children truly were, and why they'd sought refuge at the manor.

Eventually, he shut his sketch pad, gripped his cane, and, unhurriedly, headed for the front door.

He wasn't surprised to find Rose hovering in the front hall.

She didn't even wait for him to close the door before demanding, "Those men—who were they?"

Turning from the door, he studied her, took in the tension thrumming in every line of her body, tightening her features, sharpening her tone. Slowly, he went forward. Halting two feet away, voice low, he said, "They were inquiry agents. They were hunting"—and knowing the breed, the word was apt—"for a lady who had fled Leicestershire with two children in tow."

Every vestige of color drained from Rose's face.

He calmly went on, "I told them that while my housekeeper and her children might be thought to fit the description of the people they sought, I knew for a fact that my housekeeper hailed from a family from around Penzance, and that she had never been out of the county, and nor had her children."

Rose felt as if her world was disintegrating; all security, all sense of safety and comfort, had fled. Gone. She could barely breathe as, eyes wide, she searched Thomas's face . . . slowly the import of his words sank into her panicking brain.

He'd lied and protected them.

The steadiness in his hazel eyes, the acutely observant mind that lurked behind, were assurance enough that, at least in terms of the identities of the three people the men had been searching for, he knew the truth.

Dragging in a breath, she forced herself to ask, "Did they believe you?"

He hesitated, and she knew that he was deciding what he should tell her—deciding what was right for him to tell her. Eventually, he said, "For the moment. They have, at least, gone away."

The absolute truth—no more, no less.

Forcibly filling her lungs, she nodded. "Thank you."

A moment passed. Her eyes locked with his, she knew he

was waiting for her to tell him more, to explain . . . but their tale wasn't hers to tell; it wasn't she who was the focus of the threat.

When she remained standing before him and volunteered nothing more, his lips lightly twisted and he inclined his head. "We all have our secrets, Mrs. Sheridan."

Then he shifted and limped past her, making for the stairs.

Leaving Rose, puzzled, staring after him.

Rose replayed that exchange countless times through the rest of the day and into the evening. Her initial, quite staggering relief on learning that the men had believed Thomas's assurances and gone away had quickly been tempered by the realization that, at some point, they, or men like them, would be back.

Would come hunting her and the children, and next time Thomas might not be there to deflect the inquiry.

To act as her and the children's shield.

He'd told her he had come to the manor purely to await a summons that might arrive at any time.

Her mind elsewhere, she bumbled her way through lunch, then dinner, and finally got the children to bed.

After that, she paced in her small bedroom under the eaves, debating what to do, what her next move should be. Previously, whenever danger had threatened, at the very first sign, she'd taken the children and run. Even now, some deeply buried instinct was urging her to sweep the pair up and flee into the night.

But this time Thomas had intervened; his actions had bought her time to think. To plan.

They would have to leave the manor. She had started to believe that they would never have to flee it, to hope, instead, that they would be able to live there in peace until the time came to return to their world and fight the battle waiting, but her long-ago vow rang too clearly in her mind, and she would not risk all the effort she'd expended, all the sacrifices made over the last four years, on an uncertain hope. They needed to leave, but, thanks to Thomas's unconditional support, they didn't have to flee in a panicked rush.

Indeed, to make best use of Thomas's gift, she should think of what she could do to disguise their leaving as an unremarkable occurrence, as nothing worthy of note, a simple moving on due to mundane events, rather than driven by any precipitate reaction. Fleeing with the hounds too close on her trail . . . no. Better she plan; better she use her head.

She paused, verified that that conclusion was sound, and felt more settled. More sure. Decision made, then, at least in theory; the practical details would follow.

But first . . .

Going to the door, she opened it; drawing her shawl about her shoulders and knotting it, she went to Pippin's room and looked in on the little girl. Her face utterly angelic in slumber, Pippin was fast asleep.

Rose closed Pippin's door, checked that Homer, too, was sound asleep, then, determined on her course, she descended the attic stairs and set out in search of Thomas.

The attic stairs joined one end of the first-floor corridor. Stepping out of the stairwell, she walked briskly along. She hadn't brought a candle, but although it was night and the shadows were black, sufficient light from the moon and the stars reached through the big windows at either end of the corridor to allow her to walk with confidence.

She couldn't explain—for Homer's sake, she had to

keep their secret—but she needed to thank Thomas properly for his unquestioning support. She didn't want to
think of what state she and the children would have been
in at that moment had he not so calmly lied on their be-
half. Lied, and from all she'd seen, without the slightest
hesitation. At the very least, she owed him her abject
thanks, and, given he knew that she was, indeed, keeping
secrets, an assurance that her reason for refusing to con-
fide in him wasn't that she didn't trust him but that their
secret wasn't hers to share.

She was nearing the head of the main stairs when a familiar repetitive *thump* reached her. She slowed, then
halted, and waited for Thomas to gain the top of the stairs.

He did, and started along the corridor, not immediately
realizing that she was there.

Standing in his path.

This, Rose decided, was better than she'd hoped. Better
than speaking with him in his library. Pinning him down
when he had a whole room to move in . . . no; the confines
of the corridor were to her advantage.

Head rising, clasping her hands at her waist, she waited
where she'd halted, in the middle of the corridor in a spot
where a hall chest on one side and a side table on the other
narrowed the space even further.

He noticed her and paused. After a moment, he came on.
From the steady weight of his gaze, something she could
feel even through the dimness, she was certain he'd guessed
that she wasn't about to let him pass until she'd said all she
intended to say.

He halted before her, and she could almost hear his mental sigh. He arched a brow. "Yes?"

No name, she noted, but she didn't let that deter her. Fixing her gaze on his shadowed eyes, she drew breath and

stated, "I want to thank you—properly—for what you did today—"

He cut her off with a brusque wave. "You already did, as I recall."

"No, I didn't. Not properly."

"The thanks you tendered were more than sufficient. There's no need—"

"There's *every* need."

His eyes locked with hers. Rose felt the weight of his will, felt it pressing against hers almost like a physical force, but she wasn't about to give way. She held her ground and gave him back stare for stare, her determination against his stubbornness.

His lips thinned. After a pregnant pause, he drew in a tight breath. "Mrs. Sheridan." His voice had cooled, but the cutting edge that might have been there was absent; he wanted to force her to retreat, but he didn't want to hurt her. "Allow me to explain that I didn't act as I did today to garner your thanks. I acted as I did because it was the right thing to do, and I neither need nor want your gratitude—"

"You *irritating* man!" Rose finally lost her temper. Over the past weeks, she'd grown well acquainted with his constant self-abnegation, but this time, she wasn't having it. "Has it never occurred to you that people thanking you is something *they* need to do—and that you are supposed to accept their thanks with due graciousness, thereby excusing them from feeling forever indebted to you?"

Even as the words echoed between them, she recalled his confession of days before, heard his halting words in her mind: *I'm not very good at dealing with other people. I don't—habitually don't—think of how my actions will affect others, how what I do might impact on them.*

She watched his expression blank, then his gaze fell from

hers, and she realized she'd hit the nail on the head. He honestly hadn't known, hadn't seen . . . Her own expression easing, her voice lowering, she went on, "You do it all the time—you refuse to accept even the mildest, smallest expressions of thanks. You slide around them, avoid them, but, even more, you constantly downplay the good you do. You dismiss your actions, deny their importance—you denigrate the contributions you make to the lives of others . . ." All of that was true. Confused, she stared at him. "Why?"

He didn't immediately meet her gaze, but then his features hardened and he raised his eyes to hers. "If you've quite finished . . . ?"

The words . . . weren't cold. There was emotion beneath them, roiling and churning, but ruthlessly suppressed.

When she blinked at him, trying to sense, to see further, to understand, he looked away and shifted to edge past her.

"No." Brazen, Rose sidestepped and blocked his path. That brought them face-to-face, close, his coat brushing the knot of her shawl. "I haven't finished." Anger—at him, because of him—and a host of other emotions pounded in her blood. "There's this."

Raising her hands, she set her palms to his cheeks, hauled his head down two inches, and pressed her lips to his.

Damn him—he wasn't worthless!

She kissed him, pressed her lips to his, determined to express the feelings he'd denied, her heartfelt thanks, yes, but also to acknowledge the relief he'd brought her, and her appreciation of all the countless minor acts of kindness he'd lavished on her and the children.

He might not know how to deal with others, but he was trying, and he wasn't failing.

That much she could tell him—and given he wouldn't listen to her words, she told him with her lips.

Ignoring the strange feel of his scars against her right palm, she boldly did something she'd never done in her life and poured her heart and soul into her kiss.

Bold, reckless, but, on a host of levels, so very necessary.

And he responded.

Her heart leapt—literally jumped in her chest—when she felt his lips, so unexpectedly smooth and giving, ease against hers.

Just for a heartbeat.

But then he stilled, stopped, caught himself.

Oh, no—she wasn't having that.

With smooth deliberation—a determination, a decision, he wouldn't miss—she stepped into him and kissed him harder.

The dam broke.

Rose rejoiced.

And Thomas lost all touch with the world.

Stunned, amazed, he was swept up and away on a tide of feelings, of emotions whipped along by a desperate yearning, one he hadn't even realized lived within him.

Where had all this come from? How had she set it free?

He didn't know the answers. All he knew was the feel of her lips moving on his—demanding a response he could no longer not give.

All he sensed was the warmth of her body, touching his, holding out a siren's promise of succor amid the desolation his life had become.

No longer his to command, his lips parted; effortlessly—without thought or intention, much less any exercise of conscious will—he took control of the kiss, and then he was kissing her with all the pent-up longing, all the suppressed need he'd been holding back for the past months.

Ever since he'd first seen her.

Distantly, he heard a muted *crack* and realized his cane had fallen. Where, he didn't care. Of their own volition, or so it seemed, his arms rose and closed, gently yet possessively, about her.

About Rose.

Some lingering uncertainty made him wonder if she would pull back, but no—she sank against him, into him, equally caught in the tide of the moment.

In the passions, so recklessly freed, that flowed, unrestrained, between them.

With victorious abandon, she surrendered her mouth, and he claimed. Feasted. Supped, sipped, then, at her insistence, plundered, and she took, gave, and incited, her palms and fingers firm and clasping, holding, steering, directing.

Not easing. Not letting go—not even for an instant.

He'd known sensual pleasure in the past, but this was something more—something finer, something elementally precious.

Their mouths melded and she was with him every step of the way, urging him on when he wanted to pause, to savor, wanting more, taking more, driving them both to utter distraction.

The kiss grew wild, beyond all control. The physical communion swelled, expanded, and captured them, drowning them both in unexpected heat.

Their tongues tangled and danced, dueled and lured; their lips captured and teased.

And desire flared. An elemental force, it swirled up from within them, twined with their passions, and ignited.

The flames bloomed—within him, as well as in her.

He'd thought he'd lost it, that fundamental fire, but no, it was there. It had been slumbering, smoldering as barely nascent embers, until she'd fanned the blaze.

She pressed closer and the flames roared.

The conflagration consumed him, rivers of fiery need streaking down his veins. He tightened his arms, drawing her fully against him; angling his head, he took the kiss further. Deeper.

Metaphorically taking her hand, he led her on into the flames.

Rose followed him eagerly, no thought able to stand against the joy of knowing he wanted her. That was no longer in question; the hard rod of his erection pressing against her stomach was testament enough to the reality of his ardor.

He wanted her, and, good Lord, she hadn't truly realized just how much she wanted him. Hadn't realized that her reactions to him were simply symptoms of this—this greedy, ravenous, driving need.

Sliding her hands up, she speared her fingers into his hair and, up on her toes, met his tongue with hers, delighted and thrilled by the unfettered engagement. *This* was what she'd truly craved.

This closeness.

With him.

Heat and passion, need and urgency, merged and swirled through her, then pounded through her veins. Desire consumed her and cindered all thought. The only impulse remaining was *more*.

Thomas couldn't find his feet in the raging tumult of their needs. The realization struck out of nowhere; the resulting stab of panic, of being so hopelessly out of control, jarred him—fleetingly, momentarily—but it was enough.

Enough for a shaft of clarity to pierce the fog of their mutual desire and remind him of who they were.

Him, disfigured as he was on so many levels, and her . . .

Was this, her passion so warmly and freely yielded, real? Or was she offering him all this because she felt she must, because he was her employer? In return for his protection.

Some part of his logical, rational mind scoffed at the thought—she was the one who had refused to let him past—but the rest of his reeling self, so much more vulnerable than he'd ever been, wasn't—couldn't be—sure.

That uncertainty—the possibility that she might not truly feel as he assumed—made him think. Made him realize . . .

Realize the line they'd both stepped over, the barrier they'd breached, indeed, all but eradicated.

They were exposed, both of them . . .

He dragged in a deeper breath and drew back from the kiss.

Forced his lips from hers, pulled back against her hold and raised his head.

She blinked her eyes open, and through the dimness met his gaze. They remained intimately close, their lips inches apart, their breaths mingling.

For several heartbeats, he looked into her eyes. Then, unable to help himself, he raised one hand and, gently, his senses aching with the need to touch, to know, he slowly ran the back of one finger down her perfect cheek.

And felt.

So much more than he ever had before. The clash of unfamiliar emotions rocked him.

He drew in an unsteady breath, his chest swelling against the lush curves of her breasts.

Even as his senses settled, he felt beyond unsteady, as if

some internal mooring had been ripped away and he was drifting.

Still out of control.

No longer in control.

No longer the man he once had been, and unsure of the man he now was.

In this arena, too, it seemed.

But he knew what must be—he still had to pay his ultimate penance, and until he did, his life was not his own.

He didn't even know if, after, he would have a life to live.

He didn't want to let her go, but . . . slowly, he eased his arms from about her and set her back on her feet. Losing her warmth rocked him again, but he clamped down on the impulse, sharp and intense, to reach out and draw her back.

Dazed from the kiss, she'd stared—unsure, uncomprehending—at him, but now he saw confusion fill her eyes.

She opened her lips, but he spoke before she could. "That was . . . inappropriate."

She blinked. After a heartbeat's pause, in a strange tone, she parroted, "Inappropriate."

He suddenly saw that he'd misstepped again. "Not on your part," he hurried to explain, "but on mine."

She searched his eyes, her confusion only growing.

Giving in to the urge, he raked a hand through his hair—an act revealing so much weakness, so much uncertainty and vulnerability, that the logical part of him was utterly appalled. "It's not you." Lowering his hand, he briefly waved between them. "This, what's grown between us"—something not even he could now deny—"can't be. Can't come to anything, not because of you but because of me." He forced himself to add, "Because of the man I am."

She tilted her head, her gaze never leaving his eyes. After

a moment, she asked, her voice, still affected by desire, sultry and low, "And what sort of man are you that I cannot desire you?"

He knew he couldn't hesitate. "I'm a man with no future, a man with a soul blackened beyond redemption. And, as such, I'm no suitable man for you."

Rose held his gaze and weighed his words. Saw, sensed, in the steadiness of his gaze, in the unyielding cast of his features, that he believed them—that they were his truth.

She wasn't sure they were hers.

On one level, she understood what he was doing—that despite their mutual, clearly mutual, needs and wants, he was denying her, and them, for her own good.

And given she had two children she had sworn to protect, she had to give that stance due consideration.

However . . . she had to know. Arching a brow, she asked, "You're not suitable even for a country housekeeper?"

His eyes darkened. "We both know you're no ordinary country housekeeper."

Even though she'd suspected that he'd guessed, the admission still rattled her, reminded her more forcefully of the two innocents in her care.

As if reading her mind, he went on in the same dark, so very private tone, "And especially in your case, with two children dependent on you . . . no. This, between us, cannot be. I am definitely not a man suitable for you."

Thomas saw her comprehension—that it wasn't only for her that he was refusing all and everything that might be—and sought to end the discussion. "You have your life to live and the children to protect, while I—"

Epiphany struck, so powerfully that he could only stand and stare at her.

When, growing puzzled at his sudden silence, she arched

a brow, he forced himself to find some words . . . and somewhat lamely concluded, "I have my own path to find."

Had he already found it? Had it been under his nose all this time?

He couldn't think, not while she was there, standing before him, looking as if she was about to argue, and lust for her still thrummed in his veins.

Somewhat brusquely, he said, "Regardless of any arguments, I'm not going to be swayed on this." Looking around, he located his cane, bent and picked it up, then faced her. "Now, if you'll excuse me?"

When she didn't immediately respond, he gritted his teeth and pleaded, "Please, step out of my way."

Rose heard the honesty in the request. Even before she'd considered, she was stepping back, aside—allowing him to limp past her.

She stood with her back to the corridor wall and watched him reach his room, open the door, and go inside.

The door softly shut.

Still, she lingered.

And considered the heat, the longing, the sheer unadulterated need still coursing through her veins. Knowing he felt the same was a potent inducement to still greater recklessness, yet . . . he'd been right to remind her that her life was, by her own choice, not presently her own.

She needed to think, and despite his adamant declaration, she'd got the impression that he, too, might benefit from time to reassess.

After several more seconds of staring at his door, she turned and forced herself to walk on along the corridor and down the stairs to the kitchen.

An hour of sewing beside the cooling stove at least allowed the heat in her blood to subside.

Finally Rose doused the lamp and climbed the stairs to her bedroom, along the way refusing to allow even her gaze to divert to the door of Thomas's room; he'd been right to step back—she did need to think.

And to do that, she'd needed to wait for her brain to clear, for the hazy fog of desire to dissipate.

She undressed, donned her nightgown, and went through her nightly ritual of brushing out her long hair. That done, setting the brush down, she crossed to the bed, raised the covers, and slid beneath.

Settling on her back, drawing the covers to her chin, she stared up at the ceiling—and only then allowed her mind to turn to the issue at hand, and was relieved to discover that she had at least gained sufficient distance to view the matter with some measure of dispassion.

A measure of dispassion was, she suspected, all she could hope for; in the circumstances, true detachment and cool rationality weren't likely to be granted her.

Where to start? With him and his views seemed appropriate. After a moment of mulling, she decided that she couldn't feel surprised that he'd drawn the line that he had—that he'd stated, and clearly believed, that he was not a suitable gentleman for her; such a declaration was entirely consistent with the man she knew him to be.

What he didn't seem to comprehend was that his stance only made him more attractive to her—in her estimation, more right for her—not less. Yes, his constant . . . not self-denial but denial of self, his habitual self-deprecation, irritated, but . . . wasn't that, her reaction, because she felt for him? Because she cared that he didn't value himself as she felt he should?

As she valued him.

She hadn't realized that before, but yes, it was true; her irritation only existed because she cared for him. At some level, in some way, that emotional link was already there.

Admittedly, if she had a fault, it was protectiveness—she grew fiercely protective of those for whom she cared. Like the children. And, apparently, Thomas had joined that exclusive circle—whether he wished to or not.

Her gaze fixed unseeing on the ceiling, she felt her lips twist wryly. He clearly didn't—wouldn't—wish that, but that wasn't his decision to make.

Her mind, freed, continued to reassess all that she knew of him, all she'd seen of him—all that his actions had revealed. Life had taught her that when judging people's natures, one should rely on their actions rather than on their words, and Thomas's actions . . . he might have to think to know how to respond to others, but, regardless, his actions involving her and the children had all, every last one, been inspired by supportiveness and caring. And protectiveness.

His habit of putting others ahead of himself wasn't a trait a woman like her was likely to undervalue. She, more than most, needed an absolute assurance that any man she drew close to would feel for the children, at least enough to support her in her care of them.

Thomas, she knew, would unquestioningly do so. He would stand by her side and defend them.

She didn't need to fear that in pursuing a relationship with him, she would be putting the children at risk; indeed, she could argue the opposite.

Pursuing a relationship with Thomas. That was the big question—should she or shouldn't she?

Her assessment of him said she was free to do so; the lingering yearning in her blood, the whisper of temptation whenever she thought of him, the phantom memory of his lips on hers, were all powerful inducements to go forward.

He was a misfit of sorts; from all she'd seen, he was as

well-born as she. His wealth, his worldly assurance, his education, all were attributes of a man of equal station to her own. Both he and she had, for their own reasons, set themselves apart from their true social circle, and that was another link they shared—that of being cut off from their natural milieu, of having to make their way in the wider world without relying on the comforts and protections their true stations would otherwise have afforded them, and having, instead, to rely on their wits, their intelligence, their native wiles.

Quite aside from their physical attraction, they shared that, and the clarity and determination that wrought.

She didn't know how he viewed her, but, regardless, he knew her, the true her, in a way no previous suitor ever had; he'd seen the woman, not even the lady, while all others had seen her merely as a pawn to be used in furthering their social ambitions.

Conversely, he was the first man she had ever looked at, seen clearly, observed all his faults, and wanted. She'd never even vaguely wanted any man before, not even in the years she'd spent within the ton, supposedly searching for a husband.

But what of his past? The past that had, according to him, blackened his soul—irredeemably, as she understood it . . . or so he believed. Given his habit of self-denigration, she wasn't prepared to accept that last as uncontestable fact, and, in general, she believed in rehabilitation, that people could, no matter their transgressions, make amends and change.

If they truly tried. And he was trying. His actions with the children, with the Gattings, with her—he'd even bought her lace mittens simply because he had been relaxing while she'd been working—all testified to his attempts to do good.

To live by the rules of the angels, as it were.

Yes, his past was still a secret, and might very well be as black as he'd painted it, but she had her secret, too, and, more to the point, she and he had to deal with the here and now, with the man he was now and the woman she'd become.

A woman of twenty-nine who yearned for what she'd never known.

For the wonder that, when she eventually returned to her other life, she would have no chance of ever knowing.

For several long moments, she dwelled on all she felt—for once let loose all the pent-up longings of her soul, the dreams she'd left behind in order to protect the children. She could never regret doing so, yet . . .

After a time, she shook herself and refocused on the decision that lay before her.

When all was said and done, she had a simple choice. The men who had arrived at the manor that morning were undoubtedly harbingers; at some point, more would come. It was possible that, in the not-too-distant future, she and the children would have to leave the area, and she and Thomas would part.

She hoped it wouldn't come to that, but she had to acknowledge that it might.

So she could act now, and grasp the chance to explore physical intimacy with the only man who had ever appealed to her in that way—more, who had evoked such a powerful and visceral yearning that just the thought of him was enough to set desire crawling beneath her skin.

Or she could hesitate, and see the chance slip through her fingers, leaving her to mourn what she would never know.

One thing her past had taught her, and taught her well,

was that she could place no reliance on tomorrow, that seizing what she could of today was always her best choice.

So . . . she drew in a breath, then slowly released it. And felt certainty settle within her.

Another decision made. With respect to Thomas, she would seize the day and leave their tomorrow to take care of itself.

fter their interlude in the first-floor corridor, Thomas expected some degree of awkwardness to spring up between him and Rose. Instead . . . when he joined her in the kitchen for breakfast, she smiled at him exactly as she always had, and although he remained on alert throughout the rest of the day, he detected not the smallest hint that she felt any constraint arising out of that unwise kiss.

He wasn't sure what he thought of that.

He was still pondering the vagaries of the female mind when night fell and he retired to his room and his bed.

Lying back, waiting for sleep to claim him, he forced his mind from the imponderable and focused instead on the other, far more crucial revelation that had come in the wake of that kiss. Rose and the children were his purpose—the reason God or Fate, or perhaps both, had spared him. Whatever the problem besetting them was,

solving it and protecting them was the task he'd been as-
signed as his final penance.

And how like Fate to place what he was seeking right
under his nose, and then wait, laughing in the wings, for
him to stumble upon it.

But now that he had—and it felt so right that he didn't
waste time questioning it—he needed to concentrate on
that task, on completing it. That way lay his route to ultimate peace.

First step—he had to learn what their problem was.
Given the appearance of the inquiry agents yesterday, a direct appeal to Rose might just gain him the information he
needed.

The door to his bedroom opened.

Frowning, he raised his head, and from the shadows of
the four-poster bed looked toward the door.

As it shut.

Propelled by Rose, who, clad in nightgown and robe and
carrying a candle, glided toward the bed, one hand shield-
ing the candle flame, exactly as if she joined him every
night.

The candle lit her face, illuminating her expression—one
of calm certainty overlaying the steely determination he'd
seen in her from the first.

He reacted—body, mind, and soul—but not in any way
that would permit him to protest; he wanted her with a
need, a ravening hunger, that stole his breath.

How had it grown to this, that it could render him so
helpless?

Unable even to screen the greedy wanting in his gaze, he
could do nothing but watch her approach, his mind reeling
with the possibilities while, mute, he waited to see what
would come.

Rose knew what she was doing and was determined on her course. Reaching the bed, she set the candle on the small table beside its head, glanced at Thomas—at his glittering hazel eyes—then bent and blew out the flame.

Moving smoothly, serenely, refusing to pay attention to the sudden jittering of her nerves, she tugged the tie of her robe free and shrugged the garment from her shoulders. Letting it fall to the floor, she reached for the covers. Raised them. He lay in the center of the mattress. "Move over," she said and slipped into his bed.

He shifted—a little. Her shoulder bumped his and he turned onto his side, still staring, stunned, at her.

She could almost see the turmoil inside him, the battle over whether to protest, or not bother.

In the end, in a strangled tone, he asked, "What are you doing?"

Shifting onto her side the better to meet his eyes, she boldly stated, "What we've both been thinking about all day—you marshaling all your reasons against, and me amassing all my arguments for." Raising her hand, she reached for his head. "I've decided my arguments trump your reasons."

"Wait." He clamped his hands on her shoulders, clearly intending to hold her back, but, at the contact, his hands stilled, then his warm palms curved about her shoulders and his arms didn't obey—they held her, cradled her, instead of bracing and pushing her away.

Emboldened, lips lifting, she continued her advance; sliding her hand over his shoulder, she curled her palm about his nape and shifted closer still, aligning her body with his. Although torsos and limbs remained separated by dual layers of nightgown and nightshirt, the contact nevertheless sent expectant thrills streaking down her nerves, pearling her nipples, heating her blood, setting desire simmering beneath her skin, waiting to be fanned.

He wasn't immune, either; he hissed in a breath, fleetingly closed his eyes, his features hardening, lips thinning as if he were praying for strength, yet when he opened his eyes, it wasn't rejection that stared at her.

Her confidence solidified. She held his gaze. "Why? Why should we wait when we both want this, and us taking it, indulging and assuaging our needs, will harm no one?"

Burned by her touch, set afire by the promise inherent in her coming to his bed, in the supple, so-feminine length of her lightly pressing against him, for the first time in his life, Thomas couldn't think. At all. His mind had seized, overtaken by desire, by lust and passion and a torrent of feelings.

Some of which were unfamiliar enough that they should have given him pause, but nothing—no distraction or consideration—seemed strong enough to compete with the impulses, the compulsions, raging in his blood.

Clamoring for her, for release, for surcease.

For all that she promised.

Through the dimness, her eyes searched his; he had no idea what she read there, but her lips curved up, just a touch, in a smile he equated with feminine triumph, and she stretched up and brought her luscious lips to his.

Halted when just a breath separated the yearning curves to whisper, "I want you. I want your passion, your desire—I want all you feel for me. Stop holding it back."

Then she kissed him.

Not forcefully. Not even demandingly. Either, and he might have been able to resist.

Instead, she slid into the kiss, into the merging of their mouths, and took him with her.

Succulent, delicious, she lured and he followed; unhurriedly, but with intent, she enticed and he offered her everything she wished. All her heart desired.

His hands firmed and he drew her nearer, then, releasing his grip on her shoulders, he shifted, easing her half over him so he could set his hands skating down the long length of her supple back, tracing the contours of her spine, the indentation of her waist, the flare of her hips, the curves of her bottom.

Their legs twined, bare skin against bare skin as nightshirt and nightgown rode up; the feel of her smooth, sleek limbs sliding against his rougher, hair-dusted skin made him inwardly shiver.

Her fingers tangled in his hair, sifting through the thick locks, then releasing to blindly trace his features. His scars.

She didn't hesitate, nor did her touch turn tentative; she explored his scars with the same open curiosity she displayed toward every other part of his body. She treated his scars as just another part of him, another feature, one she intended to learn along with all the rest.

Her boldly inquisitive touch slayed him.

He rolled her to her back, following so that at no point did they lose the glorious pressure of body to body; the new position allowed him to caress the long line of her throat, to let his fingers sweep down and capture the firm mound of her breast, to close about the tight nub of her nipple and squeeze.

She gasped, her body arching against his. Dragging her lips a fraction from his, she breathed, "More. Show me all."

He hadn't imagined she would settle for anything less, but the demand—clear and definite—vanquished any lingering hesitation, and he set himself to obey.

Kiss by hungry kiss, caress by increasingly desperate caress, they fell victim to the building flames, to the sheer intensity of the illicit intimacy that was simply too potent, too powerful to deny.

Too scorching to even imagine drawing back from; the conflagration swelled, raged, and took them, cindering all thought, all will, all ability to stand against it.

Against the power that swelled and rose, an elemental force that drove them both.

Soft whispers of encouragement murmured through the dark—hers, his—as, with no thought of resisting the offered bounty, they went forward together, all intent aligned, and their hands quested and found, their fingers strengthened and gripped, their palms shaped and kneaded.

He caressed every hollow, every sleek curve. Never had he been this absorbed, this fascinated. This fixated.

She, her body, the promise in her dark eyes, held him enthralled. Willingly captured.

Bold and eager, she returned his gifts, her movements mirroring his, her excitement rising, feeding his.

Anticipation sank its claws into them both.

And raked.

Scored.

He answered the call, hers and that of the force that was now firmly driving them.

Wrestling with the soft fabric, aided and abetted by her, he drew off her nightgown and paused, lost, to savor. To learn anew by sight as well as touch, to know even more intimately, to worship more completely.

To pay homage.

To trace her bared curves with his lips, to savor her skin with his tongue, to claim each curve, each hollow, and let her intoxicating taste and scent claim him.

Rose couldn't catch her breath; it wasn't darkness that dimmed her vision but need—the focus of all her senses had drawn in, to this, to him, to them and their journey. Passion's landscape unfurled before her, brought to life by him, and rendered in all the brilliant hues of glittering desire, a scintillating web of sensation created by the artful sweep of his hands over her damp skin, by the pressure of his lips, the rasp of his tongue, the hot, wet heat of his mouth as he closed it over the peak of one breast and suckled.

She cried out and her body bowed; he played on her senses, on her nerves, a maestro orchestrating a symphony of delight. Of pleasure that filled her, that racked and thrilled her.

Her senses had expanded, greedily drinking in every sensation—the heat of his hard body, the reverence in his touch, the hunger still burning in his eyes.

Yet despite the fraught tension that thrummed through them both, leaving nerves stretched and quivering, he treated her with a possessive gentleness that seared her to her soul.

There was more—so much more—between them than she'd guessed.

So much more, in this, that he was showing her.

Teaching her.

Of herself, yes, but even more of him.

Of the devotion he so evocatively revealed as he caressed her, aroused her—loved her.

The need to return the sentiment grew, swelled . . . until she could deny the compulsion no longer.

She needed more—she needed to love him.

Summoning her will took effort, but she made it, gave it, finally locked her fingers in his hair, pulled back until he raised his head, drew his lips from the soft skin of her stomach, and met her eyes.

"My turn."

Thomas wasn't sure that was a wise idea; his control was a thin and fraying thread, and her passion, unleashed, might just cinder it.

He rose over her and smoothly captured her lips with his, trying to distract her with further caresses, but with a few heated, succinct phrases and a bold caress of her own, she made it clear that she wouldn't allow him to be the only supplicant. With her small hands and her woman's wiles, she insisted, persisted, until, reluctant but unable to deny her, even in this, even at this point where passion quivered in the wings, slavering and barely restrained, he clamped a ruthless hand on the reins and paused, drew in a breath, and drew off his nightshirt.

Honesty; it was a line he'd sworn to hold to, and there was little he might do that was more revealing than to let her see all his scars.

He'd anticipated some degree of revulsion, of tentativeness at the very least.

Instead, with not the slightest hint of rejection in her eyes, she viewed the mangled skin below his right shoulder and the mass of twisted, ropey scars that laced his left side, running down to the knot of darker scars over his left hip, which trailed away into raised ridges down his weak left leg. She saw, surveyed, then reached out and traced.

The flesh was damaged; he'd thought the areas would be unresponsive. Instead . . . he felt every gentle brush of her fingertips over his ravaged skin.

He held his breath as, with unwaveringly open intent, she claimed even that—the most damaged part of him.

Then she lowered her head and kissed. Lovingly traced the ridges and knots . . .

The sensations speared through him. He closed his eyes and trembled.

She continued her ministrations, and he was utterly lost, his mind awash in sensation, his wits swept away by his swirling emotions, swamped by the tumultuous tides.

Tides she evoked, that together they fed.

He'd never experienced anything like this, but the man he now was had never been with a woman before. He'd never before opened himself to this glory.

To this shattering understanding.

To this elemental intimacy that reached to the soul.

He'd had no idea such a shining glory existed, could ever be.

Finally, their now-mutual need burned too brightly to resist; the compulsion in their blood grew too heated to ignore, to delay.

It used to be such a simple act, but his twisted hip made him awkward. Without words, with just a touch and a subtle shift, she compensated, curving one lithe leg over the back of his thighs, beneath his buttocks, then urging him on, in.

Unable to breathe, much less think, he thrust into her heat, into the tight embrace of her body.

Didn't realize, couldn't halt in time, and cleaved through the barrier he hadn't imagined would be there.

What was left of his mind seized in shock as, beneath him, she arched, tensing and tightening about him, clamping about his rigid erection now buried deep at her core. Head back, a whimper of pain escaped her; her nails sank into his upper arms.

Rose couldn't think, couldn't breathe—could only feel. So much, she felt utterly overwhelmed. She'd assumed . . . clearly, she'd been wrong, but that wasn't what was important now.

The feel of his body, skin to skin against hers, had been a tactile shock, one she'd absorbed with heady, breathless anticipation. His weight settling upon her had felt equally right, equally desirable. Entirely promising.

She'd adored the heat, the fevered dampness desire had slicked over their skins.

As for the rigid, corded length of his erection, when she'd closed her hand around it and he'd groaned, she'd felt like a goddess.

And she'd wanted him inside her, had finally understood the urgent need that drove women to lie with men, the yearning that swelled like a yawning emptiness, one that positively burned to be filled.

She'd helped, almost frantic with the moment so close upon her, needy and desperate with a hunger only he, it seemed, could assuage.

And he had.

She'd urged him on, and with one powerful thrust he'd forged into her body and filled her.

Completely, utterly.

The heavy intrusion, the shocking stretching, the sharp pain . . .

She hadn't expected any of it, much less the searing intimacy—she now understood the meaning of the word as she never had before. It was that intimacy in all its myriad aspects that had swamped her mind, that now held her captive.

The pain faded, swiftly changed, overwhelmed by something quite different.

By a different wanting, a sharper need, by the sensation of being so close to something desired beyond all else.

She could feel him, hard and unyielding, within her, feel his heat, the muscled strength of his body, all around her, caging her, pinning her.

Merging with her.

Two thudding heartbeats passed, then she eased. Fractionally.

Then, in dawning wonder, she eased her muscles a little more.

Braced above her, every quivering muscle locked, ruthlessly holding to stillness, Thomas stared down at her . . . and couldn't think enough even to know what he felt.

As if she sensed his gaze, her lids rose a fraction, revealing dark eyes glittering with unslaked passion.

Releasing her grip on one of his arms, she laid her palm against his cheek. Whispered, her voice hoarse with need, "Later. Please . . ."

He knew what she was asking, and couldn't deny her. Couldn't deny the pounding need in his blood.

Bending his head, he brushed his lips over hers. "Later," he agreed, then he eased back, then pressed in again, and swept them both into the fire.

Into the waiting heat and the spiraling pleasure.

Into carnal bliss of a sort he'd never experienced, and he knew it was because the woman in his arms was her. Rose.

Intimacy had never been this physical, this able to impinge on every scintilla of his awareness, to claim every last dark corner of his soul. To rip every screen and veil away, leaving him stripped to the bone, exposed and so vulnerable, aching with need . . . a need to which she surrendered herself, that she slaked with her passion, with an open directness, a simple sincerity—her own honesty offered in recompense for his.

Eyes locked with his, she reached up, locked her hands behind his neck, stretched up, and fused her lips with his. Added her passion to his, her body freely and flagrantly riding each thrust, meeting him, matching him, joining with him and sharing in every desperate moment, spurring him on, recklessly racing onward.

She cloaked his naked need with her passion, fed his raging hunger with her desire.

And he did the same for her, openly, honestly, without reservation or hesitation giving. Simply giving.

And in that she followed his lead, and they gave and took and gave again with ever-increasing abandon.

Until the thunder in their blood was all either of them knew.

Until desperation raked, and they gasped, and reached, and drove each other on.

Until the peak rose before them and they hurtled over and beyond, driven and fused, senses awash with the glory, minds overwhelmed, suborned by bone-deep pleasure.

One last thrust, one deep penetration, and ecstasy broke, a piercingly bright wave shattering over them, blinding their senses.

He drank her cry of completion, felt his answering groan reverberate through them both.

And they fell.

Into a void of indescribable bliss where nothing beyond the beat of their hearts existed.

They shook, trembled, as the intensity of the climax slowly, so slowly, faded.

Moments passed, filled with their ragged breathing and the slowing thunder of their hearts.

Eventually, he dragged in a shuddering breath, eased his weight from her, then withdrew from the clinging heat of her body to slump alongside her.

She curled into him; he hesitated for only a second, then drew her close.

And let satiation have them both.

Later, his mind stirred, but his senses informed him that she was still asleep, sunk in sated slumber. That she remained tucked against him. Trusting.

His.

An errant thought drifted across his languid mind: Was this, too, a part of his penance?

Was this—and he wasn't fool enough to indulge in self-deception about what the power that had risen between them and had driven their acts, infusing their intimacy with such cataclysmic force, actually was—all a part of his task?

Was loving Rose part of his atonement?

On one level that seemed . . . a self-serving conclusion. Yet . . .

Now that he loved her, now he knew he did . . . what would happen, how would he feel, when he completed his penance and Fate, or God, passed judgment on his soul?

Rose's mind drifted into consciousness just enough to register the warmth and comfort enveloping her. She reveled in the sensations for long minutes, but, gradually, her mind rose through the lingering mists of slumber, and she remembered . . . where she was, and in whose arms she lay.

And why.

A torrent of feelings flowed through her, a river of silver and gold, crystal memories of the moments they'd shared—so many achingly fragile, so laden with feeling, that just the recollection left her touched, humbled. In awe.

So much had happened. So much had changed.

Her body, admittedly, felt different, somehow humming, completed, content. But that was the least of the impact, the lingering effect.

She'd had no idea that such a degree of feeling, such a depth of connection, could be achieved between two people.

But she'd felt it—in his touch and hers—had seen it in his eyes, had felt it rise through her, compelling her; she'd heard it in their ragged breathing.

They'd fused physically and emotionally, had been linked in a way that was both undeniable and unbreakable.

And she couldn't regret it; knowing she'd lived to experience such glory made her rejoice in her decision to come to his room.

But now she'd touched him, now she'd known him intimately and through that had allowed all the rest to bloom, to burgeon and come into being, real, a steady, unwavering force that, she was quite certain, continued to live within them both, a source of inner strength and certainty beyond anything she'd dreamed . . .

She wasn't going to let it, or him, go.

He, and that wonder, were too precious.

Instinctively, she tightened her arms, as if to hold on to him.

He shifted, and she realized he wasn't asleep.

She sensed him tip his head to look down at her. Opening her eyes, through the night-dark shadows, she met his gaze.

He regarded her for a moment, then asked, "Whose children are Homer and Pippin?"

Rose blinked, tried to frown, and discovered the expression still beyond her. "How . . . oh." Warmth stole into her cheeks. Then she forced herself to meet his eyes. "Given my age, I didn't think it would still be that obvious."

His brows slowly arched. "That you were a virgin?" When she pressed her lips into a warning line, he softly snorted. "Obvious enough." He paused, eyes once again studying hers, then he said, "Now we've come this far with our mutual revelations, I think it's time you trusted me with the rest."

Rose held his gaze and waited for her usual, rabid protectiveness to rise up and shut him out, but, instead, she discovered she agreed with him. He'd protected and cared for the children in myriad, not-always-obvious ways and had only yesterday blatantly lied to keep them safe. He cared for them; she didn't doubt that. She trusted him, had that night trusted him with her body, and even if he didn't know it, had already trusted him with her heart. "All right."

She paused, and Thomas waited.

Eventually, turning partially onto her back and settling more comfortably, she said, "They're my mother's and my stepfather's children." She glanced up and caught his eyes. "My mother and stepfather are dead—murdered—although I doubt many are aware of the latter fact."

Thomas inwardly stilled, then directed, "Start at the beginning. What's your real name, who were your parents, and where were you born? When did your mother remarry?"

She sighed, but obliged. "My full name is Rosalind Mary Heffernan. My parents were Gareth and Corinne. My father was gentry-born, and my mother was, too. I was their only child, and we were happy and content, living in our house in Ashby Folville in Leicestershire, until my father died unexpectedly of a fever when I was fifteen. My mother mourned him, but she was still young. Four years later, she fell in love again and married Robert Percival, Viscount Seddington, of Seddington Grange in Lincolnshire. I liked Robert and he liked me. The three of us got along well." She paused. "There's not much more to tell on that front."

"You mentioned your age, implying it was advanced. How old are you?"

Her sigh was more definite this time. "Twenty-nine. And before you ask, yes, I was paraded around the ballrooms as

Viscount Seddington's stepdaughter, but I quickly learned that my birth, gentry rather than aristocracy, meant that, in that social circle, my would-be suitors saw me purely as a pawn through which they might secure wealth, as well as a connection to the Percivals. I wasn't impressed."

She left it at that. Accepting the line her tone had drawn, Thomas shifted to the more immediate question. "Why do you think your mother and stepfather were murdered?"

Her gaze shifted, drifted; she seemed to be focusing on something distant. "Robert was an enthusiastic sailor, and he had taken Mama for a drive to Grimsby that day. Mama wasn't strong. William's birth had affected her health, and Alice's birth made it worse. Robert did all he could to cheer Mama up—he often took her out driving. So them going to Grimsby wasn't a surprise, and as Robert kept his yacht there, for him to have gone sailing also wasn't odd—but Mama getting on any boat was." Rose glanced briefly at Thomas. "Mama suffered terribly from mal-de-mer. She could barely set foot on a boat without becoming wretchedly sick. As soon as I heard they'd been found drowned in the capsized yacht, trapped in the sails, I knew something was wrong, but . . . what with the shock, the sadness and grief, and the children to comfort, I didn't get a chance to think things through, much less raise any questions—and even if I had, with Mama and Robert gone, no one would have listened to me. They would have thought I was hysterical with grief."

Thomas said nothing, and after a moment, Rose continued, "But then, on the evening of the funeral, after William had been declared the ward of my stepfather's brother, Richard Percival, I overheard Richard talking to one of his cronies—he was describing how he had poisoned my mother and stepfather, then had staged their deaths to appear to be due to a yachting accident." She drew breath and went on, "As Robert's brother—his only brother—Richard is William's heir. And I heard Richard state that his aim was to kill William, too, so that he would inherit the estate."

Thomas felt her tense.

She swallowed before continuing, "There was no one else in the house—no one to whom I could appeal who would pay attention to me and not simply tell Richard, no one who would not defer to him. His words made it clear that he wasn't inclined to wait but intended to attack William as soon as possible . . . so I fled. I went upstairs, bundled the children up—William was only five then, and Alice just two—and I took them and left. I had to, to save William. And, ultimately, Alice, too—I know she's well-dowered."

Thomas's mind was drinking in every fact, slotting each piece of the jigsaw into its proper place. "And what about you?"

"My father was wealthy—I have my own money waiting—but with Richard searching for us, I couldn't risk trying to draw on the funds. All the family's business of that sort is managed through one solicitor, a Mr. Foley in London, and I had no reason to think he wouldn't side with Richard—it would have been surprising if, in the circumstances, he hadn't."

"William and Alice—Homer and Pippin?"

She nodded. "William Randolph Percival, fourth Viscount Seddington, of Seddington Grange, near Market Rasen, and Alice Eileen Percival. I realized I would need to keep them hidden for some time—at least until William is old enough to understand the dangers and be on his guard so he could insist that there are others kept around him to protect him. I knew Richard wouldn't let us be but would come after us, searching and hunting, so I asked William and Alice what names they wanted to go by. William chose his then-hero, Homer, and Alice . . . well, she was only little, but she loved apples and had already learned the word *pippin*. It was her favorite word at that time, so she chose that."

Thomas considered what she'd said, the ramifications . . . "The men who came looking said you were all from Leicestershire, but Seddington Grange is in Lincolnshire."

Rose nodded. "Richard no doubt assumed I would go home, or at least to the area I knew best—near where I was born, where my father's house was, in Leicestershire."

Thomas studied her face. "But you're too clever for that."

A ghost of a smile tugged at her lips. "I knew he'd look there first, there and along the road to London, so I went west. To Doncaster that first night, then on to Manchester, and soon after to Chester. I had some money, so I could pay for our lodgings, but I knew that, eventually, we would have to stop, and that the money would run out, so I started looking for work—suitable work that would let me keep the children by me at all times. I started heading south from Chester, by and large avoiding the major towns. It took months, but eventually we reached the south coast at Porthleven. By then I had only a few shillings left and was close to desperate, but it was market day, and in the marketplace I ran into Elsie—Mrs. Gatting's sister. I was asking around for work, and she overheard and said she knew her sister and her husband needed help up at some manor."

Rose drew a deep breath, let it out with, "That was our biggest stroke of luck. Elsie told me how to get to the manor, and I walked up here with the children. The instant I set eyes on the house . . ." She sighed. "It was perfect.

Isolated, yet comfortable. I would have done anything to have been able to stay here with William and Alice . . . and then the Gattings fell on us as saviors of sorts, and it seemed we'd found our temporary home."

Thomas tightened his arms, held her a little closer, and rested his cheek against her hair. "When I first saw the manor, I felt the same way—the instant I laid eyes on it. I hadn't intended to buy a house at all, but I bought it on that whim, then and there." And if he hadn't? If he'd resisted that uncharacteristic whim of long ago?

Roland had been right. Fate—or God, whichever it was—moved in wondrous ways.

If he'd needed any further convincing that freeing Rose and the children from the threat of Richard Percival was his fated task, the final penance for which his life had been spared—that singular task only he could accomplish—Rose, with her tale, had provided it.

And as for the question of whether him loving her was part of that fate . . . he'd allowed himself to fall, to all but unintentionally surrender to love, and as his reward she'd trusted him with her story—trusted him with her life and those of the children.

It all seemed of a piece, a typical construct from the hand of Fate.

Rose shifted and looked up at him. "So that's what brought us here."

What about you? She didn't say the words, but Thomas saw them in her eyes.

He hesitated, but . . . he couldn't not honor her trust. He had to trust in return. "I . . . was once someone else."

Her brows arched. After a second of studying his eyes, she turned more fully to face him. "Tell me."

He did. All of it—all the past of his previous life, a full catalogue of his sins against others, his transgressions. His

arrogance and pride, his ultimate realization of the devil
he'd become, and his fall . . . and the stay of execution Fate
had handed him.

"It was . . . as if I'd suddenly woken up, and for the first
time, my eyes were truly open. Truly able to see . . . perhaps
because I'd drawn close to that couple, seeing myself in him,
or rather, seeing him as the man I might have become, so I
could appreciate their reactions, and through their eyes I
could view myself, the type of man who had, albeit without
specific intention, caused the actions I'd set in train . . . they
helped me to see myself for what I had become. And once I'd
seen . . . I couldn't not do the right thing, as far as I was able."
He paused, then more quietly said, "I couldn't go on as I had
been."

Silence fell; Rose didn't stir, nor did she press. Eventually, he drew in a deep breath and continued. Because she
knew him as Thomas Glendower, a man who had spent his
last five years in a monastery, he had started there and told
his tale more or less in reverse. It was like unraveling a long
skein of wool, tracing his life backward.

He left nothing pertinent out, but, courtesy of his time in
the priory, he'd also learned of the sin of self-aggrandizement;
he adhered to the truth and didn't make himself sound
worse than he had been—didn't pretend he'd been more
important than he had been—and made sure Rose understood that he had never actually killed anyone himself.
Hadn't, in fact, intended anyone to be killed.

"I've never been able to tell what's right from what's
wrong, not instinctively, as most do. I've never had the right
. . . framework, I suppose you might say. That, I suspect,
was due to my guardian—I was under his care from the
time my parents died when I was six years old. He, my
guardian, taught me that whatever I wanted, it was my right
to have it, and that it was entirely acceptable for me to do

whatever was necessary to attain it. That's what he did—that was how he lived his life."

"What happened to him?"

"He was found guilty of horrendous crimes and put a gun to his head." He paused, then went on, "But even so, even under his influence, I . . . not knew, but suspected that my way of arranging things so that everything fell out as I wanted it to wasn't . . . quite how life was supposed to be lived. Not quite morally or socially acceptable. One old lady saw through me and knew me for what I really was—she'd known my parents and so had a better grasp of, indeed, a sound insight into, my propensities. She warned me, but I thought I knew better and I ignored her words—words of wisdom I should have recognized, but didn't."

From those earlier times, he circled back and described how Thomas Glendower had come to be. For completeness' sake, he also explained about his current investment activities, admitting to all the funds and foundations he had put in place and actively administered, about how he was using his innate talents to make restitution as thoroughly and as broadly as he could.

Telling her everything brought an unexpected catharsis. He'd never recited the whole in its entirety to anyone, but casting himself on her mercy . . . again, that felt right.

At the end of the lengthy recitation, she studied him for several moments, then simply said, "You truly are not that other man anymore."

Absolution—precious, and of a kind he'd never thought to earn.

He closed his eyes for a moment, then opened them. He had more questions concerning hers and the children's current state, but they would keep until tomorrow; he had enough to absorb, to digest and consider, but . . . fixing his gaze on her eyes, he evenly said, "I hope, now that you've heard my story, you'll understand how important to me helping you and the children is—that you'll comprehend why it's imperative I help you to overcome the threat against William's life."

Helping you and the children is my fate. Please don't deny me my ultimate salvation.

Rose looked into his eyes and realized she could see all, all that he was, through to his soul. She nodded, instinctively at first, then more firmly. "Yes. I do understand."

So very much more than she previously had about this highly complex man.

He was no saint, but he'd never pretended to be. He was who he was—and that was the man she could see herself walking beside, into the future.

A future as yet uncertain, but one they would fight for. Together.

Oh, yes, that she would do. That she could accept.

As if reading her decision in her eyes, he said, "I'll need to know more so we can work out your options, but that can wait until tomorrow."

She nodded. "Agreed." She settled once more, pressing deeper into his embrace. "We can talk more tomorrow, but for the rest of the night . . ." She glanced up, then reached up with one hand and gently traced the marred side of his face. Now that she knew from where his scars had come, to her they held a beauty all their own. Stretching up, she touched her lips to his in an inexpressibly gentle kiss. "For the rest of tonight, let me sleep in your arms."

Thomas watched her settle, watched her eyes close.

Felt his heart swell.

Closing his eyes, he surrendered—to Fate, to her, to the warmth she'd brought into his cold life.

To the promise of absolution.

Thomas forced himself to complete his usual morning's work, reminding himself that others besides Rose and the children also had a claim on the fruits of his brain.

But he and Rose had woken early, and he'd hurried through breakfast; by ten o'clock, he was tidying away his papers. After checking on Homer—William, a name that better suited him—and ensuring the boy had enough sufficiently challenging arithmetical exercises to keep him occupied, Thomas went in search of Rose.

Rosalind, but to him she would always be Rose.

He found her in the kitchen and persuaded her to return with him to the library.

Again, he'd anticipated some degree of awkwardness, at least of consciousness, arising out of their intimacy, but, again, that didn't eventuate. He looked at her, and she met his eyes and returned his regard with her usual steady directness, and . . . they were as one. Completely open and sure of each other; it was as if through knowing each other physically, they had somehow come to know each other in a far deeper sense.

Which made going forward very easy.

He waved her to the chair he'd set before his desk. Rounding the desk, he leaned his cane against it and lowered himself into his admiral's chair. "We need to evaluate our options and decide our best way forward."

Rose hid a small smile; two "*ours*" in one sentence. Reassurance of his commitment, plus a statement of intent. Drawing the chair closer to the desk, she nodded. "Those men—even if they don't return, others eventually will."

"Indeed." Thomas set a fresh sheet of paper on his blotter, then reached for a pencil. "But as they haven't immediately reappeared, and given what I told them, combined with how few people around here know you or the children well, then I suspect we'll have a few days, perhaps even weeks, before anyone returns." Across the desk, he met her gaze. "In such a situation, the best thing we can do to improve our position is to learn as much as we can about the opposition—about our foes. And the first step in doing that is to make a list of all the questions we can think of, the things we need to learn about them in order to, first, avoid them, and, secondly, to move against them and nullify the threat they pose."

Rose leaned forward, settling her forearms on the desk. "In this case, they and them equates to Richard Percival."

Thomas nodded and wrote down the name. "What can you tell me about him?"

She frowned. "Not as much as I would like—my mother and stepfather didn't encourage him to call."

"They disapproved of him?"

She raised her brows. "I didn't think much of it before, but, yes, that's what it seemed to be, but I always put it—his effective banishment—down to his reputation as a rake. A womanizer, a gamester—not generally the sort of gentleman one encourages to spend time with a young lady of the house." Dryly, she added, "Especially not one particularly well-dowered."

"So he's in need of money?"

She considered, then grimaced. "I believe that would be the general consensus, but in actual fact, I know nothing of his financial situation. For instance, I never heard him petition, or heard of him having petitioned, Robert for more funds." She paused, then added, "Of course that might have happened and I might simply not have heard of it."

Thomas sat back, his gaze fixed on what he'd written.

Rose watched him think, and for the first time since she'd fled Seddington Grange in the wind-whipped darkness of a Lincolnshire night, she felt hope, real and solid. Hope that she would indeed see William through this danger, and see him installed in his father's shoes as the fourth Viscount Seddington.

She'd vowed to her mother that she would care for the children; she'd been twenty years old when William had been born, and with her mother so sickly after the birth, Rose had stepped in and, in effect, become William's de facto mother. And then Alice's in much the same way. She loved both children dearly, and her vow to her mother only strengthened that feeling. William and Alice were all Rose had left of her mother, and of Robert Percival, a man she'd admired, who had opened his heart to her, the daughter of his wife's first marriage.

Thomas stirred and met her eyes. "You were there when

your stepfather's will was read?" When she nodded, he asked, "And Richard Percival was named William's sole guardian?"

Rose blinked. "Yes . . . no. Wait." After a moment, she exhaled, closed her eyes, and sent her mind back to that fraught time, to the formal gathering in the library after the wake. Eyes still closed, she murmured, "The solicitor, Mr. Foley, stood beside the desk and read out the will . . . Richard was named . . . *principal* guardian." She frowned. "I remember that, but I can't recall the rest—what immediately followed—because William tugged my sleeve and I turned to him. He wanted to know what a guardian was." She tried to remember more, but then she shook her head and opened her eyes. "I can't explain what was meant by 'principal' because I didn't hear the rest of that clause."

Thomas grimaced, then sat forward. "Very well. I can think of two highly pertinent questions—the first two that we need answered." Pencil poised, he met her gaze. "But even with our queries, we'll have to move cautiously. At present, no one connected with Richard Percival has any firm idea where you are—according to the two who called here, the best they have is 'possibly Cornwall.' But even though I can, and will, make our inquiries through agencies in no way connected to you, if Richard Percival realizes that someone is asking these sorts of questions . . . well, if I were he, I would know how to trace the queries back to who was making them. To me, here. To you and the children."

"You're saying there's a risk in even trying to learn the information we need to be able to move against Richard Percival."

Thomas nodded.

Rose considered, then said, "Correct me if I'm wrong, but if we do nothing, make no effort to counter Richard, then the children will potentially, eventually, be in even greater danger. As Richard is William's guardian, and presumably Alice's as well, then once he finds them, there's nothing I will be able to do to keep them from him. He'll be able to seize them and take them away to wherever he wishes. I won't be able to stay with them, to protect them against whatever he might do."

Thomas said nothing, but returned her gaze steadily.

Rose nodded. "Write down our first two questions—we need to get started if we're ever to free William of Richard Percival's threat."

She watched as Thomas bent to the task, formulating two lines of inquiry . . . "Incidentally," she said, "what are our two most pertinent questions?"

He didn't look up, but his lips curved. "The first and most urgent question is whether the official clock has been set ticking on William's presumed death—if someone has already petitioned for him to be declared dead so that the estate can be moved through probate. If they have, that will confirm that someone—presumably Richard Percival—wants to inherit, that his inheriting is a factor at play in all this." He paused, then said, "You fled with William more than four years ago, so it's possible that there's less than three years left to run on that clock. However, the time isn't the point—it's the fact that the official petition has been lodged, and who moved for it to be so, that's critical to us in terms of understanding what's going on."

Easing back, eyes tracking what he'd written thus far, he tapped the pencil on the sheet. "Our second question is to seek confirmation of exactly who William's guardians are. 'Principal guardian' suggests that your stepfather was wise enough to put some reins on his brother's rights over William, but he might well not have wanted to take such a drastic—and potentially public—stance as to exclude Richard from a guardianship all society would have expected to fall to him."

Thomas looked up at her. "Does that sound like your stepfather? To try to do the best for his children, but at the same time to shy from any too-public declaration of distrust of his brother?"

Rose nodded. "Yes, Robert would have thought like that. He was very aware of the family's honor, so to speak."

Thomas inclined his head and continued writing, making notes on which to base the letters he would later pen and dispatch. "If someone else has been appointed co-guardian—a secondary guardian, at least—who might it be?"

Rose thought, then grimaced. "The only family member who comes to mind is Robert's uncle, Marmaduke Percival, but he, as you might imagine, is not young, and he's never to my knowledge shown any interest in the children. As for others . . . although I don't know the Percival family connections that well, I met all those who attended Mama and Robert's wedding, and, of course, all who came to the funeral, but all the others are distant cousins, and most were of the older generation, too. None of them were close."

Thomas paused in his writing, then looked at Rose. "With your permission, I'm also going to ask if there's any suggestion as to William's estate being drawn down."

She blinked. "Could it be? I assumed it would remain untouched."

"It *should,* but . . . a guardian, or in this case, both guardians, could seek to free some of the estate's income for expenses incurred in administering William's estate in his absence." He shrugged. "Something along those lines. It's easy enough to fabricate an excuse that sounds legitimate, and depending on the solicitor—this Foley, whom you don't trust—the estate might already be in the process of being carefully drained."

Rose looked faintly shocked. "I never thought . . ." Her expression firmed. "Can we stop it?"

He met her gaze. "Only by reinstating William."

Rose held his gaze for an instant, then waved her hand at his notes. "In that case, get writing."

Thomas grinned faintly, but the expression faded as he looked over what he'd written. Then he reached for a fresh sheet of paper and exchanged his pencil for a pen. "I'm going to write to my business agent and, separately, to my solicitor. Both are sound, and very used to responding to my requests with absolute discretion. They know not to make waves—not even ripples—in pursuing such inquiries." He glanced at the clock, then at Rose. "I'll write these now, then after lunch, I'll take them to Helston and put them on the mail. They'll reach London tomorrow, and then . . . we'll see."

Rose nodded and got to her feet.

She paused, looking down on Thomas's blond-brown head. The words *thank you* hovered on her tongue, but . . . gratitude of that sort would set him apart from her and the children, and that wasn't what she wanted.

They were working together now, and *he* was part of *them*.

Feeling more heartened than she had since first hearing of her mother's and stepfather's deaths, she turned and left Thomas to his task.

"**W**ell?" Richard Percival demanded.

Calmly, Curtis replied, "We found a few possibles—more than two. We need someone who can identify them—at least her, and, if at all possible, the boy." He watched eagerness transform his employer's until now grim expression. "Is there anyone you can send us—remembering that we need someone who will keep all this under his hat?"

"As a matter of fact, there is." Richard Percival met his eyes. "My brother's valet. Even though I don't need his services, I've kept the man on. He will know her, definitely, and, despite the years, he should recognize the boy, too—literally on sight."

"Excellent." Curtis felt his instincts rise as they always did when he was nearing the end of a hunt. And this hunt had been unexpectedly long and difficult. Their quarry, it transpired, had more brains than they'd expected. He glanced at Percival and decided to break with his habit of never encouraging his clients until he had their quarry bagged; the man had stayed the course long beyond what Curtis had expected of him. "I don't want to get your hopes up, but this tack is starting to feel right. I think we're nearing the end of the race, that we truly are closing in."

Richard Percival met his gaze, a powerful mix of emotions in his face. "God, I hope so." Something close to exhausted desperation colored his tone. "I don't know for how much longer I can keep the vultures at bay."

It was ten days before the replies to Thomas's first round of queries arrived, delivered by the boy he'd hired to bring the mail from Helston each afternoon.

Accepting the missives from the boy at the front door, Thomas handed him his usual coin, then watched him ride off before turning inside. Shutting the door, he saw that Rose had come out of the kitchen; wiping her hands on her apron, she stood at the rear of the hall, watching and waiting.

Thomas glanced at the open door to the dining room; Homer—for safety, Thomas and Rose had agreed William should still use that name—was reading at the dining table.

Waving Rose into the library, Thomas limped down the corridor, followed her inside, and shut the door.

She turned, her gaze going to the letters in his hand. "Replies?"

"I believe so." He went to the desk, leaned his cane against the front edge, examined the letters, then laid the one from Drayton, his longtime agent, down, and opened the one from Marwell. "This one's from my solicitor." Unfolding the sheet, he swiftly scanned it, then handed it on to Rose. While she read, he summarized, "William was reported missing, presumed dead, soon after his disappearance. As far as Marwell could learn, within a month—so yes, Percival wants the inheritance sooner rather than later."

Rose reached the end of the letter and glanced up. "But he can't get it until William's declared dead, and that won't occur until seven years have passed." She frowned. "That's correct, isn't it? I remembered a case of a soldier who went missing in the war, and his family had to wait seven years."

Thomas nodded. Easing around, he sat on the edge of the desk. "That's correct as far as it goes, but that doesn't mean that Richard Percival doesn't need to find William and ensure he never resurfaces alive. Indeed, regardless of anything else, Richard has to do that, or, on William's reappearance, the inheritance would be reversed. It can happen, although, of course, it rarely does." He paused, then, holding her gaze, went on, "However, more to the point, regardless of the seven-year rule, if Richard Percival is in dire need of the money from the estate, he might well be seeking to ensure that William's dead body is found as soon as possible, so that he can gain immediate access to the estate's coffers."

Rose didn't wince at his plain-speaking; she didn't need protecting from reality. She glanced down at the letter. "Your solicitor—Mr. Marwell—writes that Marmaduke Percival is co-guardian with Richard." She grimaced. "I doubt appealing to Granduncle Marmaduke will be of any use. He's not what one might call astute, and Richard has a much stronger personality—Marmaduke might bluster, but he could never successfully stand against Richard."

The last line in the letter made her inwardly sigh. "And Foley is still the estate's solicitor, which means he's still in control of my affairs, as well."

Thomas studied her. "Is there anything specific behind your distrust of Foley, or is it just a feeling?"

She made a moue. "I would have to admit that it's purely a feeling—I've had very little to do with him, after all. But he's a very rigid, exceedingly conservative stick—and I can readily see him doing everything and more to protect the family name from any scandal, and I can even more easily see Richard being clever enough to twist that sort of unwavering loyalty to suit his own ends."

Thomas considered her for a moment, then picked up the second letter and broke the seal. After scanning the contents, he reported, "Drayton—my agent—writes that, as far as he's thus far been able to discover, there's no evidence or suggestion that the estate's funds have been raided."

Rose nodded. "Presumably having Marmaduke, no matter how ineffectual, as co-guardian has made Richard cautious about depleting the estate."

Thomas didn't argue. Instead, retrieving the letter from Rose's clasp, he stood and rounded the desk. "I'll write back and"—he glanced at the clock as he sat—"take the letters to Helston tomorrow." Settling, he reached for a fresh sheet of paper.

Rose sank into the chair before the desk. "What are we going to ask next?"

"First, I'll instruct Drayton to start investigating Richard Percival's finances." Thomas looked up and met Rose's gaze. "We need some more definite hint of a motive for Richard killing his brother and his brother's wife—and then coming after William. We need to know, and be able to show, why he needs to inherit the estate." His eyes locked with hers, he hesitated, then more quietly said, "And I'm also going to ask Marwell to check Foley's standing."

Rose arched her brows, but then nodded and stood. "I've dinner to organize—I'll leave you to it."

Thomas watched her go, then drew Marwell's letter to him; opening it, he read again the solicitor's reference to Foley. Rose didn't trust Foley, but, reading between Marwell's lines—noting that that excellent solicitor hadn't sought to warn him in any way about Foley—Thomas suspected that Marwell saw Foley in a different light than Rose did. It was worth confirming which view was correct. As he understood it, Rose had met Foley only a few times, the last occasion being when she was twenty-five, and always in the presence of older males of her family. Foley, if he was indeed as conservative as she'd painted him, would have spoken over her head—or tried to. Which might account for Rose's negative view of him.

Regardless, as William's solicitor, Foley was an important player in the drama, and Thomas preferred to have as much knowledge about all players in a scheme before he moved against them.

Picking up his pen, he examined the nib, then, finding it

sufficiently sharp, dipped it in his inkwell and started to write.

The next morning, Thomas rode into Helston, the letters containing his second round of queries in his pocket, ready to post. It was close to eleven o'clock when he reached the town; he let Silver carry him up the long slope of Coinage-hall Street, then he turned in under the arch of the Angel Hotel's stable yard. Leaving Silver in the care of the ostlers there, who now viewed him as a regular, Thomas walked out onto the street and turned right for the post office, located a little further along on the opposite side.

A group of men—more inquiry agents—were gathered in a knot outside the post office.

Without breaking his limping stride, Thomas diverted onto the front porch of the Angel Hotel as if that had been his goal all along. Gaining the covered porch, he glanced again at the gathering across the street; at least ten agents were milling about another man, one differently dressed and with a different demeanor. Turning away, Thomas scanned the long porch and spotted two of the older men who habitually sought refuge there to while away their day. The pair was already nursing pint pots, and they, too, were observing the activity across the street.

Leaning on his cane, Thomas made his way toward them.

Both older men recognized him and nodded in greeting; Thomas had made a point of occasionally chatting with the locals whenever he came to the town—an old habit, but one which, now, as previously, stood him in good stead.

Nodding back, he halted in a spot where he didn't interrupt the men's view of the gathering along the street; leaning against the porch's railing, he joined them in silently staring for several moments, then he tipped his head at the agents. "Any idea what that's about?"

"Seems they're back to continue their search for some lass and her two children," one of the men volunteered. "There were a couple as came asking a week or so back, but they left empty-handed. Then this lot arrived just this morning, and according to Fred here, they've brought that little bloke with 'em to identify the lady and her boy."

Fred grunted. "Must've stolen something right valuable to have some lordling pay for all o' that lot."

"Aye," the other man said. "And whoever the owner is, seems he's determined to get whatever it is back. Almost enough men for a hue and cry, there."

Truer words . . . and at the mention of "lordling," Thomas realized who the "little bloke" must be. He focused on the man, so quiet and reserved, neat and precise, committing his description to memory so he could later confirm the man's identity with Rose.

The agents appeared to be getting ready to depart, but their attention seemed to be directed to the east, away from Breage.

"Any notion of where they're heading?" Thomas glanced at Fred.

Still watching the agents, Fred lightly shrugged. "Heard them mention the Lizard. Seems there's some women with children they want to check down that way, and then they'll be back here—they've taken rooms in the hotel for tonight—and plan to head off west tomorrow, searching as they go."

Thomas debated continuing with his errand. He couldn't see the agents who had come to the manor among the group in the street, but for all he knew the pair might be inside the post office; he didn't need them recognizing him and remembering that his housekeeper and children matched the description of those they sought, except for Thomas's assurance that the family were locals, born and bred.

He could post the letters later.

Stirring, he gripped his cane and straightened. "Interesting times." With a nod to his two informants, which they returned, he walked back along the porch, then turned into the hotel and made his way through the bar and the snug to the door that gave onto the stable yard.

Thomas reached the manor in time to sit down at the kitchen table and share luncheon with Rose and the children.

He said nothing of his disturbing discoveries at Helston, allowed nothing of the resulting tension to seep into his face or his movements.

When the meal ended, he left Rose clearing the table and accompanied Homer back to the dining room. He spent some minutes devising a set of simple Latin translations; once Homer was absorbed, Thomas returned to the kitchen.

Rose was standing before the sink, watching Pippin play with her dolls in the rear garden. Drawing nearer, Thomas looked over Rose's shoulder; Pippin was sitting with two dolls facing her and was passing around small bowls . . . dishes of tea?

Absentmindedly, he set his hand to the small of Rose's back.

For a moment, she leaned back into the touch, then she sighed, straightened, and turned to face him. She met his gaze, her own steady. "What did you learn in Helston that you haven't yet told me?"

He hadn't thought he was that transparent . . . looking into her eyes, he hesitated, then said, "Another band of inquiry agents have arrived. A good dozen or so, this time. They were setting out to sweep the Lizard Peninsula today, checking on various potential women with two children." He held her gaze. "They had another man, a valet by his appearance, with them." Swiftly, succinctly, he described the man.

Rose ruthlessly quashed the impulse to panic; neither she nor the children could afford that, and, this time, they had Thomas on their side. Reaching out, she drew a chair from the table and slowly sank into it. "That sounds like Robert's valet."

Drawing out another chair, Thomas sat facing her, setting his cane between his legs. "So he would recognize you?"

Rose nodded. "Definitely. And, almost certainly, William, too." After a moment, she glanced at Thomas. "You said that today they were searching on the peninsula. After that?"

"They're returning to Helston tonight, and, assuming they haven't located their quarry, and we know they won't, they intend sweeping west tomorrow."

Despite her intentions, panic clutched her chest. Quelling an impulse to leap to her feet, she drew in a breath and stated, "So we need to leave immediately."

She looked at Thomas. Sober and serious, he met her gaze and nodded. "Yes, we do. We need to go to London and get this matter resolved."

She blinked. *We?* But she wasn't going to argue with that. On the other hand . . . "London?"

He nodded. Sure, certain—resolute. "You and the children can't go on trying to run from this. While you were without help, without support and resources of the sort I can command, your original strategy was sound—

keep William out of Richard Percival's orbit for as long as
you could, until William was at least of an age he might
speak for himself, with a chance of being listened to.
Given the original circumstances, that was the best you
could do, but the circumstances have changed. Now I'm
involved, and I am much more able to bring the right sort
of resources to bear on Richard Percival and his
scheme—to expose it, including his murder of your
mother and stepfather, thus removing him as a threat to
William once and for all."

Rose studied Thomas's eyes and saw nothing but certainty in the hazel depths. "You seem very sure."

"I am." He paused, then added, "I don't imagine it'll be
easy, but exposing Richard and freeing William is achiev-
able. But to manage it, we need to go to London."

Given all he'd told her of his previous life, Rose saw no
reason to doubt his assessment. Yet still she hesitated, still
she wondered . . . "I'm sure you realize what exposing
Richard might involve." Drawing in a breath, she forced
herself to ask, "Are you sure?"

His gaze didn't waver. "Yes, I'm sure. And if you didn't
want me in your life—if you had wanted to keep me apart
from this—you shouldn't have come to my bed that night."

Or on all the nights since. Rose didn't need any further
explanation of exactly what he meant; his emotions—all of
them, all he now felt for her and the children—stared at her
from his eyes.

She felt both humbled and awed.

She had to accept that he knew what the dangers were,
probably significantly better than she did, but he'd made his
decision and was committed to his course. To their cause.

To being her and the children's champion.

She knew he viewed the role as some sort of ultimate

penance, but, regardless, she wasn't about to turn her back on him and all she saw in him. On all he offered.

Slowly, she nodded. "So . . . to London." Raising her head, she glanced out of the window, confirming that Pippin was still happily playing on the grass. "If there are searchers, lots of them, scouring the area, and at the moment they're between us and London, and we don't even know if that group you saw is all of them, then hiring a carriage and traveling with two children all the way to London . . ." She met Thomas's gaze. "They'll come here, realize we've left, guess we're the ones they're after, and come chasing after us. We'll never make it to London before they catch us."

Somewhat to her surprise, Thomas nodded in agreement, yet he didn't look downcast. Quite the opposite. He looked rather eager as, meeting her eyes, he said, "Indeed. And if I was Richard Percival, or whoever is managing this search for him, I would have men stationed along the highway back to London, keeping watch, just in case the searchers down here flush their quarry and send them—us—running." He smiled, a gesture that conveyed a certain relish. "Which is why we won't be traveling to London that way." He held her gaze. "Trust me. I know just how to escape this net."

Puzzled, Rose frowned. "How?"

His smile deepening, he gripped his cane and rose. "We go via a route he won't expect and so won't be watching, one along which, even once he realizes which way we've gone, he won't be able to easily get ahead of us."

They left the manor in the dead of night.

After Thomas had explained his plan, and he and Rose had worked through the details, Rose had called the children in for an early afternoon tea, and she and Thomas had explained to Homer and Pippin what they were going to do.

Naturally, the children had viewed the undertaking as a great adventure.

They'd all spent the rest of the afternoon and evening closing up the house, then packing all they could carry in saddlebags and traveling bags suitable for a departure on horseback. Once they'd finished packing, Rose had fed everyone, then sent the children to lie on their beds and get what sleep they could.

She and Thomas had tidied the kitchen and put everything away. Then Thomas had retired to the library to write more letters of instruction to his agent and his solicitor, letters he would post the next day, together with the two letters he hadn't yet sent. Rose had left him to it and, instead, had walked around the house, checking windows, drawing curtains, and going over her mental list of things to do before they left.

At one o'clock in the morning, they woke the children, and, with bags in hand, rugged up in their traveling clothes, they went out to the stables.

Thomas and Homer, remarkably bright-eyed after his nap, saddled Silver and the pony. Rose took the pony, riding astride, with as many of the saddlebags and bags as the beast could manage. Thomas mounted Silver, settled the remaining saddlebag across the gelding's broad back, then he took Pippin up before him. Homer clambered on behind, wrapping his thin arms around Thomas's waist.

Thomas caught Rose's eyes as, in the steady moonlight, they paused in the small court before the stable door. "There's no reason to hurry. We only have fifteen miles to cover, and we'll do it easily, even at a walk."

Rose nodded. "Lead on. I'll follow."

Thomas held her gaze for an instant, then turned Silver and set the gray trotting, first down the drive, then he veered into the field and continued on, east and a little north, riding across the moon-dappled countryside.

They rode into Falmouth while the town was still asleep. They had made good time; it was not yet four o'clock when Thomas thumped on the main door of the Seven Stars Hotel.

He'd stayed there before. It was an expensive hotel, one at which the staff could be relied on to fetch and carry, and accommodate any traveler willing to pay the house's exorbitant rates.

As he'd anticipated, the staff, roused to action, scurried

to make up beds and heat milk for the children. The horses were stabled; Thomas took a moment to speak with the head ostler, arranging for both horses to be kept in the hotel's stables until he returned for them, however long that might be.

Thomas registered them as a family—husband, wife, and two children—and in short order they were shown to a suite at the front of the hotel, with a view down to the harbor.

After approving the accommodations, Thomas dismissed the staff. Rose took the children into the smaller of the two bedrooms. Looking in from the doorway, Thomas watched her help the now sleepy children undress, then she urged them beneath the covers.

Even before she'd turned and joined him, the pair was, Thomas judged, asleep.

Rose quietly shut the door. He turned and followed her across the suite to the other bedroom.

Closing the door behind him, he watched as she searched through a saddlebag and drew out her nightgown and a brush.

Setting both on the dressing table, she started to pull pins from her hair, letting the gleaming mass swing free.

When he drew nearer, drawn, as always, by the promise of her warmth, she sighed and glanced sideways at him. "I'm tired, but I don't think I can sleep." Last pin removed, she shook out her hair.

He reached for her brush before she could. "Stop thinking." Setting his cane aside, he set the brush to her crown and smoothly drew it down. "Just close your eyes and let me brush your hair, and then we'll change and get into bed, and just rest."

Rose did as he said, felt the hypnotic tug of his slow, steady brushing.

Eventually, she followed the rest of his advice, too; sliding beneath the sheets, she turned into his arms, and he held her.

Outside, dawn was just starting to lighten the sky, but he'd closed the curtains. She lay wrapped in his arms, her head pillowed on his chest, the slow thud of his heart a steady, repetitive beat, lulling her, soothing her.

She was on the cusp of sleep when she felt him shift his head, then his lips brushed her forehead. "You and the children will always be safe with me. Sleep," he murmured.

And she did.

Late the next morning, Thomas ordered a substantial breakfast, which they consumed in the sitting room of the suite, safe from any curious eyes.

After the staff had removed the dishes and small table, he shrugged on his greatcoat, picked up his cane, and met Rose's eyes. "I'll go to the shipping offices first." If at all possible, they needed to secure passage on a ship leaving that day.

"Can I come?" Until then playing with Pippin on the floor, Homer scrambled to his feet.

Thomas glanced at Rose. They'd discussed the various dangers, and her task for the morning was to occupy and engage both children while keeping them safely inside the suite.

Their safety was one of the principal reasons he'd chosen the Seven Stars; no one could just wander up the stairs, and any inquiries as to paying guests would be met with blank looks. More, such an expensive establishment would be the last place anyone searching for a once-young lady-cum-housekeeper fleeing in panic with two children would think to check.

Rose tried to catch Homer's eye. "I brought a pack of cards, Homer—we can play any game you like."

Homer glanced at her, but his gaze returned to Thomas's face. "But . . ."

Thomas saw the avid, urgent curiosity in the boy's eyes, and understood. But . . . he sank down on the sofa beside Rose so his eyes were more level with Homer's. "We're trying to avoid the men who are searching for you, and Rose, and Pippin. None of the searchers are likely to recognize me, but they've brought along a man who might recognize you, and we can't be sure that they haven't either followed us here already, or even simply happened to come this way, so we need you to stay safely here with Rose, out of sight." Suddenly inspired, Thomas shifted his gaze to Pippin, who was watching from the floor, then he looked back at Homer. "We need you to stay here and help Rose, all right?"

Homer glanced at Rose, then sighed and nodded. "But I will see the ships later, won't I?"

Thomas smiled as he levered back upright. "If I can get us passage on the evening tide, you'll see all the ships in the harbor."

Satisfied, Homer smiled back, then turned and sat down on the floor again, returning to his game of knucklebones with Pippin.

Thomas exchanged a look with Rose. "I'll be as quick as I can, but I need to call at the post office, too."

She nodded. "Good luck."

As he let himself out of the suite, he saw her sink onto the floor with the children.

Thomas walked down the stairs and out of the hotel, then strode more briskly down the street to the wharves, savoring the sea breeze and the sharp scent of brine. He'd been in Falmouth before; he knew where he was going.

He found what he was looking for in the third shipping office at which he called.

"Indeed, sir." The shipping clerk's eyes were fixed on the notes Thomas had ready in his hand. "You're in luck—the stern cabin on the *Andover* is vacant. Quite given up hope of hiring it, truth be told. She sails on the afternoon tide, so you and your family would need to be aboard in just a few hours."

"Boarding in time won't be a problem." Thomas drew several more notes from his other hand and added them to the pile. "And how long will the *Andover* take to reach Southampton?"

"She'll be going up the Solent first thing in the morning four days from now, sir."

"Excellent." Thomas completed the transaction and quit the shipping office with four tickets to Southampton and the *Andover*'s large stern cabin and a smaller one adjoining booked for him and his family.

He looked about him as he walked deeper into the town to the post office, but he saw no sign of any inquiry agents. People in general wouldn't notice them, but to him they stood out; by the time he reached the post office, he felt reasonably confident that none of the group hunting them was presently in town.

By leaving the manor in the way they had, they'd bought themselves this day, one clear day, but beyond that he couldn't be certain. He couldn't be sure the inquiry agents wouldn't be able to track Silver and the pony across country to the port, but once they hit the busier streets, the agents wouldn't be able to track them easily, and with their having arrived so early in the morning, few beyond the discreet staff at the Seven Stars would have seen them. With any luck, they would slip away on the afternoon tide with no one the wiser.

If luck truly went their way, it would be days before the inquiry agents realized what had happened, and by then he, Rose, and the children—his little family—would have disappeared into the anonymity of the capital.

Entering the post office, he paused at one of the counters to add last instructions to the two letters he'd written the previous night, then he sealed them, put them together with the letters he had intended to post in Helston, and limped to the counter.

After paying the postage and entrusting the four missives into the postmaster's care, he gripped his cane and walked slowly out. Pausing on the steps, he looked out over the harbor, at the plenitude of ships riding at anchor there. After a moment, he stirred and, satisfied with his morning's achievements, turned and headed back to the hotel.

The most dangerous part of their day was the transfer from the Seven Stars to the *Andover*.

Although the distance was short, Thomas insisted on hiring one of the hotel's carriages; he bribed the driver to drive them onto the docks proper, all the way to where the gangplank of the *Andover* rested on the wharf.

Of course, such an entrance drew considerable attention, not least from the vocal navvies, heavy bales and barrels balanced on their shoulders, swearing as they dodged and weaved out of the carriage's way.

Homer and Pippin stared out of the windows, utterly fascinated.

Rose cast Thomas an appalled look—one that clearly stated, *Was this a good idea?*—but he just smiled and squeezed her hand. "Trust me. Such an arrival carries the stamp of some member of the aristocracy—not that of a housekeeper fleeing with two children."

The arrested expression on her face made his smile deepen.

The carriage rocked to a halt, and Thomas swung the door open and descended to the wharf. He paused, head high, looking coldly around, then he turned and gave Rose his hand. As he helped her out, he caught Homer's and Pippin's eyes. "Best behavior," he murmured.

Both children nodded, then scrambled from the carriage in Rose's wake.

Rose held her head high, lifted her skirts, and, with what she felt was commendable hauteur and nothing more than a superficial glance about, allowed Thomas to guide her up the gangplank. Her coat and those of the children were good enough to pass muster; they could have been Thomas's wife and children had Thomas been some minor scion of some aristocratic family . . . which, now she thought of it, if she'd understood his story correctly, he was.

Yet while neither she, he, nor the children were, in fact, playing a part—were, in fact, behaving as their true stations dictated—for all of them that involved the resumption of roles they'd set aside years ago.

It took a little effort to remember exactly the right tone to take with the captain, a portly, genial man who stood ready at the top of the gangplank to bow them aboard.

After greeting Thomas and the children, the captain bowed again to Rose. "If you would step this way, ma'am, the steward will show you to your cabin."

"Thank you, Captain." With a gracious inclination of her head, Rose consented to follow the captain's wave to where a neat individual in the shipping company's uniform was waiting by a door giving onto a set of stairs.

The stern cabin was a welcome surprise, more spacious

than she'd expected, and a door in one corner opened to the smaller cabin next door, one with two narrow bunks. The children made a beeline for the wide windows across the stern, scrambling onto the window seat below the panes to peer out, but then Pippin noticed the bunks, squealed, and raced to claim the lower one.

Homer glanced across but didn't follow. "I'll take the top one," he called, then returned to the view over the water and the myriad ships filling the harbor.

The instant the porters who had carried in their few bags retreated and closed the door, Rose sighed. She considered, looking inward, then across the cabin, met Thomas's eyes. "I was worried that I might have inherited Mama's affliction, but I feel well enough."

Thomas smiled and looked down at Homer. "These two seem happy enough."

Homer flashed him a grin, then looked back at the ships. After a moment, he wriggled around and looked first at Thomas, then at Rose. "Can we go up on deck and look about?"

Rose looked at Thomas.

He hesitated, then said, "Once we're properly underway and pulling away from the dock, then yes, we can go up on deck. The captain will very likely allow us onto the poop deck." Thomas pointed at the cabin's ceiling. "It's directly above us, and from the railing there you'll be able to look back and watch Falmouth fall away behind us." He glanced out of the window. "Given it's afternoon, we should have a good view."

That, as it transpired, was exactly what they did; Rose leaned against the rail along the rear of the poop deck, and with Homer on one side and Pippin on the other, with Thomas beyond, screening Pippin and Rose from the whipping wind, she watched Falmouth and all risk of immediate pursuit fall further and further behind them.

They stood watching in companionable silence until a rising sea mist obscured the view.

Thomas stirred, then met Rose's eyes. "I've arranged for us to dine in our cabin. Shall we go down?"

With nothing more to see, and the air growing cold and damp, the children were ready to descend. They went ahead, leaving Rose to take Thomas's arm and allow him to guide her back to the ladder down to the lower deck.

His arm was solid and strong, unwavering; feeling the warmth and strength of his body beside hers put the final seal on the sense of safety and comfort stealing through her. All immediate anxiety had fallen from her, the tension it wrought sliding away as in the ship's wake Falmouth had dwindled and eventually disappeared.

"Thank you," she said, letting all she felt color her tone. Glancing up, she caught his eye just as he parted his lips. "No—don't say anything." She held his gaze. "Just . . . for now, thank you."

With that she faced forward, then released him so he could go before her down the ladder.

For now. She doubted he'd understood what she'd intended, what means of later thanking him had leapt to her mind.

Once the thought, the concept, had blossomed, the attraction only grew.

She waited until night fell. Until she'd shepherded the children, drooping and yawning, into their room and tucked them securely into their bunks. After the excitement of the day, combined with the sea air, both were asleep the instant their cheeks touched the pillows.

Returning to the stern cabin, she closed the door quietly behind her. Across the room, Thomas stood beside the wide shelf of the bed, anchored to the cabin's wall. Cane resting against the nearby window seat, he shrugged out of his coat and laid it aside.

She reached him as he tossed his waistcoat to join his coat, and raised her fingers to his cravat. "Allow me."

Stilling, he met her gaze, then, as, stepping close, she unraveled the simple knot, he reached for her, slid his hands around her waist, then set his fingers to her laces.

She stripped the long, linen band away, let it fall from her fingers to join his coat and waistcoat. The scars that marred the left side of his face and head, half hidden by the heavy fall of his hair, extended down the side of his throat. Caught, unable to resist the lure, she raised her hand and slowly, gently, traced the line of scars.

He drew in a slow breath, his chest expanding, then he turned his head and pressed a kiss to her palm.

His hands firmed and he drew her closer.

Raising her head, sliding her hand to his nape, she stretched up, and their lips met.

The kiss was long, unhurried; confident and assured, they both savored.

She'd slept in his bed every night since she had placed herself so deliberately there. While she'd sensed, every night, that he'd been torn over allowing it, he had nevertheless fallen in with her wishes.

Had nevertheless succumbed to the temptation she'd realized she represented.

An affirming, confidence-building realization.

She moved with him now, sliding into passion, letting desire rise and thrum through their veins. Clothes fell, shed, whispering to the floor. They'd moved past the point of unnecessary modesty, at ease with each other's bodies, and with their own.

But when they both stood naked, locked together in passionate embrace, and he raised his head and moved to draw her to the bed, she stopped him, her hand firming on his chest. "No. My turn."

Thomas looked down at her, slowly arched his brows.

She smiled, sultry, sirenlike, then murmured, "My turn to script our play."

He wasn't sure what to think of that; searching her eyes, he got the distinct impression she had some purpose in mind, but . . . tonight they were safe, the long, rolling swell of the deck beneath their feet a reassuring reminder that for the next several days they were out of danger's reach.

Traveling through an unexpected hiatus, their peace before the storm, for once they reached London, they would inevitably be plunged back into the heart of the action, into the cauldron of whatever might come, and the dangers would escalate.

But for tonight, for these next days, they were safe, free.

Free to indulge as they wished, as they pleased.

With an infinitesimal nod, he acquiesced. "So . . ." Dipping his head, he brushed her lips, rosy and swollen from their kisses, with his and murmured back, "What's your intention?"

She smiled, soft and smug, and didn't answer.

Not in words.

Instead, lids heavy, long lashes screening eyes that smoldered with a passion she had never sought to hide, she moved into him, against him, her silken skin and supple curves a potent distraction. The grip of her hands firmed, fingers pressing into muscle, over scars, then she bent her head and pressed her lips to his shoulder, traced the line of his collarbone, diverted to lick, lave, then press a hot, wet, openmouthed kiss to one nipple.

Hands riding on her hips, he closed his eyes and let his

senses sink into the pleasure she wrought. With her kisses and caresses, her stroking, fondling, and blatantly possessive claiming, she opened his eyes to another dimension of what had grown, was clearly still growing, between them.

She showed him her passion, her possessiveness.

Showed him that her desires matched his own.

Extended his own; his reaction to her devotions, to the acceptance and open hunger she allowed to show, allowed to infuse her touch, burning him, branding him, took him unawares. Overwhelmed him and filled his mind.

He was beyond making any protest when she slid to her knees before him.

Beyond thought when he felt her breath, warm and full of promise, wash over the head of his erection.

Hands gripping her skull, fingers clenching in her hair, he rode the wave of unadulterated pleasure she evoked and, with a languid but deliberate sweep of her fingers, an achingly gentle brush of her lips, sent raging through him.

Rose curled her fingers around the heated rod of his erection; her breaths shallow, trapped in the moment, by the sensual magic she had so deliberately evoked, she touched and caressed.

And he stilled, caught, trapped in the sensual web she'd woven.

Triumph washed through her, a very feminine feeling.

Emboldened, she slowly licked the broad head and tasted the tangy salt of him; the sensation flashed like fire through her blood.

She bent her head, closed her lips about the velvet head, and slowly, savoring, drew him deeper.

He gasped and trembled.

His head fell back and his fingers tightened in her hair. Every muscle in his body locked, veins cording.

Inwardly smiling, a sense of feminine victory suffusing her, she focused on her task—on her intention.

Thanking him in words only went so far; even if, after her lecture about accepting thanks graciously, he allowed her to speak the words, even if he now listened, he didn't truly hear. Didn't truly believe that he was due such gratitude, because his actions—so he thought—were motivated by his need to atone for his past.

She understood that, in part, that was true, but was it the whole truth? His whole truth?

Or did some part of his drive to protect and care for them spring from some finer, purer source?

In her heart, in her soul, she felt the latter was true, and so she devoted herself to lavishing on him all the thanks to which she considered him due, for all his acts of kindness.

For all the things that didn't matter, that made no difference to whether they saved William, but which Thomas still did. Went out of his way to do.

Because he cared.

For that, she thanked him, in a manner he couldn't refuse to feel, to absorb and take in.

When he finally grated, "Enough," broke the seal of her lips with his thumb and freed himself from the heat of her mouth, she rocked back on her feet, smoothly rose, and, taking the hand he held out to her, joined him on the bed.

They came together in heat and in passion, with steadily burning desire, and a hunger no longer so urgent, no longer uncontrolled, but unwavering in its depth and breadth, in its towering compulsion.

Confident, assured, they rode the waves of pleasure, let them sweep them up to the pinnacle of delight, and on into ecstasy.

Into the furnace that fused them, that shattered their senses, fragmented their realities, then forged them anew.

And left them spiraling through the void, until, buoyed on the golden sea of fading bliss, they floated in paradise.

A man and a woman entwined in each other's arms, exhausted and sated, content with themselves, and at peace with the moment.

They rattled into London in the early evening. Favored by the winds, the *Andover* had sailed up the Solent and into Southampton Water earlier than anticipated. Thomas had hired a carriage and four for the journey on, and they'd made good time on the road.

Their days at sea had passed in comfort and without incident. Pippin had been content playing with her dolls in the cabin, while Rose and Thomas, freed from immediate concerns, had relaxed, strolling in the fresh air, talking and making the most of those moments. Homer had been in his element. His eager questions and polite manners had quickly made him a favorite with the crew; he'd spent most of the journey learning about the ins and outs of sailing a modern ship.

The last stretch up the Solent and through Southampton Water, one of the busiest shipping lanes in the world, had fascinated them all; there'd been so many ships to see, so many different styles and types of sails, all gleaming white against the blue-gray sea gilded by the silver brilliance of early morning.

Once they'd disembarked, bowed off the ship by the beaming captain, Thomas had led them to a nearby hotel, once again one of the more expensive variety. After arranging for the carriage to take them to London, he'd surprised Rose by hiring a room, leaving their bags there, then escorting her, Homer, and Pippin on a shopping expedition.

As Thomas had explained, given they were going into London society and would, at some point, be reclaiming their true identities, they needed the clothes to support that claim. Rose hadn't thought of the necessity, but he had.

Now, becomingly clad in a new deep-brown pelisse trimmed with gold ribbon, Rose stared at the façades lining Kensington High Street, then glanced across at the trees of Hyde Park, visible through the window on the other side of the carriage. London. They'd reached there safely, in very real comfort, and without having to weather any danger or challenge.

All thanks to Thomas.

She glanced at him where he sat alongside her, like her, rocking slightly with the movement of the carriage. He, too, was wearing new clothes, a well-cut coat of pale gray over darker gray trousers, with a silver-and-gray striped waistcoat.

When she'd asked, he'd told her that, via the letters he'd sent from Falmouth, he'd arranged rooms for them at a London hotel. He hadn't mentioned which hotel, or where it lay.

As she didn't know London well—had only spent two Seasons there, and during both had lived at Seddington House in Mayfair—she hadn't pressed him for details; after the last months, let alone the last week, she trusted him to have made the best arrangements for them, on all fronts.

In due course, the carriage turned up Park Lane, then into the quieter streets of Mayfair. After rolling slowly across the northern side of Grosvenor Square, the carriage turned left up Duke Street, then slowed even further, coming to a halt at the curb before a pair of large, glass-paned doors; the gold lettering across the doors proclaimed them to be the entrance to the Pevensey Hotel.

The hotel lived up to her expectations of Thomas. Its subdued and elegant decor, the thickness of the rugs scattered over the polished floors, and the pervasive hush that blanketed the foyer testified to the establishment's exclusivity.

Keeping Pippin and Homer close, Rose looked around while Thomas, beside her, signed the register and obtained the key to the suite reserved for them from the very deferential manager.

Pleased with Drayton's arrangements, Thomas accepted the two letters that had been waiting for him. Turning from the counter, he nodded to the hotel footmen waiting to ferry their new bags and boxes to the suite, then gathered Rose and the children and ushered them to the stairs. The manager handed the overseeing of the reception counter to a colleague and quietly followed in the footmen's wake.

Their suite was on the first floor and looked out over Duke Street. Thomas swiftly scanned the accommodations and pronounced himself satisfied. Under Rose's direction, the footmen deposited the bags in the correct rooms, then they and the manager bowed themselves out.

The door shut. Thomas arched a brow at Rose.

Tugging off her new gloves, she smiled. "Yes, this will do very nicely."

He hesitated, glanced at the doorway to the smaller bedroom into which Homer and Pippin had already disappeared, then looked at Rose. "They're known for being very protective of their guests' privacy, which means you and the children should be safe here, or at least as safe as it's possible to be. And regardless, your names don't appear in the register, so short of someone recognizing you or Homer, there's no reason anyone should come looking for you here."

Rose nodded. Sinking onto the sofa, she looked pointedly at the two letters he held in his hand. "What do they say?"

Thomas sat beside her; setting one letter aside, he broke the seal of the other. "This one's from Drayton—he organized the suite." Thomas scanned the letter. "He says he's started investigating Richard Percival's finances but has as yet turned up nothing of note. However, as he states, it's early days yet."

Setting that letter down, Thomas picked up the other, broke the seal, and read, saying, "This one's from Marwell, my solicitor." He paused, then reported, "If you recall, I asked him for his assessment of Foley."

Rose met Thomas's quick glance and nodded. "What does he say?"

"That Foley is sound—a rigid adherent of the strictly conservative approach to the law. In Marwell's view, Foley is entirely trustworthy."

When Thomas looked at her, brows rising, Rose grimaced. She thought for a moment, replaying her few meetings with the ageing solicitor, but, in the end, still shook her head. "He might be entirely trustworthy, but that doesn't mean he won't assume that everything Richard Percival says is correct, and that any suggestion that Richard might be a villain must be a ridiculous fabrication."

Thomas studied her for a long moment, then inclined his head. "Sadly, in that you may well be correct. In my experience, villains can, indeed, be represented by entirely righteous men."

Realizing he was speaking of his past self, Rose reached out and squeezed his hand.

A patter of feet had them both looking forward as Homer and Pippin came rushing up. "Is it dinnertime yet?" Homer asked.

They settled in, and the hotel proved every bit as comfortable as Rose had imagined.

The children had separate beds in the smaller bedroom, and, as on the ship, were out like lights the instant they settled under the covers.

Leaving Rose to quietly close the door, cross the sitting room, and retreat with Thomas into the larger bedroom.

They undressed, him on one side of the large bed, she on the other. Nightgown donned, she went to the dressing table and picked up her brush. As she brushed out her hair, she smiled to herself; she still half expected the floor to rock.

Finally laying aside the brush, she turned and saw Thomas already in the bed, the covers across his chest, his arms folded behind his head, his gaze, steady and somewhat pensive, resting on her.

Lips lightly lifting, she crossed to the bed, turned down the lamp burning on the side table, then raised the covers and slid beneath.

She turned to him. He unfolded his arms, closing them around her as she settled against him. She lifted her face and he met her lips, covered them with his, and together they sank into the never-fading joy of the kiss . . . but, this time, the underlying resistance that from the first she'd sensed in him solidified.

Became manifest.

When she would have pressed closer, he drew back— held her back. Their legs were tangled, their bodies in contact, their arms cradling each other, yet instantly there was space between them.

He looked into her eyes; even through the dimness she could feel the weight of his gaze. He drew breath, then quietly said, "We . . . need to speak about this." He paused, searching her eyes, then went on, "I want you, you know I do. But . . ." His gaze steadied. "I have no future—no certainty to offer you." He brushed back a lock of hair from her cheek; his hand, his fingers lingered, cradling her face. "I might want to promise you the moon and the stars, a future of togetherness, of living together . . . but I can't. I simply can't. I don't know what Fate has in store for me . . . what if you get with child?"

Something in her leapt; her heart expanded but felt crushed at the same time . . . then a surge of emotion, of determination and will, rose and steadied her. Shored her up and strengthened her. She held his gaze, then shifted to frame his face with both hands, forcing him to keep his gaze locked with hers. "Understand this." She spoke slowly, letting her determination resonate in her tone. "I don't care." She paused to let each word strike and sink in, then continued, "What I do care about is us, this, what's grown between us." Drawing breath, she forced herself to admit, "No, I don't know where this might lead us, but I'm willing to go forward and find out—and make the best of whatever comes. And if that means that we will, in the end, part—and make no mistake, I will fight that to the last—but, if it should come to pass that there's no other choice, and I am by Fate's decree left with child, a child of yours and mine, then I will treasure and love that child until my dying day."

She paused; her words, uttered with such conviction, all but echoed in the shadows. Still she held his gaze; following his thoughts, she added, "I'm wealthy enough that you don't need to worry. Once I regain my identity, I will be able to live more than comfortably and care for any child we might have."

He didn't attempt to shift his gaze. "But you will be alone."

She found the answer on her tongue. "I've always been alone, until you came."

Thomas heard her words, and all she hadn't said. Her wish to live her life with him, her determination to, if at all possible, do so. He wasn't averse—oh, no! Living the rest of his life with her, growing old with her—having children with her—was now his most yearned-for dream.

A dream he was certain he would not live to make real. Would not, one way or another, be allowed to commit to.

She seemed to understand; as had happened so often, she seemed to see deeper into his soul than he, himself, could.

Shifting, her gaze still locked with his, she reached out and clasped his hand with one of hers, urged him to twine his fingers with hers and grip. "Give me your todays." She rose to lean over him; her head above his, she looked down at his face, into his eyes, and whispered, "And if Fate takes your tomorrows, at least we'll have had . . . this." Dipping her head, she brushed her lips over his, then sank into the kiss.

And he followed.

Held her, and loved her, and followed her lead, seized their today, and left tomorrow in Fate's hands.

Chapter

9

Four days later, Thomas leaned against the railings of a town house in Albemarle Street and studied the house across the street and two doors down.

Idly twirling his cane as if he was waiting for some friend to join him, he reviewed, yet again, the events, or rather the lack of any significant achievement, over the past days. Despite Drayton's best efforts, nothing he'd uncovered in Richard Percival's finances could remotely be construed as providing sufficient motive for murder. The only thing Thomas, himself, had been able to confirm was that, if one inquired in the right quarters, it was common knowledge that Percival was, and had been for years, pushing hard to have his nephew hunted down.

That much was definitely true, which meant that the threat to William was very much an ongoing one.

Thomas hadn't been in any position to further pursue

who Richard Percival had hired to do his hunting; there was a limit to how far he could press without alerting those he was seeking—and that he was in no hurry to do. As matters stood, if anyone grew suspicious enough to follow him, he would, ultimately, lead them to William. Of course, he routinely took steps to ensure he wasn't followed, but errors could be made, even by him.

There had been no advance on the legal side, either, although Marwell was holding himself ready to act in whatever manner Thomas wished.

Thomas wished . . . that it hadn't come to this, but in accepting the need to come to London, he had always suspected that it would.

Pushing away from the railing, he looked right and left, then strolled across the street. Climbing the steps of Number 24, he halted before the town house's door, composed his mind, then rang the bell.

A shortish, slightly rotund—Thomas's gaze flicked over the man's attire—not butler but majordomo opened the door. The man looked at him in polite query. "Yes, sir?"

"Is Mr. Adair at home?"

The man didn't miss a beat. "I'm not sure, sir, but I can ask. Who shall I say is calling?"

Thomas had timed his call for ten o'clock, the earliest possible time for a polite call and sufficiently early that it was unlikely the gentleman of the house had as yet stepped out. Reaching into his pocket, Thomas drew out a calling card. "He'll know me."

The majordomo took the card; he frowned slightly when he noticed the second name Thomas had scrawled across one corner. But then the man stepped back, holding the door wide. "If you would like to wait in the hall, sir, I will inquire."

An "Honorable" on a calling card usually sufficed to get one at least into the front hall. With an inclination of his head, Thomas crossed the threshold and stood to one side of the elegant chamber. With a bow, the majordomo went off, disappearing down a corridor that led to the rear of the house.

Hands clasped over the head of his cane, Thomas glanced idly around, noting not just the elegance of the decor but also the little touches that, no doubt, had been contributed by Adair's wife. Although unmarried when their paths had crossed five years ago, Adair, the third son of the Earl of Cothelstone, had since married Penelope Ashford, daughter of the previous Viscount Calverton, sister to the present incumbent, and connected via two of her siblings' marriages to the powerful Cynster clan.

It wasn't, however, Adair's social connections that had brought Thomas to his door but rather Adair's unusual association with Inspector Basil Stokes of Scotland Yard. Along with keeping up with financial matters, Thomas had also made a point of keeping abreast of developments in the lives of those he'd known in his past life—so he could avoid them, but, as had happened with so much in this case, Fate had turned his intention on its head.

In order to successfully expose Richard Percival and remove the threat to William, and thus accomplish the task Fate had spared Thomas for—the one only he could fulfill—he needed help of a sort he didn't have access to, but to which, if the news sheets spoke true, Adair did.

If Thomas had wondered if Adair would remember him, the sudden thunder of boot heels striding up the corridor was answer enough—but the lighter, tripping footsteps following were a surprise.

Adair—older, a touch harder, definitely more mature

than he had been, but with his hair a golden halo and his frame long and lean, much as Thomas remembered—appeared in the mouth of the corridor, Thomas's card in one hand.

Incredulous, Adair's gaze pinned him.

Across the hall, Thomas met that challenging gaze calmly, serenely.

Adair slowed, confusion washing over his features. Halting, he glanced down at the card, then at Thomas. After a stunned moment, he said, "Mr. Thomas Glendower, I presume?"

He'd known Adair well enough to be certain that the man would recognize him. Thomas half-bowed, the best he could manage without risking overbalancing. "Indeed."

A dark-haired lady, the type described as petite, had come up behind Adair. She'd halted alongside him, her hand gripping his sleeve, more to ensure he took her with him, Thomas sensed, than any wish to hold her husband back. Now she looked from Adair, to him, then, releasing Adair, she calmly came forward. "Good morning, Mr. Glendower." She held out her hand. "I'm Mrs. Adair."

Thomas glanced at Adair, but the man was still staring at him, not dumbfounded but rather with his mind whirling at full speed, and with no thought to spare to give him any sign. So Thomas looked into Penelope Adair's dark eyes, took the small hand offered him, and bowed over it. "A pleasure, Mrs. Adair. But it's your husband I came to see."

Penelope Adair smiled—and Thomas realized he'd misjudged her. There wasn't just steel but iron behind that smile. "Indeed. I collect that you wish to consult with my husband, in which case, you will need to speak with us both." Boldly, she took Thomas's arm and with a wave turned him toward the doorway to his left. "Let's go into the drawing room and make ourselves comfortable, and you can tell us all. And then we'll decide whether we can aid you."

Thomas accepted the implied rebuke meekly and allowed himself to be steered into the drawing room and installed in an armchair to one side of the hearth.

Adair dallied in the hall to speak with the majordomo; Thomas didn't need to hear the words to guess what Adair's instructions were. Then Adair followed them into the room, a faint frown still hovering in his eyes—as well it might. He'd just had a man he'd thought long dead appear in his hall, damaged, perhaps, but clearly still alive.

Once his wife had sat with a swish of fashionable skirts on the sofa, Adair sank into the armchair alongside, facing Thomas.

Adair tapped Thomas's calling card edge-down on the chair's arm, then simply asked, "Why are you here?"

Thomas held Adair's very blue gaze and simply stated, "I'm here to throw myself on your mercy."

Adair's frown materialized. "Why?"

"Because I need your help. Not for me, but for three others who . . . are dear to me." The admission of vulnerability hadn't come easily, but he sensed he would be ill advised to keep even that back.

Penelope Adair leaned forward, her dark gaze acute. "Tell us."

Thomas considered her for a moment, then he ordered his thoughts and began. "Two months ago, after spending five years in a monastery on the shores of Bridgewater Bay, recovering from my injuries"—with a wave, he indicated his face, weakened side, and leg—"I returned to a house I, as Thomas Glendower, owned, a small manor house at Breage, in Cornwall, a little west of Helston. I had installed an older couple as caretakers long before, but they had retired, and when I reached the manor, I discovered I had a new housekeeper, a widow with two children. Over the course of the next six or so weeks, I learned that the widow was not a widow but a lady by the name of Rosalind Heffernan, stepdaughter of the late Robert Percival, Viscount Seddington, and the children were Percival's, Rosalind's half siblings—a nine-year-old boy, William Percival, fourth Viscount Seddington, and his six-year-old sister, Alice."

Penelope Adair looked intrigued. "How fascinating. Why were they hiding in Cornwall?"

Thomas inclined his head to her; that was, indeed, the most pertinent question. "Four years ago, Robert Percival and his wife, Corinne, who had been unwell, set out for a day's drive from Seddington Grange, which I'm told is near Market Rasen in Lincolnshire. It appears they headed to Grimsby, where Percival, who loved sailing, kept his yacht. The next day, Percival and his wife were discovered drowned, their bodies trapped in the sails of the yacht, which had apparently capsized off Grimsby. The deaths were put down to a tragic accident." He paused, then went on. "Rose—Rosalind—is twenty years older than William, and as her mother had weakened after William's birth, and weakened further with Alice's birth, Rose had largely taken over the day-to-day care of the children. With news of the deaths, quite aside from her own grief, she had to comfort the children. The funeral came and went, and on the evening afterward, Rose by accident overheard Robert Percival's younger brother, Richard Percival, boasting to one of his friends about how he had arranged Robert's and Corinne's deaths, and of his plans to do away with William so that he would inherit the estate."

"Well!" Penelope sat back. She flicked a glance at Adair,

who had been listening closely, his expression impassive. "That," Penelope declared, "is certainly a sound case for investigation."

Adair's gaze remained steady on Thomas. "What did she—Rose—do?"

"There was no member of the Percival family who lived at the Grange at that time, no one Rose knew enough to trust. As a young lady of twenty-four, as she then was, and not a Percival herself, she had no confidence in her ability to sway the family solicitor, and certainly not to have her word given credence against that of Richard Percival, who in his brother's will had been named William's principal guardian. In short, she feared to lose William and Alice— the children she'd vowed to her mother that she would care for and protect—to the man who had killed their parents. And more, Percival's confession accounted for an inconsistency Rose had seen in the verdict of accidental death by drowning. Her mother, Corinne, suffered from excessively bad mal-de-mer and wouldn't have been able to so much as set foot on a yacht without becoming wretchedly ill."

"So given Corrine was already sickly," Penelope said, "why on earth would her husband have even suggested going out on his yacht?"

"Exactly." Thomas paused, then met Adair's bright blue gaze. "Rose took the children and fled. That very night. She had enough cash to get by for some time, but she knew Richard would search for them. And he did. However, she avoided the areas in which she knew he would look. In time, she reached Cornwall and, as luck would have it, found a position assisting my then ageing caretakers. After two years, they retired, and she continued as the manor's housekeeper. The manor was the perfect refuge—it's isolated, and because the older couple had had all the deliveries arranged, Rose, much less the children, didn't need to be seen even in the villages. The locals knew she and the children were there, but in that part of the country, everyone minds their own business."

"A perfect refuge, until you, the owner, arrived."

Thomas met Adair's gaze, then said, "Even then, the fiction remained and they were safe—until Richard Percival's men appeared asking questions."

Penelope straightened. "He found them?"

"No, not yet. Apparently, he's been using inquiry agents to hunt for them." Thomas glanced at Adair. "You know the sort." When Adair nodded, Thomas went on, "I've used them in the past and recognized the two who turned up at the manor as members of the fraternity. After I sent them on their way with a believable lie, one that would at least buy time . . . after that, Rose confided in me. Subsequently, I used my own contacts here, in London, to verify much of her story. Her parents' deaths occurred as she'd described. She and the children did indeed disappear on the night of the funeral. Percival is behind the inquiry agents, is William's principal guardian, co-guardian with William's great-uncle, a much older and apparently ineffectual man." Thomas paused. "I started investigating Percival's finances, looking for the motive behind his need to inherit the estate. But then more inquiry agents arrived in Helston, a dozen or so this time, and they'd brought with them Robert Percival's valet—according to Rose, the man would recognize both her and William."

"Good heavens!" Penelope all but jigged. "How did you escape? I take it you did?"

Thomas inclined his head. "I'd seen the inquiry agents before they'd seen me, and I'd learned that we had a day's grace—they were searching in a different area that first day. So Rose and I agreed we had to come to London, face the challenge here, and resolve the issue—that we had to expose Richard Percival's scheme, his murder of Robert and Corinne Percival, and so remove the threat to William's life."

"Well, well—murder and a threat to someone's life?"

Thomas glanced toward the now open doorway and the large, dark-featured man who filled it. Thomas had never met Stokes before; instinctively, he reached for his cane to stand, but Stokes waved at him to remain seated. Thomas watched as slate-gray eyes, wintry, their expression steely, studied him.

Then, saturnine features entirely impassive, Stokes inclined his head. "Mr. Glendower." He came forward. "I believe murder and threat is my cue. It seems you have need of my services."

Thomas watched as Stokes nodded to Penelope and Adair, and with the ease of long familiarity, sat alongside Penelope on the sofa. Neither Adair nor Stokes had offered to shake Thomas's hand, but that he'd expected.

"Before you continue your tale," Adair said, "allow me to fill Stokes in on the details to this point."

Thomas inclined his head and sat back, listening as, briefly and succinctly, Adair recounted all that Thomas had thus far revealed.

While he did so, Penelope Adair rose and crossed to the bellpull, and when the majordomo responded, she ordered tea to be brought in.

It had been a very long time since Thomas had last sipped tea in a ton drawing room; accepting a cup from Penelope, he found himself somewhat cynically amused, more with himself than anyone else. But this, indeed, was the way matters were dealt with within the milieu of those of the Adairs' ilk—with all due civility.

At the end of his factual recitation, Adair cocked a brow at Thomas, clearly asking if he'd missed anything crucial. Thomas nodded. "Yes, that's it." He transferred his gaze to Stokes. "Having made up our minds to come to London and pursue Percival, Rose and I closed up the manor, took the children, and in the small hours of the following morning, we relocated to Falmouth, and from there, I arranged passage on a ship sailing for Southampton on the afternoon tide. We boarded and, after an uneventful voyage and subsequent carriage journey, reached town several days ago."

"So Percival has no notion you, Rose, and the children are in town?" Stokes asked.

Thomas grimaced. "Of that, I can't be certain, but from the moment we arrived in Falmouth, I took care to project an image entirely inconsistent with the group the inquiry agents are searching for." He met Stokes's gaze. "I'm tolerably good at concealing identities—I know what veils to employ."

Stokes snorted. He held Thomas's gaze and after a moment asked, "Why, exactly, did you come here?" He tipped his head. "To Adair."

Thomas hesitated, unsure of the ice beneath his feet. But he'd already decided on complete honesty; oddly enough, these days, with most people that seemed to serve him best. "Because I've realized that, regardless of what I might uncover about Percival, about his motives, his past actions, and his intentions toward William, courtesy of my past, I will not be in a position to take that information further, to expose Percival and remove him as a threat to Rose and the children." He kept his gaze steady on Stokes's steely eyes. "That's my aim—to ensure Rose and the children are safe. To achieve that . . . I'm willing to surrender myself, as the man I used to be, to you, to the courts." He paused, then added, "The only thing I ask is that you defer arresting me until after Percival's threat is negated and Rose and the children are safe."

Stokes stared at a man he'd never thought to see. His mind was whirling, juggling, reviewing—very close, at least on one front, to boggling. He glanced sidelong at Adair and found his friend waiting to catch his eye. What a turn-up, indeed!

It had been Adair and Stokes who had searched for Malcolm Sinclair's body, they who had found the letter he'd left at the house he'd been living in, they who had followed the trail he'd left to the murderer he had trussed and left waiting for them in the cellar, they who had subsequently followed his directions to the will he'd written and left with the local solicitor in Somerset . . . all those years ago.

Stokes and Adair knew the contents of that will. Adair had been instrumental in ensuring its provisions were fully enacted. To do so, he'd had to recruit several of his noble connections to the cause—and they, one and all, had helped. Because it had been the right thing to do.

And Stokes had done his part by assembling evidence to support his formal declaration that no man could have survived the death Sinclair had planned and executed for himself; Stokes's statement to that effect—that the Honorable Malcolm Sinclair was unquestionably dead—had been crucial in enabling probate of his will to proceed.

Both Stokes and Adair—and Penelope had later learned the details, too—knew of the extent to which Malcolm Sinclair had gone to make full restitution and more for the sins he'd . . . somewhat unwittingly committed.

Looking back at the man, if not in perfect health, then

hale enough and definitely breathing, sitting in the armchair opposite, Stokes resisted the urge to scrub his hands over his face. The very last thing he needed was to attempt to arrest an already dead man . . . but he saw no reason to explain that to Thomas Glendower just yet.

Drawing in a deep breath, Stokes nodded to Glendower. "Very well. Let's leave the question of arresting you for later, and focus on Richard Percival and his doings. The first thing I will need is to interview this Rose—Miss Heffernan. So where have you got her and the children hidden?"

Thomas didn't hesitate. "The Pevensey Hotel. We're in suite number five."

Stokes's brows rose.

Adair nodded. "Good choice." When Stokes glanced at him, he added, "They'll be as safe as they could be there. In this case, discretion equates to protection."

"Ah." With a nod of understanding, Stokes refocused on Thomas. "Once I have Miss Heffernan's statement confirming the details you've related, that will give me a sound basis for an investigation." Stokes paused, then asked, "I take it you've thus far learned nothing that would give us any clue as to why Percival needs to inherit?"

Thomas shook his head. "That's at the top of my list to pursue."

"We may be able to throw more resources behind that." Adair exchanged a look with Penelope, then said, "Montague, of Montague and Sons, occasionally works with us on cases that can benefit from his expertise."

Thomas arched his brows. "Montague—the Cynsters' man-of-business?"

Adair nodded. "The same. He has an interest in investigations, too."

"Along with his wife, Violet." When, faintly surprised,

Thomas looked at her, Penelope grinned—another of her steely, iron-willed grins. "We—myself, Stokes's wife, Griselda, and Violet—all . . ." She waved airily. "Involve ourselves in the investigations as needed. For instance, I'll call on your Rose and the children this afternoon to let her know she can call on me, or either of the others, for any assistance of a more domestic nature that she might require."

Thomas thought that surprising information through, then dipped his head in acknowledgment. "Thank you."

That earned him an openly delighted smile.

Shifting his gaze to Adair, Thomas continued, "I've already put my agent, Drayton, onto investigating Percival's finances. As yet, he's been unable to get far, but I'm sure Montague's reach will be more . . . extensive. I'll instruct Drayton to liaise with Montague's office." He paused, then added, "Drayton's areas of expertise are unlikely to be entirely overlapped by Montague's—with them working together, we should have a better chance of uncovering whatever clues lie in Percival's finances."

Adair nodded. He glanced at Stokes. "In a case like this, it's almost certain that the motive will lie there. The principal benefit Percival will get from the inheritance is access to money, both directly and via credit against the estate."

"The only other benefit he might derive is from the title itself." Penelope frowned. "And the only reason that might matter is if he's looking to marry, but I've seen and heard nothing of that." She looked at Stokes, then at Thomas. "But I will ask of those who would definitely know."

Stokes nodded. "Do—best to eliminate that as a motive if we can. Meanwhile . . . I believe I can spare a few constables and a sergeant to set up a watch on Mr. Richard Percival." He cocked a brow at Thomas. "Any idea where he lives?"

Thomas shook his head.

Stokes shrugged. "No matter. That can be the sergeant's first task—finding out."

Adair was nodding. "As it appears that William is standing in the way of Richard Percival's demonstrably very real push to inherit, and William is now in town, keeping a close eye on Percival might pay dividends on several counts." He met Stokes's eyes. "We might learn which inquiry office he's using, which will at least give us more witnesses as to his actions against Rose and William."

"Indeed. Witnesses to his active intent might very well be crucial." Stokes frowned, then said, "The only other immediate action I can think of is to see if we can interview the estate's solicitor." Stokes arched a brow at Thomas.

"Foley," he supplied. "Of Gray's Inn. Rose doesn't trust him, but she doesn't really know him. My own solicitor assures me Foley is sound, if somewhat rigidly conservative, which might explain Rose's reading of him."

Stokes nodded. "I'll have to request a magistrate's order to induce Foley to discuss his client's business, but once I've interviewed Rose, I should have enough to do so."

"I'll go with you when you visit Foley," Adair put in. "Quite aside from putting any questions, my presence alone might help."

Stokes humphed in agreement.

Thomas set down his cup and saucer on the small table beside his chair. "One thing—I know it's early days as yet, but, even if we do show that Richard Percival has been pursuing William, that, due to some financial constraint, he has reason to want William dead so that he can inherit, and we have Rose's testimony as to what she heard him say four years ago regarding him arranging for his brother and his brother's wife to be murdered . . ." Thomas met Adair's, then Penelope's, then Stokes's eyes. "Is that going to be enough?"

When no one immediately volunteered an answer,

Thomas went on, "We might be able to show motive, but other than Rose's testimony, as far as I can see we have nothing that definitively proves Richard Percival is guilty of anything criminal. And Rose's testimony will be easy to discount—a twenty-four-year-old young lady, hysterical with grief, thinks she hears . . . something Percival will insist she didn't. What judge or court would convict on that?"

Stokes grimaced. "We'll have to search in Lincolnshire for any witnesses that can link him to the murders on the yacht."

"If there were any such witnesses," Thomas quietly said.

Adair exhaled. "Sadly, you're right. Four years after the event . . . that's a very cold trail."

"But," Penelope said, "if we set the earlier murder to one side, then the critical point we have to deal with now is that William still stands between Richard Percival and what he wants." She met Thomas's eyes. "William is Richard's current target—which means that, if it comes to it, we could use William to bait a trap for Richard." She widened her eyes. "Indeed, that might be the fastest way to assemble conclusive proof against Richard Percival."

"No." His expression resolute, Thomas flatly said, "I could never allow William to be used as bait. He's intelligent and capable, but he's only nine years old."

To his surprise, Penelope smiled at him in rather fond condescension. "Of course not—we wouldn't really have William there. We would just make it appear that he, Percival's target, was there for the seizing." She looked at Stokes. "That, I suspect, would be all it would take."

Stokes grunted. "It won't be quite that easy, but . . ." He inclined his head. "I have to agree that once we've gathered all the information we can, it might come to that." He glanced at Thomas. "If Percival's searching as hard as he apparently is, then word that William has been sighted at a particular place will certainly bring him running."

Adair grimaced. "It's entrapment of a sort—never the best way forward—but I agree. It might come to that. We shouldn't turn our backs on the possibility." He looked at Thomas. "If we stage it correctly, we can make Percival's intent sufficiently clear, to the point that, along with all the rest, no judge will overlook it."

Thomas allowed his antipathy to the idea to color his features, but, reluctantly, he nodded. "Very well. We'll proceed as you've outlined, and, first of all, assemble all the information on Percival and his circumstances that we can."

Grasping his cane, he rose. The others all came to their feet. Thomas met their gazes, then inclined his head. "Thank you."

The three nodded back, and, joining Thomas, they strolled as a group into the hall.

After confirming the time for them to call at the hotel to meet Rose and the children, Thomas was about to turn away when—to his intense surprise—Stokes held out his hand.

"Until later," Stokes said.

Hiding his surprise, Thomas gripped the man's hand. "Indeed."

As Thomas released Stokes, Adair, too, offered his hand. "As well as Stokes, there'll be me, Penelope, and Montague if he can manage it—you might want to warn Miss Heffernan and assure her we won't bite."

"Naturally not." Penelope frowned Adair down, then turned to beam at Thomas and bestow her hand on him.

As Glendower very properly gripped her fingers, Penelope noticed Stokes collecting his hat from Mostyn.

"Stokes—if you have a moment, I have something for you to take to Griselda."

Stokes nodded and remained.

Retrieving her hand, Penelope smiled with real delight at Thomas Glendower. "Good day, Mr. Glendower—we'll see you this afternoon."

With a last, graceful inclination of his head, Glendower turned to the door and, with a polite nod to Mostyn, who swung the door wide, limped off down the steps.

Her smile undimmed and undimming, Penelope watched Glendower depart, then she signaled to Mostyn to shut the door.

For a moment, she stood luxuriating in the welling excitement of a new and utterly fascinating case, wallowing in the anticipation.

Stokes turned to her. "What did you want me to take to Griselda?"

Penelope blinked and returned to the moment. "Oh, that. I lied. I wanted to detain you to make sure both you and Barnaby comprehend just who Mr. Thomas Glendower is."

Propping his shoulders against the drawing room door frame, hands sunk in his trouser pockets, Barnaby smiled lazily at her. "So . . . who is he?"

"He's . . ." After a second, Penelope waved her hands. "I hardly know where to begin. He's known as an extremely wealthy, but very reclusive, gentleman—he never appears in public. Clearly, we now know why. But he endowed and manages a fund for the Foundling House—it's the largest we have, and it accounts for nearly a third of our income. That's where I first heard his name. Later, I learned that he's done the same with that new hospital south of the river, and then I discovered he's endowed the . . ." She listed charity after foundation after institution on her fingers, working through one hand, then the next, then starting on the fingers of the first hand again, ultimately concluding with, "And he's the largest individual benefactor of the British Museum."

After a moment of stunned silence, Stokes looked at Barnaby. "I suppose we now know how he's been spending his time over the last five years."

No longer smiling patronizingly, Barnaby pushed away from the door frame. "Regardless, that's impressive." He paused, then arched a brow. "I wonder what Montague's view of Mr. Thomas Glendower is."

"You can find out tonight," Penelope declared. "Dinner here at seven o'clock, gentlemen—I'll send messages to Griselda and Violet, as well as Montague, so don't be late."

At three o'clock that afternoon, in response to a polite knock, Thomas opened the door of their suite and stood back to allow Penelope, Adair, Stokes, and a conservatively dressed man Thomas took to be the great Montague to enter.

He'd told Rose of his earlier meeting and had warned her they were coming. She'd been sitting, waiting, on one of the two sofas; coming to her feet, she somewhat nervously smoothed her skirts.

Penelope Adair, in what Thomas suspected was her habitual forthright fashion, swept up to Rose, a warm and transparently genuine smile on her face. "It's a pleasure to meet you, Miss Heffernan. And might I say how indebted I am to you and Mr. Glendower"—she waved at Thomas— "for bringing us such an intriguing case. I, for one, am grateful for the distraction."

Across the room, Rose briefly met Thomas's eyes, then, clasping Penelope's offered fingers, murmured, "Please, call me Rose."

Penelope's smile deepened. "And as you've no doubt guessed, I'm Penelope Adair."

Thomas shut the door but didn't have to make the rest of the introductions. Penelope blithely did that for him, then she looked at the children, both watching from chairs at the table by the window in the far corner of the room. "And these must be . . ."

Finally, Penelope stopped and glanced at Thomas.

Obediently, he obliged. "Allow me to introduce"—at his beckoning wave, both children, openly curious, came forward—"Miss Pippin and Master Homer."

Pippin bobbed a wobbly curtsy. Homer's bow was more certain.

Penelope beamed at the pair. "Are you busy with your lessons?"

"Yes, ma'am," the children chorused.

"Indeed." Rose turned the children back to their books. "Thomas and I have promised to play a game with them later—once they finish."

Reminded of that reward, the children retreated and settled once again at the table.

Turning to Rose, Penelope arched a brow.

With a wave inviting Penelope to share the sofa with her, Rose sat, and while Penelope set aside her bonnet and reticule, and the gentlemen arranged themselves in the armchairs and on the other sofa, Rose quietly explained, "We think it best that they continue to use the nicknames they chose four years ago, when we left Seddington Grange." She met Stokes's gaze. "Using their real names might prove dangerous, and they're very comfortable with their nicknames now."

Extracting a black notebook from his greatcoat pocket, Stokes nodded. "There's no benefit in them changing back just yet." He glanced swiftly around the circle, then looked at Rose. "If you don't mind, Miss Heffernan—"

"Please. Just Rose." Rose smiled wryly. "I'm also more comfortable with that name now."

Stokes nodded easily, the expression in his eyes reassuring. "Rose. I'd like to go through the details of what happened four years ago in Lincolnshire, but it would help if we could start from further back—from your mother's marriage to Robert Percival, when you first went to live at Seddington Grange."

Fleetingly, Rose arched her brows. She understood why Thomas had taken the step he had, and if she didn't as yet fully comprehend all the ramifications, she fully appreciated that securing Stokes's—and Adair's and Montague's—support was a major advance. So she nodded and cast her mind back. "I was fifteen when my father died of a fever and nineteen when my mother remarried. Robert wooed her for several months, and I felt comfortable with him. He was kind, caring, and I was very happy that Mama had found someone who truly cared for her."

"So you weren't upset by her remarriage."

"No, not at all. I was relieved." She paused, then added, "Mama wasn't strong physically, so having Robert appear, and then be so intent on sweeping us up, into his care, was, from my point of view, a happy circumstance."

"Nineteen," Penelope said. "Did you make your come-out?"

Glancing at her, Rose nodded. "The following year. I had two Seasons, but . . ." Her lips quirked. "You might say I didn't take." She looked at Stokes. "But then William was born, and Mama never fully recovered. I helped her take care of him, and, I'll admit, as I wasn't enamored of ton entertainments, the Season, the marriage mart, and all the rest, I used caring for him, and then later Alice, too, as an excuse to avoid the social round."

"So," Stokes said, "would it be correct to say that you, the children, and your mother and stepfather were happy and content, with no acrimony or tensions, at the time of the accident?"

"Yes." Rose nodded decisively. "That's exactly how we were . . . and then, they were gone." Telling Thomas had been easier; she hadn't had to relate the details, hadn't had to relive the memories, bringing them to life in her mind. She drew in a slow breath. Stokes, to his credit, didn't prompt her, but she knew what he wanted to know. "Mama was sickly and often spent her days lying down. But on the morning they left, she was having one of her good days, so Robert thought to take her out for the day—fresh air always did her good. So they ordered a picnic basket from the kitchen, and we"—Rose tipped her head toward the children—"all three of us, stood on the front steps and waved them away. Robert was driving his curricle, and Mama was laughing."

She looked at Stokes. Head bent, he was scribbling in his notebook.

Without looking up, he quietly asked, "When did you realize something was amiss?"

"When they didn't return for dinner." She paused, recalling. "Fisk, the butler, sent a rider to Grimsby. Robert had mentioned they would head that way."

"And . . . ?" The gentle prompt came from Penelope.

Rose drew in a shaky breath, shook her head. "We heard nothing until the next day. About eleven o'clock, the head constable from Grimsby arrived with the news. Fishermen going out that morning had spotted the yacht and found the bodies." Her voice strengthening, she caught Stokes's eye as he glanced up. "I knew, then, that something wasn't right, that Mama, at least, could never have drowned, would never even have been on the yacht, but . . ." She drew in a sharp breath. "I had William and Alice to console." She glanced briefly at the pair. Heads bent, they were busy with their lessons; they were far enough away that they couldn't hear. "They didn't understand, not exactly, but somehow they knew that they would never see their parents again, that they had gone forever, and they were . . . inconsolable." She paused, then, pressing her hands together, drew in a deep breath. "It was a difficult few days."

A massive understatement; she'd been battling her own grief, compounded by her confusion, and dealing with Alice, who, at two, had worked herself into hysterics. . . . Rose pushed away the memory. She felt Penelope's hand briefly squeeze hers and spared the other woman a weak smile.

"What happened to the curricle?"

It was Adair who had asked. The question helped Rose refocus. "It was found on the headland, but the horse was wandering aimlessly, so we had no idea where they'd actually stopped. But they had eaten their picnic."

"Had anyone seen them take the boat out?" Adair asked.

Rose shook her head. "But that wasn't necessarily a surprise. If they'd gone out in the afternoon, the fishermen's boats would have been well out at sea, and when the boats returned at dusk, the fishermen might not have spotted the capsized yacht."

"So"—Stokes studied his notes—"next came the funeral." He glanced at Rose. "Anything particular about the service or the wake?"

Remembering . . . she shook her head. "No. It was all very somber. No one had expected them to die, not so young. Everyone was in shock. Both were well liked, and, of course, Robert had lived there all his life."

"Who of the family attended?"

"The Percivals—Richard, Robert's younger brother, and Robert's uncle, Marmaduke, and Marmaduke's son, Roger Percival. Beyond that, there were a great many connections and many distant cousins, but"—Rose shrugged—"no one I really knew. No one elected to stay on at the house except for Richard and Marmaduke."

"And them staying makes sense," Thomas quietly said. "Richard and Marmaduke were named William's and Alice's co-guardians. Although Richard was named principal guardian, he and Marmaduke would have had arrangements to discuss and decisions to make."

Scribbling furiously, Stokes nodded, then looked at Rose. "Tell me what you did after the guests left, in as much detail as you can remember."

Straightening, Rose raised her head and turned her mind back to that day. "I spent the next hours with the children in the nursery. I don't know who stayed to dine—I remained with the children and didn't go down. After that . . . I couldn't settle. It was still evening, not that late, so I thought to start on the task of writing to Mama's more distant friends, informing them of her death." She swallowed, then went on, "She kept her address book in the drawer of an escritoire in what was called the study. It was a room off the drawing room. Robert never used it as a study—he used the library instead—because anyone conversing in the study could be heard in the drawing room. The two rooms shared a chimney. I went into the drawing room and was crossing to the study door when I heard voices—from the fireplace." She met Stokes's eyes. "From the study."

When Stokes nodded encouragingly, she went on, "The chimney distorted the voices, but only a little—I could hear the words clearly." She drew breath, then said, "I heard

Richard say that he . . ." She blinked, then, her voice firming as exactly what she'd heard replayed in her mind, she went on, "He said that he had killed them, Mama and Robert. He was gloating over how well he'd succeeded in making it look like—*look* like—they had drowned. He made a point of explaining how he'd wrapped their bodies in the sails to make sure they were found . . ." She paused, then glanced at Thomas. "I didn't understand the significance of that at the time, but now I do. He needed their bodies found, or he would have had to wait seven years for Robert to have been declared dead."

After a moment, Stokes waved his pencil. "Return to the moment—tell me exactly what you heard, exactly what you did."

"If I might," Adair said, then he shifted his gaze to Rose. "Who was Percival speaking to?"

She grimaced. "I don't know, but he had several friends who had come up from town for the funeral. Because I didn't join them over dinner, I don't know who stayed."

"Back to the moment," Stokes insisted. When Rose looked at him, he glanced at his notebook. "You heard Richard gloat about making sure the bodies were found by wrapping them in the sails. Then what?"

"Then," she said, the words clear in her mind, echoing through the years, "he said that now all he had to do was eliminate William—that was the word he used, 'eliminate'— and he would have the estate, and he planned to make a move on that sooner rather than later. His friend, whoever he was, laughed, and wished him good luck." Rose refocused on Stokes. "To leave the study, they had to come through the drawing room. I couldn't risk them finding me there. I turned and very quietly left. As neither came after me, I assume they never knew I had been there, that I had overheard them."

Stokes, scribbling, held up a finger. When he raised his pencil, he looked at her. "How well did you know Richard Percival?"

"Not well at all. In fact, Mama warned me away from him, and Robert—he was present—agreed. Rather grimly, too. At the time, I assumed the warning was because they thought I was impressionable and might succumb to his charms or some such thing. He was—is—a notorious womanizer. But in hindsight, perhaps they meant the warning more generally." She frowned, then looked at Stokes. "Regardless, as I lived with them and saw no reason and had no inclination to go against their guidance, I never spent much time with Richard, not at family gatherings, and not socially, either. To give him his due, he never gave much sign of noticing me."

His instincts pricking, Thomas frowned, but then Stokes asked Rose, "Given your relative lack of knowledge of him, can you be certain it was Richard Percival you heard? You didn't see him, and you yourself said the chimney distorted his voice."

To her credit, Rose paused to question herself, then she replied, "True, but the distortion isn't sufficient to truly disguise a voice—for instance, I wouldn't have mistaken Marmaduke for Richard, and, as I said, the only members of the family who had elected to remain overnight at the house were Richard and Marmaduke. And, of course, as Robert's brother, it's Richard who will inherit after William. Given the words I heard—that all he had to do was eliminate William and he would have the estate . . ." She arched her brows at Stokes. "No one but Richard could have said that."

Stokes's expression cleared and he smiled in almost feral satisfaction. "And that is exactly the right answer. It *could* have been no one but Richard Percival who spoke those words." He nodded. "So, and you can be less detailed from now on—I'll ask if I need more information—tell me what you did next."

Rose obliged; Thomas listened as she described her flight from Seddington Grange and her subsequent journey through the countryside with the children, much as she'd described it to him.

At the end of her recitation, Stokes closed his notebook. "Right. That's a good start, and"—he glanced at the others—"I can confirm that Richard Percival lives in a town house in Hertford Street, the eastern end. I have three men watching the house—they have orders to keep him under surveillance and follow him if he goes out."

Rose was visibly relieved.

Then it was Montague's turn to ask questions, first verifying the members of the Percival family—Richard, Marmaduke, and his son Roger—all of whom lived in London. Montague looked at Thomas. "I've already put my people onto digging into Richard Percival's finances, but I understand you have done some work in that area, too?"

Thomas nodded.

Stokes and Adair had their heads together working out the details of how to approach the Percival family solicitor, Foley; hearing Montague's question, Adair glanced up. "We might be able to add something to that after we speak with Foley. We'll try to extract as much as we can regarding who is holding firm to the reins of the estate—" He broke off to explain to Montague, "Glendower's man has already confirmed that the estate appears to still be intact, so assuming Richard Percival is after money, that he hasn't been able to raid the estate's coffers suggests that someone—

presumably Marmaduke Percival, possibly aided by Foley himself—is resisting all such efforts." Adair glanced at Thomas. "If we can confirm that, we'll be well on the way to shoring up our motive."

Stokes grunted. "That will also explain why Percival is so hot to hunt down his missing nephew. If he can't persuade the other executors to release the funds, then he needs William dead and his body found."

"Exactly," Adair said.

Thomas caught Montague's eye. "I'll instruct my agent, Drayton in Threadneedle Street, to direct all his reports to you. Better we pool our efforts, rather than work parallel and perhaps waste precious time."

"Indeed." Montague inclined his head. "It will be an honor to work with Mr. Drayton." He glanced at the others. "As it is, thoroughly investigating the finances of a gentleman like Percival will take several days at least."

Rose, Thomas noticed, had been talking with Penelope. From the direction of the ladies' frequent glances, the children and their well-being was the topic under discussion. Sure enough, as the men fell silent, Penelope swiveled back to face them. "Rose and I have been discussing the difficulty of keeping the children constantly cooped up in these rooms. While, obviously, we can't risk simply taking them for a stroll, I was wondering if we might use my carriage."

She looked pointedly at Adair.

Who arched his brows back. "The carriage—along with the guards—is yours to command."

Penelope beamed. "Wonderful." She glanced at Rose. "It'll be perfectly safe—I'll bring all three guards. Perhaps if I call tomorrow morning"—she glanced over her shoulder at the children—"by which time those two will be climbing the walls, we could take them out for a drive around the town, stopping wherever we please, whenever the fancy takes us, whenever something catches their eye, and then quickly move on." Penelope shifted her gaze to Thomas and added, "Constantly guarded the whole time."

Thomas wasn't at all sure of the wisdom of such an excursion, but a swift glance showed that Stokes, Adair, and Montague, too, accepted Penelope's assurance at face value.

He'd also caught enough snippets of their conversation to realize that Rose was relaxing in Penelope's exuberant presence, and he could only be grateful for Adair's wife's freely tendered friendship and support . . . so he kept his tongue between his teeth and ignored the protectiveness that had closed, viselike, about his chest.

Not a sensation he'd had any experience of prior to the last weeks.

With everyone satisfied, all immediate questions answered and their next steps defined, the others rose and prepared to depart.

Stokes left first, then Montague. While Rose was farewelling Penelope, Adair turned to Thomas and smiled. "They really are guards. Coachman, groom, and footman. I vetted them myself."

Thomas read the message in the blue eyes holding his and extrapolated. "Your wife often goes into danger?"

"Too often for my liking." Adair glanced at the lady in question. "But she wouldn't be Penelope if she didn't, so . . ." He shrugged, then met Thomas's eyes and saluted. "We'll let you know what we learn."

Thomas inclined his head and watched Adair bid Rose a smiling farewell, then clasp his wife's elbow and steer her to the door.

Rose, still smiling, opened it, then closed it behind them.

Turning, she met Thomas's eyes, then sighed, relieved; her smile turned grateful. "That went better than I'd hoped."

He hesitated, then nodded at the door. "You like her."

Not a question, at least not the one it sounded like.

Understanding that, Rose nodded. "She's a viscount's daughter, but she involves herself in investigations and does all sorts of things—she's a translator of ancient languages, and she and Adair have a son, just a baby, too." Rose paused, then, attention drifting to the children, she mused, "I rather think spending more time in her company will do me, and the children, nothing but good."

Chapter 10

homas Glendower is nothing short of a legend," Montague informed the others seated about the dining table in Albemarle Street that evening. "He manages countless funds, all of which benefit various charities, but quite aside from such a gargantuan philanthropic endeavor, it's his ability to source and grow funds that is second to none. He literally grows money."

"How does he do it?" Violet, Montague's wife, asked. "I assume we're referring to legitimate dealings?"

"Indeed—entirely legal and all aboveboard. His actions are open to easy scrutiny and many, many men-of-business and all keen investors certainly do scrutinize his deals, but that's not where his genius lies. He has a nose for it—when to buy into a company, and when to sell. He doesn't hold investments for the long term—or only rarely, and then with reason. He is utterly brilliant, and I will confess that—as I'm sure many of my peers do—I run a fund within the office that operates by mimicking his financial moves. It's the most successful fund I've ever run, but because we're always moving after he's already moved, we're never making as much as he is."

Barnaby exchanged a glance with Stokes, then looked at Montague. "Do you remember, years ago, me asking you for information on a Malcolm Sinclair? It was in relation to investments in railroads."

Montague frowned, patently thinking back, then his eyes widened. "Ah, yes. A very astute investor, but as I recall, he had a shady side. No moral compass, and he'd been associated with several questionable deals."

"Indeed." Barnaby paused, then said, "Thomas Glendower is Malcolm Sinclair."

Montague stared. "No . . ." His expression blanked. A moment ticked past, then, in a distant voice, he murmured, "Of *course*." He blinked, then, features firming, he shook his head. "I should have seen it—not *quite* the same hand, and in a different class of asset, but the same . . . *innate sensitivity,* the same brilliantly incisive mind." Montague looked at Barnaby, then at Stokes. "I'm not sure I understand." He frowned. "How will this play out—us helping him?"

Stokes pulled a face. "It's not at all straightforward, but . . ." He glanced at Barnaby. "We"—he shifted his gaze to Penelope and Griselda, including them in the decision—"have come to the conclusion that there's nothing to be gained by resurrecting Malcolm Sinclair and his past misdemeanors, when all that will do is cause untold ructions and uncertainty, and possibly great financial loss, for all those who benefited courtesy of his will—all the restitution he made when he died."

"Died?" Montague blinked. "He died?"

"I'm not at all sure I'm following." Setting down her napkin, frowning, Violet looked from one face to the other. "What misdemeanors did Malcolm Sinclair commit, and why was he thought to have died?"

Barnaby explained, with Stokes and Penelope adding comments to his somewhat bald dissertation. Penelope interrupted to stress the connection that had formed between Sinclair and Barnaby and Penelope's friends, Charles and Sarah Morwellan, now Earl and Countess of Meredith, and how, through that association, Sinclair had realized the error of his ways and had then sought to make restitution, before arranging his own death. Barnaby reclaimed the stage to describe the bridge over the falls at Will's Neck in Somerset, the site Sinclair had chosen for his demise, before concluding with, "So, you see, it truly is a miracle that he lived at all, much less recovered sufficiently to be walking, talking, and able to help anyone."

After a moment, Stokes shifted, leaning forward and drawing all attention back to him. He looked around the table and succinctly stated, "Malcolm Sinclair is officially dead, and the man we now have before us is Thomas Glendower. It's he we need to judge."

"And you saw his injuries." Barnaby met Montague's eyes. "He's paid a heavy toll in pain, and I would hazard a guess that he continues to pay a price just for living each day."

"It really is a wonder that he has." Penelope looked at the others. "Continued living, I mean."

Stokes nodded heavily. "It seems almost sacrilegious to say it, but, this time, he appears to be on the side of the angels, and who are we to work against that?"

"And," Penelope said, "it's abundantly clear he's not doing any of this for his own benefit but purely to aid Rose and the children. His aim in this is entirely altruistic—he, personally, has nothing to gain . . ." She paused, then, features brightening, added, "At least, not financially."

Barnaby threw her a cynical look, then tapped the hilt of his knife on the table. When the others all turned their attention his way, he said, "We should discuss the case, and whether there's anything more we should do beyond what we've already planned."

Assessments were duly offered and discussed, but, in the end, the consensus was that they would have to await the results from their first foray of investigative actions the next day.

Penelope was the only one to make any addition to their program. "The grandes dames—at least, all those I generally consult—have retired to Somersham for a mid-Season rest, but I'll see who else I can find and ask what they can tell me about Richard Percival." She pulled a face. "I was never much interested in his sort, so I don't know anything about him myself."

Stokes nodded. "Yes, ask—one never does know, and you've uncovered useful information from such sources before."

They all rose and repaired to the drawing room. Once they were settled comfortably and sipping tea, Stokes, who had been faintly frowning, volunteered, "I can't help but think that, despite this case seeming so very straightforward, we'll still need to exercise some degree of ingenuity to catch Richard Percival in such a way that he gets no further chance to pose any real threat to the boy."

Barnaby grimaced but didn't disagree. The others, likewise absorbed in thinking over the case, murmured agreement.

Eventually, after good-byes had been said and they had seen the others off home, Barnaby twined his fingers with Penelope's, and, side by side, they headed up the stairs.

As they always did, they went straight to the nursery. Leaning against the door frame, Barnaby watched Penelope look down on their sleeping son. She delicately adjusted his blanket, then stooped and brushed a kiss to his fair head, then, straightening, she turned down the nightlamp to just a glow and returned to Barnaby.

Stepping back into the corridor, he drew the door closed behind her, then he paused and looked down at her until, feeling his gaze, she looked up.

Briefly, she searched his eyes, then arched a brow.

He held her gaze and softly said, "Tomorrow, when you go out with Rose and the children, you will take all due care, won't you?"

Of yourself, because you are the most important being in the world to me and to our son.

Penelope heard the words Barnaby didn't say; she smiled, raised a hand to his cheek, stretched up on her toes, and lightly kissed him. Then, taking his hand, she tugged him back to the stairs, toward their room. "Yes, of course." As he fell in beside her, she slanted him a glance, then grinned, confidence personified. "Quite aside from my rather obvious guards, all three of them, I'll have my lovely little derringer with me."

Barnaby smiled, inwardly shook his head, and allowed her to tow him to their bed.

Later that evening, safely ensconced in the comfortable luxury of the Pevensey Hotel, Rose checked on the children one last time, then, assured they were sleeping peacefully, she crossed the sitting room, paused to turn down the last lamp, then continued to the large bedroom she shared with Thomas.

He'd left the door ajar; going through it, she closed it behind her. He was already undressing, laying coat, then waistcoat, over the stand on his side of the bed.

Hands going to her hair, Rose pulled pins as she walked to the dressing table; setting the pins down, she shook out her hair, letting it tumble, free, down her back. She hesitated, then, rather than lift her brush and stroke it through the shining mass, as she usually did, she turned and, determined, crossed the room to Thomas.

Engaged in undoing the buttons at his cuffs, he saw her coming and paused. Hands lowering, he straightened.

She didn't halt until she was all but chest to chest, her bodice brushing the fine fabric of his loosened shirt. Looking into his face, she locked her eyes on his. "How did you do it? What did you do to gain the support of Adair, and Stokes, and all their helpers?"

They hadn't had a chance to discuss it before, but she knew him, and she had enough insight into how things worked to doubt the likelihood of him simply asking and being granted that sort of assistance.

Thomas looked into her eyes, the brown more stormy than soft. He hesitated, uncertain and, as usual, questioning what he should do, which way he should jump—how much truth he should tell—but . . .

He'd always been honest with her, had vowed on his private altar never to lie to or mislead her. "I . . . offered to surrender myself as the man I used to be, to stand trial for the crimes I committed in the past, in return for their assistance in helping to protect William and safely reinstate him to his rightful position."

She held his gaze as she digested his words. "You knew Stokes . . . from before?"

He shook his head. "I knew Adair—he wasn't married then. He was in Somerset—Charlie Morwellan summoned him to look into the odd happenings I had been behind. That I had caused to happen. Adair was, even then, known as something of an investigator. Subsequently, I learned that, in recent years, Adair and Stokes had formed an ongoing connection. From what I've gathered, Adair had, at the end, summoned Stokes into Somerset, so Stokes does indeed know all about the doings of . . . the man I used to be." His gaze locked with hers, he paused, then added, "Stokes understood what I was offering. He, and Adair, accepted."

Rose didn't know what to do—how to react. She felt as if her heart had stopped. Yes, it still beat, but . . . she had to be sure. "So . . . once Richard is exposed and his threat to William is no more, you—Thomas Glendower—will . . . what? Simply cease to be?"

He looked into her eyes, and nodded. "In a nutshell, yes. That's how it will be."

She stared at him. She wanted to rail at him, to ask how he could have done such a thing—to have so calmly set the clock ticking on the existence of the man she had come to love, the man who had woken her heart and touched her, and to whom she'd given herself heart and soul . . . but she knew the answer.

He didn't try to cut short the moment, to turn away from her scrutiny.

Finally, seeing the truth in his crystal-clear eyes, she dragged in a tight breath and said, "You're going to tell me that I have to accept this"—*your sacrifice*—"graciously, aren't you?"

His expression had remained impassive throughout, serious but unyielding, but her comment broke through; his lips quirked. He glanced aside, but then again met her eyes. Fractionally inclined his head. "The argument had occurred to me."

She could imagine. She managed not to glare at him. After another long moment lost in his eyes, she heaved a huge sigh. "Very well. But understand this." Her voice strengthened; refocusing, she recaptured his gaze. "I will not give you, or what has come to be between us, up without a fight."

He started to frown, but she held up a hand. "No. That is not something you have any right to argue against or attempt to influence. Just as I must accept your stance, knowing as I do that you see saving William as some sort of final penance, and so your surrender to the authorities to achieve that seems all of a piece, so you must accept that my stance is my own to make."

She held his gaze. "There is nothing you can say that will make me stop praying that whatever happens, you will be spared. Nothing you can do to prevent me living each day as it comes—and loving you through every hour. Nothing you can say will stop me from waiting for you, from being yours, even if I have to wait until eternity to be with you again."

Without hesitation, Thomas spoke from his heart. "I wish there was." Between them, his hands found hers and gently squeezed. "For your sake, I wish that."

She searched his eyes, then inclined her head. "That, I can accept. But it changes nothing."

He studied her eyes, her face, then drew a slightly shaky breath. "We're a pair, it seems."

And doomed.

Rose heard the unspoken words, but she hadn't battled through all the difficulties of her life to be cast in the role of a heroine in a tragedy. "We are, and until the last roll of the dice, until the dice settle, we won't know what they say— won't know what the final outcome might be."

His brows rose fractionally, but he made no response.

She didn't wait for him to agree. "So." Sliding her fingers from his grasp, placing her palms against his linen-draped chest, she slid them slowly upward, feeling the heavy muscles firm beneath her touch, the scars at his right shoulder pinch and tighten. Then she stepped forward, into his arms, breast to chest, and reached up to cup his nape.

His arms closed around her and he allowed her to draw his head down.

Just before their lips met, she breathed, "All that's left is for me to thank you—appropriately—for your sacrifice."

She kissed him, then issued an invitation impossible to mistake—one Thomas immediately accepted, only to discover just how much he hungered, how much he desired.

The day's portents had affected him, too. His rational mind might have seen his sacrifice, delayed though he'd made it, as an inevitability, impossible to escape, but some much more deeply buried part of him—that part she so effortlessly drew forth—railed against the decision and all it would mean . . .

She twined around him; sliding from his arms, she disrobed—herself, and him—and he let her.

She drew him to the bed and he went, as hungry as she, as needy for the warmth and comfort and the inexpressible closeness . . .

That closeness—that true intimacy—rocked him, racked him; it anchored him, all his wits and every one of his senses, ruthlessly in the here and now, and made him an unresisting, willing captive to the delicious give and take, to the moments of scintillating, breath-stealing wonder.

To the unalloyed joy.

Caresses rained; lips supped, sipped; tongues rasped while hands gripped and fingers shaped.

As they loved.

She came over him, rose up, and took him in. Sheathed him in her slick heat, and then rode him.

He gripped her hips and held her as they raced through the landscape they now knew so well, to the peak that beckoned, the pinnacle that waited.

Their hearts thundered as one; skins slick with desire, their flesh burning with a flame they both embraced, they drank in the glory and raced on.

Up and over the peak, leaping from the pinnacle as nerves fractured and senses fragmented, and then there was nothing beyond the blinding glory.

Ecstasy shone, a never-dying truth, between them.

That sun in all its splendor slowly faded, leaving them not bereft but comforted.

She collapsed onto his chest and he closed his arms around her.

The spark that fueled their glory didn't leave them but sank back, into their flesh, retreating more deeply to take refuge in their hearts.

Neither needed to say the word—it was there, hovering, in them, about them.

Forever a part of them, something neither could deny.

Eventually they parted and lay side by side, arms loosely draped around each other.

He pulled the covers over them; laying his head back on the pillows, he closed his eyes and waited for slumber to claim him.

Settled against him, through the dimness, Rose watched his face, watched the lines Fate had carved upon it ease and soften as sleep neared.

She waited, then, pressing nearer, fitting her body to his, she relaxed into his arms. Pillowing her check on his chest, she gently kissed his cooling skin. "Come what may, Thomas Glendower, I will love you forever, until the day I die."

She'd whispered the words, but from the momentary stillness that came over him, she knew he'd heard.

Closing her eyes, she surrendered, to the latent pleasure in their embrace.

To whatever came. To whatever Fate thought to make of their lives.

It was nearly midnight when Richard Percival let himself into his house in Hertford Street and found Curtis sitting on a chair in his front hall, waiting for him.

Shutting the door, Percival immediately asked, "You have news?"

Slowly, Curtis got to his feet. He was nearly as tall as Percival, and half again as wide. "Of a sort."

Percival's expression said he didn't like that answer, but, tossing his hat, gloves, and cane on the hall table, he waved down the corridor. "In the library."

Curtis followed; he'd entered the house as he usually did, via the back alley and the kitchen door. He probably didn't need to take such precautions with Percival's job, but old habits died hard.

A bare minute later, they were seated on opposite sides of Percival's desk, the lamp that Percival had lit and turned low casting a soft glow that reached not much further than the pair of them.

Percival tried to read Curtis's utterly impassive countenance, gave up, and somewhat brusquely asked, "What have you learned?"

"I believe"—Curtis met Percival's dark blue gaze—"and I stress it's no more than that—that I know who the young lady has been masquerading as, and where she's been hiding the children."

Percival had learned to trust Curtis's "beliefs." "Where?"

"I believe she's been calling herself Mrs. Sheridan, and

she was the housekeeper at an isolated manor house near Breage, on the Cornish coast."

"Who owns the house?"

"A Mr. Thomas Glendower, but, until recently, he wasn't in residence. He's been an absentee landlord for many years, but he reappeared a few months back and has remained at the manor since then."

Percival frowned. "If you know where she and the children are—"

"No—I know where they were. Where I believe they were. The housekeeper and her children fit your bill to a T, but when two of my men questioned Mr. Glendower, he claimed they were from a local family, with their roots firmly in Cornish soil."

Percival's frown deepened. "So why do you imagine they are who we seek?"

"Because when my men stopped there with your brother's valet to confirm they weren't, they found the house closed up and no one at home."

"No one? But . . . if she's taken the children and run, what about Glendower?"

"That's why I'm here. He wasn't there, either. My men took a day to check, to ask around, but no one had seen him since the day before—in Helston, when my men were standing in the main street, organizing their sweep of the Lizard Peninsula. He saw them, that much I do know."

Percival's eyes narrowed on Curtis's face. "You think he went back to the manor and then . . . fled with her and the children?"

Curtis nodded. "It took a few days, but eventually we found his horse and the manor's pony in the stable of the best inn in Falmouth. He'd arrived there in the small hours of the morning on the day my men reached the manor.

From there, we learned he'd booked passage on a ship to Southampton, and he was on it, with his wife and two children, when it sailed that afternoon." Frowning blackly, Curtis growled, "My men spent weeks setting everything up, and yet he slipped through our net, neat as you please."

Percival eyed Curtis. "Possibly not your average customer, then."

"No. A very cool head, and a quick thinker." Curtis met Percival's gaze. "Which is why I'm here—to warn you."

Percival had been sitting with his chin sunk in his cravat; now he raised his head and looked directly at Curtis. "About what?" Then he frowned. "What I don't understand is why this Glendower, if it is indeed he, is helping her. Assuming it is, indeed, her and the children."

Curtis snorted. "That's about the only certainty in all this. The descriptions of the young lady and the boy, as well as what one can infer for the little girl—those descriptions fit. As for Glendower, he's been in some accident and so is scarred and walks with a cane, so he, too, is easily identified. And all the descriptions match this party—the one Glendower brought to Southampton. And, yes, I've sent men down to see whether they can pick up any trail from there, but given the days that have elapsed, I'd say it's fairly certain that Glendower brought 'his wife and children' to London—and you know how hard it will be to find them here."

Frowning, Percival nodded. "Yes, that seems likely, but I still can't understand *why* he's helping her."

Curtis quietly sighed. "That's what I came to warn you about. The question you should be asking yourself is not why he's helping them but *whether* he's helping them."

Percival stilled; his expression leached to impassivity. His voice was cool as he asked, "What do you mean?"

Curtis ran a hand over his close-cropped skull. "I mean that it's possible he—this Glendower—has discovered their secret and thinks to use it and them to his advantage." Curtis met Percival's gaze. "The lady and the children might, or might not, be his willing companions." Curtis paused, then said, "I think it's possible that he'll contact you himself."

A long moment passed, then Percival said, "To get me to ransom them?"

Curtis held his gaze. "To sell them to you."

Chapter

11

Montague could barely wait to get down to his office the next morning. As soon as he did, he summoned his staff to his inner sanctum.

Settling behind his desk, he smiled at them all. "We have a new investigation to pursue."

They had collaborated with Adair and Stokes on several such investigations in recent months, the first of which had brought Violet into Montague's life. Indeed, into the lives of all his staff; glancing across his desk, he found her eyes, too, on him, waiting to hear how he would handle the necessary explanations. Violet spent three days a week acting as his personal secretary and the rest of her week assisting Penelope.

Now Violet nodded at him to start. Clearing his throat, he glanced around at the eager faces, and did.

All had been with him long enough or were—as was Pringle, the most recent addition— experienced enough to quickly grasp the implications.

"So." Frederick Gibbons, Montague's senior assistant, straightened away from the bookcases against which he'd been leaning. "We're looking for some debt sufficient to make Percival desperate enough to act—and that four years ago."

Foster, Montague's junior assistant, snorted. "If he was moved to murder four years ago because of this debt, it must be gargantuan by now."

"Hmm." Eyes narrowing, Montague tapped a finger on his blotter. "I'm not sure we can make such a leap." He glanced at Foster and Gibbons. "Percival's affairs may simply constantly be underwater—enough to be a goad, an ever-present anxiety, but not enough for anyone else to see it as a massive debt."

Gibbons nodded. "Chronic debt, rather than acute." He met Foster's eyes. "Could be just as pressing—indeed, even more of a motive than a single major debt."

"Exactly." Montague glanced around at the others— Slocum, his longtime head clerk, Pringle, also an experienced clerk who had joined the firm some months earlier when Montague and the others had investigated Pringle's previous employer's murder, Slater, Montague's junior clerk, and lastly Reginald Roberts, the office-boy-cum-runner. "Does anyone else have any observations?"

Somewhat to Montague's surprise, it was Violet who said, "Actually, yes—there's a point I find confusing." She met Montague's eyes, and when he nodded encouragingly, she went on, "This Richard Percival is known to be hiring professional searchers—inquiry agents, as you, Stokes, and Adair called them. If I'm remembering aright, the suspicion is that he's been using them for some time, and recently Mr. Glendower saw two agents on one occasion, and on another occasion, at least a dozen." Violet paused, then, head tipping, said, "Does that not argue that Percival has considerable financial resources? Don't such professionals cost money?"

Montague's eyes widened, then, slowly sitting back, he nodded. "An excellent point, but I believe I can guess the answer." He glanced at Gibbons and saw the same suspicion in his eyes. Looking at Violet, Montague explained, "As many such things are in the less-than-legal world, I suspect the fee for the search will be contingent on its success."

Violet frowned. "So none of those men will get paid unless they find the boy?"

Increasingly sober as he thought through the ramifications, Montague nodded.

Foster grimaced. "No wonder, then, that they're hot to find him." He turned to the door. "I'll get on to the banks and see what I can learn."

Gibbons, too, nodded somewhat grimly. "If they've been strung along for years on the promise of what will come once they find and hand over the boy . . ." He shook his head and started for the outer office. "After I finish with my day's meetings, I'll go out and see what I can learn from among the fraternity." He glanced back at Montague. "Any idea who his man-of-business is?"

Montague shook his head and looked at Slocum.

Who inclined his head. "I will endeavor to find out while Mr. Gibbons is in his meetings."

Montague nodded, then spoke with Pringle, Slater, and Reginald to ensure that the day-to-day business of the office continued to run smoothly. When they left to return to their desks, he turned to Violet, to discover her still frowning, albeit in a distant way. "What is it?"

They had recently learned that she was expecting their

first child, and any frown or grimace made his lungs constrict.

Her gaze lifted to his face and she focused . . . and her frown dissolved into a sweet and gentle smile. "Nothing about that—I'm perfectly well and would tell you if I wasn't." Her frown returned. "I was thinking about this new investigation. Who are these professional searchers? Is there any way we might"—she waved vaguely—"subvert them to our cause? Might we persuade them to bear witness against Percival, at least as far as his orders to them go?"

Reassured of her health and that of his child—his *child,* a word he'd never thought to have the chance to associate with himself—Montague considered, then grimaced. "No, I can't see it. And us approaching them might backfire— they are more likely to notify Percival that someone's asking about his case than be of any help to us." He met Violet's gaze. "Professional searchers, be they inquiry agents, debt collectors, or simply so-called hounds—people who find others for a finder's fee—are only as successful as their reputation for absolute discretion allows them to be. One slip on that front, and no one would ever hire them again—and, sadly, most of the outfits depend on jobs from the less-than-legal side to stay in business."

Violet pulled a face. "Well, it was worth a thought. Now!" She opened a ledger she'd held in her lap. "You have at least two meetings you cannot wriggle out of today."

Montague smiled, listened, and allowed her to order his day.

An hour later, Stokes slouched into Hertford Street and ambled to the eastern end, where the street ended in a small court.

Almost at the end of the street on the southern side, two

men, beggars if one judged by their outer clothing, were sitting on the pavement, their disreputable backs propped against the front railings of one of the town houses.

They were quietly chatting. The only thing notable about them was that they hadn't yet been moved on by the local constabulary.

Not exactly surprising, given they were the local constabulary.

Stokes halted by the men's feet. He looked down at their regulation boots and nodded at them. "I'd get those out of sight if I were you."

Both men colored and drew in their legs, hiding their boots under the skirts of their rough frieze coats.

Briefly, Stokes glanced around the street. He didn't stare at any one house in particular but confirmed that there was nothing remarkable about Richard Percival's house—it was a terrace town house, typical of the area. He looked down at his men. "Where's Philpott?"

"Off on a break," Sergeant O'Donnell replied. "He'll be back shortly, then I'll move to the corner and take up my street-sweeping duties again."

Stokes nodded. "So what have you learned?"

"He came in last night, just before midnight. Went into one of the downstairs rooms for a while, then he went upstairs to the front room to the left above the door, then it was lights out. This morning, the curtains were opened at about ten o'clock. We've seen neither hide nor hair of him since."

Stokes looked at the younger constable. "What's the household like?"

Baby-faced, and with a certain easy charm, Morgan had proved adept at getting kitchen maids and even cooks to talk. In this instance, he pulled a noncommittal face. "I thought as how there'd be sure to be stories, but no—seems his staff is small and keeps to themselves. Quiet household—I got that from the scullery maid next door."

Stokes frowned. "No hints of any wild parties, orgies, that kind of thing?"

Unblushing, Morgan, who was older than his looks painted him, shook his head. "Not a peep. Could be a country vicar for all I heard."

Inwardly frowning more definitely, Stokes said, "Keep up the watch. You know what to do if he moves?"

"Aye." O'Donnell lumbered to his feet. "Two to follow, and the other to alert the station and then you."

Stokes hesitated, then said, "If he doesn't move other than this evening, and that only socially, I'll come by tomorrow sometime, and we'll reassess."

He saw both men fight the urge to snap off a salute.

"Aye, sir," they chorused.

Without any further sign, Stokes strolled on around the court, then back up the other side of the street.

As he walked, he pondered the picture of Richard Percival his men had painted.

Not at all the portrait Stokes had expected.

"Then again, being strapped for cash, perhaps he's simply living as he must, and as for today, he's on edge and waiting for news." That was a reasonable, perfectly plausible explanation. Stokes raised his head, lengthened his stride, and headed back to his office.

Later that morning, Thomas climbed the stairs to Drayton's office, which was located on the first floor of a narrow building off Threadneedle Street.

Drayton's office overlooked the street. Reaching the door at the end of the corridor, Thomas opened it and went in.

He'd sent word he was coming; the clerk, seated behind his desk, looked up, then, a smile blooming, leapt to his feet, rattled off a welcome, and rushed off to fetch Drayton.

Although they corresponded regularly, Thomas hadn't set eyes on Drayton for more than ten years, yet the man who followed the clerk from Drayton's inner sanctum was instantly recognizable, at least to Thomas. Physically, Drayton was average in every conceivable way, the sort of man who could disappear among five others and not be remembered. But it wasn't for his physical attributes that Thomas had hired him; Drayton's mind and attitudes meshed well with his own. Mild manners and an easy temperament, combined with an astute wit and an almost obsessive thoroughness, along with inviolable discretion and a willingness to trust in his client and act on orders without requiring explanations, had long made Drayton the perfect man-of-business for Mr. Thomas Glendower.

To his credit, Drayton, who was aware that Thomas had been in a serious accident from which he had spent literally years recuperating, took in Thomas's state in one swift but comprehensive glance, then, a smile wreathing his face, held out his hand. "Sir! It's a pleasure to see you again."

Smiling easily, Thomas grasped the proffered hand. "Indeed. I'm pleased to have this opportunity to catch up with you." He was somewhat surprised to realize that the words were true. Drayton had been one of the few constants in his life, an association that had survived untainted by the actions of his other persona.

"But come in, come in." Drayton waved Thomas to his inner office. "I take it you wish to confer regarding this matter you've asked me to look into?"

"Yes." Thomas waited until he was settled in the chair before Drayton's desk and Drayton had shut the door and resumed his seat before continuing, "I believe we are currently up to date and as one regarding my own affairs. Unless you have anything urgent to lay before me, I suggest we leave those to one side."

Drayton nodded. "I'm aware of nothing that requires our attention at this point. All the funds are performing as expected, and we've executed your last orders. As usual, they proved prescient and well timed. Your affairs are in a very sound state."

Thomas shared Drayton's smile. "Indeed. So, to the other matter. There have been developments." Smile fading, he went on, "The reason I requested you to look into Richard Percival's affairs is because somewhere in those affairs lies a motive for murder, or so I and others believe. Our understanding is that Richard Percival has some compelling financial need such that he must inherit his late brother's estate in order to meet it. Indeed, there are sound reasons to believe that Percival arranged the murders of his late brother and his brother's wife in order to achieve that end. At present, only Percival's young nephew stands in his way." Thomas met Drayton's increasingly wide eyes. "The boy—Viscount Seddington—is currently under my protection. In light of the seriousness of the situation, I have enlisted the aid of Mr. Barnaby Adair and, through him, Inspector Stokes of Scotland Yard."

Drayton straightened, surprise giving way to interest.

Thomas paused to assemble his words, then went on, "We are now all investigating in our various ways. Adair and Stokes count Montague, of Montague and Sons, who I am sure you know of, as one of their colleagues, and he, too, is now actively involved. What Montague and his people, and I, and through me, you and your staff, need to define is Percival's motive. Why is he so desperate to inherit the estate?" Thomas paused, then allowed, "There could be reasons other than money, and others are investigating that possibility, but such reasons appear much less likely than a need for funds. So." Glancing up, he met Drayton's eyes. "You've already canvassed Percival's standing in the general sense, and I've passed that information on to Montague. He, I believe, will use his contacts to investigate what one might term the establishment side of things—the banks, Percival's man-of-business, the Exchange. We can, I think, reply on Montague to cover those angles and uncover whatever is there to be found."

"But there might not be anything." Drayton, growing progressively more intrigued, was now leaning forward, forearms on his desk. "Percival's need might stem from a different arena."

"Indeed." Thomas exchanged a knowing look with Drayton. "While we've never dabbled in such arenas ourselves, we've often had a need to learn whether others we've considered allying ourselves with have associations in such spheres. In investigating Percival, what I would like you to do is make inquiries in the . . . shall we say more shady side of business? See if you can find any whisper of his name in relation to any less-than-straightforward venture, any questionable investment, any high-risk game. There must be some revealing association somewhere, but it might well date back four, or even more, years. Alternatively, this may be an ongoing, constantly changing, and escalating situation, with him rolling investment debts from one vehicle to another, increasingly desperately, so cast your net wide, and don't discount any connection you might find."

Eyes narrowed in thought, Drayton was nodding. Refocusing on Thomas, he asked, "Do you want me to start now, or wait until you see what Montague turns up?"

"No. Start now. Normally, yes, we would investigate sequentially, moving from the aboveboard to the less-regulated spheres, but, in this case, we don't know how much time we have. If Percival was desperate enough to commit murder four years ago, and has pursued his nephew doggedly ever since, then we can't afford to dally over exposing him—every day he remains free, the boy remains at risk." Gripping his cane, Thomas rose. "I'll inform Montague of the tack we're taking."

Drayton came to his feet. "Yes, of course. We'll get onto the matter right away."

Rounding the desk, Drayton shook Thomas's hand, then opened the door and escorted him through the outer office. Pausing before the outer door, Drayton asked, "Where should I send my reports?"

Thomas met his gaze. "Send them direct to Montague. It'll be best if he coordinates our efforts. I believe his offices are off Chapel Court."

Drayton nodded. "Yes. They are. Well"—he grinned a touch sheepishly—"in the realm of finance, Montague is nearly as revered as you are."

Thomas laughed. "I hadn't thought . . . but I suppose that's true." Drayton opened the door. Thomas stepped out, pausing to add, "I'll tell Montague you've been conscripted to the cause so he'll know to expect to hear from you."

With an exchange of courtesies—a bow on Drayton's part, a nod on Thomas's—they parted.

Thomas made his way slowly back down the stairs. Reaching the pavement outside, he stepped to the curb, hailed a hackney, gave the jarvey the direction, and climbed inside.

Settling on the seat, he used the moments as the conveyance rattled toward Lincoln's Inn to reflect on the sharpening of his senses, an increased engagement with everything about him; it had been a long time since he'd felt that—the drive that came from having a real purpose.

Of being committed to seeing something done and acting to make it so.

He dwelled on the change for several minutes, then turned his mind to his destination.

Like Drayton, Marwell, his solicitor, would be pleased to see him, and would be happy to undertake whatever tasks he required. With Marwell, there were several issues Thomas wanted addressed, and not all concerned Richard Percival. But aside from those other matters—all straightforward enough—he wanted to hear Marwell's assessment of Foley firsthand, after which he intended to explain the situation with Richard Percival as they understood it, much as he had with Drayton, and then invite Marwell to speculate on any legal twists or turns Percival might think to use, either as hurdles in their path or routes to victory.

It would be just as well to have some inkling of any other fronts that might open up in their battle to contain, and then expose, Percival, and reinstate William to his birthright.

It was just short of midday when Barnaby and Stokes arrived at Mr. Foley's offices in Gray's Inn. The morning had gone in convincing a magistrate to grant them an order sufficient to compel Foley to reveal the details about the Percival estate that they needed to confirm; from everything they'd learned of him, there would have been no point calling on Foley without that order in hand.

Foley's chambers occupied a prime position at one corner of one of the inn's buildings. A sober clerk who bore all the hallmarks of being wedded to the neat and precise consented to allow them to enter. Asking them to wait in the foyer just inside the outer door, the clerk retreated with both Stokes's and Adair's cards in hand to inform his master of their wish to consult him.

The clerk tapped on a door leading off a short corridor at the rear of the reception area, then entered. He did not immediately return.

Arching his brows, Barnaby looked around. "He'll be trying to imagine what we're here about."

Stokes snorted. "By all accounts, he's not the sort to entertain the police on a regular basis—you'd think he'd be curious."

Barnaby chuckled. "I think it's more likely he'll view us as a damned nuisance."

The door opened and the clerk reappeared. Frowning down at the cards he still held, he approached, then, looking up, handed both cards back. "Mr. Foley says he can spare you a few minutes. But only a few minutes."

Tucking his card back in his pocket, Stokes smiled one of his more cutting smiles. "We'll see about that."

The clerk threw him an uncertain look but opened the gate in the low wooden railing and waved them through. He then hurried to take his place ahead of them, leading them to his master's presence. Opening Foley's door wide, the clerk stepped inside; standing with his back to the panels, he announced, "The Honorable Barnaby Adair, and Inspector Stokes of Scotland Yard, sir."

Stokes threw the clerk a resigned look as he passed. Following Stokes, Barnaby offered the clerk a grin and forbore from commenting that his performance would have done Barnaby's mother's butler proud.

It was, after all, Foley they had come to tease.

Dressed in severe black, Foley rose from his chair behind a large, black-stained desk. The bow window behind

him was diamond-paned and fractured the sunlight pouring
in from the court beyond. The walls of the room were covered in bookshelves hosting countless legal tomes, but it
was the desk, and the man behind it, that dominated the
quietly comfortable room.

Despite the glare behind him, Foley's desk was sufficiently far into the room for his features to be readily dis-
cerned. From beneath thick, but slightly straggly, white
brows, dark eyes regarded them with no hint of welcome.
Foley's cheeks were sunken, his lips thin. After considering
them for a silent second, he waved to two chairs angled before the massive desk. "Gentlemen, please be seated."

Foley didn't offer to shake anyone's hand, but he nodded
to each of them, a reserved and carefully polite inclination
of the head for Barnaby, and a somewhat brisker nod to
Stokes.

They sat, and Foley settled once more in his chair. Leaning his forearms on the desk, he clasped his hands and
looked first at Stokes, then at Barnaby. "I understand you
wish to speak with me, gentlemen—might I inquire about
what?"

Foley's tone was distant, not arrogantly so, but in keeping with his image of rigid correctness.

Unperturbed, Stokes replied, "We're here to ask for information on the Percival estate." When Foley opened his
mouth, Stokes held up a hand, staying the obvious protest.
Reaching into the inside pocket of his coat, Stokes continued, "Understanding, as we do, the constraints of client
privilege, we have obtained a magistrate's order covering
the issues about which we need to interview you." Drawing
out the order, Stokes unfolded the sheet, glanced at it, then
handed it across the desk.

The first sign of a frown tangling his white brows, Foley

accepted the document. Groping for, then raising, a pair of pince-nez, he perched them on the tip of his patrician nose and focused on the formal order.

Foley read the order line by line. By the time he reached the end, his features had set in a patently disapproving cast. Setting the order down, he studied it for several seconds, then raised his gaze to Stokes. "Very well, Inspector. You may ask your questions." Foley lifted his head a fraction, in subtle defiance. "However, please understand that I will not be volunteering anything beyond the issues detailed in the order, nor will I indulge in any speculation that in any way concerns the Percival family or the Seddington estate."

Sound, but rigidly conservative. Barnaby recalled Thomas's description of Foley's reputation; everything Barnaby had thus far seen, from the office, to the clerk, to the man's private office and the man himself, confirmed that assessment.

Stokes didn't immediately respond to Foley's declaration but instead studied the man with a somewhat piercing and steady gray gaze. Then he slowly arched a brow. "I understand the heir to the estate, William Percival, Viscount Seddington, is currently missing, having disappeared on the evening of his parents' funeral."

Stokes now had Foley's complete and unwavering attention; the man's face gave little away, but the tension in his hands, his frame, suggested he was hanging on Stokes's every word.

"Our current investigation," Stokes smoothly continued, his gaze fixed on Foley's face, "concerns the matters leading up to the boy's disappearance, and what forces, if any, might be standing in the path of his return."

Foley frowned, a genuine expression. He shook his head. "I don't understand." His eyes locked again on Stokes's face. "Are you saying that William is alive and that he might return, but"—Foley's expression grew openly confused—"there are those who might not wish him to?"

Stokes dipped his head in response.

Foley drew himself up. "I assure you, Inspector"—his gaze switched briefly to Barnaby—"and you, too, Mr. Adair, that everyone in this firm, as well as the Percival family, would be thrilled to have William returned to us. More, that we would do everything in our collective power to effect such a happening."

Stokes held Foley's gaze, no longer so distant and remote, then, in acceptance, inclined his head. "In that case, Mr. Foley, as the police are now working to resolve William Percival's disappearance, I would respectfully suggest that it would be in yours and the Percival family's interest to assist us in whatever way you can."

Foley was clearly caught on the horns of a dilemma—should he bend his rigid stance against revealing anything about his clients and perhaps assist in the return of the young heir, or hold to his line and . . .

"If I might make an observation?" Barnaby said.

Foley looked at him. "Yes?"

"When William returns, even though he's a minor, *he* will be your principal client with regard to the Percival family's holdings and the Seddington estate."

That was a simple statement of fact, but as William had been a small child when Foley had last seen him, it wasn't a fact Foley had truly considered. . . . He did now. After several moments, his features eased. Slowly, he nodded, then he looked at Barnaby and inclined his head. "Thank you, Mr. Adair. That is, indeed, a pertinent point."

Returning his gaze to Stokes, Foley reclasped his hands. "So, Inspector, let me hear your questions, and I'll answer as best I can without infringing on my duty of discretion toward my other clients. In this matter, I am still constrained, as I act for all the Percivals, not just the principal line and the estate."

"That shouldn't be an issue at this point—our questions today concern William Percival and the Seddington estate." Stokes consulted the notebook he'd settled on his knee. "The first matter we wish to confirm is that Richard Percival was named William's principal guardian, with the late viscount's uncle, Marmaduke Percival, as co-guardian."

Foley nodded. "Yes, that's correct." He glanced at Barnaby. "But that's a matter of public record."

"Indeed," Stokes continued, "but we wondered if you could explain why a *principal* guardian and a co-guardian were appointed."

Foley clearly debated, then offered, "The late viscount, Robert Percival, was well aware of the foibles of certain members of his family, and so he, very wisely in my view, insisted on two guardians."

"So the appointment of two guardians," Barnaby said, "came about because Robert Percival didn't trust one or the other, at least not entirely."

His gaze on Barnaby's face, Foley's lips slowly compressed, then he shook his head. "I cannot comment on anything specific regarding either Richard Percival or Marmaduke Percival. Both are private clients of mine."

Barnaby nodded in acceptance. He glanced at Stokes.

"Our second question," Stokes said, "relates to the estate itself. We are in the process of confirming that the estate is intact—our contacts have led us to believe it is. Can you add anything to that confirmation?"

Foley hesitated, then, clearly choosing his words carefully, said, "To my knowledge, the estate remains intact in all ways. It has been preserved as it was at the time of Robert Percival's death. And while I am unable to disclose any specifics as to the people involved, the wisdom of Robert Percival in appointing co-guardians, where the approval of both must be gained for any change to the estate, has proved critical in protecting the estate from depredation."

Barnaby and Stokes shared a glance; that was more than they'd hoped to learn.

"Thank you," Stokes said. "That brings me to our final question." He looked up and met Foley's gaze. "Is the estate entailed?"

Foley nodded. "Yes, sadly, it is—virtually in its entirety."

"So," Barnaby confirmed, "if William were to die, the estate, virtually in its entirety, would pass to William's next of kin."

A faint expression of distaste on his face, Foley nodded. "Indeed—just so."

Barnaby and Stokes shared another loaded glance, then both rose and thanked Foley. He'd answered all the questions they had for him to that point, and, despite the constraints under which he'd labored, he'd given them more than they'd hoped.

Barnaby could barely wait to get outside and into the sunshine bathing the court to confer with Stokes, thereby fixing all they'd heard, and so learned, in their minds. They paused under a tree. "Let's see if we both received the same messages."

Stokes halted beside him and lifted his face to the breeze. "Cautious beggar—it was like reading in code."

Barnaby grinned. "The legal profession doesn't approve of simple and straightforward. So." He settled his greatcoat across his shoulders. "First, we now know that Robert Percival distrusted the person who would normally have been appointed William's sole guardian—namely Robert's brother and William's immediate next of kin, Richard Percival."

Stokes nodded. "More, we now know that Foley, sound and conservative as he is and well acquainted with the family, considers the co-guardianship a wise appointment, and that attempts to draw on the estate have proved that to be true."

"Which tells us that Richard Percival has indeed attempted to draw on the estate, but because of the co-guardianship—which Foley took care to tell us requires both guardians to agree to any such action—Richard has been blocked from doing so."

"By his uncle, Marmaduke Percival." Stokes's expression hardened. "It all adds up nicely."

"Indeed. And to cap it all off," Barnaby said, "Foley just told us that on William's death, Richard Percival will inherit the entire estate. So that, all along, has been his aim, exactly as Rose suspected."

Stokes stood in the dappled shade under the tree and thought through the case. He stirred, then glanced at Barnaby. "The one thing we're still missing is proof of his motive—the reason why Richard Percival needs to inherit and gain access to the estate."

Barnaby grimaced. "True. Sadly we can't just say he wants to be wealthy."

Stokes snorted. "Right. So I'm heading back to see if my men watching his house have anything to report."

"And I," Barnaby said, "rather think I'll do a circuit of the clubs and see if I can pick up any whispers concerning Richard Percival and his compelling need for cash."

Side by side, they ambled out of the inn's court, then hailed two hackneys. With genial waves, they went their separate ways.

Thomas had to exercise a certain degree of care in limping over the lush lawns in Kew Gardens; if he didn't pay attention, the tip of his cane would sink into the thick mat of grass and the softer earth beneath, throwing him awkwardly off-balance.

Despite Adair's assurances regarding the quality of his wife's "guards," Thomas had been unable to quiet his protective instincts, so he'd invited himself along on Penelope and Rose's planned excursion. Somewhat to his relief, Penelope had rethought her original notion of simply bowling around the city's streets, stopping wherever the children's fancies dictated, in favor of a more formal day's outing in the fresh air at Kew.

As he limped along in the ladies' wake, admiring the view, he had to approve of the choice. It was highly unlikely that Richard Percival or any of his minions would happen upon them amid the garden beds, lawns, and winding paths, not even when they dallied in the new conservatory, admiring the exhibits housed within in company with dozens of other fashionable females and their children.

Not only was the location safe enough, but Conner, Penelope's groom, ambled ahead of the ladies, and James, the footman, hovered close, at Penelope's elbow, and Phelps, the coachman, was following behind Thomas, bringing up the rear.

Thomas paused in the shade of a tree. Ahead, the ladies availed themselves of an empty bench and sat, their parasols deployed to shade their delicate features. The children—not just Homer and Pippin but also Penelope and Barnaby's young son, Oliver, a bouncing toddler still not quite steady on his chubby legs—settled in a group on the grass before the bench, gathering around Oliver's nurse, Hettie.

As Thomas watched, Hettie drew a set of knucklebones from the pocket of her pinafore, and Homer and Pippin fell on them. Then the pair realized that Oliver wanted to play, too, and soon a rambunctious game was underway, with much overacting and antics to amuse the baby.

Hands folded over the head of his cane, Thomas stood and watched, and realized he was grinning.

Phelps came up and settled beside him. The coachman nodded to the group. "Sounds like they're having fun."

"Yes, they are." Thomas realized he hadn't heard the children laugh quite so freely before. Even on the decks of the *Andover* they'd exhibited a certain sense of awareness, of caution with respect to those around them. Here, surrounded by Penelope's guards, with Hettie close at hand, Rose and Penelope nearby, and no one else but other mothers and children within sight, the pair had finally relaxed enough to laugh unshadowed by any lingering care . . .

Thomas decided he could forgive Penelope the look—one filled with far too much understanding—that she'd slanted his way when, back at the hotel, he'd declared that he would be joining the party.

After a while, when the lure of knucklebones waned, the party rose and ambled on. Growing tired of the baby and the company of females, Homer dropped back to walk beside Thomas.

"I was wondering," Homer said, "how they keep the conservatory so warm." He looked up at Thomas. "I didn't see any fireplaces."

Thomas smiled down at him. "Steam. I read somewhere that there's a patented system of metal coils carrying steam that heats the place."

Homer's lips formed an O. Several steps later, he said, "It seemed a very *fine* building, if you know what I mean."

Thomas grinned. "You have a good eye. It was designed by Nash—architect to kings. It was one of a pair of pavilions Nash designed for Buckingham House, but the king sent one to these gardens, probably in honor of his father, who used to love walking here. And another famous architect, Wyatville, worked on changing what was originally designed as a pavilion into the conservatory."

Several steps later, Homer glanced up at him. "Where do you learn things like that? About the steam and the buildings?"

"Mostly from the news sheets. I have a good memory."

Homer looked ahead; they were nearing the gates and the wide drive along which the carriage waited. "I've a good memory, too. Perhaps I should start reading the news sheets?"

Thomas met Homer's up-slanted glance, hesitated, then said, "If you like, after I've finished with mine every morning, you can have them."

Homer nodded. "I'd like that." Taking hold of Thomas's arm, he walked with him to the carriage.

They bowled back into London at a brisk pace. Seated alongside Penelope, with Thomas opposite and Homer and Pippin beside him, Rose felt more content, more relaxed, than she had in years.

An entire afternoon and she hadn't had to worry. More, the need to feel concerned, the anxiety she'd carried constantly for the past four years, had, over the hours they'd spent in the gardens, lifted. Eased.

That weight would return now they were reentering Mayfair's streets, where turning any corner might bring them face-to-face with Richard Percival or one of his friends, or someone who knew them well enough to recognize them and inform Richard that they were there, but for the past hours . . . she had breathed freely, easily. For the last hours, she had been without care.

And although it had been Penelope's suggestion, and her guards who had hovered close, the thanks for Rose's hours of simple pleasure primarily lay at Thomas's door. The fact that he'd accompanied them, that he had been there and she trusted him—more than anyone else—to keep her and the children safe, had been the necessary final criterion that had allowed her to let go and simply enjoy the flowers, the sights and scents, and give herself over to the distraction.

Looking at him across the carriage, she waited until she caught his eye, then smiled—in gratitude, in acknowledgment.

From the corner of her eye, Penelope glimpsed Rose's smile; glancing swiftly across, she saw Thomas smile in response and pretended not to notice, letting her gaze drift unconcernedly on while inside she positively gloated.

They were so . . . connected. Connected herself to Barnaby, she recognized the signs; those shared smiles were so revealing. Almost as revealing as Thomas's insistence on joining them today, when any sane gentleman would rather have done anything but.

Careful to keep her delight concealed—she wasn't, she told herself, a matchmaker per se, but she came from a long line of matrons whose primary purpose in life had been arranging marriages, so her interest really wasn't surprising—when the carriage halted outside the hotel, she declined Rose's invitation to come in for afternoon tea. "I need to get on."

She accepted Rose's, Homer's, Pippin's, and lastly Thomas's thanks with due graciousness, then, once she'd seen the party pass safely into the hotel, she sat back and frowned.

"Ma'am?" Phelps called down through the ceiling trap. "Where to?"

Penelope considered Oliver, fast asleep in Hettie's arms, then looked up and quietly called, "St. Ives House, Phelps. And then you and Conner can drive Hettie and Oliver home, and James can wait and walk me home later."

Phelps hesitated but then said, "Aye, ma'am," and lowered the trap.

Penelope leaned back, anticipation rising; St. Ives House was only around the block, and there, with any luck, she would find not just afternoon tea but information as well.

On being admitted to St. Ives House by the inestimable Webster and inquiring as to the possibility of partaking of afternoon tea in the company of his mistress, Penelope wasn't surprised to be directed to the back parlor.

There, she discovered a relaxed female gathering. As she had hoped, Honoria, Duchess of St. Ives, was playing host to two of her husband's cousins' wives, Patience, the wife of Vane Cynster, and Alathea, who was married to Gabriel Cynster. With all their children at either school or university, the three fashionable matrons often spent their days together. Now that the last of the Cynster girls had married, with none of the next generation as yet old enough for the marriage mart, there was little incentive to keep up with the social round; although needing to remain in town to support their husbands in their political and business activities, to act as their hostesses and partners at the dinners, soirees, and the occasional formal parties, daytime life for the three ladies was no longer the hectic progression of events it once had been.

As Penelope marched in, three heads turned her way.

Recognizing a diversion when they saw one, all three matrons smiled delightedly.

"Welcome, Penelope." Honoria held out her hand.

Penelope took it, squeezing the duchess's fingers as she

bent to kiss her proffered cheek. "Thank you." Straightening, she moved to greet the others in the same way. "I had hoped to find at least you three here."

"Aha!" Patience grinned as she released Penelope. "You *do* have a query for us, something we can help with."

Penelope nodded and settled on the chaise beside Alathea. "As I'm sure you know, all the elders have gone off to the country. Even my mama has retreated to Calverton Chase to play with Luc and Amelia's children, and Amanda and Martin and their younger ones are there, too—Mama is determined to enjoy them while they're young, or so she says. So with no one of greater experience to consult, I'm here to appeal to you." Pulling off her gloves, she surveyed the offerings displayed on the tiered cake plate that sat on the low table before the chaise.

Alathea chuckled. "We'll try to live up to the elders' standards, but I'm not sure any of us can as yet claim such all-encompassing knowledge."

Leaning forward to pour Penelope a cup of tea, Honoria snorted. "In truth, I doubt any of us will ever be a match for Therese Osbaldestone—or Helena." Lifting the cup and handing it to Penelope, Honoria paused, then amended with a smile, "Except, perhaps, for *you,* Penelope, dear."

Laughing at Penelope's arching brows and doubting expression, Honoria sat back. "But ask, and we'll do our best to stand in for those not presently available."

Penelope nodded, sipped her tea, then lowered the cup. "The Percival family. Viscounts Seddington, of Seddington Grange, in Lincolnshire. Robert, the late Viscount Seddington, died in a boating accident four years ago, and his son and heir vanished on the night after the funeral."

"Ooh, yes. I remember that." Patience looked intrigued. "Quite a to-do it caused—such a gothic tale—but as I recall, it happened in summer, so by the time the ton reconvened in September, it was old news."

Penelope nodded. "What I need to know is everything you can tell me about the late viscount's younger brother, Richard Percival."

"Hmm." The sound came from Alathea, but all three matrons frowned in thought.

Honoria spoke first. "I have met him socially, but only briefly. In age, he falls between us and you—mid-thirties . . ." Honoria focused on Penelope. "Actually, he must be around the same age as Barnaby. I take it Barnaby doesn't know him?"

Penelope made a mental note to specifically ask, but . . . "I don't think they move in the same circles."

Patience humphed. "That rings true. Richard Percival is the sort all sensible mamas warn their daughters not to look at—in case they lose their hearts."

"Indeed." Alathea shifted on the chaise to face Penelope. "I vaguely remember Robert Percival—he was older than we are, but, as I recall, he was a handsome man. His younger brother, however, is a *dangerously* handsome man."

Penelope straightened. "Dangerous in what way?"

Honoria waved. "Black hair, dark blue eyes—a touch darker than even Richard's or Alasdair's—a face like a fallen angel, all long, lean planes and squared chin, with a long, lean, rider's body to match." Honoria caught Penelope's eyes. "He dances like a dream, has manners polished to the extreme, is always elegantly, but faintly negligently, dressed, and can charm the birds from the trees. *That* sort of dangerous."

"And," Patience pointed out, "when it comes to 'that sort of dangerous,' we are the reigning experts."

All four laughed, but, after taking another sip of her tea,

Penelope returned to the meat of her inquiry. "I need to know . . . for want of a better way to phrase it . . . if he has a darker side."

Alathea narrowed her eyes. "Whether he could be a villain?"

Penelope nodded. "I don't want to tell you why we think he might be, because I want your untainted views."

All three matrons fell silent, clearly consulting their various memories of Richard Percival. Penelope nibbled at a sweet cake and patiently waited.

Eventually, Honoria drew in a breath, exchanged a glance with Patience, then Alathea, then said, "I haven't any idea why you think he might be involved in something . . . dishonorable, but, for my money, no. He isn't that sort." Honoria met Penelope's eyes. "Yes, he's dangerous, but in the same way that Devil was—or any of the others."

Alathea was nodding. "In the same way Chillingworth was, and, if it comes to it, Luc, and even Martin."

"I agree." Patience sat forward. "And I just remembered a pertinent point. One summer several years ago, before the death of Robert Percival, Vane and I visited with the Dearnes—Christian and Letitia Allardyce—at their house in Lincolnshire. Robert Percival and his wife . . ." Patience narrowed her eyes. "Corinne, I think her name was, were guests, too. It was a weeklong house party, and after a few days, Richard Percival arrived—he had a message from London for Robert. After Richard delivered the message, Letitia prevailed upon him to stay for a few days. Of course, he spent most of that time with the gentlemen, but—and this is my point—I had plenty of opportunity to observe Richard with our men. And you know what they're like—they aren't much good at concealing their feelings toward other men, at least not from us."

Penelope was riveted. "So how did the other men treat Richard?"

"As one of them." Patience held her gaze. "In age, Robert and Richard were something like ten years apart, but they were clearly close, truly close. And as for the others—Christian, Vane, and all the other men there—they welcomed and included Richard without reservation." Patience paused, then added, "Now that you've posed the question of whether Richard Percival could be a villain, looking back, I would cite all that I saw, all that I witnessed of him then, as speaking most emphatically against such a notion."

Honoria regarded Patience for a moment, then caught Penelope's eye. "Our men might not be terribly intuitive, but I really cannot see them welcoming any man who has what you term a 'darker side' into their circles."

"Not even the propensity for a 'darker side,'" Alathea confirmed.

Penelope frowned. Slowly, she set down her empty cup, then she pulled a face. "Well, that does rather put a wrinkle in my thesis."

The others laughed.

"Now that we've helped you with your problem as far as we're able, don't you have anything else to report? No pending scandals?" Patience's wave included the others. "We're in dire need of divertissement here."

Penelope raised her brows. "Well, I can report that I have met the elusive Mr. Thomas Glendower."

"The secretive philanthropist?" Alathea asked. When Penelope nodded, Alathea said, "Great heavens! Roscoe, and Gabriel, and Gerrard, and any number of others will be lining up for an introduction. Where did you meet him? Is he in town?"

Penelope considered before admitting, "Yes, he is in

London at present." *Just around the corner, as it happens.* "But he's not going about socially." She tipped her head. "I'll make a point of telling you if that changes, but somehow I doubt it will—the social arena holds no lure for him. He truly is a recluse."

Rising, she picked up her gloves and reticule. "Thank you for your insights." She faintly frowned. "I'm not sure if they will prove useful, but knowledge is always valuable."

The others didn't rise but farewelled her from where they sat.

As, with a last wave, Penelope headed for the door, Honoria called, "And don't forget—if Mr. Glendower changes his mind and consents to indulge us with his presence, I'll host a dinner for him here, and it can be as private as he wishes."

From the doorway, Penelope called back, "I'll tell him."

Then she escaped.

Chapter

12

Two mornings later, Montague sat at his desk and surveyed the accumulated results of their investigations into Richard Percival's finances.

From her chair on the opposite side of the desk, Violet studied his expression, drank in the solid focus that was so quintessentially him. When he remained silent, a frown growing in his eyes if not on his face, she glanced at the documents spread over the desk. "Well? What have we found?"

"Nothing," Montague all but growled. "Everything we've thus far uncovered looks to be aboveboard." Sitting back, he waved at the various papers. "Drayton—Glendower's agent—has sent all the information he's collected to date, and Marwell, Glendower's solicitor, has sent word, too—in his case clarifying and expanding on the details Foley gave Stokes and Adair, which is undeniably helpful. In cases like this, the legal aspects can be the trickiest. However"—Montague drew breath and went on—"to summarize, what we've so far uncovered paints Richard Percival as a gentle-man who is, at least currently, living much more quietly than anyone would expect a man of his social ilk to do." Montague flicked a glance at Violet. "And that fits with what the men Stokes has watching Percival have reported. He doesn't go out much at all, and his household is small, and he lives quietly."

Violet nodded. Leaning forward, she scanned the papers. "But is there nothing in all this that's at all unusual?"

Frowning, Montague reached for the pair of pince-nez hanging on a ribbon around his neck. "There's one oddity, but what it might mean I don't know." Perching the pince-nez on his nose, he selected a set of papers; fanning them out, he scanned, then pointed. "Here. And here. And here again. Not huge sums, but out they go, to whom we don't know. We've checked, and the bank has confirmed that the payments are made via money orders submitted every month. They're too regular not to be going to the same sup-plier, but, again, the bank can't say, as the orders are for cash, and the varying sums suggest the payments aren't to do with any debt per se, but . . . they continue throughout the period we've looked at, going back at least four years." Sitting back again, he said, "Taken all together, they amount to a small fortune, and have been a steady drain on Percival's wealth over the last four years at least."

Setting those sheets aside, Montague picked up another set. "Against that, however, Percival has a sound investment portfolio, rather conservative, if anything, but it provides him with a solid income, and as far as Gibbons, Foster, and I have been able to see, he is living within his means. He's definitely not outrunning the constable."

"But where is all that money—the small fortune—going?"

Lips tight, Montague nodded. "That, indeed, is the question."

After frowning at the documents herself, Violet wondered aloud, "Could it be gambling?"

Montague opened his mouth to refute the suggestion, but then hesitated. After a moment of juggling possibilities, he replied in much the same wondering tone, "I'd discounted that because of him not going out much, but . . . once a week or so might account for what we're seeing." He blinked and looked at the evidence they'd assembled. "And that might explain the widely varying size of the payments—if he gambles on credit extended from the house, and then repays the next day or under some such arrangement . . ."

He looked up and met Violet's eyes. "It's a possibility, and one we can easily follow up."

He started clearing his desk. Violet rose and helped him stack the papers neatly to one side.

Leaving her to complete the task, Montague drew out a fresh sheet of paper, set it on his blotter, and reached for his pen. "And I know just who to ask for that sort of information."

Thomas walked into Montague's office late that afternoon.

The previous day he'd accompanied Rose, Penelope, and the children, along with Penelope's guards, on a daylong excursion that had taken in the sights of Fleet Street, St. Paul's Cathedral, and the Tower, then the carriage had rattled across the bridge and followed the river to Greenwich. They'd spent the afternoon in the park there; there had been plenty to keep Homer and Pippin amused. At one point, Thomas had found himself observing the unexpected sight of Conner and James teaching Homer and Pippin various ways to escape the clutches of any villain who sought to seize them.

Once she'd mastered the knack, Pippin had insisted on demonstrating to Thomas. Again and again. She'd demanded that he hold her trapped against him, his arm locked across her thin shoulders, then she would go boneless and fall, sliding out of his hold. Her last and, as ever, successful attempt had forced Thomas off-balance and he'd landed on the grass in an ungainly heap—causing Rose to rush over, concern flaring in her eyes and suffusing her face.

He'd been startled, but he'd drunk in the sight—worth any embarrassment—then he'd soothed and reassured, and done his best to calm everyone and assure them that he was perfectly all right.

Today, when, after luncheon, Penelope had called to take the others to Kensington Gardens, and then shopping along Regent Street before heading on to the British Museum, where, apparently, she was well known and had the entree into areas not generally open to the public, Thomas had decided that he didn't need to go. He'd held firm in the face of Penelope's persuasion; through her connections at the museum, she'd learned that he was one of that institution's largest sponsors and had wanted to introduce him to the directors . . . he'd hidden his instinctive shudder and politely, but firmly, declined.

When she'd humphed and all but glared at him, he'd invented a visit to Montague's office on the pretext of collating financial information to account for his time.

Penelope had had to accept that and, however reluctantly, leave him in peace.

So when he walked through the door to Montague's office, he had no specific investigative direction in mind. He was, however, curious, in a purely professional sense.

Handing the clerk, a sober and experienced individual, his card, he asked to speak with Montague. The clerk, who had already taken in his injuries, merely glanced at the card for confirmation, then, with a bow and a "One moment, Mr. Glendower," hurried as fast as dignity would allow to the door Thomas assumed led to Montague's private office.

The clerk returned almost immediately, with Montague on his heels.

"Glendower." Montague advanced across the office. "It's a pleasure to see you, sir."

It was Thomas's place to extend his hand, which he smoothly did.

Montague gripped and shook, then, releasing him, turned to wave expansively. "But come into my office and we can confer in comfort."

"Thank you." Thomas didn't hurry as he crossed the outer office—there were times when his infirmity proved a boon; he used the moments to glance about and observe, to drink in the quiet, steady thrum of financial industry.

It was a milieu he found soothing, an ambiance more in keeping with his true talents and skills.

They reached the inner office, and Montague waved Thomas to an armchair before the desk. Thomas limped to it; sinking into the comfort, he caught Montague's eye and smiled. "Your office"—he tipped his head to the activity beyond the door Montague had left open—"appears as prosperous as I'd imagined."

Montague smiled, clearly taking the comment for the compliment Thomas had intended. "Indeed. We're at full stretch, but we all like to be kept busy."

"It's good of you to find time for this investigation, then."

Montague waved that aside. "No, no—I find that these challenges keep one on one's toes, and, even more, keep one abreast of how matters might go wrong." He met Thomas's gaze. "I would far rather learn about how people get themselves into financial difficulties without it being one of my clients involved."

Thomas chuckled. "I see your point." He glanced at the stack of papers Montague was lifting from one side of his large desk. "Is that our accumulated wisdom to date?"

"On Richard Percival? It is, indeed." Setting the pile on his blotter, Montague started separating sheets. "And I'm glad you called, because I would greatly value your assessment of what we have. Because, in my view, it amounts to precious little, and that's even combining what we've found with what Drayton and Marwell have contributed."

After handing over a sheaf of what, accepting it, Thomas saw were summaries, Montague clasped his hands. "There's only one set of expenses that's even mildly unusual, but perhaps if you look over those, you might see something that has thus far escaped us."

Thomas doubted it, but he looked. He swiftly identified the expenses Montague had referred to; after confirming that that was the case, he continued scanning what amounted to a consolidated report on the movement of funds into and out of Richard Percival's accounts.

After checking through the summaries twice, Thomas sighed, tossed the pages onto Montague's desk, then sat back and met Montague's gaze. "Other than those expenses, there's nothing there. But those odd payments add up to a tidy sum, yet the variation in them makes no sense to me. When we first pick them up four or so years ago, they're high, and stay high for several months, but then they dwindle, almost to nothing at one point, then increase again, then decrease again."

Reaching for the summaries, Montague nodded. "And so

on, increasing and decreasing, then increasing again, up to last month's payment, which was on the higher side." He grimaced. "I twisted the figures every which way—I looked to see if there's any unit cost buried in them, and checked with others to see if the pattern rings any bells, even unexpected ones, but no. Those payments match no pattern that I or my colleagues have ever seen."

"Nor I," Thomas murmured.

"*Except*"—Montague placed the summaries back on the stack—"as Violet reminded me this morning, if Percival is gambling on tick regularly, and has some arrangement with some club, den, or hell to pay off his slate on a monthly basis . . . that might account for the odd pattern of amounts."

Thomas raised his brows. "I have to admit that's one vice that never called to me—losing money was never my style."

Montague snorted. "Nor mine. However, I do have contacts in that arena, and—" The sound of the door to the outer office opening had him pausing, then leaning forward to look out of his open office door. His expression lightening, he continued, "As I was saying, I sent word to my principal contact this morning, and, unless I miss my guess, the answer has just arrived."

Pushing back from the desk, Montague stood.

Hearing a pleasant male voice greeting the clerk, then footsteps approaching, Thomas gripped his cane and the desk and got to his feet.

A man whom Thomas judged to be his late thirties strolled through the door. He was tall, dark-haired, well turned out, and neatly, if a trifle soberly, dressed. Not a gentleman, Thomas's instincts informed him, but the man's easy confidence, open expression, and twinkling smile suggested he was well accustomed to dealing with the breed, and entirely at ease among his social betters.

"Montague." The man held out his hand.

Montague grasped it with every evidence of friendship. "Jordan. Thank you for coming." Montague gestured to Thomas. "Allow me to introduce Mr. Thomas Glendower. He's involved in this latest investigation."

Having noted Thomas's injuries with a single general glance, the man nodded easily and extended his hand. "Jordan Draper, Mr. Glendower." As he shook Thomas's hand, Jordan glanced at Montague. "Any friend of Montague's, and we're pleased to help."

As they all sat, Jordan taking the empty chair on the same side of the desk as the armchair Thomas occupied, Montague continued, "Jordan is employed by Neville Roscoe."

Thomas blinked, then inclined his head. "I know the name."

"Just to confirm," Jordan said, "as we are all sitting here together, I take it that I can speak freely before Mr. Glendower?"

Montague nodded. "Indeed. It was Mr. Glendower who brought this investigation to us."

"Oh."

When nothing more came, Thomas glanced at Jordan to find the younger man's gaze on him, his eyes rounding.

Jordan waved. "Sorry—I just registered the name. You're *that* Mr. Glendower, the one the boss has always wanted to meet." Jordan focused on Thomas. "I say, as you are in town, you will meet him, won't you? He—and Miranda, too, she's his wife—will never let me live it down if I don't manage to twist your arm."

Confused, Thomas looked at Montague.

Who was trying unsuccessfully to hide a grin. "Your . . . ah, generosity precedes you."

"Oh, of course," Jordan rattled on. "You wouldn't know,

but aside from being London's gambling king—and he definitely is that, as I'm the one who manages his books—Roscoe is also one of the founding members of the Philanthropy Guild. He and like-minded others have been supporting various charity projects up and down the country for the last . . . well, fifteen years." Meeting Thomas's eyes, Jordan added, "He—and the rest of the guild, too—would be thrilled to meet you."

Thomas hesitated, then said, "Perhaps, after this present matter is concluded, if I'm still in town, we might arrange a meeting." He wasn't at all sure Thomas Glendower would still be around afterward, but that seemed a safe enough commitment, and the notion of a gambling-czar-cum-philanthropist was intriguing.

"Excellent!" Jordan beamed, then looked at Montague. "You realize, of course, that this means you can ask for damned near anything and the boss will oblige?"

Montague smiled. "I'll bear that in mind, but to return to our present inquiry, can you shed any light on any gambling debts or line of credit maintained by one Richard Percival?"

"With no intention of being coy, the answer to that is yes, and no." Sitting back, Jordan steepled his fingers, and a certain steeliness infused his expression. "We do know of Richard Percival—he's a regular enough customer, but he's never been in any way difficult. Yes, he loses, just like anyone, but, notably, he's quite a creditable hand at most card games and, overall, rarely loses much. I've asked around and got nary a whisper that he ever plays deep—that's not his style. In our sphere, he's what we call a dabbler, one who gambles purely for the social interaction rather than from any real addiction, not even from any true desire to win."

"This isn't sounding hopeful," Montague said.

Jordan inclined his head. "And it only gets worse, at least if you were imagining Percival has some gambling-related problem. I mentioned your query to the boss, of course, and he, too, was puzzled. He said that although we know Percival as a sound man, given it was you who was asking, I should look deeper. He told me to ask Symonds." Jordan broke off to explain to both Montague and Thomas, "He's the one who took over Gallagher's patch when the old man passed on."

Thomas arched a brow. "And Gallagher was?"

"The man to go to to learn anything about the seedier side of life in the capital—its underworld, if you like. Gallagher wasn't a player himself—his business was information." Jordan paused, then went on, "So I went to Symonds and asked."

"And?" Montague prompted.

"Nothing immediately known, but, as it was me asking, and so the boss, Symonds was thorough and put the word around, and even asked his friends, the moneylenders. He sent what he'd learned in a note an hour ago. Seems no one holds any vowels of Richard Percival's, but he has occasionally been gambling in some of the lower hells, so to speak, and that at a level deeper than we've known him to play at in any of the boss's venues. However, again, no one knows of him being in debt to anyone. More, one hell reported that he'd won a cool fifteen thousand in a single sitting a few weeks ago."

Jordan looked at Montague. "So if you're trying to identify where Percival got some sudden influx of cash, that's the source. But if you're looking for some ongoing debt, then the tables are the wrong place to look."

Montague sighed. "Thank you. At least we now know we're looking in the wrong direction."

With a what-would-you gesture, Jordan rose, and Thomas and Montague got to their feet.

With handshakes and expressions of goodwill all around—and a reminder to Thomas of his agreement to meet with the Philanthropy Guild at some future date—Jordan departed.

Both Thomas and Montague remained standing. The instant the outer door shut behind the younger man, Thomas looked at Montague. "Where did the fifteen thousand go?"

Montague met his eyes. "There's no hint of it going into any of his accounts."

Thomas shifted his grip on his cane. "Fifteen thousand isn't the sort of sum you put under any mattress."

Montague humphed and tapped the stack of papers detailing Percival's finances. "I wonder if that fifteen thousand, the disappearance of same, might be in any way linked to the irregular but constant drain on his coffers."

"He's paying for something." Frowning, Thomas added, "But what?"

"Indeed." Montague moved back to his chair. "I'll keep looking. Sometimes perseverance is the only way."

Thomas nodded absentmindedly, then remembered. "Incidentally, Penelope has summoned us to dine this evening in Albemarle Street. Apparently your wife will already have received a note."

Brows rising in resignation, Montague met Thomas's eyes and nodded. "I'll see you then."

"Indubitably." With a nod and a salute, Thomas headed for the door.

But once he gained the street, he paused, thinking over all he'd just learned, then, determination firming, he turned toward Threadneedle Street. With Drayton's office so close, the chance to mount one last-ditch effort to identify the debt it appeared Richard Percival must, in some fashion, be servicing was too good to pass up.

It was early evening when Percival went upstairs to change. Walking into his bedroom, he heard feet pattering up the stairs behind him, and left the door open.

A second later, his gentleman's gentleman, Wilkes, came rushing through, whirled in something approaching a frenzy, and shut the door.

Before, frowning, Percival could ask what the devil the man was about, Wilkes turned a face alight with excitement his way. "Sir! I saw them! Here! *In town*."

Percival blinked. "What?"

"I saw them, large as life, in Conduit Street. I'd taken your brown jacket to be mended and was walking back, and there they were, getting into a carriage with some others."

For a moment, he couldn't breathe. *Here?* He hardly dared hope. Still stunned, and more than a little disbelieving, he studied Wilkes. "Are you sure?" Even as he asked, he remembered that Wilkes would know.

The euphoric certainty lighting Wilkes's face didn't dim as he nodded emphatically. "I had a clear view, sir. It was her and the boy—I'm absolutely certain."

Wilkes was all but bouncing on his toes in his eagerness.

Percival could empathize; he—they—had been waiting for so long . . . gradually, Wilkes's excitement reached him. An even stronger euphoria bloomed and surged through him, and he smiled. "Well, well—who would have thought dear Rosalind would be so . . . bold. London, here, right under the family's noses."

And just in time. The reason he needed William dead was daily growing ever more pressing, but, it seemed, salvation was at hand.

"Indeed, sir—but there's *more*!" Wilkes could barely get the words out. "I think I know where they're staying."

Percival refocused on Wilkes's face. "Indeed?" His smile grew intent. "Do tell."

They started sharing all they'd learned of Richard Percival the instant they gathered in the drawing room in Albemarle Street. By the time they sat down to dine, all their latest findings had been aired but, by common consent, not yet discussed; as the courses came and went, it wasn't purely the food they were digesting.

A comment from one of them, most often in the vein of thinking out aloud, or of asking for clarification on some point, would set their collective minds whirling again; Rose found it strange as well as reassuring, having such a company of supporters all plotting and scheming and actively seeking for ways to bring Richard Percival down.

To expose him and free William of any threat; none of them seemed to lose sight of that goal, no matter how absorbed or distracted by specific details they became.

"Right, then." With dessert consumed, Penelope set her napkin beside her plate and looked around the table. "If you gentlemen wish for brandy, you may drink it in the drawing room, but I suggest we all repair there, summarize our case, and then decide what we need to do next."

No one demurred. Denying any wish to dim their wits with liquor, the gentlemen followed at the ladies' heels.

As soon as everyone was settled, from the corner of the sofa closest to the armchair in which Barnaby sat, Penelope looked around the group. "So, where do we start?"

"Let's briefly revisit the evidence we have." Stokes paused, gathering his thoughts, then proceeded, "First, Robert Percival, Viscount Seddington, and his wife were found dead, wrapped in the sails of the viscount's yacht off Grimsby. However, it's known that the viscountess would never have boarded the yacht willingly. That's the first clue that some crime was committed, that the pair might have been murdered. Our second clue is what Rose overheard." Stokes proceeded to lay out the facts as they knew them, through Rose's flight and the eventual arrival of inquiry agents at the manor, concluding with, "So it appears that our prime suspect, Richard Percival, has been mounting a search for Rose and the children, and he's been employing professional searchers to do so." Stokes shifted, straightening. "Today, the watch my men have been maintaining on Percival bore fruit. He's been staying put, only going out to his club of an evening, then coming straight home, but midmorning today, he traveled into the city, to the office of a man named Curtis."

Barnaby nodded. "So the searchers came via Curtis."

Thomas frowned. "I've used Curtis myself on occasion. His reputation paints him as highly effective while always operating within the law."

Montague was nodding. "That's my understanding, too. Curtis and his firm are well known, well established."

Stokes inclined his head. "Be that as it may, that's where Percival went. He was there for over half an hour, then returned to his house."

Penelope made a *more* gesture. "What do we know about this Curtis—more specifically, about how he runs his business?"

"His firm," Barnaby said, "specializes in finding people, nothing more. They don't apprehend. They don't get involved. They simply locate people. Most often, those people are debtors hiding from their creditors, but, of course, there are other reasons people go into hiding."

Stokes pulled a face. "I can't say I've ever heard of Curtis finding someone when that person didn't deserve to be found, so to speak."

"Then again," Thomas dryly remarked, "if Curtis was engaged in such pursuits, essentially finding innocents for villains, would you necessarily know?"

Stokes grimaced. "Good point."

"There's also the fact that few villains would be in a position to, or even wish to, pay Curtis's fees." Montague looked around the group. "His services don't come cheap."

"However," Barnaby said, "what we don't know is if Percival has been using Curtis all along, or whether this is a recent association."

"True," Stokes said. "And there's no denying an outfit like Curtis's would be just the thing for hunting down a missing heir."

"And"—Thomas shifted, straightening his weak leg—"as William's legal guardian, it would be easy enough for Percival to convince Curtis that he, Percival, was acting legitimately."

Stokes looked from Thomas to Montague. "So where do we stand regarding Percival's motive?"

Montague pulled a face. Briefly, he summarized the avenues he, Drayton, and Marwell had between them canvassed. "From all the sources we've accessed, from the entirely legitimate to the underworld, we've established that Percival has a steady income, doesn't in general gamble heavily, but on occasions might, and that usually in the lower of hells. He does, however, have some as-yet-unidentified drain on his purse, amounting to a considerable sum, and it's paid via a most peculiar monthly system that dates at least from the time of the murders, and might, conceivably, be an outcome of some debt that occurred prior to the murders. That said, the monthly payments are highly irregular—they start out quite high in the months after the murders, then decline almost to nothing, then rise again, then fall again, and that goes on through the years. The recent payments are high, and rising. Needless to say, the payments are untraceable. In addition, Percival won fifteen thousand pounds at the tables recently, and that money has not appeared in any of his legitimate accounts."

Montague paused, clearly gathering his thoughts, then stated, "We are left to conclude that there might well be some very large debt that Percival contracted before the murders, one sufficient to provide his motive for the murders, but as for that debt's specific existence and any description of what it might be . . ." He met Stokes's steady gaze. "We still don't have any evidence of that."

Stokes frowned, then, leaning forward, rested his forearms on his thighs and clasped his hands. "So you *have* evidence of payments that might be occasioned by some large and significant debt, but you can't yet identify the debt itself."

Thomas stirred. "As to that, I've asked my agent, Drayton, to inquire, very quietly, among the lowest ranks of capital suppliers." Meeting Montague's gaze, he went on, "The moneylenders who operate below the level that even Symonds would know of."

Expression turning grim, Stokes nodded. "The real bloodsuckers."

Thomas inclined his head. "Given the oddity of the payments Percival has been making, it occurred to me that he might have fallen into their hands—some have been known to demand a percentage of a man's income, month to month, rather than a fixed figure."

Montague was nodding. "I've heard the same, and yes, it might be some payment system of that nature."

"However," Thomas continued, "as neither I nor anyone else I know—including, I suspect, even Symonds—have any direct contacts in that exceedingly murky sphere, the approach will have to be handled very carefully. Any answers we get won't come quickly."

"Regardless," Penelope said, "such inquiries must now be made." She looked at Stokes. "As I understand it, we need to prove either a solid and believable motive or, alternatively, actual intent—meaning catch him in the act."

With a grim twist of his lips, Stokes nodded. "The way this is shaping . . . yes, that's it."

"Hmm." It was Penelope's turn to grimace. Somewhat glumly, she looked around the circle of faces. "As I mentioned, after our outing a few days ago, I called on several ladies older than I am who would know more about Richard Percival. Sadly, the grandes dames I normally rely on for social insights are presently in the country, but the three matrons I consulted, although not directly acquainted with Percival, did know something of him." She drew breath and went on, "And I have to report that, in their view, Percival is . . . well, not a villain. That he doesn't possess a 'darker side.' I would be the first to admit that that's a very subjective judgment. On the other hand, such judgments from such ladies are rarely wildly wrong."

Barnaby turned to regard her. "You're saying that they don't believe he's evil. That he doesn't have the necessary propensity."

"Yes, exactly." Penelope sighed. "I went to them expecting to hear that Richard Percival was a shady character, one they wouldn't personally trust. Instead, while they labeled him 'dangerous' in the social sense, they see him as similar to their husbands, and their husbands' friends. Even more telling, they are quite certain, and had firsthand evidence to support the view, that their husbands saw him in that light—as one of them."

Barnaby's lips twisted. "I couldn't unearth much via the clubs—Percival hasn't been spending much time in them, not since his brother's death—but what I heard largely supports that. The view that he's an honorable gentleman is widespread."

Griselda, Stokes's wife, who until that point had remained silent, listening and observing, but not commenting, said, "So social opinion contradicts our view that Percival is the villain."

Stokes grunted. "Maybe so, but how much reliance can we place on social opinion? The annals of crime are riddled with instances of a pretty face and fine manners very effectively cloaking the black soul beneath."

Barnaby nodded. "That's all too true. While in general such observations might be sound, there will always be exceptions." He met Penelope's rather disgruntled expression and faintly smiled. "Without such instances, there would be very much less drama within the ton."

"And with that," Thomas dryly stated, "I would most certainly agree."

No one missed the reference to his past, but it was, indeed, proof that society didn't always see people clearly.

Penelope humphed but appeared to accept that, in this case, her information wasn't definitive.

Griselda stirred, drawing the others' attention. "One possibility we don't seem to have addressed." She looked at Montague, then at Thomas. "Could those varying monthly payments Percival has been making be Curtis's fees?" She glanced from one to the other. "You said they commenced soon after the murders—meaning, I take it, soon after Rose fled with the children. If Percival immediately hired Curtis, presumably his fees would have started falling due from that point on."

"And," Stokes said, clearly struck by the idea, "the monthly amounts would vary according to how many men Curtis sent out, and into which region, and many other factors."

Rose, along with all the others, stared at Griselda.

Unperturbed by the scrutiny, she mildly arched a brow. "Well?"

Thomas gave a short laugh. "You're right." Meeting Griselda's gaze, he inclined his head to her. "You are our detached observer—the only one not immersed in the active investigation—and so you've seen more clearly than the rest of us. You are, indeed, correct—that is a possibility. But, if so"—he looked at Montague, then Stokes—"that leaves us with no initial motive at all."

Silence fell while they all digested that, then Barnaby shifted. "I don't know about you, but I'm growing increasingly uneasy over our lack of real progress. As to Griselda's suggestion, we're getting ahead of ourselves there, too—we have no reason to suspect that Percival hired Curtis until recently, shortly before the inquiry agents appeared in Cornwall. That's the first evidence we have of someone like Curtis being involved. Prior to that"—he shrugged—"who knows?"

"Who, indeed?" Violet glanced around the circle, finally meeting Montague's eyes. "There's another possibility we haven't canvassed, and given the social evidence, which suggests that, if Richard Percival is our villain, then he's an accomplished chameleon and so we shouldn't pay attention to appearances, what if he is, indeed, desperately in debt, but that debt is held under another name?"

His expression unchanging, Montague held Violet's gaze for several seconds, then he sighed and, rather bleakly, looked at Stokes. "If that's the case—and I agree it might well be—then our chances of identifying that debt, which might have been incurred more than a decade ago, are . . ."

"Not nil, but as near as makes no difference?" Stokes supplied.

Lips setting, Montague nodded. "Much as it hurts to admit it, yes."

Rose glanced at Thomas, but his expression was as bleak as Montague's, and he said nothing.

Glancing around, Rose cleared her throat. "I acknowledge that we've had no suggestion of any attack against William since we arrived in London, but I have to admit . . ." She drew breath and felt Thomas shift; his hand closed over one of hers, and she lifted her head and continued, "To an increasing nervousness over how much longer our luck will hold."

Rather than dismissing her concerns, Barnaby gravely inclined his head. "I feel the same—the sense of a clock ticking, of time running out."

Stokes nodded curtly; Griselda looked sympathetic.

Sitting back, Violet stated, "I can only imagine the anxiety you must feel, waiting for the moment when something *does* happen."

"Exactly," Rose said.

Somewhat to her surprise, sitting beside her, Penelope, who had been frowning at the carpet, sighed heavily. Raising her head, she looked at the others, then grimaced. "As to something happening, I'm not sure that something hasn't."

"What?" Stokes asked, instantly alert.

Penelope held up a staying hand. "This happened this

afternoon, and I have no idea how meaningful it might be. It was when we were coming out of the lacemaker's shop in Conduit Street." Penelope glanced at Rose. "Our last stop, and the carriage was there, by the curb, waiting." Penelope looked at Stokes. "Some man, a gentleman's gentleman by his attire, came walking around the corner from Savile Row. He saw us—and stopped and stared. He looked at Rose, then at Homer and Pippin. We were all there, gathering to get into the carriage. Then he saw Conner and James, and he turned around and walked quickly away." Penelope glanced at Rose. "I would lay odds he recognized Rose and Homer." Penelope looked back at Stokes. "But it all happened so quickly, I can't be certain I would recognize the man if I saw him again."

Silence held for several moments, then Stokes blew out a breath and sat back. "Well, I'd say that's torn it, but it was bound to happen sometime, and at least there was no immediate danger."

"I suspect," Barnaby said, his tone much harder, "that from this point on, we should assume that Percival knows that Rose and the children are in town."

"At least he won't know where they are," Griselda said.

Under cover of the wider discussion, Rose turned to Penelope. "You didn't say anything this afternoon."

Penelope met her gaze. "I didn't want you to react in front of the children, and later . . . well, there was no point. The damage, whatever it might prove to be, was already done, I knew you would be bringing the children here tonight, and so you and they are still safe and guarded, and telling you then . . ." Penelope looked into her eyes. "You would only have worried for longer."

Rose couldn't deny that; with a wry grimace, she accepted the explanation, felt Penelope squeeze her fingers and squeezed briefly back, then they both returned their attention to the discussion that had raged, but which, it seemed, had already reached consensus.

"So we're in agreement," Barnaby stated. "We've become distracted by our investigation and have forgotten the simple fact that Rose *heard* Richard Percival declare himself a murderer and state that his next target was William. It was that unequivocal statement, directly from him, that started this entire sequence of events. As identifying his motive for the initial murders is taking too long, and, indeed, may never be achieved, we have nothing to lose, and everything to gain, by pursuing the alternative strategy of proving Percival's guilt via his intent toward William." Barnaby glanced around the circle. "In short, we need to set a trap and lure him into incriminating himself."

Stokes didn't disagree, but he wasn't happy. "Trapping him, meaning catching him in some revealing act and thus unequivocally demonstrating his intent, might sound easy, but it has to be very craftily done so that there's no chance he can explain his actions in any acceptable way."

All eight of them fell silent, thinking of what scenarios might serve.

It was Stokes who, eyes narrow, eventually suggested, "If we can set things up so that Percival turns up at a certain spot in the clear expectation of illicitly seizing the boy . . . put together with what Rose heard him say, that ought to do it."

"Indeed." Thomas's voice was harder, colder, and more utterly implacable than Rose had ever heard it. As she glanced at him, he continued, his expression matching his tone, "But we cannot risk Homer—William—even for that. Even to secure his ultimate safety." No one argued; along with Rose, the others all waited.

Thomas seemed to look inward, then, lips cynically

twisting, he refocused and glanced around. "Courtesy of my past, I'm really very good at devising schemes. So . . . what about this?"

The plan he outlined was straightforward and clear, and not at all difficult to execute. More, even Rose could see how it would play into Richard's desires, how it would, indeed, lure rather than overtly force.

Stokes, Barnaby, and Montague all grew increasingly eager; Violet and Penelope both grew animated, adding various touches of verisimilitude to the evolving plot.

Even Griselda ultimately gave a nod of matriarchal approval.

Finally, Thomas turned to Rose; on the sofa between them, he gently grasped her hand. "We can plot and plan and hold ready to act, but it's you who must decide." He searched her eyes, then arched a brow. "Will you trust us to pull this off?"

Drawing in a breath, she looked around at the faces, all eager, but waiting on her word, then she looked back at Thomas, met his eyes, and faintly smiled. "Yes. Of course."

That decision hadn't been difficult; Rose trusted Thomas—with herself, with the children, on every level and in every way.

When, with their plan fully detailed and everything arranged, they'd finally left Albemarle Street, Pippin had been too deeply asleep to rouse, so Thomas had carried her. Rose hadn't been certain he could manage it, but he'd settled Pippin in the crook of one arm, held her safely against his chest as he'd negotiated the three steps down to the pavement, then, used to the awkwardness, it seemed, he had pulled himself up and had ducked into Penelope's waiting carriage without even jiggling Pippin.

When they'd reached the hotel, he'd continued carrying the sleeping child upstairs to their suite and on into the children's bedroom, with Rose steering a sleepy Homer in their wake.

She and Thomas had switched charges and, between them, got the children into their beds; both were asleep before, following Thomas from the room, Rose drew the door shut behind her.

She followed Thomas into their bedroom. As the distraction of having things to do—children to manage, other people to speak with—faded, her mind calmed and her rising anxiety shone through.

Not for William; he wouldn't be anywhere near danger and would be kept safely guarded throughout. Thomas's plan had ensured that.

It was Thomas who was the focus of her concern, his safety the question that now dominated her mind.

That, and the prospect of losing him.

When he turned and glanced at her, she smiled and went forward. To him, into his arms.

He was a little surprised, clearly wondering at her tack; they usually undressed separately. But he closed his arms around her and looked down into her face.

Studied it, then his gaze steadied on hers and he raised his brows.

She looked into his eyes, into the crystalline-sharp medley of greens and golds, and saw him, the real him, the gentle, loving, caring man he now was, looking back at her, and she simply said, "I don't want to talk."

Freeing her arms, she reached up and framed his face, setting her palms to his lean cheeks, one perfect and cool, the other knotted with scars; the feel of both was now dear to her—a distinguishing feature that meant him. "Not about anything."

Stretching up, she set her lips to his and kissed him—supped from his lips, and in return allowed all the pent-up yearning inside her, all the feelings that were welling and burgeoning, to flow through the caress into him.

She might have loved him before, but now she knew the depth of her longing, the breadth and strength and power—the reality of what he now meant to her.

He was safety and security; he was passion and wonder.

He was joy.

The kiss deepened, and she encouraged, evoked, and set the magic free so that it could sweep them both away.

As ever, he went with her, ready and willing to follow wherever in their landscape of passion and desire she led.

Drawing back from the heated melding of their mouths, feeling desire rising in a warm wave beneath her skin, with passion already a low thunder in her veins, she stepped away and disrobed . . . for him.

He held still and, his chest rising and falling dramatically, watched her unveil herself, the gold in his eyes glinting hot as the flames that rose beneath her skin.

Naked, bathed in the wanton glow of her desire combined with his, sensing the power that was hers flowing through her, she returned to him, placed her hands on his chest, stretched up—and touched her scorching lips to his.

The kiss scalded; their tongues tangled and flames ignited, desire erupting, hotter and sharper—more compelling.

She broke from the engagement, drawing back, stepping back.

He made an inarticulate sound and reached for her, but she caught his wrists, trapped his gaze. "No—let me."

He hesitated; eyes locked with hers, he teetered . . . but then he hauled in a huge breath, and nodded.

Once. As if once was all he could manage.

She didn't ask for more, but set herself to strip him. Slowly, lingeringly.

Drinking him in.

She had no guarantee that this wouldn't be the last time, the last chance Fate allowed her to set her hands to his skin, to pay homage to the undeniable strength of the heavy muscles cording his torso. His injuries had distorted what must once have been male perfection; he was no longer symmetrically shaped, but in her eyes, that only added to his beauty.

He was real. No polished god, no false icon.

He was true. Steady and strong, and always as he appeared.

And that, she worshipped. All that he now was.

Just as he had committed, unasked and willingly, to give his all—his freedom, his future, his life if need be—to saving William and freeing her, too, so she, now, gave herself to him.

Without reservation, without restraint.

Without guarantees.

Without thought for tomorrow.

She put all her anxieties aside and devoted herself to this, to now, to him.

To them.

As she had accepted, so, too, did he—guided, it seemed, more by instinct, by fate, than by any logic or deliberate thought.

Thomas couldn't think, too overwhelmed by the feelings. Not by their passions, not by their desires, potent though both were.

It was that deeper power—the one he still refused to name, still refused to acknowledge because he couldn't bring himself to believe he would be allowed to keep it—

that surged through him and overwhelmed his mind, leaving him no option than to follow her lead, to let her take his hand and lead him to the bed.

They sank into each other's arms; eyes wide, gazes locked, they caressed, and knew again.

Learned again all the joys they'd previously found, indulged again. With passion and abandon, with growing hunger and escalating need, they gave and took, and shared.

They came together in a rush of wild delight, on a sweeping flight of passion so intense he could barely breathe.

He bent his head and their lips locked; his body surged and plundered, and hers flowered in welcome and she clung.

They rode their wild ride into the heart of passion's storm, up and over the crest into ecstasy.

Into the sun of that ineluctable glory, to where their senses fragmented and their souls fractured, then melded into one.

To where bliss waited to cradle and soothe them, to fill the achingly empty void.

To where togetherness and closeness welled and overflowed, and eradicated the loneliness of two originally separate hearts.

Later, long after they'd eased apart, turned down the lamp, and drawn the covers over their cooling bodies, Rose lay in Thomas's arms and listened to the slow cadence of his sleeping heart.

For long moments, she simply wallowed.

Of their own volition, as if instinctively seeking to imprint every last minute detail of him on her senses, her hands gently drifted over his damaged side, her fingertips tracing his scars, the knots, whorls, and ridges she'd come to know so well.

Those scars marked him more than he realized; they were the physical signs that he had changed so very much from the man he once had been. They were the markers of his journey; they stood in silent testimony to how far he'd traveled from the identity that now threatened to reach out and reclaim him, and make him pay for those past sins.

And what of her?

Was she to pay, too?

If she lost him, she would. And if it came to that, she would.

If Fate forced her to let him go, she would.

Not for Fate, but for him.

Because she knew what he thought, knew how he saw himself; she knew she had to let him walk into the darkness of whatever lay ahead—so he could learn what lay beyond.

And so she would.

But until she knew that there was no hope, no possibility, not even a tiny kernel, until the last bell tolled, she would fight and hold fast. To the chance, to the promise.

To their love.

hey set their plan in motion the next morning. Regardless of to whom the man who had recognized Rose and William might report, the risk that Percival had already been notified that William was in London, most likely in Mayfair, left them no real choice—no further time to investigate.

As William's principal guardian, if Percival got William into his hands, getting the boy free again . . . none of them felt confident that could even be done. Rose's testimony alone could be too easily dismissed as the hysterical imaginings of a female mind weakened by understandable grief.

Stokes reached Hertford Street before the bells tolled eight, and he joined his man on the South Audley Street corner. Dressed in an old coat the better to blend with his men, Stokes nodded to O'Donnell. "Any movement?"

"No, sir. Not yet." O'Donnell, again dressed in the garb of a street-sweeper, leaned on his broom. "But Morgan slipped close before first light and pushed your note under the front door, just as you ordered. The maids would've found it by now."

Stokes nodded. Their scheme to elicit a sufficiently incriminating reaction from Percival was simplicity itself. The note in question, courtesy of Phelps, Barnaby's coachman, written in an unpolished, masculine hand, read:

We heard as you want the boy, William Percival, to disappear. If such is the case, bring one thousand pounds to the Salisbury Stairs at eleven o'clock today and speak to the man in the plaid cap and mayhap we'll be able to help you out.

With advice from Barnaby and Montague, Thomas had crafted the wording. When, on reading the script, Stokes had looked doubtful, Thomas had pointed out that if Richard Percival was an honest man, on receiving such a note, his first stop would be Scotland Yard. If, instead, he elected to go to the Salisbury Stairs and paid the cash, what would that say of his motives?

Stokes had had to agree. If Percival left his house and went to the Salisbury Stairs, a set of water steps on the banks of the Thames, and paid the man in the plaid cap one thousand pounds . . . together with Rose's testimony, that would be enough to at least get Percival into police custody. And then they would have time to wring more from him, his staff, Curtis, and whoever else Percival had been consorting with.

Thomas. Stokes realized he'd thought of the man by his first name, not the more distant *Glendower*. Stokes wasn't sure when the change had occurred, when he'd started acknowledging the man more personally, but after last night, when Stokes had seen Thomas carrying young Pippin to the carriage, seen the nature of his smile as he'd encouraged Homer—William—to follow with Rose, Stokes couldn't doubt the reality of the man's feelings toward his charges, charges he hadn't had to assume yet had, apparently without hesitation.

The feelings that had shone so clearly in Thomas's face were feelings with which Stokes was intimately familiar. The fact that Griselda, who was no easy mark, and who, Stokes had been aware, had observed Thomas with an initially highly critical eye, had been moved to wholeheartedly approve of the man—not his standing, his actions, but the man himself—had further shifted and solidified Stokes's view.

Quite how this would end Stokes didn't know, but he no longer bore Thomas any ill will. The man had paid, comprehensively and on many levels, for his past misdeeds. If Fate consented to allow him a second chance, Stokes, for one, wouldn't stand in his way.

Beside Stokes, O'Donnell shifted. "Daresay we won't see any action until himself consents to get out of bed."

Stokes considered, then grimaced. "We wrote 'Urgent' on the note, so with any luck his staff will see the sense in putting it on his breakfast tray and setting that before him soon." He pulled out his watch and consulted it. It was already fifteen minutes past eight o'clock. "He'll have to move by ten-thirty at the latest if he's to reach the Salisbury Stairs in time."

Eyes flicking down the street, O'Donnell straightened. "Speaking of the devil, that's Morgan's signal that Percival's curtains have been opened."

"Excellent." Tucking his watch back into his pocket, Stokes looked down the street. He couldn't immediately spot the younger man. "Where is Morgan?"

"Area steps opposite and two doors further down. We realized the house there's closed up, and so the area down the steps leading to the servant's door is the perfect spot to keep an eye on Percival's house. The staff of the surrounding houses just think as we're beggars looking for a place to kip."

"I think," Stokes said, "that I'll go and join Morgan. Where's Philpott?"

O'Donnell tipped his head back along South Audley Street. "He's keeping watch in the lane behind the houses in case Percival heads out that way."

"Good. And the others?" Stokes had sent orders to the Yard for two more men, one another constable and the other a runner, to join them.

"Philpott dropped in at headquarters earlier, and he said the desk said as the pair you'd asked for would report to me here by eight-thirty."

Stokes nodded. "Keep them with you for the moment. Whenever Percival leaves, however he leaves, we'll follow, all of us, but we'll need to keep well back."

"Aye, sir."

Leaving O'Donnell to mind his corner, Stokes crossed to the opposite side of Hertford Street and ambled along, apparently idly, but, in reality, scanning the houses opposite. Eventually reaching Morgan's refuge, reasonably sure no one was watching, Stokes smoothly stepped onto the area steps and descended to where Morgan was perched, the top of his head barely clearing the pavement as he kept his gaze trained on Percival's house.

"Sir." Morgan flashed Stokes an expectant grin. "Looks like we might see some action soon."

"Here's hoping." Stokes hunkered down, remembering why surveillance was one of his least favorite aspects of his job.

Morgan's position gave them a clear view of Percival's bedroom window. Within a short space of time, it was apparent that there was considerable movement inside the room, with people rapidly moving back and forth, interfering with the play of light on the pane.

"Well, well," Stokes muttered. "Looks like our note has, indeed, spurred him to action." He paused, then added, "Now we wait to see which way he heads." Down the path of an innocent man to the Yard, or along the road of a murderer toward the Thames.

Percival surprised him by doing neither. When, just after nine o'clock, the front door opened and Percival, in breeches and boots, jacket, and a loosely tied scarf in place of a cravat, his dark hair looking as if he'd run his hands through it, grim-faced and sober, strode down the steps, he turned right, his deliberate strides carrying him rapidly along the pavement to the intersection with South Audley Street.

Morgan frowned. "Bit early to be heading to the river, isn't it, sir?"

"Indeed," Stokes muttered. But it wasn't too early to head for Scotland Yard.

Even as the thought formed in Stokes's mind, Percival reached South Audley Street. Passing between the buildings and the group of three men gathered at the corner—O'Donnell and the two recent arrivals from the Yard—Percival turned north.

Away from Scotland Yard. Also away from the river.

"Where the devil is he going?" Stokes glanced at Morgan. "Come on."

They reached the corner in time to see Percival, further along the pavement, hail a hackney. They weren't close enough to hear what directions he gave the jarvey, but his wave indicated somewhere north and east.

Stokes immediately hailed a passing cab. "Morgan and Davies, with me." Davies was the young runner, already eager and straining at some metaphorical bit to race off with a message. "O'Donnell—get Philpott, find another cab, and follow as fast as you can."

Morgan had already swung up to share the jarvey's bench, was already directing the driver's notice to the cab carrying Percival north. Stokes hopped into the carriage; immediately Davies scrambled in, slamming the door behind him, the hackney started rolling.

Trusting Morgan to keep Percival in sight, to keep their hackney unobtrusively following, Stokes sat back and watched the streets slip by, plotting their route in his head.

When the hackney turned right into Oxford Street and continued at a steady clip east, Davies, leaning forward to peer at the façades sliding past, asked, "Where do you think he's going, sir?"

Stokes was wondering that himself. "It could be that he has an accomplice. We hadn't considered that, but it's certainly a possibility."

When, fifteen minutes later, the carriage had continued through St. Giles Circus and onto High Holborn, then had rattled past Chancery Lane and Gray's Inn Road, Stokes suddenly realized, "He's going to Curtis's office." Leaning forward, he peered through the window, looking ahead. "It's just ahead, this side of Holborn Circus."

Sure enough, the hackney slowed, then pulled into the curb. Stokes and Davies got out; after paying the jarvey, Morgan joined them on the pavement.

Facing Stokes, Morgan tipped his head back and to his right. "Saw him go into that building along there."

"That's Curtis's office." Stokes scanned the area, picking out several likely spots from where his men could watch the building. To Morgan he said, "Take Davies and scout around the back—see if there's a way out on that side. I'll wait here for the others, then we'll deploy to cover all entrances. Report back to me here."

Morgan nodded, jerked his head, summoning Davies to follow, then melted into the stream of passersby.

After a moment, Stokes drew out his watch. It was a little after half past nine. Tucking the watch away, he glanced along the street to where Curtis's office lay; if Percival had arrived in search of support for his meeting at the river, then it would be a little while yet before he moved again. Stokes and his men would have time to get into decent positions.

Another hackney pulled up, disgorging the rest of his small force; they hadn't been that far back, had been able to follow purely by sight, but the traffic had slowed them.

Morgan and Davies reappeared. Morgan shook his head. "No way out that way, sir. The building backs onto another, and that one's a warehouse and we checked. There's no way through."

If it hadn't been Morgan, Stokes would have been skeptical—he found it hard to believe Curtis wouldn't have another way out—but it was Percival they were after, and the man had no reason to imagine he was under surveillance. "Right, then." Stokes looked down the street. "We'll cover the front only, but we need to make sure we raise no hackles. Curtis is no fool, and his men aren't, either, so we need to ensure they get not even a whiff of us. Understood?"

There were nods all around. Stokes had handpicked this crew from the most experienced and talented men the Yard had on roster for surveillance work; Davies was new and too eager to be left alone, but all the rest Stokes knew he could rely on.

He let them pick their own places of concealment, then watched as they drifted and ambled into position.

Stepping back under the overhang of a tobacconist shop's canopy, Stokes leaned his shoulders against the rough brickwork and slouched as if waiting for a friend. Davies all but quivered alongside.

After several minutes of silence, Davies whispered, "The boy who just left Curtis's office—he's a runner."

Even as Stokes glanced briefly along the street, another young lad came barreling out of Curtis's door and raced toward them; he passed Stokes and Davies, flying along at a good clip. "So," Stokes murmured, "Percival arrives, and ten minutes later, Curtis sends messengers out."

The boy's headlong dash past them seemed to have infected Davies with a similar urge. He shifted back and forth on his feet. After a moment more, he offered, "I could duck down and tell those at the river our mark's up here—I'd be back before anything happened."

"No." Stokes softened the prohibition with, "We don't know what might happen. We need to know Percival is definitely on his way to the river, *and* whether he has anyone with him, before you hare down."

He also planned to order Davies, once he'd warned those at the Salisbury Stairs, to hie on to the Yard and let those there know that their scheme had borne fruit, so they could prepare . . . Stokes ducked his head as a large, thickset man, along with his slightly smaller crony, walked briskly past.

Glancing sideways, without lifting his head Stokes watched as the pair reached the entrance to Curtis's office and disappeared inside.

Davies, who, to give the lad due credit, had had the sense to look vacant, murmured, "Were they Curtis's men—inquiry agents?"

Stokes nodded. Like Thomas, he could recognize the type on sight. Something about their elevated alertness instantly triggered his inner alarms.

Not that inquiry agents who worked for men like Curtis were dangerous . . . or, at least, not generally. Not in Stokes's previous experience.

As he watched more agents, doubtless summoned by the boys who'd been sent out, walk through Curtis's door, Stokes wondered if, today, previous experience would hold true. All told, six men had responded to Curtis's summonses.

Stokes pulled out his watch; it was twenty minutes past ten o'clock. He glanced at Curtis's offices; if Percival wanted to make the rendezvous at the Salisbury Stairs at eleven o'clock, he would have to move soon.

Ten minutes later, the door to Curtis's office opened and Percival strode out. He paused on the pavement, and Curtis joined him. After glancing over his shoulder, Percival stepped out. Checking the traffic, he crossed the street, Curtis following.

The six inquiry agents who had answered Curtis's call streamed out of the building, fanning out in three pairs, then following in staggered formation in Percival and Curtis's wake.

Davies bounced on his toes. "Should I go now?"

"No." Stokes pushed away from the wall. "We need to be sure before you take off." Hands in his pockets, head down, Stokes strode easily along, following the last of the inquiry agents.

He hung back, letting the considerable number of pedestrians in the area provide cover, just in case any of Curtis's men had hyperaware instincts.

Stokes's men gradually drifted closer, following several paces behind him, a loose net set to catch anyone among the party they were pursuing who might fall back. None did, and as they trailed down streets leading south and slightly west, it was soon apparent that Percival and Curtis were heading toward the Salisbury Stairs.

Their quarry reached Fleet Street, just east of The Temple, and turned west; Stokes continued ambling in their wake. The men ahead of him strode along easily enough, yet there was an air of purpose in their steps, a sense of focus. Percival, in particular, moved with single-minded determination; he barely seemed to see the people around him—he was always looking ahead.

Keeping pace at Percival's shoulder, Curtis seemed rather more laconic, or perhaps more taciturn. Or perhaps he was simply harder to read.

Finally, approaching the Strand, with Davies all but straining at an invisible leash, when their quarry reached the point where the road split into two around the Church of St. Clements and Percival led his party onto the south arm, Stokes nodded to the north arm. "Go that way, and you'll pass them without them noticing you. To Adair first—tell him and Sergeant Wilkes that it's on, then straight on to the Yard and report to Ferguson on the desk—he'll be waiting to hear."

"Aye, sir!" With that, Davies was off. Fleet of foot, he flew down the street, dodging and weaving; within seconds, he was out of sight.

Suppressing a grim, rather feral smile, Stokes continued in Richard Percival's wake.

The Salisbury Stairs were the first set of waterman's steps west of those under Waterloo Bridge. The stairs lay at the end of Salisbury Street, a middling-sized street of old houses. The stones of the quay where the street met the river's edge were dark gray, their upper surfaces above the waterline etched with lichens. Below the tideline, the stones were coated in slime.

Sitting in a rowboat, holding it in position just off the stairs with an occasional wielding of the oars, Thomas had plenty of opportunity to observe the sights and the smells. He'd forgotten that particular delight of the capital.

He was dressed like a waterman, his normal clothes entirely covered by an oilskin cape, his features shadowed by the peaked hood he'd pulled low over his head. The cape spread all around him, concealing his awkwardly placed left leg and his cane.

In front of him in the body of the rowboat lay a trussed bundle of cushions designed to realistically represent William; Penelope and Rose had, quite literally, matched the bundle to William's height and girth.

The children were safely stowed under constant guard, while both Penelope and Rose were waiting—no doubt impatiently—with Montague at Scotland Yard, ready to assist with the subsequent interrogation, assuming Percival took their bait.

Violet was manning Montague's office in case any further information came to hand. Griselda, much to her dismay, had had to remain home with her and Stokes's young daughter, who had apparently woken with a cold.

A sudden patter of flying feet on cobbles, and a young man came pelting out of the shadows of Salisbury Street. He raced directly up to Barnaby, who was playing the part of the man in the plaid cap; in an ancient frieze coat over rough workman's trousers, Barnaby was loitering, clearly waiting for someone at the head of the stairs.

The young man came to a skidding halt and breathlessly gasped, "They're on their way. Guv'nor said as it was on." He glanced around. "Where's Sergeant Wilkes?"

"Here, lad."

The young man glanced up a narrow alley behind Barnaby, spotted the grizzled sergeant, dressed like a drunk, crouching there, then nodded, gave a weak thumbs-up, and spun on his heel. "I've to warn the Yard." He flung the words at Barnaby and took off again, long legs extending as he raced along the river's edge, then dodged into the alleyways to the west.

Barnaby glanced at the sergeant, who raised a hand in salute and drew back into the shadows.

Turning, Barnaby looked at Thomas. "Ready?"

Thomas merely nodded. There weren't that many watermen plying their trade at that time of day; glancing to right and left along the water, then out over the river, Thomas confirmed that there were no other craft approaching the stairs. Leaning on one oar, he steered the rowboat closer until its prow grazed the side of the narrow stone platform at the bottom of the stairs.

In the distance, drawing nearer, he heard the tramp of booted feet. Not the stride of one man but of several.

Eyes narrowing, Thomas glanced at Barnaby—who was standing still and silent, looking into the maw of Salisbury Street. A moment passed, then Barnaby glanced Thomas's way and flashed his fingers. Five, plus another three. Eight men, then.

They hadn't expected that many.

Thomas felt a sudden surge of emotions. The excitement, the thrill, was something he recognized from his far-distant past, the anticipation of impending satisfaction when he'd closed a difficult deal, or made an unprecedented financial strike, but this time, other feelings—surprisingly potent and strong—were laced into the roiling mix. The strongest, most powerful, was a form of anger—a latent fury blazing up like touch-paper at the lick of a flame at the prospect of finally coming face-to-face with the man behind the cold-blooded murders of Rose's and the children's mother, of William and little Alice's father, who had stolen so much from the three. The man who had forced Rose to forfeit the life she should have had to keep her half siblings safe and alive.

To survive herself; Thomas harbored no illusions over what Percival would have done to Rose had he ever caught her.

That righteous fury flared and Thomas welcomed it, embraced it—surprised to realize he'd felt its like once before, over Charlie Morwellan's refusal to accept the freely offered love of his wife and openly admit to her that he returned it.

But that time righteous fury had been fueled largely by frustration. This time . . . it was that other emotion, the one Rose, and, in a somewhat different version, the children, too, evoked.

That was what made today's fury burn so much hotter than in the past.

The city's bells started tolling the hour, and Thomas had a blinding flash of insight. He felt so strongly—because he truly cared.

Because those three were so important to him now.

Because he loved.

A gentleman came striding out of Salisbury Street. Behind him, the tramp of boots slowed. From where he bobbed on the water, Thomas saw six men—inquiry agents all—fan out to block the end of the street.

Richard Percival—it could only be he—strode boldly forward, eyes narrowing as he scanned Barnaby, noting his plaid cap. Then Percival's gaze moved on to the boat and Thomas, and finally came to rest on the bundled cushions at Thomas's feet.

Percival halted an arm's length from Barnaby; his gaze remained locked on the bundle representing William.

To Thomas's eyes, Percival's gaze looked hungry, drawn.

Close behind Percival, a heavyset man with a close-cropped head and the build of a brawler, garbed in a plain but good-quality suit, ambled with deceptive gentleness to a solid halt.

Curtis. Thomas kept his head angled so the cape's hood shaded his features. He'd dealt with Curtis several times in his previous life; there was a reasonable chance the highly observant man would remember his face if he saw it, scars notwithstanding.

Curtis noted him assessingly, measuring also the distance to the boat, but then looked at Barnaby.

Thomas transferred his gaze to Percival; the blackguard looked . . .

The word that leapt to mind was tortured, but there was no sympathy in Thomas's soul; his fury welled, pure and hot, and he had to fight to suppress a snarl.

Percival had been sizing up Barnaby, who Thomas now wouldn't have recognized. The man was a chameleon; he appeared shorter, more hunched, definitely seedier.

Percival's gaze fixed on the plaid cap atop Barnaby's dusty—liberally dusted with ash—curls. "So." Percival's voice was hard, rigidly controlled. "You say you have the boy."

Barnaby glanced briefly at the bound lump at Thomas's feet. "Right little beggar, he is."

"He's alive?"

Thomas blinked at the desperation in Percival's voice.

Barnaby bobbled his head. "He's well enough. You got the cash? Thousand pounds, or me mate sets sail." Barnaby gurgled a short, rather ugly laugh.

Percival spat an oath and turned to Curtis, who reached into his jacket pocket, drew out a wad of notes, and handed it to Percival, but Curtis's watchful gaze never left Barnaby.

"Here's your money." Percival thrust the notes at Barnaby. "Now"—Percival turned to the boat, his gaze once more locking on the trussed bundle—"give me the boy. And for your sake, he'd better be alive."

Percival's tone and the look on his face made Thomas frown, but Barnaby, deep in his disguise and busy ostentatiously counting the notes, only bobbed another bobble-headed nod. "Comin' right up, guv'nor. Jest as soon as I knows you haven't diddled us."

Turning slightly as he counted, Barnaby slid his left hand into the pocket of his horrible coat and drew out a silver whistle. Shooting a glance at Thomas, Barnaby raised the whistle to his lips and blew.

The shrill note sliced through the morning.

Percival leapt as if whipped. "What the . . . ?"

Curtis spun toward Salisbury Street, but then he saw Sergeant Wilkes come barreling out of the alley making for Percival. Curtis swung back and nimbly intercepted the burly sergeant, engaged, and threw him back.

Curtis's men didn't wait for any signal but came charging out onto the quay.

As they did, the rest of Stokes's men, all in disguise, poured out of the mouths of the tiny alleys and lanes.

Curtis's men swung around and met them in a snarling, fist-swinging clash.

Fleet of foot, Barnaby ran down the stairs and stepped into the rowboat as Thomas pushed off with an oar.

Richard Percival, momentarily distracted by Sergeant Wilkes's charge, and then the swelling melee, spun around, saw . . . he roared and charged down the stairs.

Thomas swung one oar out and fended off Percival, then the rowboat floated out of reach.

"*Bring him back!*" Percival swore. "What the devil do you want with the boy?" Then, his gaze falling on the bundle from a different angle, his expression changed. "Did you ever have him?"

Another whistle sounded, two short, sharp blasts, followed by Stokes's bellow: "*Police!*"

The effect was instantaneous. Curtis's men froze.

"What?"

"Police?"

One minute, Curtis's men were brawling; in the next, they disengaged from their opponents and stepped back. Slowly, openly puzzled at the sight of the squad of beggars facing them, they lowered their fists.

After several seconds of total astonishment, as one, the six men looked at Curtis.

Who had stopped fighting Wilkes. Even though the sergeant maintained a dogged hold on one of Curtis's arms, the man ignored him, instead staring across the quieting quay at Stokes. Then Curtis glanced at Thomas and Barnaby in the rowboat, then swung his gaze to Richard Percival. His face a mask of confusion, Curtis demanded, "What the hell is going on?"

Richard Percival returned his look with one of equal incomprehension.

Stokes pushed through the large bodies crowding the quay. He glanced at Barnaby and Thomas, then went down the slick stairs to where Richard Percival stood on the narrow shelf at the bottom. "I'm Inspector Stokes of Scotland Yard." Meeting Percival's gaze, Stokes clamped a heavy hand on Percival's shoulder. "Richard Wyman Percival, I'm arresting you on a charge of conspiring to kill your ward,

William Percival, Viscount Seddington, and with having caused or conspired with persons unknown to bring about the deaths of the late Robert Percival, Viscount Seddington, and his wife, Corinne."

Percival's features showed nothing but utter astonishment; his jaw had dropped. "What?" The word was weak; he swallowed, then stated, "No! You have it wrong."

He went to shake off Stokes's hold, but an enterprising constable was already there, waiting with shackles to assist Stokes.

Percival saw, stiffened, but then gave up the fight. "Very well." The words were spoken with a cutting edge. He glanced, narrow-eyed, at Barnaby and Thomas. "I don't know who you are, or what your game is, but if you believe I'm guilty of any of those charges, you are beyond misguided."

Barnaby just looked at him, then shook his head. "All villains say that, you know."

"Indeed," Stokes said. "So why don't you and your small army just come along quietly, and you can explain our errors to us at Scotland Yard."

Percival shot another lingeringly lethal glance at Barnaby and Thomas, then, jaw clenched, lips set in a thin line, allowed himself to be escorted up the stairs.

Thomas didn't like it, and said so as he and Barnaby trudged behind the others—the platoon of police escorting Percival, Curtis, and his six inquiry agents westward through the laneways that led to Scotland Yard. "Too many things don't ring true."

He'd shrugged off the oilskin cape and carried it over one arm. They'd returned the skiff to its owner by the Adelphi Stairs, and Barnaby was lugging their trussed bundle, gripped in one hand.

Pulling off the plaid cap, Barnaby stuffed it in his pocket, then ruffled his hair, shaking ash everywhere, and grimaced. "I wish I could disagree. It all went so neatly. But something's off kilter." He looked at the men walking ahead of them. "Not least the way Curtis and his men stopped fighting the instant they heard the word 'police.'"

"One couldn't help noticing," Thomas dryly observed, "that it seemed they thought they were fighting on the side of right, and that we were the villains."

Barnaby nodded. "Of course, we may find that Percival is such a convincing fiend that he's managed to pull the wool over Curtis's eyes."

"Indeed," Thomas retorted. "And pigs might fly."

Eyes on the ground, Barnaby grunted. "I haven't used Curtis myself, but once his name cropped up, I checked, and his reputation hasn't changed since you would last have dealt with him—he's known as hard, but rigidly honest and straighter than a die."

"I haven't heard anything different, but to my mind, Percival's reactions were even more telling—he was desperate to find William alive. Not dead, but alive. You heard it—his desperation at the end."

Barnaby nodded and looked ahead. "I'm getting the distinct impression we have something fairly major wrong with our hypothesis, but for the life of me I can't see where, let alone what."

The cavalcade of prisoners and police finally reached Great Scotland Yard and filed into the building that housed the headquarters of the Metropolitan Police. The desk sergeant, Ferguson, warned by Davies, had several holding cells and an interview room waiting. Thomas and Barnaby stood back while Stokes made his dispositions, sending Curtis's men to one holding cell, and Curtis himself to a smaller one. Then, with a glance, Stokes collected Thomas and Barnaby, and they followed as Stokes escorted a silent, but acquiescent, Richard Percival, his hands shackled, down a corridor to a largish interview room.

Led inside by Stokes, Percival's gaze initially passed over the other occupants—Penelope, Rose, and Montague, seated in chairs along the wall beyond one end of the plain interview table—with nothing more than cursory curiosity, but then his gaze abruptly backtracked and fixed on Rose's face.

Percival halted. Even as he surrendered to the pressure of

Stokes's hand and subsided into the chair on one side of the table, Percival continued to stare in increasing astonishment at Rose. "Rosalind . . . ?"

His tone suggested complete bafflement. He stared at Rose, and she stared back.

Rounding the table, Stokes said, "You're acquainted with Miss Heffernan. Flanking her are Mr. Montague and Mrs. Adair, both of whom have been assisting us with our investigation, along with Miss Heffernan." Taking the center chair of the three facing Percival, Stokes gestured to Thomas as he drew out the chair to Stokes's right. "And these gentlemen are Mr. Glendower, and"—Stokes indicated Barnaby, who slouched in the chair to Stokes's left— "Mr. Adair, who have also been assisting us."

As Stokes sat, Percival swung to face him. "My nephew, William Percival, and his sister, Alice. Are they safe?"

Stokes held Percival's gaze.

Thomas studied Percival's expression, too, but all he could see was genuine concern, even anxiety.

Eventually, Stokes replied, "William and Alice Percival are safe and well guarded."

The tension in Percival's shoulders eased. He studied Stokes, Barnaby, and Thomas, his expression growing steadily harsher. "In that case, where are they, and what the devil is going on?"

That demand was more peremptory, more what one would expect from a scion of the aristocracy.

Unperturbed, Stokes checked that Sergeant O'Donnell had entered and settled by the wall, notebook in hand, and that Morgan had followed O'Donnell in and shut the door, then Stokes rested his forearms on the table, hands loosely clasped, and brought his gray gaze once again to bear on Richard Percival. "Let's start at the beginning. Four years ago, on the day your older brother, Robert Percival, and his wife, Corinne, disappeared. Where were you that day?"

Percival blinked. "I was in London." He glanced from Stokes, to Barnaby, to Thomas; his expression grew increasingly confused. "I don't understand. What's—"

"Mr. Percival. We've got rather a lot to discuss. If you will allow us to pose our questions in the order that makes sense to us, we'll get through them more quickly."

Expression hardening, Percival returned Stokes's gaze, then he shot a sharp glance at Rose. Then, curtly, he nodded. "Very well, Inspector." Settling in the chair, Percival returned his attention to Stokes. "What do you wish to know?"

"You, in London, on that day four years ago. Is there anyone who can bear witness that you were, indeed, in the capital throughout that day?"

Percival thought, then nodded. "Several people." He rattled off four names, all gentlemen of the ton. "And there were others, as well. We met for a private luncheon at Kings in St. James. None of us left until nearly six o'clock, and I went on to a dinner with Ffyfe, Montgomery, and Swincombe at Lady Hammond's. We were there until after midnight."

Stokes nodded. "When did you learn of your brother's death, and what did you do once you had?"

Percival frowned. "I got word the next day, late in the afternoon. I sent a message to Foley, the family solicitor, to make sure he'd been informed. He had been, and replied that he would be traveling up the next day. I also sent word to my uncle and cousin—Marmaduke Percival and his son, Roger—but I didn't wait for their reply. I drove up to the Grange in my curricle—I left Hertford Street about six o'clock, so I ended up driving through the night."

"What did you do once you reached Seddington Grange?" Stokes asked.

Percival frowned at his shackled hands, now clasped on the table before him. "The household was in predictable chaos. I saw Rosalind and the children briefly, but they were . . . caught up in their grief." Percival paused, as if remembering, then his face hardened again. "I couldn't make head or tail of what they—the staff—could tell me about what had supposedly happened, so I drove to Grimsby."

He flicked a glance at Stokes. "All the Percival men sail—even my uncle, Marmaduke, and he's as far from athletic as one could imagine. It's something that runs in the blood, and so all the sailors in Grimsby know us." Percival shifted, then continued, "I went there and asked around . . . and none of the sailors could understand what had happened any more than I could." Percival met Stokes's gaze, his own steady. "Robert was an expert sailor, and very well able to manage his yacht on his own. The day they'd gone out . . . it was dead calm. No sudden squalls, nothing. They hadn't hit any rocks." He hesitated, then went on, "I spoke with those who found the yacht. The bodies were tangled in the sails, all but wrapped in them—which is hard enough to understand on its own. To pull in the bodies, they had to cut the sails loose, and once they had, the yacht's hull went down—otherwise they would have towed it to shore and we might have been able to determine what had happened."

Percival lifted his shackled hands as if to rake his fingers through his hair, then realized and lowered them. "So we were left to accept that Robert, expert sailor though he was, in a waterway he'd grown up on, in a craft he owned and knew down to the last inch, capsized the boat on a clear day on a dead calm sea." He met Stokes's gaze, then Barnaby's and Thomas's. "I also found it odd that no one had seen them go out. No one even knew when they had. Yet Robert was a gregarious sort. If he'd gone down to the wharf where the yacht was moored, he would have spoken to anyone around, and there are always people around on the wharf. I asked, but no one had any clue. No one even realized the yacht wasn't at its moorings until it was found capsized."

Stokes, Thomas noted, was also frowning faintly, as if he, like Thomas, could hear the straightforwardness—the simple honesty—in Percival's recounting.

After a moment, Stokes volunteered, "We now have information, courtesy of Miss Heffernan, that it is highly unlikely that the accident—if it was an accident—could have happened as it was made to appear."

Percival glanced at Rose. "What information? And why the devil didn't you tell me then?" The last was said without heat.

Narrow-eyed, clearly distrusting Percival, Rose replied, "Mama, as you know, wasn't well. And she suffered terribly from mal-de-mer. She would never have set foot on the yacht."

Percival blinked, then softly said, "Even more to the point, Robert wouldn't have suggested it, much less permitted it, not with Corinne's health in the state it then was." He swung back to Stokes, but then sank back in the chair and grimaced. "I wish I'd known that, but, in reality, it would have made no difference. I spoke with the Lord Lieutenant at the funeral, pressing for an investigation, but he was firmly of the opinion that there was no proof of any crime, and that further investigating would only create unnecessary scandal for the family." Percival's next grimace was cynically disgusted. "*I* didn't care about any scandal, but the rest of the family—even Foley—were horrified by the suggestion." Percival drew in a tight breath, then slowly exhaled. "And so Robert and Corinne were buried, and that was that."

Stokes's frown was growing ever more definite. "That brings us to the hours after the funeral. Who remained for dinner at the house on that evening?"

Percival's expression grew distant as he thought back. "Other than myself, Marmaduke was there, and Roger, along with several of his friends, both from London and nearer at hand. Robert's, Corinne's, and my London friends had already left to return to town, but two local gentlemen, friends of mine, remained to dine. There were several distant cousins, too, but they were planning on departing soon after. And Foley was there, as well."

"Miss Heffernan has told us that only you and your uncle stayed at the house overnight." Stokes looked at Percival for confirmation.

He nodded. "Yes—we were the only two. We'd been named co-guardians of William and Alice, and were therefore co-custodians of the estate. We'd both known that was how Robert had written his will, so had expected to stay for several days to . . . sort matters out." Percival glanced at Rose. His gaze hardened. "But then Rosalind fled with the children, and threw all Robert's careful planning into chaos." Disapproval and more rang in his tone.

Rose held Richard Percival's accusatory gaze and, her eyes narrowing, returned it in full measure. "I *heard* you," she said. When he only looked puzzled, she raised her chin and clearly stated, "That evening, after dinner. After all the others had left. You were in the study, speaking with one of your friends. You boasted about how you had killed Robert and Mama, and arranged their deaths to appear to be an accident, and that now only William stood between you and the estate, and that you planned to eliminate him as soon as you could."

Percival's jaw dropped. He stared at Rose. After several

moments of utter silence, Percival looked at Stokes. "That's . . ." Shaking his head, Percival appeared lost for words. *"Nonsensical,"* he eventually managed. "How could I have said that?" He spread his shackled hands. "Quite aside from it being untrue, I wasn't even in the house at that time."

Stokes blinked. "You weren't?"

Percival glared. "No. Immediately after dinner, which was served early, at six o'clock, I drove Foley to Newark-on-Trent so he could catch the mail back to London."

Stokes glanced at O'Donnell, confirming that his sergeant was scribbling like fury, getting all the information down. Looking back at Percival, Stokes paused, then asked, "Foley is the family's and also your personal solicitor, correct?"

When Percival curtly nodded, Stokes asked, "Did anyone else see you in Newark-on-Trent, or did you stop anywhere along the way where someone might have noticed you?"

Percival frowned. "We didn't stop on the way. Foley was anxious to ensure he caught the mail, and I wanted to get back as soon as I could—it's a good four-hour round trip from the Grange. I didn't get back until midnight, which the stable hands could verify . . ." Abruptly, Percival's expression cleared. "Wait—there *is* someone other than Foley who can place me in Newark-on-Trent on that night. When we reached the coaching inn, there was a private carriage in the yard, getting horses put to. The owner was some judge . . . Hennessey. Judge Hennessey. He recognized Foley and offered him a lift back to London, which Foley gratefully accepted." Percival met Stokes's gaze, then looked at Barnaby and Thomas. "Foley introduced me to the judge—so Judge Hennessey can swear I was in Newark-on-Trent at about ten o'clock."

Flicking a glance at Rose, Percival added, "Which means I couldn't possibly have been the man Rosalind heard speaking in the study."

After a moment of studying Rose, Percival swung to face her. "Where were you that you heard someone in the study—in the drawing room?"

When, still frowning at him, Rose nodded, Percival looked sideways at Stokes. "I grew up in that house. I knew as well as Robert did about the problem of speaking privately in the study. If I had been so stupid as to want to boast to a friend about committing a double murder, I wouldn't have chosen that room in which to do it."

"But . . ." Rose couldn't work it out. "I know your voice. I heard you say the words—it certainly wasn't Marmaduke. But aside from all that"—she searched Percival's face— "who but you could say that only William stood between you and the estate?"

Percival's expression blanked. Slowly, his gaze on Rose, but not as if he was seeing her, he straightened. "Ah." A second later, he looked at Stokes, then at Thomas and Barnaby. "So that's what this"—with the fingers of one hand, he gestured at himself—"suspecting me stems from. You think I'm William's heir."

Barnaby asked the obvious question. "Aren't you?"

Percival held his gaze, then quietly said, "Robert Percival wasn't my brother. He was my half brother. I'm illegitimate, which is why there were so many years between us in age— our father dallied with my mother long after Robert's mother had died. My mother was a widow and didn't wish to re-marry, but she died soon after birthing me. My father and Robert didn't care about my birth. To them, I was always my father's son, Robert's brother." He glanced at Rose. "Which is why Rosalind never knew of that, and, indeed, few outside the immediate family do." Looking back at Stokes, he said, "But my illegitimacy does mean that I cannot inherit either the title or the entailed estate. If William dies, the estate will pass to Marmaduke, which is why Robert made a point of making me William's principal guardian—he would have made me William's only guardian except Marmaduke got . . . huffy. As it was easy enough to appease him with co-guardianship, Robert did so, knowing he, Robert, could rely on me and Foley to keep William and the estate safe through any term of minority." Percival paused, then went on, "Robert and I were close—he knew I would protect William and Alice, and Rosalind, too, if anything happened to him, and, in fact, I swore I would." He glanced at Rose. "It was that vow that's driven me to search and search for William, Alice, and Rosalind through the last four years."

Rose held his gaze; it remained steady, unwavering—true. She frowned. "But who, then, did I hear? I will swear on any Bible that I definitely heard all I've said I did."

Percival's gaze narrowed fractionally, then he nodded. "That's why you fled." His jaw firmed. "Because you thought . . . I was going to kill William."

"I had no idea you'd sworn to Robert and Mama to protect them." Rose paused, then added, "Mama had previously asked me to promise to always keep them safe, so I felt I had to act—immediately, that night."

Percival grimaced. "In hindsight, that was an error on Robert and Corinne's part." He flicked a glance at Thomas, Stokes, and Barnaby. "The pair of them feared I would, entirely unintentionally, simply by being me, turn Rosalind's impressionable head, so they asked me to keep my distance from her, which I dutifully did. But once they were gone"—Percival looked back at Rose—"that meant that I did not know Rosalind well. I had no idea why she had so precipitously, without any apparent reason, fled with the children. Conversely, she had no basis on which to judge me—neither of us knew the other well, certainly not enough to trust."

After a moment, Stokes tapped the table. "Back to the point—if it wasn't you Rose heard, who was it?"

Percival looked at Rose. "It couldn't have been Marmaduke—you wouldn't have mistaken his voice for mine, not even allowing for the distortion of the chimney." Percival glanced at Stokes. "Marmaduke booms."

Rose shook her head. "It definitely wasn't Marmaduke."

Percival searched Rose's eyes . . . then his expression hardened. "Roger." His tone was harsh. Turning to Stokes, Percival said, "It had to have been him. He and I sound alike enough to pass, certainly heard through that chimney. And although it's Marmaduke who inherits after William, Marmaduke is . . . not a strong character, and very easily led. He's most easily manipulated, virtually constantly, by his only son—Roger. That's a large part of the reason why Robert made me William's principal guardian."

"And," Penelope said, speaking for the first time although she'd been following the unfolding story avidly, "because of that, Roger might, indeed, have stated that only William stood between him and the estate." She appealed to the others. "Roger didn't need to inherit himself. He just needed his father to, and that would achieve the same purpose—the same access to the estate's funds."

Barnaby straightened. "When we interviewed Foley, he intimated that one of the co-guardians had tried to tap the estate for funds. That wasn't you?"

Percival shook his head. "That was Marmaduke, almost certainly at Roger's behest. Foley can confirm that. That was exactly what he and I were there to prevent, and we did."

"We also learned," Thomas said, "that someone set the legal clock ticking on William's presumed death shortly after his disappearance." He raised his brows at Percival.

Who nodded. "Marmaduke again. Foley and I held back as long as we could, but Marmaduke is the legal heir, so could push the point, and we had to give way."

Montague cleared his throat. "Our investigations have been wide-ranging, and we noted that you have a steady drain on your income. More, you recently won fifteen thousand pounds at cards, and that has apparently disappeared."

Percival stared at Montague for a moment, then, almost reluctantly, with resigned acceptance, inclined his head. "Curtis and his men don't come cheap."

"Damn!" Stokes muttered sotto voce. "Griselda was right."

When Percival cocked a brow at him, Stokes waved the point aside. "But speaking of Curtis, and all this searching you've been paying him to do, why didn't you come to us—the police—when Rose and the children disappeared?"

Percival grimaced and threw a sidelong look at Rose. "As I said, I didn't know Rosalind well. I didn't know anything about what she'd overheard—all I knew was that she was grief-stricken over the loss of both her mother and Robert, and that she loved the children—I did know that. Then, the next morning, she and the children were gone. We knew she'd taken them, that much was obvious, but in light of my vow to Robert and Corinne, the last thing I wanted to do was bring the law down on Rosalind's head."

He sighed and looked up at the ceiling. "We—me, Foley, and Marmaduke—reasoned that Rosalind had had some sort of hysterical breakdown and had, due to some imagined cause, for some unreal and therefore incomprehensible reason, kidnapped the children. We felt confident she wouldn't harm them, and I assumed that by hiring Curtis we would track her down soon enough and rescue the children as well as her. We thought she needed care." He glanced again at Rose, this time with a certain level of respect. "But we never caught up with her, not until recently, when we got some decent sightings in Cornwall."

Rose had been following the revelations, but distantly. Now she nodded, but, still frowning, said, "I still don't see how it could have been Roger I overheard." She met Richard's gaze. "He wasn't staying overnight."

"No," Richard said. "But he was still at the Grange when Foley and I left. And he had a friend with him—they were intending to leave later and drive to town together . . . Atwood . . . no, Atwell. Ambrose Atwell." Percival looked at Stokes. "That was Roger's friend's name. They were thick as thieves, and had been since their schooldays. That Roger would have so openly boasted to Atwell isn't all that surprising."

Stokes's expression blanked. Then he blinked and looked at Sergeant O'Donnell.

Who had stopped writing and was staring at Stokes.

"Ambrose Atwell," Stokes said. "Am I thinking of the right man, O'Donnell?"

"If you're thinking of that incident 'bout two years ago, then yes, sir—that's the name I recall."

His expression growing grim, Stokes faced Percival. "Ambrose Atwell was found bludgeoned to death in a wood in Exeter about two years ago. It's an unsolved murder. It was one of my cases. Atwell was well down on his luck and owed significant amounts to all sorts of people—we never got a whiff of who did it, and put his death down to falling foul of the wrong sort of creditors."

Percival didn't say anything for several moments, then he

sighed. "If Atwell was the friend Rosalind heard Roger boasting to, at some point in time, Atwell, pressed for cash, might have tried to blackmail Roger."

Stokes caught Percival's gaze. "In your view, could your cousin have bludgeoned a friend to death?"

After a long moment, Percival replied, "If all we're thinking is correct, and, finally, we seem to be unraveling the truth, then Roger killed Robert and Corinne, two people who had never done him the slightest harm. Could he have killed again to hide that fact?" Gravely, Percival nodded. "Yes, I believe he could."

Stokes grimaced, then gestured to Morgan. "Get those shackles off."

Morgan came forward, key in hand. Percival held up his hands. While Morgan unlocked the shackles and removed them, Rose, studying Percival, said, "I've spent the last four years thinking you murdered my mother and Robert, and planned to kill William, but you're innocent."

Percival shot her a faintly rueful glance. "I've spent the last four years thinking you had lost your mind and had kidnapped the children, but, clearly, you haven't."

Rose could barely believe the sense of relief that was flooding her; she found herself returning Richard's faint smile.

A sudden tapping at the door drew everyone's attention. Returning to his post beside it, shackles dangling from one hand, Morgan opened it.

"I have a message for Inspector Stokes and must see it into his hands."

They all heard Violet's clear tones. "Let her in," Stokes ordered.

Violet swept into the room. She noted everyone, then her gaze fixed on Percival. After a second of studying him—a regard he returned without reaction—she drew in a breath, glanced at Montague, then looked at Stokes. "If this man is Richard Percival, then he's not the one who is in terrible debt. It's his cousin, Roger Percival, who is under threat from his creditors." Violet handed a note to Thomas. "Your man Drayton sent this an hour ago. I thought you might need to see it straightaway."

Unfolding the note, Thomas scanned the contents. "Drayton reports that Roger Percival is under mounting pressure to start paying off the quite mountainous debts he's incurred . . . from the worst of the worst of the money-lenders operating out of the slums near Seven Dials."

Looking up, Thomas smiled at Violet. "Thank you." He handed the note to Stokes.

Who received it with a sharklike smile. Verifying the note's contents, Stokes passed it on to Barnaby, then looked first at Percival, then at Rose. "Despite our wrong assumptions and the false trails we've pursued, we have, indeed, got to the truth. That"—he tipped his head at the note now in Montague's hands—"is the final nail securing our case against Roger Percival."

Chair legs scraping on the wooden floor, Stokes stood. "Now." He looked at Richard Percival. "Where can I lay hands on your cousin?"

Percival drew out a fob-watch and checked the time. "As it's not yet one o'clock, if you're quick, you should be able to catch him before he leaves home."

The others all stood. Stokes stepped back from the table. "And his home is where?"

On his feet, too, Percival replied, "He lives in my uncle's town house in Mayfair—Number five, Albemarle Street."

The shock on everyone's faces had Percival glancing around.

"Oh, *no!*" The exclamation came from Penelope.

The others all looked at her; she appeared utterly shocked and had paled.

"What?" Barnaby demanded, his tone like a whip.

Penelope met his gaze. "That gentleman's gentleman who saw us in Conduit Street—the one who recognized Rose and William. I just realized—he also recognized me!"

Along with all the others, Barnaby stared at her, then he looked at Richard Percival. "Does your cousin or your uncle have a gentleman's gentleman?"

Richard Percival nodded. "Marmaduke's valet is old and rarely leaves the house. Roger's man, on the other hand, is a slimy character." He glanced at Penelope. "Shorter than average, a trifle rotund, slightly bald with thinning brown hair, a round face with pasty complexion, and a sad liking for paisley waistcoats."

Penelope swallowed; eyes widening, she nodded. "That's him."

Silence fell as everyone extrapolated what that news might mean.

Richard Percival was growing increasingly restive. Glancing from face to face, he eventually demanded, "Where are the children?"

Stokes met his gaze, then shoved his chair under the table and turned for the door. "We left them under guard at the Adairs' house. In Albemarle Street—Number twenty-four."

Rose uttered a choked sound and raced for the door. Thomas beat her to it, held it open for her, then, his expression grim, his jaw set, followed at her heels.

They piled out of police headquarters and rushed down the steps and across the street to where a row of hackneys idled. People were constantly coming to and leaving the building, so the hackneys waited expectantly.

Thomas reached the first coach in the line and wrenched open the door. "Albemarle Street, as fast as you can," he called to the jarvey as Rose caught up with him, gathered her skirts, and climbed up.

Following her into the carriage, Thomas was about to slam the door when Richard Percival caught the outer handle.

Percival met Thomas's eyes, then his gaze shifted to Rose. "Please. I need to see that William's all right."

Rose paused only for a second, then nodded.

Thomas released his hold on the door and Percival opened it wider, climbed in, then shut it.

The driver snapped his whip and the hackney pulled away from the curb, quickly picking up speed.

Richard Percival dropped onto the seat opposite Thomas and Rose. Sitting back, he met Rose's eyes, then grimaced and looked away . . . but then he forced his gaze back to meet hers. "I'm sorry. I feel like I failed the children, and you, and even more, Robert and Corinne." He shook his head. "I knew Roger was always hungry for cash, always pushing for more, but I never imagined . . ." Gesturing help-lessly, Percival looked away.

Rose stirred. "Roger's actions, and all the repercussions to date, are not your fault any more than they're mine." When Percival glanced at her, she continued, "As I see it, what's happened so far is a . . . concatenation of events aris-ing from the impact of Roger's murderous actions on the careful arrangements Robert and Mama had set in place. If they hadn't protected me from you, if they hadn't hidden your illegitimacy from me, I would have known better than to think it was you I overheard speaking about killing Wil-liam in order to inherit the estate. But I didn't know, and so I acted."

Percival all but shuddered. "Thank God you did. I've been heaping oaths on your head for years, but if you hadn't taken them and fled . . . who knows what might have oc-curred even on that night. We can never know."

"True. But my point is that both you and I acted as we did from the purest of motives—to protect the children. Neither of us, in my view, needs to apologize for that."

Percival held her gaze for a long moment, then inclined his head. "Thank you. In return, let me state that I in no way hold you responsible for the last four years' difficul-ties."

Rose nodded in acceptance.

Thomas shifted his gaze to the façades whipping past; their jarvey had taken him at his word and was weaving in and out of the traffic thronging Cockspur Street. As the jarvey somewhat enthusiastically took the turn into Waterloo Place, Thomas and Rose swayed, shoulders brushing.

Percival, righting himself as the hackney straightened and pressed up Regent Street, glanced somewhat grimly at Rose. "I can't help remembering how Roger used to put himself out to charm the children. Do you remember?"

Thomas glanced at Rose as she shivered.

"Yes." She paused, then, sensing Thomas's gaze, she elaborated, "Roger used to come up to the nursery and spend time with the children, playing silly games with them, making them laugh. That sort of thing."

Thomas hesitated but then voiced his inference. "So they will most likely view him as a friend."

Rose nodded. "If they remember him at all, and William certainly will, they'll remember him as a family member, one they like." She drew in a shaky breath, held it for a second, then said, "If he asks them to go with him . . . they very well might. He can be extraordinarily charming when he wants to be."

Percival leaned forward, resting his forearms on his thighs; light fell across his face, revealing lines of mounting anxiety. "I swear," he said, his voice low and thrumming with latent anger, "if Roger has hurt them in any way whatever, I will literally wring his neck."

Thomas studied the other man's face, then looked out of the window. If Roger Percival had done anything to harm William or Alice, all others would have to wait in line.

Despite his rising protectiveness—stronger, finer, more powerful than any compulsion he'd ever felt before—he kept his mind focused and refused to let it fragment, to plunge into assessing this scenario and that. There was no point. They needed to find out if anything had happened to the children and, if so, what, before wasting energy in futile, too-early planning.

Eyes on the passing streetscape, he waited . . . for Fate to reveal her full hand.

The others were following in two other hackneys that drew up outside the Adairs' house immediately behind theirs. Percival descended first and paid off the jarvey. Thomas stepped down, then gave Rose his hand.

By the time she was on the pavement, Barnaby was already striding up the steps to his front door. He opened the door with his latchkey; everyone fell silent as, in a close group, trepidation rising over what they might find, they stepped over the threshold and into the front hall.

Everyone stood and listened, but nothing beyond the usual muffled sounds of staff busy in the rear of the house reached them.

Quietly, Montague shut the front door.

Barnaby signaled for them to remain silent and stay where they were. He walked into the drawing room but returned almost immediately.

A second later, Mostyn came hurrying through the door at the rear of the hall, summoned via the bellpull in the drawing room. The majordomo all but skidded to a halt when he saw the assembled group waiting.

Recovering his dignity, Mostyn drew himself up and bowed. "Sir, madam—my apologies. I didn't hear you arrive."

"Is everything in order here, Mostyn?" Penelope quietly asked.

Mostyn frowned. He glanced at Barnaby. "I think so, ma'am."

The prevailing tension noticeably eased.

Rose all but sagged with relief. "Where are the children? Homer and Pippin?"

Mostyn's expression remained unperturbed. "They've gone out for a drive with Mr. Roger Percival—he told me he's cousin to Mr. Richard Percival, and Master Homer recognized him . . ."

Seeing the shocked dismay writ large on their faces, Mostyn floundered to a halt. He looked at Barnaby. "It is Mr. Richard Percival who's the villain, isn't it?"

Barnaby sighed through his teeth, then waved at Richard. "This is Mr. Richard Percival. And no. Sadly, we made a very large mistake. The villain in this case is Roger Percival."

Stokes growled, "He must have had his man watching the house. He would have seen the children brought here this morning, and would, soon after, have seen you all depart, leaving William and Alice here with the staff."

"And now he has them." The quiet anguish in Rose's voice raked them all.

Thomas reached for her hand, gripped it.

"Well," Mostyn said. "Not exactly."

All gazes whipped back to Mostyn's face.

"By which you mean?" Barnaby prompted.

"Well, when he called and Master Homer was so delighted to see him, and Miss Pippin, too, we saw no reason to prevent him playing with the children in the parlor, although James remained with them the whole time, of course."

"Are you saying our guards are with the children?" Penelope demanded.

Mostyn nodded. "Indeed, ma'am. The children have gone for a drive with Mr. Percival, but in our carriage, with Phelps and Conner to watch over them. And, I have to say, the drive wasn't Mr. Percival's idea—it was the children's. They got it into their heads to go to Gunter's for ices, and Mr. Percival asked if that was all right, given he was willing to escort them. The arrangement was that they would go to Gunter's, then perhaps drive through the park before returning here." Mostyn glanced at the clock on the hall table. "I would expect them back within the hour."

Everyone looked at everyone else. No one was sure quite what to make of that.

Eventually, Violet voiced the question revolving in all their minds. "So what do we do? Wait in the drawing room for them to return, or . . . ?"

Richard Percival shifted. "No. We need to find them." He met Rose's gaze, then looked at Thomas. "That idea to go to Gunter's? It might have seemed to be the children's idea, but Roger would have seeded it. He's an expert at steering people to do what he wants, and planting ideas in the children's heads would be . . . well, child's play for him."

"But why would he want them out of the house?" Even as the words left her lips, Penelope waved the question aside. "No—that's obvious. What I mean is, why did he bother going in our carriage with two large men guarding the children?"

Barnaby glanced at Mostyn. "Did he—Roger Percival— try to get you to let them go with him alone, without the guards? In a hackney, perhaps?"

Mostyn looked concerned. "Not exactly, but . . ." He glanced at Penelope. "I got the impression that he'd imagined doing that—taking them off in a hackney—but when James and I explained about the carriage and the guards, that we couldn't agree to let the children go out without them, Mr. Percival fell in with our arrangements without any argument."

Thomas met Stokes's gaze. "Consider this—in arranging the deaths of Robert and Corinne Percival, Roger could not have known they would go for a drive until they did. Those murders were very neatly carried out, left no hints or clues that he was involved, yet he had to have been forming and re-forming his plan as he went. The murder of Atwell—I'm sure there's no evidence there either, and almost certainly that would have happened in the same way, with Roger Percival reacting to an unfolding situation." Thomas shifted his gaze to Richard Percival. "And as Richard said, Roger will continue to work the situation to his own ends, step by step making adjustments, until he gets what he wants."

Rose nodded emphatically. Grasping Thomas's arm, she locked gazes with Stokes. "Thomas and Richard are right. The children may *appear* to be safe, but they're not. They're with a man who wants to murder them—William, at least. And he *will* find a way, an opening, an opportunity, guards or not."

Abruptly, Richard ran a hand through his hair. "He'll probably view it as a challenge—him against Fate. Him succeeding in bending the situation to his own ends."

Thomas stilled. Richard's words resonated through him, a clarion call, and he knew. He looked at Barnaby. "We have to find the children."

Barnaby met his gaze and didn't argue.

Stokes stirred and growled, "I want to rush around to Gunter's, but they most likely won't be there."

Barnaby glanced at Mostyn. "How long have they been gone?"

Mostyn looked at the clock. "They left at about twenty minutes past twelve, so they've been gone for close to an hour."

"Long enough to have gone to Gunter's and left." Penelo-

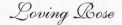

pe's eyes narrowed. "But I suspect none of us are imagining they're currently bowling along the Avenue." She looked at Barnaby, then at Stokes, at Richard, and finally at Thomas. "So where will he take them? How will he engineer the opportunity he wants?"

After several moments of silence, Richard said, "If he's had murdering William in mind all along, and has come here today and succeeded in inveigling the children out of the house . . . he won't stop there. He won't pass up the chance."

All color drained from Rose's face.

Noting it, Thomas closed his hand over hers where it gripped his sleeve. He looked at the others. "We have to start thinking like him. We have to look at the challenges, the hurdles he has to overcome, from his point of view." Something Thomas himself was exceedingly well qualified to do. "Whatever he does, he has to make sure he can either claim it was an accident, or, as with Atwell, and Robert and Corinne, not be identified as being with the victim when they died."

Grim-faced, Barnaby nodded. "You're right. So in this instance, given he's known to be with the children, he'll need to make William's death appear to be an accident, and for that, he'll need to get rid of the guards in some way."

"Or," Thomas said, "find somewhere Phelps, with his coach, and Conner, being a groom, can't readily enter."

"And which they won't see as a dangerous place," Violet put in, "and so won't prevent the children from going in with Roger."

"Exactly." Thomas looked around the circle they'd formed. "So where will he—has he—taken them?"

They all cudgeled their brains, then Penelope volunteered, "The Royal Exchange?"

Thomas thought, then shook his head. "No—too public. It qualifies otherwise, but there will be too many others about, and from memory, there's only one entrance." He paused, then said, "So we can add the stipulation that it needs to be somewhere either deserted, or close to it—and preferably somewhere the children themselves will be keen to go." He glanced at Rose, then Richard. "Roger got the children to suggest going to Gunter's, and he'll do the same again—he'll lead William and Alice to desire to go somewhere, to demand to be taken there, rather than Roger suggesting it himself. Only in response to their entreaties will he offer to take them, and that will help sway Phelps and Conner."

Barnaby, Stokes, Penelope, Violet, and Montague were all nodding, all following the logic.

Thomas looked from Richard to Rose. He tightened his grip on her hand. "So where? *Think*—where's the place the children will want to go to, a building of some sort, deserted or close to that, somewhere the guards will let them go into with Roger alone?" Thomas paused, then added, "And it has to be somewhere reasonably close—Mayfair itself or in areas close by."

"Because," Barnaby filled in, "Phelps and Conner would never countenance being away from here for more than a few hours, and they've already been—"

"Seddington House!" Richard Percival looked at Rose, then raised his gaze to Thomas's face. "It's in Tilney Street, so quite close. It's been closed up for the last four years, but Roger almost certainly has a key—Marmaduke has, so Roger will have."

"Yes!" Gripping Thomas's arm more tightly, Rose met his gaze. "William will remember the house—he was five when last he was there."

"And now it's his." Richard raised his hands. "So easy for someone like Roger to spark William's curiosity, and then fan it to a blaze."

"Oh, yes." Thomas met Barnaby's gaze. "I can definitely imagine that."

Penelope frowned. "But would Phelps and Conner let the children go with anyone into a deserted house?"

Thomas stared at her for a second. "But will they know it's deserted?" He looked at Richard.

Lips compressing, Richard shook his head. "No. They—neither the guards nor the children—would know, not unless Roger tells them, which, of course, he won't. Because of the risk of burglary, we've taken care to keep the house looking like it's occupied. Gardeners come in regularly, and the curtains aren't all drawn. Occasionally, I send my staff around to clean the main rooms . . ." Richard looked at Rose. "I always wondered if you might, at some point, seek refuge there."

"So you're telling us," Stokes said, his voice hard, "that there's nothing that would alert Phelps and Conner to the fact that Roger Percival is taking the children into a deserted house?"

Richard nodded. "Exactly." His expression hardened into a grim mask. "We need to get around there." He turned to the front door.

"No—wait!" Stokes caught Richard's arm and bodily hauled him back. "We can't just go barging in. If we're right, and Roger's there, he'll have William with him, and we don't know how Roger will react. We can't predict what he might do if we charge in."

"Indeed." Penelope nodded. "Roger sounds like the sort to seize the opportunity and take advantage of the clamor to push Homer—William—down the stairs, and then claim that William was startled and tripped." From behind the lenses of her glasses, Penelope held Richard's gaze. "That's not the outcome we want."

The heightened, battle-ready tension that had gripped Richard eased—a fraction. Curtly, he nodded. When Stokes released him, he shrugged his coat into place, then raked the group with his dark gaze, finally looking at Rose. He studied her for a second, then looked at Thomas. "We can't just wait and see what happens—we have to go there and get William and Alice away from Roger. We can't take the risk of leaving them with him for a moment longer than necessary."

Thomas inclined his head. "No, we can't." Even he heard the harder, more incisive note in his voice. "But we have to go in with a plan—one with a decent chance of succeeding, of allowing us to bring William and Alice safely out of that house." He drew breath and turned his mind to the game. Focused on that and blocked everything else out. "Roger doesn't know we suspect him. He has no reason to imagine we know anything at all about the previous murders, much less about his murderous intentions."

Letting the scenario unfurl in his mind, Thomas drew in a deeper breath, then looked at Rose. "Roger can't know what Rose's standing is with Richard, Foley, and even his father—you all might have met this morning and sorted everything out. What Roger does know is that Rose and the children have been in London for the past few days, living openly, and are welcome visitors to this house. He won't think it odd if, having been out for a walk and noticing the Adairs' carriage drawn up by the curb before Seddington House, after speaking with Phelps and Conner, Rose enters the house, thinking to join Roger and the children in reacquainting herself with her old home." Thomas glanced questioningly at Richard.

Richard nodded. "True. So I can go in with Rose and—"

"No." Thomas's tone brooked no argument. He caught Richard's frustrated gaze and spoke decisively and increasingly rapidly; time was, indeed, running out. "You can't accompany Rose because Roger will see you as a threat. We can't know what the situation will be when we enter the house, where Roger will be in relation to where Homer and Pippin—William and Alice—will be at that moment. We can't risk spurring Roger into deciding to act first, and think up his explanations later."

Thomas glanced at the others—Penelope, Barnaby, Stokes, Montague, and Violet. "Rose has to go in, but the only one of the males here who can go in with her is me. Roger will see me as a semi-cripple with no connection to the Percival family and no reason to suspect him of anything. He'll dismiss me as of no real importance and will focus instead on talking his way around Rose."

Of them all, it was Penelope who, with critical detachment, studied him most closely, then she nodded. Decisively. "I agree. You are the best chance William and Alice have for leaving that house alive."

A split second later, Barnaby also nodded. "You're right." He started hunting through the pockets of the old coat he still wore. "For today, for now, it has to be that way. We don't need to capture Roger today, we just need to stymie him." He, too, was speaking rapidly, urgency mounting in his tone. "What we need to do now is stop Roger from killing William and get the children back in our hands."

"Yes." Stokes, too, nodded. "We can deal with Roger Percival later. The rest of us will hang back, out of sight of the house, and watch, but we can't go in—not until the children are safe."

"Here." Barnaby handed his police whistle to Rose. "Blow on this and we'll come running."

"But don't use it until you know William is safe," Stokes warned. "Until you have him and Alice in your keeping."

Rose took the whistle and tucked it into her pocket.

Like her husband, Penelope had also been hunting, in her case in her reticule. She'd pulled out a small pistol and expertly checked it; she handed it to Thomas with a simple "It's loaded."

He took it and slipped it into his pocket.

Looking lost and a trifle wild-eyed, Richard looked from Rose to Thomas, then at the others. "I can't believe I'm going along with this, but . . ." He handed Rose a key he'd removed from his keychain. "The key to Seddington House, in case Roger has locked the door behind them. No reason you wouldn't have had a key from before."

Rose took the key. "Thank you." She met Richard's eyes. "We will do our best to bring them back."

"No," Thomas said, taking her hand as they all turned to the front door. "We *will* bring them back, safe and sound."

"Right, then." Stokes pulled open the front door. "Hackneys to the corner of Tilney Street and South Audley Street—we'll walk in from there."

Arm in arm with Rose, Thomas strolled along Tilney Street, cane gently swinging, an easy expression on his face, as if he and Rose were merely out to take the air, their goal most likely the grassy expanses of Hype Park, just across Park Lane. Penelope's carriage drew his attention; it was drawn up outside one of the large old houses on the southern side of the street.

With his cane, he pointed it out to Rose, and after exchanging a comment, they crossed the street to investigate.

As Richard had told them, Seddington House appeared well tended and lived in. Windows were clean, and no litter, cobwebs, or other signs of neglect marred the face it showed the world. Wrought-iron railings separated the neat garden from the pavement. The house comprised two full stories, the upper topped by a low parapet overlooked by the dormer windows set in the steeply sloping slate roof. The ground floor was raised and small windows below suggested a working basement beneath. Architecturally, the house was a hodgepodge of older styles; a wide bay on the ground floor to one side of the front door supported a balcony above it, the balcony's surrounding wall matching the parapet above.

Reaching the carriage and Phelps, who was standing beside his horses' heads, Thomas smiled as the coachman bobbed a bow to Rose, then him. "Any sign?" Thomas asked with an innocent smile.

Alerted by Barnaby, who, still in his disguise of lowly workman, had sloped past and stopped to exchange a comment with Phelps, who had subsequently passed the message on to Conner, Phelps was understandably tense but strove to hide it. "No, sir." Phelps touched a finger to his forehead. "None at all. They've been nowhere near any windows—least not the ones we can see."

"Thank you." Thomas glanced at Rose, who had been studying the house. She was doing well enough at concealing her agitation. Catching her eye, Thomas kept his smile in place. "Shall we go in?" The gesture that went with the words would, he hoped, be pantomime enough should Roger Percival be watching from anywhere inside the house.

Rose looked at the house, then forced a bright smile and nodded. She glanced up and met Thomas's eyes. Her fingers tightened on his sleeve. "Yes. Let's."

With every evidence of embarking on a pleasant diversion, they walked through the gate Phelps swung open and continued up the gravel path to the steps that led up to the front porch. Standing apparently at ease beside the bottom step, Conner inclined his head as they approached. "Sir. Ma'am." Only his eyes gave away his tension.

"Have you heard anything?" Thomas quietly asked.

"I'm pretty sure they went upstairs, and I haven't heard them come down—the children were running, so I heard their footsteps."

Thomas held to calm, stopped his eyes from narrowing. "How long ago did they go up?"

"About ten minutes ago." Conner's jaw tightened. "Call if you need us."

"We will." Thomas steered Rose on; the urgency riding her was becoming increasingly apparent, at least to him.

They reached the front door—and found it unlocked. Far from being at all reassured, Thomas found the blatant confidence of Roger Percival alarming. He'd left the door open so if—when—there was a scream or any such noise, Conner would rush in without encountering the oddity of an unexpectedly locked door, a door only Roger could have locked, and would then have to explain.

The man did, indeed, think quickly and was unquestionably, demonstrably, very thorough in dealing with details, with the minutiae that would have tripped up lesser men.

Ushering Rose over the threshold, lowering his head, Thomas whispered, "Remember your role." She needed to cling to it, to preserve the façade of not suspecting Roger of anything.

Following her inside, Thomas looked around with mild interest as he slowly closed the door.

Rose halted in the middle of the front hall. She listened,

straining her ears, but heard nothing. No giggles from Pippin, no scrape of Homer's shoe. Inside, she felt as if her entire body had stopped, shut down—waiting. Turning, she looked at Thomas as he came to join her.

He caught her gaze. Smiled easily, and at normal volume said, "I wonder where they are."

His gaze held hers, gave her strength, and encouraged her. Prodded her to keep to the script they'd rapidly devised as they'd walked down the street.

Turning to face the stairs once more, she raised her head and her voice. "William? Alice? Roger—are you there?" She paused for a second, then went on. "It's Rose—Rosalind. Thomas and I were passing, and we thought we'd come and join you. I haven't been here . . . well, since you two were last here. Years and years. So . . . where are you?"

With bated breath, both she and Thomas listened—and yes, that was a distant scuff, a shoe scraping.

She met Thomas's eyes; he'd heard, too. He nodded at her to proceed.

Dragging in a breath, she infused her words with as much happy gaiety as she could. "Oh, is it a game, then? Are we supposed to search and find you—a game of hide-and-seek? Well, all right, but you know Thomas can't run, so we won't be quick, but . . . we're coming to find you!"

Thomas nodded in approval and, still smiling amiably, walked with her to the stairs. "Up," he murmured, "but don't rush. Whatever happens, don't run."

They started climbing; Thomas had to take stairs like these one step at a time.

Reaching the landing, they started up the second flight. As they neared the top, Thomas murmured, "Cling to your act as long as you possibly can—don't drop it until we have them in our arms and you've blown that whistle."

She merely squeezed his arm in confirmation.

Stepping into the first-floor gallery, they looked around.

Thomas had been in deserted houses before. His senses remained well-honed, even more so after his accident, and they informed him that this house wasn't empty, devoid of life, but he didn't think the sound they'd heard had come from this floor.

He caught Rose's anxious gaze. "Is there a nursery?" he whispered.

She nodded and, turning, pointed across the gallery to a narrow archway; in the shadows beyond the arch, stairs led upward.

Leaning closer to Rose, he murmured, "Describe what's up there."

She met his eyes, then whispered back, "The stair has three short flights. You'll step out"—she looked up at the ceiling—"virtually directly above. There's a corridor that runs above the one we're standing in, forward and back through the house. If you go forward"—with her hands she directed—"the first rooms you come to are maids' rooms and nurses' quarters. The last four rooms, two on either side, are the children's bedrooms—William and Alice had the two closest to the schoolroom. That's the room at the end of the corridor—it runs along the front of that floor."

Thomas nodded. "Start talking. Tell them you're coming to look for them—keep talking and move to the front of the house." He pointed ahead. "Pretend to search the bedrooms at the front on this floor."

Her face clouded. "What are—"

He gripped her hand, squeezed hard. "We don't have time. They're upstairs, and it's too silent up there. I'm going up, but I need you to distract them, to make them think we're searching down here."

She stared at him for a second, then she stepped close, framed his face, and kissed him.

Briefly.

Pulling back, she looked into his eyes. "Be careful."

Releasing him, she whirled, and started along the corridor. Raising her voice, she called, "We're starting to search for you along here. Pippin? Where are you? Are you hiding in Mama's room?"

Thomas limped to the archway, cast a last look over his shoulder, and heard Rose continuing on. Then he gripped his cane and started up as fast as he silently could. As fast as he dared.

It still took too long, but, eventually, he paused on the top step. Rose was still calling out now and then, marking her progress through the lower rooms. At her next pause, Thomas listened—and detected an odd, sliding, scraping sound, then muted voices reached him.

From the direction of the schoolroom.

Stepping out from the cover of the stairwell, his cane held off the thinly carpeted floor, he made his way swiftly but silently toward the schoolroom door.

It stood half open; beyond, the room was bright, full of light. Presumably, the dormer windows had no curtains.

The voices were nearer, had grown clearer; although Thomas couldn't yet make out any words, he identified Homer's boyish tones, then on a rush of relief, he heard Pippin's piping squeak—immediately drowned by a deeper, darker, seductively lethal male voice.

Roger, Homer, and Pippin were together somewhere beyond the door.

Cloaked in the shadows thrown by the door, Thomas scanned what he could see of the room but saw no one and nothing of note. Putting out a hand, very carefully, he eased the door further open.

One part of his mind gave mute thanks that the door didn't squeak; the rest rapidly absorbed and analyzed what his eyes were seeing.

One of the dormer windows stood open, the long casement pushed wide. Roger had taken—forced—both Homer and Pippin out onto the roof. At pistol-point.

A few feet from the open window, the blackguard held Pippin loosely against him; the little girl wasn't struggling because Roger was holding a pistol in his right hand, with the end of the barrel tucked under Pippin's chin. The girl was terrified.

No doubt using the threat against Pippin for leverage, Roger had forced Homer to climb out onto the roof first. Standing heartbreakingly straight and tall, his fists clenched at his sides, his chin tipped defiantly, the boy was further away from the window, a good five paces from his would-be murderer. Who was holding a gun on his little sister.

The section of roof on which they were standing was a flat expanse no more than two feet wide that ran between the parapet and the steep upslope in which the windows were set.

Conner was standing too close to the house to notice the action occurring two stories above. Thomas glanced toward where Phelps waited with the carriage and realized a tree blocked the coachman's view.

Roger's attention was fixed on Homer, and Homer was staring back at him. "Just remember," Roger murmured, "if either of you raise your voice, much less think to scream to your sister or the others for help, I'll almost certainly startle and pull the trigger . . . and you wouldn't want that, would you?"

After a moment of fraught silence, Roger smiled. "Excellent. So, now, here's what you're going to do." He continued in the same low, murmurous, almost mesmerizing voice to direct all to his liking . . .

Thomas teetered on the brink of rushing forward.

He caught himself.

Dragging in a huge breath, his gaze locked on the scene playing out before him, he ruthlessly quashed the emotions geysering through him, clamoring for immediate, impulsive actions, and reached deep, deeper, and found and hauled forth his old persona.

Deliberately wrapped it like an old and well-worn cloak about him.

Malcolm Sinclair had never felt emotion. Had never had to contend with its distraction.

Malcolm Sinclair was who he needed to be to rescue Homer and Pippin.

His vision cleared, sharpened.

Everything, he immediately saw, hinged on how close he could get to the open window without Roger seeing him or either of the children noticing him and reacting.

Leaning his cane against the door frame, he glided forward. One step. Two. His need to limp was still there, but he ignored it—blocked out the pain not limping sent shooting through him.

He didn't matter. Homer and Pippin did.

"I won't!" Fists clenched hard, Homer flung the words, quiet but implacable, at Roger. "We thought you were kind—we liked you. But you're a *monster*." Homer jerked his chin at Pippin. "Let her go!"

Roger smiled, all charm and deadly calm. "I'll let her go after you jump—you have my word."

"Your *word*?" For a nine-year-old, Homer managed to infuse an incredible amount of scorn into the phrase. "What is that worth? I know you won't let her go—you'll throw her off after me or she'll tell everyone what you did."

Roger's smile changed, taunting and openly evil. "Very well. In that case, how about I throw her off first?"

Homer's face blanched.

Malcolm reached the open dormer.

Homer saw him—his gaze locked on him and his expression changed.

Roger noticed and glanced at the window.

He panicked and swung around, lifting the pistol from beneath Pippin's chin.

Malcolm didn't look at the pistol. He looked at Pippin, trapped the girl's gaze. "Pippin—*drop*!"

Her eyes widened.

Then she did.

Roger tried to grab her suddenly boneless little body, but she slid through his hold.

Swearing, he glanced at Malcolm. Lips lifting in a snarl, Roger gave up on Pippin, who scrambled and scuttled to Homer. The boy grabbed her and bundled her behind him.

Roger held Malcolm's gaze for a split second, then straightened, turned, and leveled his pistol on Homer.

No thought was required.

Malcolm grabbed both sides of the window frame, hauled himself up, and launched himself at Roger Percival.

He slammed into the man. Hands locking on Percival's arm, Malcolm forced the pistol barrel up and back.

They wrestled. Percival cursed. Malcolm tightened his grip and forced Percival's arm higher.

The pistol discharged harmlessly into the sky.

Percival roared. With his free hand, he pushed Malcolm away.

Pushed himself backward.

The top of the low parapet caught Percival across the backs of his knees.

Eyes flaring wide, arms flailing, Percival started falling backward.

Unsupported, unbalanced, Malcolm staggered forward.

In utter desperation, Percival lashed out—and caught the side of Malcolm's coat.

Then he fell.

And took Malcolm with him.

He was falling.

Again.

And as it had on the first occasion, time slowed.

But, this time, instead of myriad flashes of his life, his senses replayed that time before, the deafening thunder of the water, the icy chill as the tumult soaked him. Most especially he remembered the savage terror that had ripped through him, body and soul, as he'd plummeted toward the jagged black rocks . . .

That picture faded.

This time, there was only peace.

A sense of finality.

Of completeness.

Of end.

A scream pierced the enveloping silence.

Rose. His Rose.

His loving Rose.

His route to peace—his salvation.

Something struck his ribs; a sharp crack sounded.

He couldn't see. His vision had dimmed.

His body tumbled; pain shot through him.

Overtook him.

He landed with a thud.

On soft, dark earth instead of jagged rocks.
It didn't matter—he was done.
Closing his eyes, he let Fate have him.

Standing on the semicircular balcony at the front of the house, tears clouding her vision, her heart in her throat, Rose blew and blew on the whistle.

*H*e heard murmurs, whispers, but couldn't tell who spoke, nor what they said.

Perhaps it was St. Peter deciding where he should go? Up, or down? But he didn't believe in God—so perhaps it was the Fates, deciding his.

Either way, he'd done all he could. His life was over.

He drifted. Pain had no purchase here, on this plane where nothing existed.

But *he* was here, wasn't he? He was real . . . or was he?

The questions were too hard, the mists shrouding him too dense to penetrate.

He let go, stopped wondering, and simply drifted.

He came to his senses and realized that they, and his wits, were once more his to command.

Of his body, he was not yet sure.

Before testing the latter, he let his senses expand, let them tell him what they might.

He was . . . lying in a bed, with plump pillows beneath his head, with covers, warm and soft, tucked about him.

Not what he'd expected.

It took effort to lift his lashes, but, eventually, he managed it. Blinked.

Rose sat in a chair by the bed, head bent, busily sewing.

He'd seen the sight so often in the kitchen at the manor that for several seconds he didn't dare believe this was anything more than a memory . . .

Then, as if sensing his regard, Rose looked up—and met his eyes.

"Thank God," she breathed as joy suffused her face. A smile brimming with love and gratitude lit her countenance.

Laying aside her sewing, she rose and drew near.

Placing her hand over his where it lay on the counterpane, she held his wondering gaze. "I love you."

Her smile didn't dim; her gaze remained steady and sure. *He was alive.*

Emotions battered him, left his wits giddy, reeling, intoxicated with welling happiness. He studied her face, drank in her beloved features, soaked up the emotions he could see in her eyes. He let his lips curve wryly. "Not the monastery again, then."

The words came out in a raspy rumble. His tongue felt thick, his throat dry.

Rose laughed, all but delirious with relief and happiness. Lifting a tumbler of water from the bedside table, she held it for him and urged him to sip.

Once he had, she asked, "How do you feel?"

He frowned, transparently taking stock.

Setting the glass down, she sat on the bed beside him, taking one of his hands between hers—unable not to touch him, to hold onto him now he was back.

After a moment, he raised his gaze and met hers. "I'm not sure. I was certain I would die."

There was a question in the last sentence, one she answered. "No—according to the doctor, you were never in any danger of dying. You hit the tree as you fell, several times, and that slowed your fall, and also turned you so that you landed fully in the garden bed, rather than on the gravel or across the bed's stone edge. You've broken several ribs, but they're set and are healing, and the doctor believes you wrenched your already damaged hip and weak leg, and you suffered a bad wound across your back where you hit a large branch, but"—she paused to draw breath—"in time, the doctor believes that all you'll have to show from the incident is a scar across your back."

She watched him trying to assimilate that. "The doctor said that in a roundabout way your previous injuries protected you this time—he said your joints and muscles have grown unusually strong, having been forced to compensate for your earlier injuries. They held up better under the stress than an uninjured man's would have."

That seemed to help.

Then he turned his hand and grasped hers, and refocused on her eyes. "Homer and Pippin—William and Alice. How are they faring?"

She grinned and returned the pressure of his fingers. "Better than anyone else. They were as shocked as all we adults were, but as soon as they heard of the doctor's verdict about you . . ." With her free hand, she gestured. "Their shock turned to excitement, and they've been busy telling everyone who'll listen about their thrilling escape from Roger's villainous clutches. He now features as 'that very bad man.'"

"From the mouths of babes—he *was* a very bad man."

Thomas—he realized he was, indeed, Thomas again—remembered Roger's voice on the roof. Heard again the cadence, recalled the darkness dripping from every syllable, and suppressed a shudder. Glancing up, he met Rose's eyes. "I've met evil men before, several, of various different stripes. Roger was neither the highest nor the lowest in standing and scope. But he was the worst."

He shifted in the bed, then asked, "What happened to him?"

"He's in hospital, under guard, but not expected to live."

There was, he noted, not a shred of gentleness, of compassion, in her voice; Roger was dead to her, regardless.

He couldn't find any fault with that.

Letting his head sink back on the pillows, he looked around, taking in the furniture and trappings of a regular bedroom. Beyond the window, the sky showed blue, the leafy canopies of trees ruffling beneath the hand of a playful breeze. "Where are we?"

He looked back at Rose in time to see her smile.

"In Barnaby and Penelope's house. They insisted that we all stay here until you've recovered enough for us to think of what we wish to do next, of where we want to go."

He held her gaze for a long moment, then quietly said, "Us?"

She nodded decisively. "Us." Her tone was determined. Her eyes narrowed fractionally, as if daring him to argue.

Us. His gaze locked with hers, he hesitated—struggled to define the logical way forward, to shape words to give it reality—but, in the end, he bowed to the moment, to the overwhelming emotional compulsion welling within, and said nothing.

He wasn't sure . . . what should be. What could be.

He knew he needed to think things through, but . . . heaving a sigh, he realized he was still too weak.

His lids grew heavy and drifted down. He started to fight, to try to stay with her, but then he felt her hand stroke over the back of his, then she shifted forward and he felt her lips brush his forehead.

"Sleep," she whispered. "We'll be here when you awake."

Reassured at some primitive level, he let go, and did.

More than a week passed before Thomas could manage the stairs. The day after he proved he could brave them, Penelope organized a dinner party.

"Come along." Her arm looped through his, Rose steadied him as he paused at the head of the stairs. "Everyone's waiting in the drawing room."

It took another five minutes of careful, step-by-step negotiation, but, at last, he gained the tiles of the front hall and straightened.

Rose smiled encouragingly. Arm in arm, they turned toward the door that Mostyn, beaming, stood ready to open.

As they approached, Thomas still nursing his mending ribs and leaning heavily on his cane, Mostyn obliged and sent the door swinging wide, and they walked into a celebration.

The others were all there—Barnaby and Penelope, Stokes and Griselda, Montague and Violet, and Richard Percival—the people Thomas had come to know over the last weeks, those he'd worked alongside to save William, Alice, and Rose.

The children were there, too, not just William and Alice, who were gradually learning to respond to their real names, but also Barnaby and Penelope's son, Oliver, and Stokes and Griselda's Megan, rambunctious toddlers both, and it was now more apparent that Violet and Montague were expecting a child, albeit several months from now.

All the adults were on their feet, watching Thomas, glasses in their hands and huge smiles on their faces.

He halted, bemused. He'd assumed this was to be an ordinary dinner party; he hadn't imagined . . .

Barnaby raised his glass. "To our own conquering hero."

"To our conquering hero!" the others echoed, raising their glasses to Thomas, then drinking his health.

He blinked rapidly. He was, indeed, Thomas again, with his inconvenient emotions and their consequent distractions.

Someone pressed a glass into his hand.

He looked at Rose and saw she already had a glass and was sipping, drinking to him with the others.

He met her eyes, saw them brimming with happiness, and hesitated—and looked inward, as he so often had to, for guidance. As Thomas, thanks to her, he knew what to do.

Raising his head, he lifted his glass to the others and said, "Thank you." He paused, then added, "I couldn't have saved the children without the support and help of you all."

Everyone grinned, laughed, inclined their heads in acknowledgment, then all turned and found their seats and sat so they could talk and share the latest news.

Limping forward to the small sofa that had, apparently, been reserved for him and Rose, Thomas carefully sat, then eased back. Rose sat beside him. He glanced at her and felt gladness—a sense of gratitude, of simple joy at being alive—well and flow through him.

The talk, unsurprisingly, had turned to those critical moments at Seddington House.

Stokes, Barnaby, and Penelope, and Montague and Violet, and Richard Percival, in various positions along and across the street, had all had a clear view of the action on the roof.

"But we couldn't see you," Richard explained. "Not until you flung yourself at Roger."

"We didn't know what to do," Violet said. "Whether to scream at Phelps and Conner to look—"

"Or to run inside ourselves." Stokes shook his head. "It was a horrible few minutes."

"Minutes the likes of which I never want to live through again." The iron-willed declaration came from Penelope.

Griselda's brows rose, as if she couldn't believe her ears.

Penelope saw, and raised a shoulder. "Well, not if I can avoid it."

Griselda laughed. Barnaby caught his wife's eyes and smiled.

They adjourned to the dining room and the conversations rolled on.

Penelope had seated Richard Percival, the odd man at the table, alongside Thomas. Richard seized a moment between courses to capture Thomas's attention. "I've spoken with Rose, and William, too, of course. Given that summer's approaching and the schools will soon close, we thought, if you're agreeable, that it would be best for William if we could leave him in your care, to continue his studies under your guidance, at least for the next few months. We have plenty of time to assess schools and decide which one will best suit him, and, of course, he will need to start to get to know the estate, to spend more time there."

Thomas hadn't thought . . .

Richard tried to read Thomas's suddenly impassive expression but couldn't. More tentatively, Richard said, "We realize, of course, that it's an imposition, and if you don't feel inclined to take on the responsibility, I'm happy to arrange for Rose and the children to live in Seddington House. We can hire tutors, and—"

"No." The word spilled from Thomas's lips, driven purely by emotion. By reaction. But he didn't yet know what was to happen. He glanced across the table at Stokes; engaged in an earnest discussion with Montague, Stokes appeared oblivious of, and had certainly given no sign of remembering, their arrangement, but Thomas couldn't believe Stokes had forgotten it. "It might be best," Thomas quietly said, bringing his gaze back to Richard's face, "if we left things as they are for the moment. Until I have time to sort out how matters stand."

Richard's gaze moved past Thomas to Rose, sitting on Thomas's other side. With a smile, Richard nodded. "Yes, of course. As I said, we have several months before any decisions regarding William's personal life need to be made."

And Thomas's relationship with Rose was another issue that hung in the balance. A balance that, as far as he knew, was firmly weighted against.

Eager to deflect any further comments on such issues, he asked, "What about Marmaduke? He's still William's co-guardian, I take it?"

Richard nodded. "However, when it comes to it, Marmaduke has never had any interest in running the estate, and neither Foley nor I imagine he'll show any more engagement over the details of William's personal life now William has reappeared—and, incidentally, Foley has notified the courts of that fact, that William is hale and whole and very much alive."

Richard paused, then went on, "As for Marmaduke himself, he's in a sorry state. At the moment, he's keeping vigil by Roger's bed. On learning what Roger has been up to, Marmaduke was stunned, shocked—indeed, beyond horrified. He found it hard to accept, at first, but now he knows it's the truth and he's a shattered man. I seriously doubt we, or William, need fear any further interference from that quarter."

Thomas glanced across the table to where William sat, with Alice beside him; both children were thrilled to be dining with the adults. "What of society?" Thomas asked. "How much does the ton know?"

Richard had followed his gaze and understood why he was asking; the ton had a habit of looking askance at the family of blackguards like Roger. "We've endeavored to keep the matter as quiet as possible, and, thanks largely to the Adairs, we've succeeded well enough. Many do know, of course—that was unavoidable—but all of those are of the ilk to appreciate the need for discretion."

Relieved, Thomas nodded. "Good."

Rose claimed his attention, and he and Richard were drawn into the wider discussion.

When the meal was at an end, the trifle disposed of and the poached figs all gone, they repaired to the drawing room. The conversation veered into more general spheres as, with Thomas's encouragement, Adair and Montague brought Thomas up to date with all the happenings he'd missed during his recent convalescence.

The children started to yawn, and Rose urged them to retire.

With sleepy smiles, a bow, and a wobbly curtsy, the pair took their leave of the company and departed for their beds, passing Mostyn in the doorway as he rolled in the tea trolley.

Stokes shifted in his armchair. "I didn't want to mention this until the children left—they've heard enough of such things and can be told the salient points later, should they ever need to know." He looked around the group. "Roger Percival breathed his last about noon today, but before he did, he made a full confession."

"Wait!" Penelope held up a staying hand. "Let me hand

around the cups, then we can all sit back and you can have the floor."

Thomas duly accepted a cup and saucer. He took a sip, then caught Stokes's gaze. "Before you start, perhaps you could fill me in on what actually happened when Roger and I fell. I'm a little hazy on the details after we left the roof."

Stokes looked at him, then said, "Because Roger pulled you over, you fell forward, more or less headfirst, closer to the house and somewhat to the side of where he fell. You hit several large branches of a tree and landed in the flowerbed that ran along the front of the house. Roger, in contrast, fell backward—he fell further out from the house, and clear of the tree. He landed half on the gravel path, half in the flowerbed. The raised stone edging of the bed broke his back and punctured a lung. He was never going to recover, but he lingered until today."

Thomas nodded. "Thank you."

Stokes took the cup and saucer Griselda handed him, sipped, then glanced around the circle of now expectant faces. "We—the police—are now confident that Marmaduke Percival had no idea what his son was about, not at any time. As Richard mentioned, Marmaduke is . . . not exactly simple but very easily led. His son knew that and used it as far as he was able."

Stokes paused, sipped, then went on, "Roger was in crippling debt. He first started borrowing money while at school, he and his friend Atwell. Both liked to pretend they were much wealthier than they were, and lived well beyond their means. They egged each other on, and, from the first, both borrowed from the most unscrupulous lenders—the ones willing to lend to schoolboys from good families. Roger never attempted to get money from his father because, by the time he realized how deeply he was sinking and wanted to pay his way out, he'd discovered Marmaduke had very little funds, not enough to make any serious dent in Roger's debts. So Roger sank deeper and deeper into the mire. He had always played on his connection to the Seddington estate, but as time went on, and William was born, for Roger, matters grew increasingly fraught. Eventually, he had to do something to appease his increasingly aggressive creditors, so he calmly and cold-bloodedly planned to murder his cousin Robert and Robert's wife, Corinne, and then subsequently to do away with William. After that, Roger's father would have inherited the estate, and that would have been enough to save Roger.

"Roger bought a potent sleeping draft, enough to kill Robert and Corinne, and William, too. He drove to Seddington Grange, but as he was nearing the entrance to the drive, he saw Robert drive out, with Corinne by his side. They turned north, away from Roger, so he followed. He saw them halt on a grassy headland above Grimsby and lay out a picnic. He quickly found an inn, bought a bottle of wine, and joined them. He slipped the sleeping draft into their glasses, but he was clever enough not to give them too much. They slept, but they didn't die."

Voice darkening, Stokes went on, "Roger waited until night fell, then he took them in his curricle down to the wharf. He put them on Robert's yacht, then—and remember all the Percival men can sail—he took the yacht out, wrapped the two bodies, still alive, in the sails, and then capsized the yacht. He made sure the sails would stay with the yacht and that the yacht would float, then—it being a calm sea—he swam back to shore and drove back to London."

Stokes looked at Rose. "What you heard on the evening after the funeral was Roger boasting to Atwell, telling Atwell how he'd got himself out of the mire. Atwell hadn't yet, you see—he was still sinking. And it was just as well that you reacted as you did—Roger planned to dose William with the draft the next day. When you and the children disappeared . . . Roger decided it didn't really matter. His cousin and wife were dead, and the only person who stood between him, or rather his father, and the estate was a five-year-old boy who had vanished. Roger artfully led his creditors to believe that William would never reappear, that it was simply a matter of waiting out the seven years and then he would have unfettered access to the estate. His creditors were willing to continue to lend to him on that basis. For Roger, William's disappearance was merely a temporary delay."

Switching his gaze to Richard, Stokes went on, "And then Roger realized that you were searching for William, and that made everything, in his eyes, so much easier. Through Marmaduke, he learned of your progress, and he kept a distant watch on Curtis and his men. Regardless, Roger felt that, if and when you found William, he would have plenty of time to act. He wasn't worried either way. But, of course, as time went on and his debts continued to mount, his creditors grew increasingly demanding. That happened recently. However, two years ago, Atwell—school friend and confidant—reached point-non-plus, and, as we'd surmised, on the strength of his knowledge of Roger's murder of his cousin and his cousin's wife, Atwell tried to get money from Roger. Atwell died at Roger's hands. So that's that murder solved, too."

Stokes paused, clearly ordering his thoughts, then continued, "But returning to the present, for Roger, matters were growing increasingly pressing. He had to find William, murder him, and have his body found—he now needed that to assure his creditors that he would one day be able to pay his debts. Roger started watching Curtis's men. He knew Richard, through Curtis, was closing in on Rose, and he was holding himself ready to act. When his man saw William, Rose, and Alice getting into Penelope's carriage, Roger could barely hold himself back. He needed William dead as soon as possible, and he was willing to work with whatever situation eventuated." Stokes paused, then looked at Thomas and dipped his head. "He nearly succeeded, but he didn't."

"And now he's dead." Richard Percival didn't add "and a good thing, too," but the sentiment hovered in the air, nonetheless.

Stokes nodded. "The commissioners are delighted that we've closed several cases, all nice and neat, with nothing left hanging."

Thomas glanced at Stokes, but the man was draining his cup; Thomas concluded that Stokes hadn't meant anything specific by the remark.

Penelope, Griselda, and Violet stepped in, introducing and pursuing topics that drew them all from the darkness that had been Roger Percival, that had emanated from him and driven his deeds.

Gradually, under the ladies' determined influence, the atmosphere lightened, and, one by one, they were able to laugh and smile again.

Thomas looked around the circle, listened to the others' plans for the future, immediate and more far-reaching, and found himself wishing that he, too, had a future he could look forward to, one he could share with friends like this. Instead, he listened to them expound, and artfully slid around any questions aimed at him. For their part, they assumed he was still recovering and hadn't yet had time to think further, so they—even Penelope—didn't press him for answers.

Letting their warmth, the ambiance of friendship, wash over him, he looked at each one and had no doubt that their friendship would be there, already was there, offered and extended to him should he wish to claim it; he'd gained enough insight into these people to read them clearly, to appreciate and understand.

To feel their sincerity when the evening finally wound to a close and they all walked into the front hall to make their farewells, and they, each of them, turned to him and wished him well, wished him a speedy and continuing recovery, shook his hand or kissed his cheek, and bade him adieu until next they met.

He had no idea whether they would ever meet again.

That was up to Stokes and the police. It was they who held his future in their hands.

They who would determine what that future was.

He'd made an agreement, and he wasn't about to resile from it. Stokes, and Adair, too, had more than delivered on their side of the bargain; it was now up to Thomas to pay the agreed price.

Stokes and Griselda were the last to leave.

After farewelling Barnaby, Penelope, and Rose, Stokes turned to Thomas and held out his hand. When Thomas gripped it, Stokes met his eyes. And nodded. "I'll call tomorrow morning. It's time I brought you up to date on the police file on Malcolm Sinclair."

Thomas felt a chill touch his soul, but, without allowing his easy expression to change in the least, he held Stokes's gray gaze and inclined his head. "I'll be here, waiting."

With an acknowledging nod, Stokes released his hand and turned to take Megan from Griselda's arms; a minute later, they'd piled into their carriage and were gone.

Mostyn closed the front door. Turning away, Rose and Penelope led the way upstairs, heads together as they

planned some outing. With a grin, Barnaby fell in by
Thomas's side, and, together, they followed.

He'd known she would come to him that night. But having
no faith in his future, he'd already made the necessary arrangements, had, weeks before, made a new will so that if
anything happened to him, she and any child she bore
would live a life of luxury. He didn't know what tomorrow
would bring, and with regard to her future well-being, he
was not of a mind to court any risk.

He was already in bed, lying back, his arms crossed behind his head when she slipped through his door. Her nightgown glimmered white, the pale pink of her robe muted in
the soft light of the candle she'd used to light her way.

Coming to the bed, she saw he was awake, and smiled.

Joy and more shone in her eyes, and although he still felt
he should make some effort to dissuade her, as she set the
candlestick down on the bedside table, then shrugged out of
her robe, he remained mute.

Just watched. Let his eyes drink her in as she bent and,
holding back the heavy fall of her hair, blew out the flame.

Darkness descended, but the moonlight was strong
enough for him to see the delight, the expectation of happiness and pleasure, that lit her face as she accepted the covers he'd raised and slid into the bed, into the space he'd
shifted to create for her alongside him.

Turning to him, she placed her hands on his chest, looked
into his eyes, searched his face, then tipped her head.
"What? No attempt to tell me that you have no future, and
that I shouldn't—that we shouldn't—do this?"

She hadn't forgotten, any more than he had.

He covered one of her hands with one of his, raised her
fingers and gently brushed his lips over the slender digits,
then, unfurling them, his eyes never leaving hers, he pressed

a hotter, more potent kiss to her palm. "I've given up pretending." Through the dimness, he held her stare, then he lifted his gaze to her hair, let it sweep down, over her face, over her shoulders, and beyond. "Pretending that I don't want you." He returned his look to her face. "That I don't love you. That you aren't as essential to me as the sun and the moon and the wind and the rain."

She stared up at him, then she reached a hand to his nape and drew his head to hers. "Good. So let me love you."

He let her have her way—or, at least, think she was getting it. Let her draw him into a kiss that quickly grew heated. Then hotter. More needy, hungry, and demanding, until it held them both, consumed them both, and drove them onward.

Into a spiraling storm of passions, of desires held back, denied by circumstance for the last several weeks, but now let go, released, unleashed.

Hands drifted, stroked, caressed—possessed. Her nightgown was shed, tossed onto the floor. She came into his arms, and with her body, her hands, her lips and tongue, she boldly, brazenly, demanded more.

And, this time, it was his turn to give. His turn to love her without reserve, without restraint.

To show her.

All. All that lived inside him. All that had claimed his heart.

He laid it all—everything—at her feet, openly, without reservation.

He had no idea what tomorrow would bring, for him, for them, but for tonight, they had this.

Each other.

And their love.

Naked, she writhed, her hands locked about his, clamped about her hips as he held her immobile, and lapped and tasted her, and drove her wild.

Bare; he stripped himself of every last shield and screen, and let her see how deeply he felt, let her touch, taste, and know his vulnerability.

The depth of all he felt.

For her.

Loving Rose.

That had grown to be so much more than simply his salvation.

She was his all, and he gave to her unstintingly. Lavished every last iota of his devotion on her.

Here, tonight, was the time of his choosing, his moment of revelation.

Yet when he would have risen over her and joined them, she pushed and wrestled him onto his back. "No," she murmured, her voice thick with passion. "You still hurt."

How she knew he didn't know, but as she straddled him and, with sublime confidence, sheathed him in her body, took him in and held him, he gave her even that—his surrender.

She rode him through the landscape that together they created, one of passion and heat, of desire and hunger, and he went with her, gladly sharing every molten moment, until the inevitable peak rose and they swept up and on, surging powerfully into their sensual sun.

For that one, bright, brilliant moment, ecstasy held them, sharp as any crystal, as scintillating as any diamond.

Then it shattered. Them, the moment—all imploded in a nova of golden pleasure.

Joy and happiness and shining love radiated through them; pleasure thrummed deep in their veins.

Then it was over and they slumped, and satiation enfolded them.

Wrapping his arms about her, holding her close, he yielded to their joy, and to their happiness.

And, most of all, to their love.

Chapter
17

Thomas was standing by the window in the back parlor, watching Rose, Penelope, and Griselda play with all four children on the rear lawn, when Stokes walked into the room.

Thomas glanced around, then turned, expecting Stokes to wish to speak with him in a more formal setting, but Stokes walked forward and, his gaze resting on the tableau outside, settled beside him.

Seeing no reason to argue, Thomas turned back to the scene outside.

And waited.

Eventually, Stokes said, "Just to be clear, this wasn't only my decision. I've discussed it with Adair, as he, too, was involved. His father and the Chief Commissioner have also considered the matter in some depth. This isn't a straight-forward situation."

Thomas gave no response; there was none he could make.

He waited.

But Stokes said nothing more.

Gaining the impression the other man was having difficulty finding the right words, Thomas quietly volunteered, "I take it you've come to arrest me."

Clasping his hands behind his back, Stokes drew in a deep breath. "No." He paused, then, his gaze still fixed on the scene outside, went on, "I've come to inform you that as far as the Metropolitan Police and all others involved are concerned, Malcolm Sinclair died five years ago, when a bridge collapsed over the falls at Will's Neck in Somerset, immediately after Sinclair had assisted Charles Morwellan, Earl of Meredith, to escape a similar fate."

Thomas blinked. "But I didn't."

"Die? You, the man, might not have, but, I assure you, Sinclair did. He was declared dead—on my recommendation, I might add—and his will passed through probate, and the dispersal of his estate was overseen by several of the most senior peers in the realm . . . do you have any notion of just how difficult resurrecting Malcolm Sinclair would be?" Jaw setting, Stokes shook his head. "And for what? Just to hang you—or more likely transport you—courtesy of that long-ago confession?" Stokes snorted. "The courts, the police, and I have better things to do with our time."

Thomas frowned. This was not what he'd expected; he wasn't sure what to do, how he should react—whether the impulse to simply accept and go forward was the correct thing to do or simply a craven longing.

Finally, Stokes glanced at him, saw the dilemma writ large in his face, and for a wonder seemed to understand. "You need to consider this from the perspective of wider society. That was our perspective—always is our perspective—when deciding issues such as this. While Malcolm Sinclair's actions may have indirectly led to crimes, and even tragedies, his death brought a great deal of good to a very large number of deserving souls. His will ensured that, and, as I mentioned, a great many people devoted time and effort and lent their standing to make sure that will was properly executed." Stokes paused, then said, "If you think of true justice as the balancing of a scale, then the details surrounding Malcolm Sinclair's death and the impact of his will outweighed the sins of his life. He made reparation, and his account is closed."

Stokes paused, then went on, "Which brings us to you— Thomas Glendower. The man you now are is no threat to anyone. More, you are an asset to society, and that on many levels. Through the funds you manage, you support a range of institutions, from those helping the most needy to the wider arts." Stokes humphed. "If the police were so foolish as to move against you, we'd have a good half of the ladies of Mayfair, and a good portion of the gents, too, knocking on the Chief Commissioner's door, demanding to know what we think we're about."

Shaking his head, Stokes went on, "Don't imagine that we're simply looking the other way—I've checked. And while it's unclear how you, Thomas, got your initial funds, given those initial funds were relatively small, and, regardless, even if they were ill-gotten gains, the subsequent growth of those funds was entirely due to you, through the exercise of your remarkable talent for a certain type of high-return investing—and yes, I got that from Montague— and the amount of money you've since given away to a range of charities literally dwarfs those initial funds and renders them insignificant."

Stokes looked down, and this time his pause was more reflective, more weighty.

Thomas waited, sensing there was more but knowing better

than to prompt. Despite the direction of Stokes's disclosures, Thomas couldn't yet allow himself to believe . . . to hope.

"There are times," Stokes said, his deep voice low, "rare times in a policeman's life when he's faced with the choice between adhering to the letter of the law or acting for the greater good of the community he's sworn to serve. Adair, his father, the Chief Commissioner, and all the others involved in this case know that, in this instance, that's the choice we're facing—and we all know which way that choice should be made." Stokes looked up, and for the first time since he'd walked into the room, his gaze met Thomas's squarely; there was compassion and understanding—an unexpected wealth of it—in Stokes's slate-gray eyes. "Malcolm Sinclair is dead. Thomas Glendower lives, and is a respected member of society."

Thomas held Stokes's gaze—and felt weak, suddenly detached. Light, as if his soul was floating . . .

Relief, he realized, deeper and more profound than any he'd previously felt. He hadn't, truly hadn't believed that this moment—this pardon, this freedom—would ever be granted him.

"Thank you." That was all he could say.

Stokes's lips lifted lightly and he turned once more to the scene beyond the window. "It's not me you need to thank, but if you wish to repay not just me but the world"—Stokes nodded outside—"there's your way forward. Rose, William, and Alice—they need you. Not anyone else but specifically you—someone who knows the ropes, who knows how to get things done. Who knows how to watch over them."

Thomas had followed Stokes's gaze to where Rose, William, and Alice cavorted with the others in some riotous game. "They have Richard Percival—he's their family, their nearest kin."

"Perhaps, but they don't trust him, not as they do you, and they never will. Rose in particular will never feel as safe with him as she does with you. And as for William . . . he's too damned intelligent for his own good, but you have experience of that. You know how to handle that, as very few others do."

Thomas tried to absorb, to fully comprehend and accept, the implications of Stokes's words; the prospect was more than he had ever imagined he might aspire to. So much more that he was having difficulty getting even his mind to cope. He felt like a child offered his dearest dream on Christmas morning, and being too afraid to reach out and touch, just in case it was an illusion . . . he dragged in a breath and forced himself to put that fear into words. "So I . . . what? Continue as Thomas Glendower and . . ."

This time Stokes seemed unaware of his state, of his shattering uncertainty. Eyes on the group on the lawn, Stokes shrugged. "You live a normal life." He nodded outside. "You marry Rose, and help her bring up William and Alice, and have children of your own." Stokes's lips curved appreciatively. "Trust me, having children of your own changes a man more than anything else in life—and all to the good. Speaking of which"—Stokes glanced at him—"I rather think I'll join them."

Thomas found himself nodding in agreement. He drew in a deeper breath and tightened his grip on his cane. Moving to follow Stokes through the open French door, he murmured, "Your proposition . . . is going to take a little getting used to."

Stokes snorted. "Don't take too long—you're no spring chicken."

Stepping onto the rear terrace, Stokes waited for Thomas to join him, then said, "Incidentally, one thing I, we—our band of investigators, which includes the commissioners—would appreciate is being able to call on you and your particular knowledge of raising capital, should we run into future cases in which that features."

Thomas readily inclined his head. "All the knowledge I have is at your disposal—you have only to ask."

"Excellent." Stokes rubbed his hands together. "Now . . . what the devil is the point of this game they're playing?" Stepping down from the terrace, he started across the lawn. "Does it even have a point?"

A valid question, Thomas thought as he followed more slowly.

His mind was still reeling. He was still grappling with the realization that all he now desired of life was his for the claiming. As he limped across the neatly clipped lawn, he felt shaky, unsteady, as if taking his first steps into a new life . . . he supposed that was, in effect, what he was doing.

Stokes had paused a little way from the garrulous group of ladies and children, the women seated on the grass, their skirts billowing about them, with the children crawling in and out of the spaces between in what appeared to be some peculiar game of tag.

Halting beside Stokes, Thomas, too, watched, but his mind was still searching for perspective. "Looking back," he murmured, "I could wish that, in my youth, I had met men like Montague, Barnaby, or even you, anyone who might have introduced me to the challenge of bringing wrongdoers to justice, or even simply the challenge of making money to help others, rather than the challenge of self-interest, which was all my late and unlamented guardian taught me."

His gaze on the women and children, he drew in a deep breath, then exhaled—and it felt as if he was letting go of the past, releasing it and letting it slide back into the past, where it belonged. "Then again, if that had happened, would I be standing here now?" He dipped his head toward Rose and the children. "Watching them, planning a life with them—having the chance of a life with them now?"

Stokes met Thomas's eyes and smiled. "Fate does, indeed, move in mysterious ways."

With that, Stokes looked at the group, then, smile deepening, went forward to ask if he might join the circle.

He was welcomed with eager delight.

As she shifted to make space for Stokes, Rose looked up, met Thomas's gaze, and arched her brows.

Thomas smiled. He hesitated for only an instant, then he limped forward, ready, very willing, and, at last, free to take his place.

Malcolm Sinclair was dead and gone. Thomas Glendower lived.

It was Thomas who loved Rose, and who, one gentle August morning, had married her in the chapel on the Seddington estate, with William and Alice, now fully restored to their dignities and their proper names, standing alongside them, with their London friends, and Richard Percival, and the entire Seddington Grange household in beaming attendance. Roland had traveled from Somerset to bless their union with his grace; even Foley had come up for the day.

Despite the crowd, Thomas had only had eyes for Rose, and she for him.

He'd spoken his vows clearly and had meant every word—to love, honor, and cherish.

Forever. Until death finally and truly parted them.

And even after that.

The day had been a golden one; the celebrations had

lasted for days. The warmth with which so many had embraced him remained with Thomas, a potent reminder that, indeed, he was no longer the man he once had been.

Autumn spiced the air on the day they returned to London over two months later, and, at Thomas's insistence, he, Rose, William, and Alice went walking up South Audley Street, then turned off to stroll past the Audley chapel and into the graveyard beyond.

Her hand tucked into the crook of Thomas's arm, Rose walked beside him along the paved path that led through the graveyard. He had recovered from the injuries sustained in his fall from the Seddington House roof, and, once again, carried his cane more for safety's sake than any constant need.

William and Alice ranged ahead, one on either side of the path, reading the names on the gravestones and calling out the more remarkable for each other's amusement.

Rose—now Rosalind once more, but to Thomas she would always be his Rose—hugged his arm and looked up at him. Caught his eye when he looked down at her. "Why are we here?"

Rose hadn't pressed for a specific destination when they'd left Seddington House, now fully staffed and functioning again; when she'd asked where they were going, Thomas had said that there was one place he needed to visit before they headed off to Cornwall, to claim the belongings they'd left at the manor, hire new caretakers, and put all in order for their return to Seddington Grange for Christmas. Now, surrounded by the graves of the fashionable, Rose wondered what particular piece of his complex past he'd come there to put to rest. Glancing around, she asked, "Have we come to visit a grave?"

"Yes, we have. Or"—he looked ahead—"I have, at least."

After a moment—his usual moment of considering how much to reveal—he looked down at her. "Her name most likely will mean nothing to you—she was an old lady when I knew her, and that was twenty and more years ago. But I wanted to pay my respects . . . before moving on."

Raising his head, he faced forward. Intrigued, Rose looked around as they walked on.

He pointed with his cane. "Her grave should be somewhere around there, I think."

They detoured into that section, taking the narrower paths between the sets of graves.

"There it is." He waved his cane at a neat, elegant, but not ostentatious marble-topped grave. The headstone, surmounted by a lute-playing angel, was clean, the plot well-cared for.

Settling her arm snugly in his, Rose halted by his side at the foot of the grave. "Edith Balmain." She glanced up at Thomas—her husband—and felt the thrill that still skittered through her every time she realized that that was now a fact, now true. His face was calm; his normal expression was less impassive than it used to be, but other than the fact that the old lady hadn't been someone he'd disliked, she couldn't read more from his face. "Who was she?" *Most especially, who was she in relation to you?*

As usual, he answered her unspoken question, the one most important to her. "She was an old lady who, from the very first, saw me as I truly am. She gave me advice that I didn't heed at the time—back then I was young enough, arrogant enough, to think I knew everything—but, in time, I came to value her words. She saw my weaknesses and my strengths, as well as my potential. She understood me in a way that no one else did."

He shifted his gaze to her. "Until you."

Rose looked into his hazel eyes and saw the devotion that would always be hers, his biggest gift to her, shining steady and strong. After a moment, she drew breath, then, together, they looked at the grave.

"Ros-a-lind!"

William; Rose glanced around.

Thomas gently squeezed Rose's hand. "Go. I won't be long." He met her gaze as she looked back at him. "I'll catch up—we can walk on and leave through the gate at the end of the path."

She held his gaze for a moment, then nodded. Drawing her arm from his, her hand from his sleeve, she turned and walked off to where William and Alice were investigating a particular grave.

Thomas watched her go. Fate had obviously thought Stokes's advice sound, and Rose was already expecting their first child, a boon and a future prospect just the thought of which held the power to make him weak.

With joy.

With a gladness of heart he'd never before truly known, not until he'd gone to Breage Manor, knocked on his own door, and met Rose.

Looking back at Edith Balmain's last resting place, that welling joy still buoying his soul, he smiled. "I think you would be pleased with how everything's turned out." The murmured words fell from his lips, spoken without his usual restraint, the distance he instinctively preserved between him and most of the world. "You told me the truth about myself so long ago—you were the only one who ever did. You were the only one who ever tried to reach me, who understood enough about me to make the attempt. But, back then, I was too young, too immature, too flown on my own brilliance to pay your words due heed." He paused, then admitted, "Even so, even then, I knew you were right, but it took me a long time—and the example of another of your descendants, Sarah, now Countess of Meredith—to make me look, and see, and finally acknowledge that. And to change."

Shifting to fold both hands over the head of his cane, his gaze on the grave, he went on, "I made the change and I thought that was the end, but, apparently, it wasn't. Having changed . . . it seems that for me that was only the beginning, that, despite my age, I've only recently started living—started living the life I'm supposed to lead. The fact that I'm still here . . . I'm sure you would tell me that that's a sign, a directive from above as to how things need to be. So . . . for however long I'm granted, I will take your long-ago words to heart and endeavor to live wisely."

He paused, remembering the old lady with her piercingly acute gaze, hearing again her insightful words, then he refocused on the headstone and smiled. "In many ways, all the good I do, and might do throughout my life, stems from those words of yours. I never thanked you while you were alive, but I thought you might appreciate knowing that the impact of those words and your influence has continued, and is continuing on, long after you died."

After a moment, he gripped his cane and started to turn away, then he paused and said, "One thing you didn't tell me, although I'm sure you knew—love truly is the most transformative power in heaven and on earth."

Turning away, he looked around, located Rose's shining head—focused on her, on his future, and went forward to meet it.